D A V I D

Redemption

THE STANFIELD CHRONICLES

Published by Pond House Books LLC
www.davidtoryauthor.com

Cover design and composition by Stewart A. Williams
Author photograph by Jemma Tory

Print ISBN: 979-8-9861434 -8-4
Ebook ISBN: 979-8-9861434 -9-1

First edition

This book is dedicated to Rue and Pippa

ACKNOWLEDGEMENTS

I am hugely grateful to Julie Tibbott, copyedit and final proof, and Stewart A. Williams, cover and interior design, both via Reedsy, for their invaluable and highly professional service. In addition, Jack Armitage who read and corrected the early draft and Anne Easter Smith for her review and advice. But above all I am grateful to my wife Helen, who provided steadfast encouragement and support, as well as being advisor, brainstormer, critic and editor.

AUTHOR'S NOTE

The Mayflower left Plymouth England in 1620 bound for the Hudson River. It didn't get there. Was it bad weather or something clandestine? The Stanfield Chronicles is Isaac Stanfield's story. He escapes from a disastrous fire to become an eager, adventurous young sailor. By happenstance he is recruited as an agent for Sir Ferdinando Gorges and faces torture, humiliation and death in Sir Ferdinando's efforts to establish settlements in New England.

Isaac's adventures and misadventures take him to New England, Holland, France, Spain and Bermuda. He becomes a successful merchant, ship owner and farmer, only to face the prospect of ruin.

His story is also the story of his love for two women.

MAIN CHARACTERS

(REAL NAMES IN BOLD)

Ahanu	Indian
Beamish, Arthur	New Settler
Blackstone, Rev. William	**1623 Settler**
Braddock, James ("J.B.")	Sailor
Burch, Obediah ("Obi")	Sailor
Burden, Giles	Farmer
Chandler, Tobias	First mate, *Abigail*
Chogan	Indian tribal leader
Conant, Roger	**Old Planter**
Darnell, Richard	**New Settler**
Dawkins, Jeannie	Housekeeper, Johnny's wife
Dawkins, Johnny	Former ship's boy aboard the *Sweet Rose*

Endecott, Capt. John –	**New Settler** **interim Governor**
Gardner, John	**Old Planter**
Gauden, Capt. Henry	**Skipper of *Abigail***
Garcia, Ezra	Bermudian farmer
Gott, Charles	**New Settler**
Grindle (Carson), Septimus	Isaac's antagonist
Hadfield, Tiny	Bosun, *Abigail*
Hallet, Jacob	Bermuda Government official
Hendry, Gavan	Carpenter
Hoekstra, Anton	Dutch trader
Hopkins, Stephen	**Separatist**
Kimi	Squaw of Chogan
Masconomet	**Indian Sagamore**
Maverick, Samuel	**1623 Settler**
Milsted, Patience	Housekeeper
Morton, Thomas	**1623 Settler**
Nootau	Indian

Pedro, Anthony	Bermudian fisherman
Scroud, Ebenezer	Isaac's business manager in England
Spiggott	Sailor
Sprague, Ralph	**New Settler**
Squires, Thurloe	Second mate, *Abigail*
Stanfield Abigail	Daughter of Isaac and Annie, born 8 July, 1623
Stanfield, Annie	Isaac's wife, born 4 September, 1597
Stanfield, Hannah (Nan)	Daughter of Isaac and Annie, born 19 December, 1630
Stanfield, Isaac	Narrator, born 6 January, 1597
Stanfield, James	Son of Isaac and Aby, born 6 December, 1619
Stanfield, Nathaniel (Nat)	Son of Isaac and Annie, born 19 December, 1630
Sykes	Sailor
Thomson, Mrs. Amyse	**1623 Settler, wife of David Thomson**
Trask, William	**Old Planter**

Tremaine, Beth	Kate's daughter
Tremaine, David	Sea captain
Tremaine, Kate	Farmer, David's wife
Tremont, Seth	Annie's cousin
Trescothick, Jason (Argie)	Bermuda merchant
Walford, Thomas	**Old Settler**
White, John ("Patriarch", "P.")	**Rector of Holy Trinity Church in Dorchester**
Whiteway, Will	**Friend of Isaac in Dorchester, England**
Winthrop, Jack	**Son of John**
Winthrop, John	**Governor**
Wood, Capt. Henry	**Governor of Bermuda**
Woodbury, Humphrey	**John's son**
Woodbury, John	**Old Settler**

Salem Peninsula
1630

1500 ft

North River

Old Settlement

Naumkeag
(Salem)

New Settlement

South River

Boston Shoreline
1630

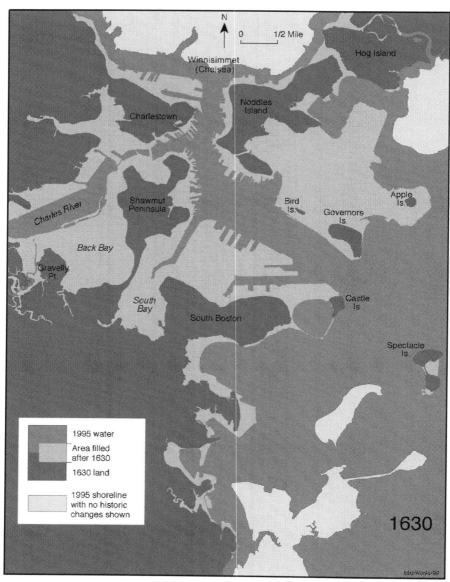

Map Works, Inc. "Boston shoreline 1630." Map. 1999. *Norman B. Leven-thal Map & Education Center*, https://collections.leventhalmap.org/search/commonwealth:q524n430n (accessed February 26, 2024).

New Barrow
Farm

Merrimack River

Agawam

(Ipswich)

Cape Ann

Coastline
Merrimack ~ Shawmut

(Gloucester)

Beauport
Harbor

Salem

2 miles

Shawmut
(Boston)

Bermuda

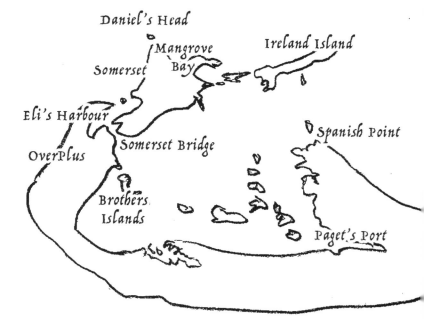

Daniel's Head

Mangrove Bay

Ireland Island

Somerset

Eli's Harbour

Spanish Point

Somerset Bridge

OverPlus

Brothers Islands

Paget's Port

St George's

Coney
Island

Flatts

Harrington
Sound

Southampton Harbour

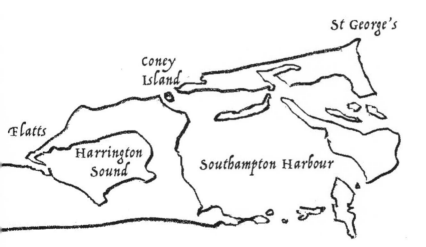

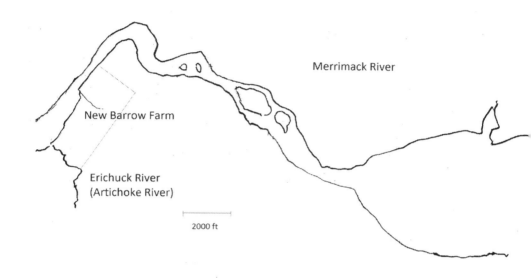

New Barrow Farm

Merrimack River

Erichuck River
(Artichoke River)

2000 ft

Merrimack River

NEW ENGLAND TOWNS
MENTIONED IN *REDEMPTION*
(FROM NORTH TO SOUTH)

Piscataqua	Portsmouth NH
Agawam	Ipswich
Beauport	Gloucester
Naumkeag	Salem
Winnisimmet	Chelsea
Mishawum	Charlestown
Shawmut	Boston
Nantasket	Hull
Wessagusset	Weymouth

PROLOGUE

EXPLORATION: THE STANFIELD CHRONICLES, BOOK 1

After a devastating fire strikes Dorchester, England in 1613, sixteen-year-old Isaac Stanfield leaves town to become a sailor on a merchant-man, *The Sweet Rose (Rosie)*, leaving behind his love, Aby Baker.

Isaac's lifelong friend Will Whiteway asks him to keep a journal of his adventures and send his writings to him on a regular basis.

Rosie takes Isaac to La Rochelle in France. He rescues a crewman Johnny Dawkins from an officer's lecherous clutches. In La Rochelle, Isaac becomes involved with a covert spying operation orchestrated by Sir Ferdinando Gorges, Governor of Plymouth Fort. He meets the spy, David Tremaine. Isaac returns to Plymouth to work for Sir Ferdinando (Sir F). His home there is the Minerva Inn where he meets and becomes friends with Annie Potts, barmaid and niece of the landlord.

Sir F has established the Council for New England which has been attempting, unsuccessfully, to establish settlements in North America. Isaac becomes involved with Sir F.'s efforts in that regard. A number of Indians have been brought to England to share their knowledge before being sent back to support further exploration in New England. Sir F asks Isaac to spend time with two of the Indians to gain their trust and learn what he can about the people and land from whence they came.

Back in Dorchester, Isaac's guardian, the Reverend John White, called by his parishioners the Patriarch (P), is an active supporter of the Puritan movement and is in touch with the Puritan Separatists who had fled persecution in England to go to Leiden in Holland. He supports their efforts to leave Leiden to go to North America. P asks Isaac to keep him abreast of Sir F.'s activities.

Sir F sends Isaac on a number of exploratory trips to New England in the furtherance of his aims. Sir F comes to understand that the Leiden Separatists' desire to emigrate to North America intersects with his increasingly desperate need to establish a settlement in New England. With Isaac's help, he uses guile to ensure that the Puritans aboard the *Mayflower* in 1620 arrive in New England rather than on the Hudson River where they had planned to go.

Aby and Isaac, although separated for months at a time, through absence, misunderstandings, and miscommunication, retain their love for each other, become engaged and marry. The couple finds a home in Plymouth. Aby becomes an indispensable member of Lady Ann Gorges' household while Isaac continues to be sent on assignments by Sir F. Their son James is born. Annie Potts becomes housekeeper and child carer in the Stanfield household. While helping the sick and indigent, Lady Ann and Aby are infected by a fever and die. Shortly thereafter, the *Mayflower* leaves Plymouth for North America.

RETRIBUTION: THE STANFIELD CHRONICLES, BOOK 2

Retribution begins in 1620 after the *Mayflower* has sailed from Plymouth. A grieving Isaac Stanfield heads out across the Atlantic Ocean, sent by Sir Ferdinando to accompany David Thomson's expedition to start a settlement on the Piscataqua River, and to find out how the Puritans survived their first winter in New England.

Annie is left to manage the household and look after James. In Isaac's prolonged absence she assumes the role of mother to James. On Isaac's return to England, he remains confused about his feelings for Annie and his duties as a parent.

Isaac is sent on further assignments by Sir F and begins to develop his own business interests as a junior trading partner. He is sent back to New England to support Robert Gorges' efforts to become established as the Governor of New England. That attempt ends in disaster.

Isaac is embroiled in a series of increasingly dangerous escapades and entanglements with pirates from which he barely survives, but in the process, becomes a part owner of his beloved *Rosie*. He also takes ownership of *The Swallow*, a coastal trading sloop.

Through all this, the patient Annie remains loyal to Isaac and a fierce and loving protector of James. Isaac comes to realize that he loves Annie, and they marry. Then, James is kidnapped. He is traced to Bermuda. Isaac follows on *The Swallow* and rescues him.

Annie and Isaac have two daughters, Abigail and Miranda, and the family moves to a new home, Barrow Farm, near Dorchester in Dorset.

Just when Isaac's fortunes seem blessed, retribution strikes: *Rosie* is sunk after pirate action, *The Swallow* has to be sold, and baby Miranda dies. Those disasters coupled with a worsening economic and political environment in England persuade Annie and Isaac to emigrate to New England.

—— CHAPTER 1 ——

Letter to Will Whiteway – *5 September, 1628*

Dear Will,

It has been a long, strange, and worrying journey across the Atlantic. I feel lucky to be alive after a number of alarming incidents on the way over. I am enclosing my journal entries which describe what happened. Cape Ann is in sight from the masthead. We expect to arrive at Naumkeag tomorrow.

I am leaving this packet for you with Tiny Hadfield who, you will remember, was bosun on the dear old *Rosie* when she foundered after the incident with the pirate vessel in September '26. Was it really two years ago? Tiny is now bosun on *Abigail* which has carried us to New England and will be returning to Weymouth. He promised to deliver the packet into your hands.

I hope that you, Elenor, and your family remain in good health. Annie sends her love.

Isaac

Journal entry –*June 1628*

In the early pre-dawn hours of 20 June, we left our home, Barrow Farm, by cart, piled with our possessions, and three goats in a cage, to ride to Weymouth to board *Abigail*, bound for New England. Annie, Jeannie, and our two children, James, aged eight, sturdy, short golden brown hair, large brown eyes watching the world go by and Abigail, four, her long auburn hair framing her face, blue eyes sparkling, were travelling on the cart, Johnny and me riding borrowed horses. My beloved wife, Annie, excited about this new adventure and what the future has in store for us, anxious to leave her unhappy past behind; me torn, sad to be leaving my past behind, concerned about the challenges we were sure to face as settlers in the new world. Jeannie was a bundle of nerves, terrified of the impending trip across the stormy Atlantic, Johnny focused on trying to calm his adored wife. James, eager to be back on board a big ship, Abigail, distracted by the goats. Overriding my thoughts was the euphoria of having my family with me on this Atlantic crossing. Our new life had begun.

We headed for the harbor and were deposited on the quayside close to *Abigail*. We seemed to be early. There were a few people about with more arriving, adding their possessions to the piles of baggage, boxes, and barrels ready to be taken aboard. I was hailed from the main deck. I looked around. It was Tiny Hadfield. Tiny, so called because of his massive size, waved to me. I waved back, surprised and delighted to see my old shipmate. At that moment a familiar figure appeared at the quarterdeck rail. It was Henry Gauden, a longtime acquaintance, skipper of *Abigail* whom I, in my trading days, had met many times. We greeted each other and he invited us aboard. Johnny said that he and Jeannie would wait and keep an eye on our pile of baggage (I think he wanted to delay Jeannie's boarding as long as possible) and Abigail preferred to stay in Jeannie's arms, looking apprehensive. Tiny welcomed us as we boarded. He told us he was the bosun, led us to the steps to the quarterdeck and said, "The captain awaits."

Henry Gauden was a squarely built man of thirty-five, five years my senior, short grey hair, a clean-shaven, weathered, brown face, deep set, blue eyes under grey eyebrows. He shook my hand, bowed over Annie's, and tousled James' hair. Henry had a strong uncompromising character. A good friend but not someone to cross. He was as pleased to see us as we were him. He advised us that we were a little early, which was probably not a bad thing, as it would allow us to become familiar with our home for the next few months. He said he and his crew were going to be busy for the next few hours and suggested we stay in his cabin or on the quarterdeck out of the way of all the bustle. Annie said that she would prefer to wait with the Dawkins on the quayside. She had a hamper with food and drink for their breakfast. James pleaded that he be allowed to stay on board, so he and I remained on the quarterdeck while Annie went ashore.

It had been three years since we had rescued James from Bermuda on the *Swallow*. I wondered how much he remembered of what he had learned sailing back to England. Quite a bit, apparently—the observant boy was quick to point out that the rigging was different, *Swallow* was a single masted sloop, *Abigail* a three masted barque. Seeing his father impressed, with increasing confidence he pointed out and named the spars and lines for each mast, the names of the furled sails. Now in his stride, he pointed to the various parts of the ship, giving me the names, only occasionally having to be corrected. Looking forward from the quarterdeck, where we stood, below us was the main deck, beyond that the forecastle (or fo'c'sle). I told him that the main deck between the two was also called the waist. I told James to think of a buxom lady with a big bum and large bosom, with her waist in between. He told me that under the main deck was the lower deck, where the guns were, so it was also called the gun deck. Below the lower deck was the hold, which he said, held the freight. Under the quarterdeck were the gun room and captain's quarters. The fo'c'sle held the forepeak and cook room. James wanted to go below but with the passengers' possessions being hoisted and stowed in the hold, I suggested we go back ashore and have something to eat.

By now the passengers had assembled quayside in a confused gaggle, children out of control in their excitement, women in high-pitched chatter, hiding their apprehension and the men in small groups trying to look casual, telling each other old, tired jokes, betraying their own nervousness by laughing too heartily. I was pleased to see John

Woodbury and William Trask there. I had met them in Cape Ann in February 1624. They had returned to England last year to request support for Naumkeag from Rev. John White (called the Patriarch or P., in Dorchester) and the Dorchester Company, the settlement Roger Conant had persuaded them to move to in 1626. They were now returning there, with Woodbury's son Humphrey. Sadly, they were accompanying Captain John Endecott, Roger Conant's successor as Governor of the settlement. They told me they were not looking forward to that meeting, especially as Conant had not been informed he had been replaced.

In the bright early morning sun, with all baggage loaded, we were invited to board and told to assemble in the waist of the main deck where we would be addressed by the skipper. There was a rush precipitated by the young and followed by anxious mothers. I told Annie to hold hard to James, while Jeannie held Abigail, we should wait until the gangplank was clear of bodies. Eventually, we were all aboard and milling around in a confused, tightly packed group waiting for something to happen and to be told what to do. Gauden came to the quarterdeck rail, looked down at us for a moment and called for quiet, easily heard over the chatter. Captain Endecott, previously invited to the quarterdeck by the skipper, stepped forward to the rail, and then, interrupting the skipper, demanded that he should be speaking to the passengers first. Endecott was of average size, ruddy complexion, with bushy, dark eyebrows over piercing brown eyes, a long nose, moustache and a narrow beard. He was about forty years old.

We looked at each other, surprised and in my case, embarrassed by his presumption. Gauden took Endecott by the arm and led him back from the rail out of direct sight of us passengers below on the main deck. There were sounds of a slight altercation between the two. The quiet, reasonable voice of Gauden made it clear, over the loud objections of Endecott, that there was one skipper on board, and that Endecott would be in a position to assume his role as Governor once arrived in New England and ashore. Sanity returned and, with a truculent Endecott remaining in the background, Gauden resumed his address.

He advised us of the rules of passage and that it was our responsibility to manage our own affairs while aboard. He and his crew would have their hands full ensuring the safe passage of the ship to our destination. Passengers would be allowed on the main deck only when weather and sea conditions permitted. The gunroom and forepeak were out of bounds to all passengers as they comprised the crews' quarters. The quarterdeck was the preserve of the captain and on-duty watch. Passengers were allowed rarely and by individual invitation only. We were advised that, notwithstanding the optimistic promises we might have received, the journey would be long, possibly very long, and most uncomfortable. Such confinement would lead to frayed tempers. Discipline must be maintained. If the passengers were unable to maintain that discipline, he, the captain, would step in to administer suitable punishment in line with that meted out to the crew, including flogging.

Mr. Gauden then introduced his officers, first, second mate, bosun, carpenter, gunner and cook, describing their responsibilities. The second mate, Mr. Thurloe Squires would be responsible for liaison between the crew and the passengers. With that, Mr. Squires was asked to continue to brief the passengers about what was required of them and the details of the accommodation available.

Squires spoke simply, slowly and clearly so there would be no misunderstanding. *Abigail* and crew were to deliver the passengers, with minimal loss of life, to their destination. The passengers were to fend for themselves as much as possible. They were to stay out of the way of the crew and organize themselves into a functioning community for an unknown duration. The voyage could take two or even three months, depending on the weather. During the day, the lower deck (the gun deck) would be rigged much as it was set up now. He recommended that by two bells first watch (9:00pm), with tables and benches cleared, it should be rigged for sleeping and by two bells morning watch (5:00am), the gun deck restored for day use. Certain passengers, most notably Captain Endecott and his immediate party, had paid for cabin space, cabins made of wooden stretchers and canvas. The remaining passengers would be using paillasses and hammocks as desired.

Mealtimes would be determined by the passengers as long as supplies lasted. The use of the passengers' brazier would be strictly controlled. The cook room had a stove that, depending on the weather and circumstances, might also be available under the control of the cook. Depending on the length of the voyage and the quantity of provisions that the passengers had brought aboard there might be a need to supplement their diet from the ship's stores—at which time, meals would be regulated.

Anyone who might need to wash self and or clothes would be limited to the amount of rainwater available. First priority would always be to replenish the butts containing drinking water. Squires said that he was aware that many more hogsheads of beer than water had been stowed. Water turns foul quickly, but it could be replenished on board; beer couldn't. Sea water was available for washing, although he advised against it as clothes and bodies do not react well to prolonged exposure to salt. I had the impression that there would not be much washing done over the next few months, which did not bode well for the living conditions in such a cramped and overcrowded space. I remembered the increasingly fetid atmosphere on the voyages I had made previously to New England, and those were with few passengers. I also thought back to the winter we spent at Saco in 1616 – 1617 and the noisome huts we had to live in until the spring, so foul by then that we burned them and their contents, to build afresh.

Squires described the dimensions and constraints of the living space for the 38 passengers for the duration of the voyage. It was going to be tight. After he had finished, the passengers were asked to go below and sort themselves out while the ship was made ready for departure. Passengers were given limited space to stow the possessions and provisions they required, ready to hand, for the voyage; one small chest for each passenger. The rest of their possessions would remain in the hold. Once underway, we would be invited to return to the main deck to witness our departure from England.

We went below. The deck space of the lower (gun) deck was about thirty-five feet long and half that wide with a maximum height of six feet. How were we all expected to live, eat, and sleep in such confinement? In that space, there were four minion cannons, two per side, as well as ladders fore and aft to the upper deck, with mast trunk, capstan fittings and hatch to the main hold. Eight tables with benches were the only furniture for the entire voyage, apart from each passenger's small chest, that had to be stowed hard up against the hull or bulkhead walls, with hooks above to hang clothes. I supposed that everyone would get used to the conditions with which they were presented, but what of the night? The tables and benches would be folded up and stowed; palliasses brought out and laid on the deck between the guns, mast, hatch, and capstan. For the men, hammocks could be swung from the beams six feet above the floor, so would dangle, like so many large moth cocoons, to within almost touching distance of the people sleeping below them. I tried to imagine it. Every bit of deck space covered with sleeping bodies. No room to move about, and hammocks blocking the way, as well. What about relieving oneself during the night? The boat's piss pots should be used but, surely, not possible at night in the dark with nowhere to tread. That meant using the chamber pots belonging to the passengers, ready to trip the unwary and likely to tip over. And to think, we had been firmly told that the heads, open to the elements at the bows, were off-limits to the passengers for safety reasons.

James gazed around, eyeing the large cannons. He tugged my arm. I looked down and he whispered something. I couldn't hear with the bedlam about us, so knelt down and asked him what he had said. He whispered in my ear, "Daddy, what happens when the guns are needed? Where do we go then?"

"The passengers will be asked to go to the forepeak and the hold. It will be an unforgettable experience."

James nodded slowly, eyes wide, trying to imagine such a calamity.

The six collapsible cabins, set up at night, further reduced available space. In addition to those booked for Governor Endecott, I had booked a couple. The space at the aft end, between the guns and the bulkhead, was taken by Captain Endecott and his entourage. A screen was going to be set up to separate that space from the rest of the lower deck. My two cabins would be used by Annie with James, and Jeannie with Abigail. Johnny and I would use hammocks, swung adjacent to the cabins, although I suspected James, on occasion, would persuade Annie to sleep with Abigail, so Johnny could sleep with his wife, thereby allowing James access to Johnny's hammock.

It quickly became clear who were the leaders and who were the led in the resulting chaos, as everyone milled about. Heated discussions erupted on who should sit at which table and where the passengers' chests should be placed. Endecott remained on the quarterdeck with Captain Gauden while his entourage moved into their space at the aft end of the main cabin. It was clear that Annie, ably assisted by Johnny, was a capable organizer. Her years working for her uncle at the Minerva Inn in Plymouth had taught her how to deal with a boisterous crowd in a confined space. She was able to help everyone sort themselves out without causing offence and by her cheerful demeanor, gained the respect of the passengers and restored good humor. Jeannie, meantime, had taken control of James and Abigail. She set them to playing a game in a corner. As for me, I did whatever I was told to do by Annie, which included helping the other menfolk in the hold, ensuring that each family's possessions were stowed together and their location known.

Our goats, a buck and two does, were penned at the aft end of the main hold, together with two other does, with plenty of fodder. All four does had recently produced offspring and were in milk. Longer term, I had asked David Tremaine to arrange shipment of two cows to come with him or otherwise on one of the vessels leaving at the same time. I knew there were several bulls already at Naumkeag, with more being shipped, as part of the Dorchester Company's final gesture of support before the company was subsumed within the New England Company. Assuming my cows survived the crossing, there would be plenty of opportunities for them to be served in time for calving in the early summer of next year.

CHAPTER 2

Journal entry *– June 1628*

By the time everything was shipshape, with my family and me topside, *Abigail* was working her way out of Weymouth harbor.

Johnny and Jeannie joined us at the starboard, leeward rail on the main deck tucked in the corner of the aft bulkhead with the quarterdeck above us, trying to shelter from the brisk breeze out of the east. Twenty-three year old Jeannie with red hair, a mass of freckles, an upturned nose, green eyes, and a Cork brogue, had been Annie's housekeeper and child-minder for five years: Johnny twenty-seven, looking younger, below average height and slim, with blond hair, blue-green eyes and a happy countenance was my factotum and companion. I had first met him in 1613, when we were both ship's boys on *Rosie*. After he suffered a terrible sexual assault on board, I took the broken boy home and lost touch with him, only to have him reappear seven years ago, fully restored and having led an adventurous life, to renew our friendship.

The wind had a nip to it. The sea, reflecting the morning sun, sparkled with an intensity that blurred the eyes. The waves were friendly, slight chop, dark blue green with little caps of white feathered by the wind. An abundance of bad-tempered seagulls followed in our wake, screaming their demands for food, dropping down to look for anything edible, fighting each other as they flapped, frustrated, to soar up and rejoin the throng. The motion of the boat increased as we rounded Portland Bill and headed southwest out to sea, wind veering to the southeast and increasing, the sea now more boisterous, waves creating little troughs, gullies and peaks, a slow swell causing *Abigail* to lift and fall with a rolling motion from side to side, the feathered white caps becoming wind driven spray. Annie, looking slightly green, led Jeannie below with the children, James protesting, leaving Johnny and me enjoying the feel of the boat and the decidedly mixed experience of regaining our sea legs. Suddenly, Johnny leaned towards me.

"Isaac, if looks could kill, you'd be rolling in the scuppers. What on earth have you done to our estimable Governor?"

Johnny was staring up above my head toward the quarterdeck. I sighed, not turning to look.

"Johnny, do you remember me coming back from a meeting in Dorchester about New England that the Patriarch had asked me to attend? It was the first time I had met Captain Endecott. At the time, I didn't know why he was there. I was asked by P. to speak to the attendees about my experiences in New England. Endecott inserted himself and dominated the meeting, asking me questions, admittedly to the point, but not allowing anyone else to ask theirs. P. told me later that Endecott was being considered to replace Roger Conant at Naumkeag. Once it was known that I planned to move the family to New England, I was pressured by many influential people to agree to work for Endecott there. Endecott became rude and insistent. I explained that I had no interest in being part of his administration. I told him that we are moving to New England to be farmers and I want to rebuild my shipping business. I've had my fill of being forced to help establish governing structures in New England. Sir Ferdinando Gorges had made an ill-fated attempt to install his son Robert as Governor in 1623. He pressured me to go, against my wishes, ignoring my foreboding." For a moment I got lost in my own thoughts, recalling how many people suffered under that ineffectual and inexperienced leader.

"What happened" Johnny asked. I shook my head.

"It had been a disaster. There was a subsequent meeting in London that I was asked to attend to provide potential investors with an account of my experiences. Endecott was there. He spoke at length about what he intended to do when he got to Naumkeag. To my dismay, he stated that he would take over ownership of the settlement. Such a preemptive action disregarded the extraordinary work Conant had done to rescue the Cape Ann settlement from demise. Endecott then introduced me as his assistant. I ignored the reference, although it made me angry at the man's bullheaded refusal to accept what I had so repeatedly told him. I spoke for a few minutes before he stopped me. Afterwards, I was surrounded by a ring of attendees wanting more information. Endecott thrust himself through the ring and demanded that all questions should be referred to him and not directly to his assistant. I took him aside and forcefully rejected, once more, his notion that I was in any way associated with him and his intended administration."

I then told Johnny of my meeting earlier that morning. I explained that Captain Henry Gauden was a friend of Isaiah Brown, one time skipper of *Rosie*. Gauden and I had become friendly over the years. He knew much of my background.

While the passengers were below, sorting out their possessions, I was relieved from my duties in the hold by being invited to the captain's quarters under the quarterdeck. While we were engaged in updating each other on our lives and prospects, Endecott entered and reacted angrily, shocked to see me present. He demanded to know why his subordinate, Stanfield, was being honored with a private meeting with the captain. Gauden invited Endecott to sit, offered him a glass of madeira and expressed surprise that he deemed Mr. Stanford to be a subordinate. He turned to me with eyebrows raised. I responded, as meekly as I could.

"Captain, I fear Mr. Endecott is mistaken. I and my family have, as you know, paid for and are making our way on *Abigail* to start a new life and rebuild my business in New England. Mr. Endecott is being sent by the New England Company to become Governor upon his arrival there. In spite of repeated requests, I have stated before and remain determined that I will not to be a member of his staff or of the Company."

Mr. Endecott, bristling with a red face, accused me of insolence and insubordination. Gauden intervened.

"Surely, sir, you overstep the mark. Insolence and insubordination assume rudeness and Mr. Stanfield actually being subordinate to you, He has, in my humble opinion, adequately and politely exposed those presumptions. I can understand you wanting to employ Mr. Stanfield for his knowledge of New England. He seems to have decided otherwise. I have known Mr. Stanfield, personally, for several years and by reputation many years longer. I can vouch for him."

I smiled, hoping that would be an end to it, and rose to my feet offering my hand to Mr. Endecott. He sat stiff and silent, one hand grasping his wine glass, the fingers of the other hand drumming on the arm of his chair. He also rose, nodded towards Gauden, ignoring me and my outstretched hand, turned and, gathering his cloak around him, swept from the cabin.

"Isaac, I apologize for that most unbecoming behavior from the impending Governor. Since he first came aboard, I have been watching and conversing with him. He is overweening, impatient, impetuous and stubborn, quick to pass judgement and loathe to change his mind. I believe he hides his grave misgivings about the responsibilities he has taken on and his competence to carry them out. I will attempt to mitigate his sense of inadequacy by providing him with access to the quarterdeck and myself. You, Isaac, I will leave to the tender mercies of my first mate, Tobias Chandler and my bosun, your old acquaintance Tiny Hadfield."

At the end of my account, Johnny frowned.

"Isaac, you might be able to keep your independence on *Abigail*. I believe Endecott to be an implacable enemy. Once we land, if you don't bow to his authority, he will see you as a threat, even a pretender to his position. I agree with Captain Gauden, if he can't control you he will want to remove you by any means. He will have ultimate authority to do with you whatever he wants."

"Don't worry, Johnny. I will endeavor to keep out of his way to the extent possible in this small universe we will be living in for the next few months. Once ashore, he will be too busy to worry about me and he will have the counsel of Roger Conant and others who have much more immediate and relevant experience to call upon. However, I do worry how Mr. Conant will react when Mr. Endecott arrives and snatches the proverbial chain of office from around Conant's neck and hangs it around his own. I know Roger Conant to be a wise and steady man. He has achieved his position as the current Governor of the Naumkeag settlement through hard work and strong leadership. Endecott can not afford to alienate him."

Johnny looked puzzled.

"If Conant is such a person, why was it thought necessary to replace him with Endecott?"

"A combination of political and commercial expediency with a mixture of opportunism, nepotism, and ambition. The old Dorchester Company, largely controlled by the Patriarch, had established the Cape Ann settlement in 1623 which proved unsuccessful, with poor leadership and even poorer planning. Roger Conant was recruited to take over that settlement in 1625. The company's expectation that a profitable trade in fish would result, to the benefit of the original investors, was found to be unrealistic. "

"So what happened?"

"Conant decided to move the remnants of the settlement to Naumkeag in 1626 and with considerable strength of character, and the respect he had gained in trying circumstances, convinced a core group of the settlers to move with him."

Johnny was still puzzled.

"P. should have been pleased with Conant, not replace him."

"Earlier this year, the Dorchester Company was folded into a new company, the New England company, under new leadership with additional investors. P. and a number of the original subscribers continued with the New England Company. Matthew Cradock was elected to lead the company. He was not only a major investor, he was also able to bring in others. To satisfy them, a new governor in New England needed to be appointed, using the existing settlement in Naumkeag as the foundation for a much more substantial undertaking.

"What about Endecott? Where did he come from."

"Johnny, it is understood that Endecott was chosen because he is a nephew by marriage of Matthew Cradock. Almost nothing is known about Endecott's background or even where he was born and brought up. He talks of having a Dorchester background. I was born and raised in Dorchester and had never heard of him, nor had P., which is pretty damning. With the wholehearted support of Cradock none of the investors thought to question his credentials."

— CHAPTER 3 —

Journal entry – *July 1628*

After a spritely start out of Weymouth, the onshore breeze died by early afternoon and we lay becalmed, the tide and adverse current denying us further progress. Eventually, we struggled as far as Exmouth, where we anchored offshore overnight. Next day the wind, light as it was, veered to the southwest, our intended heading, so we had no option but to stay put. It remained so for the next few days then backed to the southeast, the wind scarcely filling the sails allowing us some forward motion. The passengers spent time on deck, enjoying the summer weather and the calm. They were able to organize themselves, establishing day and night routines without having the added challenge of bad weather and rough seas. I stayed clear of Endecott. Annie made friends with Mistress Ann Endecott, a gentle lady, dutifully following her husband to the new world but, according to Annie, with much trepidation.

It was 1 July, before we rounded the Lizard and turned to head west and then northwest, our last sight of land for the next many weeks. The weather changed as we headed out into the Atlantic. With the rain, the winds increased and the seas became rough. The passengers were confined to the main cabin on the lower deck and living conditions quickly deteriorated. While the first fortnight aboard had enabled most of the passengers to gain their sea legs, the increased and unsteady motion of *Abigail* hit a number of them hard, including Mistress Endecott, who took to her berth. Annie's offer to attend to his wife was begrudgingly accepted by Mr. Endecott and she spent much time comforting the ailing lady while Endecott spent his time on the quarterdeck or in the captain's cabin.

The calm of the preceding two weeks had not prepared the passengers for the prevailing conditions that I knew from experience would be with us for most of the rest of our journey. In the frequent, prolonged periods of heavy weather the noise was deafening, of the wind in the rigging, the rush of seas rolling past the hull, the crack of sails as they spilled and filled, the constant beating of lines on masts and spars, the shouted orders and pounding of the crew's feet on the deck above us. During the day, down below, the rise and fall of the boat and the rolling from side to side made it difficult to sit at our tables. Anything moveable moved, sliding across tabletops. Falling objects poorly stowed escaped our clutching hands. It was wet. The closed gun ports leaked sprays of water, the battened main hatch dripped sea and rainwater. Clothing remained damp. Little daylight filtered in, so lanterns were lit and hung from beams, swinging to and fro, casting continuously changing shadows that confused the mind. The smell of vomit, spilled chamber pots, dank and foul clothing, unwashed bodies, rancid milk and rotting food waste; at night, lying on moldy, musty palliasses under thin, damp blankets, caused tempers to fray and for animosities hidden during the good weather to become more evident.

In spite of my attempts to stay clear of Mr. Endecott, the boat was small and confining, I was having an increasingly difficult time with him. Henry Gauden tried to mitigate the rancorous interactions, keeping us apart. Endecott, clearly concerned about his lack of practical knowledge of the conditions he and his settlers would find in New England, continued to try to enlist my active support by threat or favors. He offered me a senior position in his administration, presumably something more than to be his chief of staff. I would have none of it. From then on, whenever we were alone, which was rare, he threatened me with dire consequences if I didn't submit to his authority.

One cold and blustery evening while we were all confined below,

I was invited by Mr. Gott to join a group of men seated at a table in Mr. Endecott's reserved area behind a screen at the aft end of the main cabin. I had had few dealings with these men so far. My time had been spent with my family enjoying the weather and the sailing conditions of the first two weeks. James fretted about being confined but was able to establish friendships with the few other young people on board. Abigail, James, and Jeannie enjoyed going down to the hold to visit with the goats, when it wasn't too rough. We made sure that part of each day, we were all together at our table. We read books to each other, told stories, played games. We had played checkers at home, but Johnny taught us chess. To Annie's and my amazement, even young Abigail became adept. I also spent time with Tiny Hadfield reminiscing and catching up on his activities over the past few years. It gave me joy to see him in action. I had the memory of him, huge, blackened and bloody, standing on the quarterdeck of the sinking *Rosie*, surrounded by death and destruction, driving the surviving crew members to try and save her.

Mr. Endecott was not present at this gathering. It seemed that Mr. Gott was the spokesman for the group. I was offered a beer from a flagon on the table. The others all had beakers in front of them, clutched in their hands, braced against the ship's movement.

"Mr. Stanfield, we understand that you are at odds with the Governor, which is causing him much distress. This concerns us as we seek harmony and good fellowship on board and a shared commitment to support the Governor with our undivided loyalty when we reach New England."

I was surprised and said so. I too wished for harmony and good fellowship. I asked what gave them the idea that I was in some kind of adversarial relationship with Mr. Endecott.

"Mr. Stanfield, when you refer to the Governor you do not give him the courtesy of addressing him by his title. An indication perhaps that you are opposed to him in some way."

I pointed out that his appointment was effective from when he arrived at the settlement he had been chosen to govern—a comment dismissed with a wave as irrelevant. Clearly, Mr. Gott understood that the issue was more than a problem with Endecott's title.

"I understand he has offered you a senior position in his administration which you have turned down. I can only believe that you are opposed to him, then?"

"No, Mr. Gott. I am not opposed to him being the Governor. He was appointed by the New England Company and, therefore, has the necessary authority. However, I am opposed to attempts to coerce me into working for him."

At that point, a young man who had been slouched over his beer, sneered and demanded to know who the hell I was to be so insubordinate. Again, I was surprised. I replied that I was at a disadvantage as I surmised that I had been the subject of discussions that had taken place about which I knew nothing. It was, therefore, difficult for me to respond. The young man, Mr. Richard Darnell, then proceeded to interrogate me. I looked around at the other men at the table. They were silent, some grim, some looking embarrassed.

"Mr. Stanfield, you came from nothing and became a ship's boy and an ordinary seaman. Is that true?" Darnell demanded.

"Yes."

"It was in that capacity that you went to New England and you were returned incapacitated, in fact, barely alive?

"Yes."

"How then did you gain the reputation of being a know-it-all about all matters relating to New England?"

By now I was becoming a little peeved at the questioning from a young man who appeared inebriated and more so by the silent acquiescence of the group. I shrugged and said I had been lucky. That flippant remark enraged Mr. Darnell. He accused me of being arrogant, worthless, traveling under false pretenses, causing dissention, being a danger to the enterprise, and that I should be dealt with. His remarks were so outlandish that I didn't bother to respond. After a long silence Mr. Gott apologized, saying that Mr. Darnell was merely repeating what had been said elsewhere.

"It is clear, Mr. Gott, that you know little about me and what you have learned is not accurate. You need to return to the source of that information and make sure that what you understood to have been told or implied was actually what was said. You should also question the source as to the extent of their knowledge of my background. I worry, in the meantime, that the threat delivered represents an opinion shared by others. Now, if you will excuse me, I will return to my family."

Annie recognized my expression when I reappeared from behind the screen. We retreated to a corner and with the noise around us were able to talk without being overheard.

"Isaac, my sweet, you look as if your old teacher, Mr. Cheek, has just given you a beating. What happened?"

I laughed. "No, Annie, nothing quite like that although I have been chastised for not being loyal to Endecott. I need to pay attention to the undercurrents of the attitudes being developed and evolving. I have been naïve in believing my relationship with Endecott was something private between the two of us. It seems that is not the case."

"Are you saying that Mr. Endecott is spreading dissension among his people?"

I nodded and wondered how far it had gone. Annie thought for a moment.

"You know that I have established good relations with the women on board and especially with Mistress Endecott. They would be a useful source. They do like to pass on what they hear from their men-folk. Johnny and Jeannie have become friendly with a number of the indentured servants aboard. They can sniff out what their masters are saying. You should have a word with Johnny and I can talk to Jeannie. Don't you know Mr. Woodbury and Mr. Trask? They are certainly not part of what you call Mr. Endecott's entourage."

The moments we had alone were few. I took her in my arms and we kissed demurely. Annie's softness melding itself to me had me catch my breath. Annie was quick to see the tell-tale signs put a finger to my lips, smiled, gently shook her head and moved away. This was going to be difficult. I knew Annie was of the same mind though clearly much more disciplined than I was. I had to admit that the thought of making love cheek by jowl with forty other men, women, and children, even divided by a thin canvas screen, greatly reduced our physical desire.

—— CHAPTER 4 ——

Journal entry – *July 1628*

As the weeks went by, in spite of the discomfort, the routines of the day were maintained in all but the worst weather. Early rising, palliasses and hammocks stowed, chamber pots emptied, breakfast prepared, heated if possible, morning prayers were said. We made a special occasion for Abigail's fifth birthday on 8 July, on a clear day with a steady southerly breeze. Children were allowed on deck under strict supervision, to fill their lungs with fresh air and watch the waves swirling past the hull, to see what was causing the constant whistling, clatter, and thunder of the wind in the rigging and sails, that they had lived with day and night since they came aboard. For Abigail it was a special day. Members of the crew, made aware of her birthday, greeted her when she came up on deck. She was invited to the Cook room and given a sugared biscuit. Her obvious happiness was infectious and brought smiles to the faces of our fellow passengers.

James and Abigail had the important positions of shepherd and assistant shepherdess of our flock of goats, under Jeannie's watchful eye. Their care and attention greatly contributed to the goats' continuing good health, which meant fresh milk, butter, and cheese were available. Jeannie taught James to milk and showed Abigail how to keep the doe's attention while James was milking.

The passengers became a community and followed a daily routine, together. After breakfast, readings from the bible followed by groups sitting at their tables, the women stitching and knitting, the men gathered together talking, reading to each other, playing board games, writing journals. A midday meal with more prayers and the afternoon spent in much the same way as the morning. In the evening, a service with singing from the psalms and reading from the bible. We sufficed without a minister aboard. Every attempt was made to adhere to the Book of Common Prayer, the more separatist-minded offered their own prayers. There was lively debate questioning and defending the different religious attitudes being professed. Some were persuaded to the Puritan desire to purify the Church of England of its dogma. A few remained firm in their loyalty to the Church. The children, including other children of passengers, had been taken in hand by Johnny and Jeannie who appointed themselves their teachers. From the noise at the table they had taken over as a school room they seemed to be thoroughly enjoying themselves. I wondered what was being taught.

Whenever the passengers were allowed on deck, the fresh air, the wind in their faces, the bright daylight seemed a miracle. In those rare moments, James was my constant companion. I remembered when J.B. had taken me in hand after I had first joined *Rosie* as a ship's boy fifteen years ago. He had taught me what everything was and did, every rope and sail, every spar, every device. I now had the fun of doing the same for my son. He was a quick learner, he had already had two voyages across the Atlantic, between England and Bermuda, so he was much more experienced than I had been. For the first time, I came to understand how much James loved sailing. I remembered Anthony Pedro, a simple fisherman in Bermuda teaching James how to work the sails to catch the wind shifts, how to steer. I could see James on the *Swallow* on the return from Bermuda delighting in the surging motion of the boat through the tumbling seas. How many eight-year-olds can there be making their third Atlantic crossing?

Annie and Johnny kept me aware of the mutterings that continued among Endecott's entourage. It seemed that Darnell was a hothead, held in check by his older colleagues. I attempted to be courteous to them all. It was difficult to remain distant, especially as we all suffered the same privations and discomforts in that noxious space we co-habited. For the most part I was either ignored or treated with bare civility. However, John Woodbury and Trask were pleasant. I enjoyed their company. They were keen to talk about our separate experiences in New England and were puzzled that neither Endecott nor his entourage wanted to learn from them. Johnny had become friendly with Humphrey Woodbury, twenty-two years old and five years younger than Johnny. Horrors of cramped, sordid, frightening life aboard were mitigated by Johnny, who was also the entertainment manager, having spent many years with an acting troupe. One of the passengers, a maid of Mistress Gott, had a lovely voice. She and Johnny would sing together, with passengers joining in to sing the chorus. There were periods of violent weather which drove us off course or required *Abigail* to lie a-hull with sprits'l, main and fore sails furled, top masts brought down and helm lashed to leeward. Other times we were becalmed and left to drift with the currents, losing the miles we had gained.

Endecott became increasingly and actively hostile towards me, resulting in strong words. Endecott's party started following their leader's example. This divided the passengers—there were a few, such as Woodbury and Trask who were supportive of me. They were in a delicate position with their obvious loyalty to Conant, yet having to be part of the settlement that Endecott was to govern. One evening, Johnny and I were on deck sheltered from the strong winds in the lee of the quarterdeck. The sound and fury of the wind and sea with the repeated thunderclaps of the course and main sails above our heads, being braced in response to the shifting wind, made talking difficult, just the occasional grunts of our pleasure as we embraced *Abigail's* battling of the elements. A sharper shift, a shouted order to brace the mainsail above us. Johnny grabbed my arm and hauled me away from the rail we had been leaning against. A large turning block crashed down bounced off the rail and disappeared overboard, trailing a line behind it. Johnny attempted to grab the line, too late.

"Thanks, Johnny. That would have caused serious damage if it had hit one of us. Look at the damage it has done to the rail. How in heaven's name did you see it?"

"I was looking up at the sails, wondering if we needed to shorten them when I noticed the block hanging from the end of the main yard. I was just trying to work out what it was when it let go."

Thurloe Squires, watch officer, leaned over the quarterdeck rail and asked if we suffered any damage. He asked us both to come up to the quarterdeck. Captain Gauden had been alerted. Squires had seen the block fall out of the corner of his eye. The helmsman had confirmed what he saw. Gauden joined us.

"There is no reason for that block to have let go like that. I'm concerned. Both of you should go below. I will investigate this incident in the morning. Good night to you both."

With that we were dismissed. Later the next day, I was called to the captain's cabin.

"Good morning, Isaac. I hate to say this, my investigation leads me to the conclusion that there has been a possible intentional attempt to kill or seriously damage you. That block should not have been on the main yard, the two lift blocks at the end of the yard are still in place. No blocks are missing from the rigging. Therefore, it must have been put in place for the specific purpose of injuring someone. There was no one in the rigging at the time. The fact that there was a long line attached to the block means that it could have been held by a light line around a cleat at the end of the yard, the line led back to the crosstree under the maintop and then led down the mainstay to the head gratings where the bitter end was belayed. Releasing the line at the head would cause the heavy block to fall taking the line with it and over the side. God knows how it could have been rigged without any of the crew noticing, unless one or more crew members were involved. However, every one of the crew denies that. Given the conditions, the on-duty watch were at their stations on deck. It seems nobody saw anything untoward. What needs further investigation is when the block was placed there. In daylight it would have been seen."

I was puzzled. It seemed a chancy way of trying to get rid of someone. It depended on the block being let go, hitting the intended victim, and disappearing over the side without anyone seeing what had happened. With the block identified, it clearly didn't take long to work out what must have occurred. I was more of the opinion that it was an ill-thought out scare tactic which had potentially more lethal consequences than had been planned.

Johnny and I went below, the southeast winds of the night before had increased and veered to the south and then southwest causing *Abigail* to head north of her track. If the wind shifted further we would need to tack. In addition, the main and fore courses were taken down, all passengers confined. The bad weather continued for the next two weeks. We made little headway. We had been at sea for six weeks.

The conditions below went from bad to worse—the odors, unwashed bodies, mildewed clothes, urine, feces, vomit, the bilges, fouled water, rancid, spilled milk and butter, the cold, the constant damp, filthy clothing, skin sores, teeth and gums aching, stomach and head aches, women's complaints. Skin lesions, sprains, bruises poorly cared for. Constant use of nit combs to remove nits and lice. Wooden and pewter chamber pots were in constant use. In the rough seas they often emptied themselves onto the deck. Sea water that regularly streamed into the cabin mixed with spilled human waste found its way into the bilges at the bottom of the boat making the overpowering smell a permanent feature. Algae, green, slimy growth appeared on the wood surfaces. I was reminded of the unsavory living conditions that caused us to flee Plymouth. At sea it was horrifyingly worse. The passengers who had come from towns seemed more inured to the smells. Those of us from the countryside were not so lucky. On days of prolonged calm, Annie organized the women to scrub the lower deck, the walls, and beams with a vinegar solution. They threw out lice, nit and flea ridden straw from old palliasses, and replaced it with new straw stowed in the hold. The hard work provided a short respite, hardly improving the general humor. When the smell from the bilges became overpowering, they were flooded with seawater and pumped out. The odor endured, as did the passengers.

On another day of severe storms, the conditions required *Abigail* to lie a-hull, sea anchor deployed, all sails struck except the reefed mizzen. Lifelines had been set for the benefit of the crew. Annie had sent me on an urgent errand to the cook room which meant I had to mount the for'ard steps to the main deck close by the cook room door. While in lengthy conversation with the cook over a beaker of hot soup, there was a muffled shout from outside requesting Mr. Stanfield's attendance in the captain's cabin. I finished my soup and went out on deck. A lifeline led from the fo'c'sle steps aft to the steps to the quarterdeck. In the howling wind, horizontal rain and bucking seas I dragged myself down the lifeline bracing against the pressure of wind trying to tear me away when, of a sudden, the lifeline went slack and I was blown across the deck and over the lee rail. I just managed to save myself by grabbing hold of a main shroud lanyard and was able to haul myself back onto the deck. Two crewmen tending the capstan holding the anchor line came to my aid and I was assisted aft.

The captain was surprised to see me. I had not been summoned. I told him what had happened. He looked grave and told me to return to the main cabin while he investigated this new incident. I was later informed that on close examination, the lifeline had not been belayed properly or had let go, accidentally or otherwise. Mr. Hadfield had interrogated the on-duty watch, a senior seaman who had been assigned to set the lifelines as a standard part of heavy weather sailing preparation. He insisted he had set them correctly. The two crewmen manning the capstan had not noticed anyone approaching the cook room. Mr. Gauden was now convinced that I was the intended target for both this and the first incident with the block. I still found it difficult to believe. The only animosity I had experienced was over my relations with Mr. Endecott. Notwithstanding the threat made to me, I couldn't believe these incidents had been engineered by any of the passengers. Apart from anything else, it would have required an experienced seaman to do so.

I told Gauden to leave it with me. He should not further damage his relationship with Endecott by suggesting his direct or indirect involvement. I would work with Tiny Hadfield with regard to the crew and Johnny Dawkins, who had a number of pairs of eyes and ears open among the passengers, Jeannie, who had her own circle of friends, as well as Annie, who was friendly with the ladies, to come up with ways to uncover what was going on. I promised to keep the captain informed before any plan was executed.

The voyage continued without any more idea of who might have organized or participated in the two incidents. The worsening conditions on board were of more concern and over the next two weeks the passengers' attention was reduced to endurance. People were ill, some with serious stomach complaints that caused further burdens on attempts to deal with noxious outflow, others with a fever, and scurvy was beginning to appear. With all fruit and vegetables consumed, crewmen were ordered, to their complete satisfaction, to fish from the gallery at the stern or if the weather was sufficiently benign from the towed longboat . However, little was likely to be caught until we were closer to the fishing grounds off Newfoundland. While soundings were made daily, it was still too deep for the lead to reach bottom.

Mistress Endecott was, perhaps, the sickest of everyone and remained prostrate. Annie was her constant companion and did what she could to make her comfortable, bathing her head, making her broth to eat. Endecott was grateful and worried, angry at his own helplessness. Gauden offered him the freedom of his cabin and the quarterdeck, of which he made extensive use. His entourage were quiet around him. Sharing the same dismal conditions, they engaged much more with the other passengers. Aware of the incidents that had threatened my life, they had commiserated with me and became more civil, the angry young Darnell being the sole exception. Johnny had also been telling his friends among the indentured about some of my exploits, including how part of an ear was missing together with why I had a blaze across my cheek where a part of my beard had turned white, inflicted when saving *Rosie* from pirates. These exploits filtered back to their masters which further eased the tension.

—— CHAPTER 5 ——

Journal entry – *August 1628*

Abigail's progress towards New England was being made in spite of the gales, calm, fog and contrary winds. Squires invited me onto the quarterdeck whenever he was the watch officer. If the weather permitted, he let me bring James with me. James was fascinated, observing Squires use the backstaff (whenever the sun showed itself) to determine our latitude. Interesting, as I had been taught in my days as a sailor to use the cross-staff, an earlier design. He also used the traverse board to note our log speed, knots through the water and heading. In the many days I was with him I was able to gain some idea of our progress. The distance travelled in a watch might vary between 4 – 20 nautical miles. We saw whales, grampus, and porpoises, even the occasional sunfish. As we approached Newfoundland there were many seagulls that screamed and soared above and around the boat, feeding off the refuse that was chucked over the side. We also saw clumps of seaweed and other vegetation which showed we were close to land.

Early one morning, I went on deck to find we were in thick fog, with no wind, sails flapped disconsolately shaking off the dew and soaking anyone underneath. Dodging the drops, I made my way for'ard to the forbidden head, so thick was the fog I could barely see a few paces ahead of me. Certainly, no one could see me from the quarterdeck using the facility that was denied to all passengers. While sitting there I was struck from behind and knocked unconscious. Next thing I knew I was being hauled aboard the longboat by two crewmen who had been fishing from it and seen me barely conscious float by out of the fog. I was returned to *Abigail*. Henry Gauden had me taken down to his cabin, put into his berth, and sat waiting until I was sufficiently awake to question me. Meantime, Annie had been called and was kneeling beside me tending to a bloody wound on the side of my head.

"Why, Mr. Stanfield," she said, "this is quite like old times. What have you been doing to yourself?"

Beneath the apparent cheer there was a desperately worried woman. Someone was trying to kill her husband and had almost succeeded. She looked up at Gauden, who saw the concern in her face.

"A question I was about to ask your husband."

I admitted I had gone to the head and had been struck by someone that I did not see and woke up lying on the floor of the longboat with two anxious looking crewmen peering down at me. Startled, I had wondered where I was and why before falling back to sleep, awaking a short time later comfortably settled in the captain's berth.

Gauden jumped to his feet and paced, barely avoiding Annie. Having mopped up the blood, she felt it safer to retreat and sit on the vacated chair and listen to the Captain.

"Isaac, this is the third and much more serious incident—no, attack. If it hadn't been for the fortuitous presence of fishermen you would have gone without a trace. There is no doubt in my mind that you have been the victim of three attempts on your life. The perpetrator is aboard *Abigail*, a passenger with or without the help of a crewman. I can think of no reason why a crewman would have carried out these attacks on his own initiative. As soon as you feel able, you should return to your own berth and I will have a word with Governor Endecott."

Annie escorted me and my sore head back to the main cabin and put me into her berth, ordering that the cabin be left in place. She reclined, leaning against the side of the boat with her arms around me, my eyes closed and head resting on her sweet bosom. Her hand reached under my shirt and started caressing me. I looked up at her. Her eyes were closed. My movement in response to her fingers brought her back. Her eyes opened, startled, and she withdrew her hand. It had been an unthought, unguarded moment and she whispered a regretful apology. I sighed and slept.

Meantime, I was informed later, Captain Gauden called Mr. Endecott to his cabin and told him what had just happened to me. He gave me a detailed account of what was said.

"Mr. Endecott, someone has been trying to kill Mr. Stanfield, be it a member of the crew or a passenger, possibly with the help from a crewmember. You, Mr. Endecott are responsible for your people. However, given your attitude towards Mr. Stanfield, I will have my first mate, Mr. Chandler, interview you and the passengers to account for each person's whereabouts and seek confirmation from other passengers. He will provide me with a list of those without that confirmation. I will have Mr. Hadfield do the same with the crew."

Endecott bristled and protested that no one under his command would have done such a thing. Gauden responded:

"There appears to be an understanding among your entourage that Mr. Stanfield is an imposter, unremittingly insubordinate to you and a threat to be dealt with. I have to believe you are fully aware of his reputation and yet your awareness has not been shared with your people. Perhaps you do not know that in addition to his perhaps unmatched knowledge of New England he is a successful businessman, ship owner, and property owner. He counts among his many friends and acquaintances highly influential people, some of whom are a part of the company that employs you. Without wishing to belabor the point, I must remind you that it is my intention to deliver you and all the passengers to your destination. To do so requires everyone to be civil and not physically attacking each other. I would be grateful, therefore, if you would alert your people to what has happened and what I am proposing to do about it. I want you to pass on to them that not only is Mr. Stanfield not your subordinate, he is an experienced and influential resource that should be cherished not vilified."

Endecott was furious at the dressing down he received from Gauden.

"How dare you speak to me that way. I am Governor Endecott! If I was ashore, you would be arrested and whipped."

"You are not ashore. You are not Governor here. As Captain, I have absolute authority. I also should remind you that you have been appointed to lead a small, isolated settlement in a large and potentially hostile country. You are totally dependent on ships' captains like myself for everyone and all provisions that come to your settlement and all produce you might wish to send back to England. You are also subject to the reports that returning ships' captains must provide to the Company that charters those ships. I advise you, therefore, to be civil. Now, good day to you."

Tiny Hadfield had been interrogating the crew one by one after each of the incidents. He had kept a record of each interview and had asked each crewman what they were doing, who they had seen or been with at the time. It seemed that everyone's presence was accounted for by at least one other crewman. I asked Tiny whether that was probable. Surely, there must have been times when a sailor would have been on his own. No, crew worked in pairs, or more, on watch and were normally overseen by their officers. What about off-watch crew? Down below together. When anyone went on deck, they would have been seen by the on-watch crew. Tiny had made a list for each of the incidents, of anyone unaccounted for, and compared the lists to see if there was a match. There wasn't and everyone on the lists seemed to have a plausible alibi. Though not convinced, I thanked Tiny for all the hard work he had undertaken in addition to his normal duties. I also didn't like to raise the possibility that there might have been collusion among the crewmen.

When I was back on my feet, Tiny, Johnny, and I agreed that I would be accompanied by Johnny at all times and when on deck should keep to the quarterdeck under the watchful eye of the watch officer. Everyone, passengers and crew, now alerted, it became somewhat unnerving. I seemed to have the eyes of the world on me wherever I went. Our voyage was nearly over, but the problem would almost certainly accompany me when we were ashore.

CHAPTER 6

Journal entry – *September 1628*

Masthead lookout sighted Monhegan Island on the 4th day of September, to much celebration, standing in the turbulent sea, a fortress imperturbable, two points off the starboard bow, an added reason to wish Annie well on her 29th birthday. We arrived in Naumkeag 6 September, 1628. Captain Gauden, guided by John Woodbury, worked *Abigail* past a large, wooded island, marking the entrance to a broad bay lined with trees, through a scattering of small islands into an inlet, then through a narrowing passage into a pool with three rivers feeding into it. We turned south into one of the rivers that Woodbury said was the North River. On our larboard side lay the Naumkeag peninsula. The sails furled and the anchor dropped, *Abigail* swung round to settle head to wind. We could see a few houses on the higher ground above the water, among the trees and a number of people on the shore waving. I sighted the imposing figure of Roger Conant, with his wife watching us. A shallop was rowed out. Endecott and his entourage quickly boarded it and were rowed back to be greeted by the Conants. Mistress Endecott was too ill to be moved.

The remaining passengers on deck pressed against the starboard rail. Having been used to the squalid, fetid, cramped and dark atmosphere during the trip over, the fresh, scented air that greeted us was intoxicating. We couldn't wait to disembark. Annie, Jeannie, and the children continued to drink in the sights, sounds and smells that over-whelmed their senses. After the constant, unremitting clatter and thrumming of a ship at sea, the lap of the water and cries of birds, re-laxed muscles and eased tensions, A sense of peace returned for the first time in eleven weeks.

I told Annie that she and the family should stay aboard, despite the conditions, until I could arrange accommodation for us all. I was concerned that provision had not been made for the arrivals and their possessions. I did not want us to be caught up in a confusion of pas-sengers and settlers, brought to land and nowhere to go. The crew had launched *Abigail's* longboat to begin off-loading supplies. Johnny and I took advantage and slipped away to be rowed ashore to find out what awaited us.

I had sent word from England to Roger Conant that my family and I would be coming on *Abigail*. I wasn't at all sure the letter had arrived. Perhaps it was with the bundle of company correspondence waiting to be offloaded. I wanted to meet with him as soon as possible but he was with Endecott. Neither Trask nor Woodbury were on the shallop with Endecott, so they were unable to soften the blow of an imperious Endecott announcing his immediate replacement as the new Governor of the settlement. With Conant busy, we were free to explore. It quick-ly became apparent that my fears were well founded. There were no dwellings prepared for an influx of thirty or more new settlers.

The settlement is on raised ground on a spit of land that protrudes into the bay between the river to the north, called the North River, and a further river to the south. The land is also called Naumkeag after the local Indian tribe. The spit is perhaps a mile or so in length and a half mile wide at its widest point. Its shape is like a prancing horse, its body to the southwest, head and neck to the northeast, front legs to the southeast with a wide cove between them. It is wooded with a cleared open area where the settlers had planted fields of maize, tobacco, and other crops, now harvested or ready for harvesting. The settlement has good views, when not blocked by trees, landward to the north and west and out into the bay to the east. There are some ten or so dwellings, some more substantial than others, haphazardly scattered among the trees close to the mouth of the North River, with paths connecting them to each other. The houses have gardens, fenced with wide planks of rough sawn wood, similar to those I had seen in Plimouth. With no obvious, well-trodden paths to the southwest it seemed that travelling was done by boat beyond the immediate area.

We met up with one of the old settlers, Mr. Thomas Gardner, whom I had met four years back on Cape Ann. Mr. Gardner with his family, wife Margaret and four boys, Tom, George, Tim, who were around the same age as my son James, and baby Samuel, have a house on the fringes of the settlement close to the planting fields.

I asked him if he had temporary accommodation for four adults and two children. He showed us a rough storage hut, ten by ten feet, some distance from the house. It was framed and had a roof with walls on two sides. I asked whether we could make it more habitable to which he agreed. He said he had a store of rough planking and some canvas which we could use. We thanked him and I told Johnny to start preparing the hut for the construction we would need to undertake, while I went in search of Mr. Conant. I promised I would return later that day. We would make ourselves a temporary home while the others stayed on the boat.

When I went back to the landing place, many of *Abigail's* passengers had been ferried ashore and the locals were making similar arrangements with them. Those first passengers to disembark, being primarily in the Endecott entourage, were taken in hand by Mr. Conant and housed at or close to his own dwelling, with their servants set to establishing a military style encampment on open ground further west, down Naumkeag. What I found was that Endecott and Conant were at odds with each other. I saw John Woodbury and asked him what had happened. He motioned me to step away out of earshot.

"Governor Endecott, I fear, is not the most tactful person I have met. Unfortunately, Trask and I weren't able to get to Mr. Conant in time to prepare him. When we arrived Endecott had already announced to everyone that the Dorchester Company, which had paid for and supplied the original settlers that he insisted on calling Old Planters, had been dissolved and the new company, the New England Company, had taken ownership of everyone and everything and as he had been appointed that company's agent he was taking possession and command. He did not, alas, have the common courtesy to take Mr. Conant aside and forewarn him that he had been replaced. Several of the Old Planters had paid their own way and took exception to the fact they would now be considered Company employees by Mr. Endecott. As you can see, not only is Mr. Conant upset, the Old Planters, who had been persuaded to come with Conant and who respect him as their leader, are angry."

Endecott had by his arrogant assumption of power set up a confrontation with the people, most of those who came on *Abigail* siding with Endecott, the others, mostly the original Naumkeag settlers, the Old Planters, who had begun to adopt the name for themselves, siding with Conant. Leaving the discontent unresolved, Endecott decided he wanted to explore Naumkeag. He was disdainful of the settlement Conant and his followers had built and dissatisfied with the lack of preparations that should, in his opinion, have been made for their arrival. William Trask offered to take him up the North River by boat to investigate further.

I was able to meet with Conant, who welcomed me warmly. We had spent time together when he was with the Separatists in New Plimouth, several years ago. I knew that Conant had the strength of character to deal with Endecott's abrasiveness and would, once tempers had been cooled and a more reasonable Endecott emerged, be prepared to accept his being replaced as the Governor of the settlement. I pledged support to Conant and left him to deal with the situation.

I boarded a shallop returning to *Abigail* that had been making repeated journeys to offload supplies, passengers, and their possessions. Annie, Jeannie, and Abigail had been invited onto the quarterdeck and were watching the bustle on the ship and ashore. I told Annie we would have temporary accommodation ready for us all the next day and I would be back to get them. However, she was worried about the weakened and ailing Mistress Endecott. She felt duty bound to continue to assist her while the poor lady was confined to her berth. Annie told me to take Jeannie and the children when I came back tomorrow. I described the Gardner house, in a clearing, surrounded by trees and close to cultivated fields, and the Gardner family. James and Abigail were happy to learn about the children. They had only a few older children to play with on the long voyage.

I returned to the Gardner house with some of our provisions. Johnny had been hard at work, clearing out the hut, retrieving and stacking the planks of wood, and measuring out on the ground the dimensions of the expanded accommodation he felt we needed. We showed Gardner what we planned. He was pleased because after we had moved on, he would be getting back his hut, transformed into a substantially better barn. Johnny and I set to, constructing our first home (even if temporary) in New England. One large room, that at night could be divided by a canvas screen. We constructed an outside firepit and a privy at the edge of the clearing. By late afternoon on the following day Johnny and I returned to *Abigail* to fetch our families. Leaving Johnny to organize the disembarkation, I went to see Captain Gauden, Tobias Chandler, and Thurloe Squires, who were on the quarterdeck overseeing the unloading of the freight destined for Naumkeag. I thanked them for ensuring we all arrived safely. Gauden laughed, somewhat ironically.

"No thanks to us. Isaac, you were fortunate. I am most concerned that we did not find the culprit or culprits. However, Mr. Hadfield has some information which might be relevant."

He leaned over the quarterdeck rail and shouted for the bosun, who was working with the crew by the main hatch. Tiny came up to the quarterdeck. He was told to report his findings about missing crew.

"Yes, Mr. Stanfield. We have two crewmen who have gone missing, called Spiggott and Hendry. They disappeared soon after we arrived. They were taken on shortly before we left England, as were many of the crew. Not unusual when making an Atlantic crossing. Not much known about them. Competent seamen. Don't know whether they knew each other before. They did share a watch and seemed close."

The names meant nothing to me. I would probably recognize them if I saw them but couldn't put faces to the names. I would ask Johnny if he knew them. With no suspicious behavior or rumors concerning the passengers identified through Johnny's and our wives' contacts, Spiggott and Hendry were all we had to go on.

I wished Captain Gauden good sailing and a safe return to England. Tiny accompanied me back down to the main deck. I handed him a package containing journal entries and letters for Will Whiteway back in Dorchester and my business manager Mr. Ebenezer Scroud in Plymouth. He promised to see them into safe hands when he got back to England.

"Mr. Stanfield, pardon my boldness. With your experiences as ship owner and trader I do not find it difficult to imagine you being tempted back into that business."

I laughed and admitted the thought had crossed my mind.

"If and when you do, please keep me in mind. I have the fondest memories of *Rosie* and your role in the latter part of her life. I would deem it an honor to serve with you again."

I was touched, promised I would certainly keep him in mind, shook his hand and he returned to his duties.

CHAPTER 7

Journal entry – *September 1628*

Johnny and I were able to load our possessions onto the hard-working shallop and together with Jeannie and the children returned to the settlement. Abigail burst into tears as we left.

"What about Amos, Nanna, and Beatrice?"

I looked startled. James reminded me, "The goats."

"Well done, assistant shepherdess, Mummy will take care of them until tomorrow. Then they will be brought ashore and join us in our new home."

As we passed through the settlement on our way to the Gardner house, the children were fascinated by the loud and contentious arguments among the adults. The arrivals at first thankful to be ashore were now realizing that nothing had been planned to house them. The Old Planters were defending themselves by accusing the new arrivals of lack of planning and coming unequipped. I had been away a couple of hours and Endecott was back from his trip up the North River and retrieved his wife, carried on a litter to his house. It was clear he had taken time to think in the hours he was away. He needed to work with Conant to bring everyone together with a clear plan of action. Now was not the time to worry about protocol and his position. The population had more than doubled, everyone to be housed, their provisions and the supplies needed to finish being brought ashore and stored under cover. *Abigail* was due to sail to New Plimouth and then back to England. Gauden was keen to be away.

Over the next weeks I stayed clear of Endecott and with Annie, Johnny, Jeannie, and the children (taken in tow by the three eldest Gardner boys), we settled into our new, temporary home. I had few moments alone to enjoy with Annie, especially our much-cherished intimacy. One thing we needed to do was to confirm our recordkeeping responsibilities. Annie had become, of necessity, the family bookkeeper many years ago, when I had taken myself away from her and James for long stretches of time. Once back together again and even when we were married, she continued that role, to the delight of Mr. Ebenezer Scroud. Now that we could no longer depend on him, the roles of record and bookkeeper became more critical.

I had brought funds with me. Anything to be acquired and brought from England could be paid for with a note to be dealt with in England by Mr. Scroud. But all acquisitions and services that we required over here must be accounted for and paid from our immediate resources. With those resources finite, we had to keep accurate records of our expected expenditure. Where possible we also needed to barter or otherwise charge for produce and services we might offer. Obviously, when my farming and trading enterprises started becoming productive we would require a local Mr. Scroud. Until then, Annie agreed to continue to be the mistress of the purse.

To regain our fitness, Johnny and I took to our swords and began a daily practice fencing session, which we continued whenever we had the opportunity. We agreed that it wasn't just fitness. We were in a new and raw environment without functioning law and order. There was a possible assailant afoot. We needed to be able to defend ourselves and our family. For hunting, we had a fowling piece, but Johnny preferred his bow. He suggested we should somehow upgrade the fowling piece to a flintlock rifle if one could be found over here, something we should order from England, if we can't get a ship's captain to sell us one. I told him I had brought a brace of pistols with me, including balls and powder.

We built a pen to house our three goats. They were delighted to be eating fresh vegetation again. Thomas Gardner advised us that we needed to protect the goats from wolves and coyotes so the pen had to be sturdy. Gardner told us about their move from Cape Ann to Naumkeag in 1626. Roger Conant, Allen, Balch, Gardner, Gray, Knight, the Normans, Palfrey, Tilley, Trask and Woodbury, together with their families, about twenty total including women and children were there when *Abigail* arrived, together with twelve cows, a bull, and their progeny. When they first arrived at Naumkeag, they had found a seemingly abandoned Indian village with several wetus. These were round huts made of long stakes sunk into the ground in a wide circle and bent and lashed together at the top leaving a round hole. The stakes were then covered in hides and bark. Inside, a firepit with the hole in the roof allowed smoke from the fire to escape. The description fitted the huts we used and built in Saco ten or so years earlier. Conant and his followers took over the wetus while they built houses for themselves. The wetus were then taken down or used for storage. It was only later that Conant realized that the native Indians were somewhat nomadic and moved between different locations depending on the season and the availability of food. They had only temporarily left the village. It took Conant's considerable diplomatic skills to reach an acceptable accommodation with the returning residents. So much so that the Indians adopted the settlers and provided invaluable support in the provision of food and teaching what, when and how to grow their own.

Gardner told us that the tribe were friendly towards the settlers, these foreign and strange invaders of their land. He was amazed at how gentle they were and kind. Ten years ago they were almost wiped out by diseases that they knew had come from the English. In spite of which, they taught the settlers how to plant corn from good seed into small mounds of earth, with rotting fish buried in the mounds. I remembered learning the same in Saco. Gardner said the Indians also persuaded them that the corn seedlings needed to be tended throughout the growing season.

I asked about the lack of preparedness of the Old Planters for the

arrival of Endecott and the new settlers. He was a little defensive, saying they were not fully aware of when we were to arrive and how many
there were of us. Life here was a constant struggle and there was little
time to divert their attention to preparing for an unconfirmed arrival.
Everyone, he said, was responsible for building their own house. He
hoped that among the new arrivals there would be carpenters with the
tools and materials needed to build houses, such as nails and glass for
windows. Better still, send over blacksmiths to make the items needed together with quantities of iron and steel to make the nails, locks,
as well as fittings for ploughs and carts. How about livestock, I asked
him. He said he was pleased we had brought the three goats and that
they had survived. The settlement desperately needed more horses, cattle, sheep, goats, pigs, hens. Sadly, many failed to survive the crossing.
    I told him that it was costly especially when the losses were so high.
He shook his head. We will not survive without the means to build
sustainable farms, which means farm animals. I noticed there were no
horses that I could see, and I understood why. While it costs £5 to ship
one person over here, it costs twice that to ship a horse for the space,
including fodder needed. He nodded and added, it is rare to lose a person on the voyage, however up to 80% of livestock is lost. The reason
we still have our goats is because they were the only animals aboard
and, therefore, had space, fodder, and were well cared for. It is foolish
to pack too many animals into too small a space and expect them to
survive. I asked him about provisions, food stocks for the new settlers.
    "We have enough for ourselves with what we grow and kill. Our
friends, the Indians, help us, if necessary, during the winter when they
are here. We have not had the time to build substantial harvests to feed
so many additional mouths. Everyone arriving here needs to come with
a year's worth of victuals to give them the time to plant, grow, and harvest the food for themselves."
    "Do you share what you have?"
    "Of course, to the extent we have anything to share. There is nothing
to buy so the settlers must bring everything needed, wool and linens,
axes, saws, spades, every kind of tool, utensils, dishes, cutlery, leather.

If someone has extra, I suppose it's possible for them to sell it to some-one else by bartering—money has no value here."

Annie spent many days with Mistress Endecott who did not seem to be responding well to coming ashore. Annie told me that the Governor, as we all now called him, was worried. He was working with Roger Conant trying to placate the Old Planters while, at the same time, at-tempting to settle the new arrivals. Apparently, the growing of tobac-co is a major bone of contention. Endecott wants to ban it even though it is a source of livelihood and is being sent back to England as trade.

I had asked Johnny if he knew Spiggott and Hendry. He said he knew what they looked like but had not had many dealings with them. He did a thorough search of the Naumkeag peninsula and found no trace of them. They could have gone to a number of the settlements in Massachusetts Bay, even further north to Piscataqua and beyond, or joined the crew of one of the many fishing boats that were a constant presence. I was concerned that the incidents remained unresolved. Annie was more forthright.

"Isaac, my sweet, we can't just ignore the fact that someone or other is determined to kill you. Each successive incident on *Abigail* became a more serious attempt on your life. The last was the worst. Each could only have been carried out by a member of the crew."

"No Annie, the first attempt I agree with you. It was clearly pre-meditated. Only a crewman could have set up that block. A passen-ger wouldn't have had the skills and experience. Also, crewmen were up the mast and tending sail all the time. A passenger up there would have been seen and hauled down as soon as he started up the ratlines. The second and third attempts were or seemed more spontaneous and anyone could have committed them."

"Alright, why would a sailor want to kill you? The only ones that you say know you are the captain and the bosun. The Governor is your enemy and there are members of his entourage who have made threats against you. It seems to me quite possible that a crewman was bribed to do these dastardly attacks."

"Annie love, what does concern me is that our family might also be a target. All the more reason that we keep out of the way of Endecott and the new settlers. While we are currently housed and welcomed by a friendly family, it has to be a temporary accommodation. The Gardner family are on the fringes of the old settlement and Endecott plans to build a new larger settlement a little bit further down the peninsula. I want us to move further away, for safety and also to enable us to start our new life on our own land where we can build a more suitable home."

CHAPTER 8

Journal entry – *October 1628*

Early one morning, at the beginning of October, Johnny and I borrowed the Gardners' light shallop and went exploring, determined to establish a more permanent home as far as possible from Endecott and Naumkeag. It was a warm, clear day with a light, steady breeze from the south, the water reflecting the blue sky, cool to the touch and soft. From Naumkeag we sailed a mile or two southeast across a small bay, rounded a headland then southwest between the mainland and a densely wooded island. After about a half mile we had to sail back as we saw that, at the far end, our way was blocked. What we thought was an island was a peninsula attached to the mainland by a sandbar, blocking our way. We had sailed into a sheltered natural harbor, with room to moor a hundred ships.

After rounding the eastern end of the peninsula, we continued sailing southwest along the tree lined coast, the autumn colors of the changing leaves adding warmth and lifting our hearts. Working our way past many islands, most covered in trees, some cleared for grazing, we passed an island to starboard, where an early settler called William Noddle lived, and into the large harbor that Reverend William Blackstone and I had explored in 1624. Blackstone was then a young man of twenty-eight, a year older than me, but seemed much older with his wisdom and tranquility. We made our way across the harbor towards the Shawmut peninsula where Blackstone had his house. Keeping it to larboard we headed directly for Mishawum, working the shallop into the Mystic River passing Winnesimmet to starboard, the home of Mr. Samuel Maverick, who had built a substantial, fortified house there, Gardner told us. A place I wanted to visit at another time. We beached the shallop and went to meet with Thomas Walford.

I had known Walford in 1623 when he was part of Robert Gorges disastrous expedition to New England that Sir Ferdinando had persuaded me to accompany, much against my will, to help in his son's attempt to establish the first government in New England. We had set up the Gorges base at the Wessagusset settlement established by Thomas Weston in 1621. I remembered Walford, a hardworking blacksmith. When Robert Gorges and I returned to England in '24, Walford and his wife left Wessagusset and moved north to Mishawum. He had built a substantial, stockaded house with a thatched roof.

He greeted us cordially and, once he recognized me, expressed his surprise in meeting me again after so long. I told him that I had always wanted an opportunity to return with my family, despite that abortive trip with Gorges. I said that I was sailing with my friend Johnny Dawkins along the coastline, hoping to make contact with the people that I had left behind in 1624. He told us that he and his wife came to Mishawum because it was isolated, with local Indians that were hospitable and had welcomed them as neighbors. He suggested we might like to meet up with Reverend Blackstone at Shawmut, a short boat ride away, William Noddle on his island, and Samuel Maverick across the river. Sadly, until recently we would also have been able to visit David Thomson on his island in the outer harbor.

I asked where David had gone. I was shocked to hear that he had died, and that Amyse Thomson had married Mr. Maverick. Walford was loathe or otherwise unable to answer my questions and suggested I should talk to Blackstone, who he thought might know more. I remembered Walford as being a somewhat taciturn individual so didn't push him. After showing us around his property which was on open land that sloped down to the water, and on which he grazed a few cows, a bull and goats, we parted in friendly manner happy to meet again at some time in the near future.

In the late afternoon, we sailed into the Charles River, named for the then Prince Charles, by Captain John Smith in 1614, around the northern shore of Shawmut then doused the sail and rowed northwest into an inlet, making for a muddy shore with the tide beginning to ebb. Blackstone's house was on high ground. We walked up a well-used path through trees to a wide clearing. The house, made of clapboard timber, had a steeply pitched, thatched roof with a brick-built center. It was small, a window either side of a solid door. A well-stocked, fenced garden surrounded the house, with flowers on either side of a path from a gate to the front door. Behind the house, the garden, full of rows of vegetables some already gathered, a small orchard with harvested apple and plum trees, a few windfalls still on the ground with a number of chickens pecking away at them. Beyond, a field on which stood an animal barn with hay loft. We knocked on the door. There was no response. I remembered that Blackstone was not easily distracted from his books so knocked again more loudly. Sounds of movement and the door opened.

In the four years since I had last seen him, William Blackstone remained as I remembered him. He looked at me and then at Johnny. Then a flicker of recognition. No surprise, just a pleasant smile and a simple

"Welcome, Mr. Isaac Stanfield and your companion. Come in."

He then turned and led the way back to his living room. There was a central hall with two open doors to the left, a bedroom and what looked like a kitchen further down the hall. To the right a large room with two comfortable armchairs by a hearth with a small fire, a window on each of the three outside walls, a table, laden with books, some open, with four chairs and the walls hidden by bookshelves which included interesting natural specimens, presumably collected from woods and shore. He pulled up a further chair by the hearth and invited us to sit.

"Some refreshment, gentlemen?"

Before we could reply he had left the room and gone to the kitchen, we could see him through the hearth, which served both rooms. A pitcher of ale, three beakers, a loaf of bread with butter and cheese appeared and we moved to the table. Books cleared away, we sat with beakers of ale in our hands and saluted each other. I introduced Johnny and said we had travelled from Naumkeag in order to meet up with my old friend again. William smiled.

"Mr. Dawkins, I must tell you that your friend Isaac Stanfield must share responsibility for my being here on Shawmut. In 1623, we explored the area, and both agreed that the hill on which we sit would make an ideal location for me to establish my own home, which I proceeded to accomplish shortly after Isaac returned to England."

He settled back and waited for me to explain why we were there. He nodded occasionally as I spoke and when I had finished, he asked me what I intended now I had moved my family to New England. I replied that my first intention was to settle my family and establish a self-sufficient homestead even half as welcoming and attractive as he had done, then to rebuild over here the business I had left behind in England as a ship owner and trader. He smiled and rose to put another log on the fire, then lit candles on the heavy oaken mantelpiece.

"Gentlemen, I would be pleased to continue our conversation another time. It is getting late. I fear you will not be able to find your way back to Namukeag in the daylight remaining and I suggest you do not try to at night until you learn the tides, currents, sandbars, and rocky ledges that abound in these waters. I suggest you stay the night. I can offer you these two chairs by the fire or you can make use of the hay loft in the barn out back, whichever you prefer."

Johnny suggested the hay loft, to which I agreed. Satisfied, he said he would prepare supper for us, and we should make ourselves comfortable. He also pointed to the privy through a window. Johnny asked if we could have a look at his garden and barn before it got too dark.

"Help yourself, I will be preparing the food."

Once away from the house, Johnny asked me how and when I expected to restart the business I had left behind in England. He said he thought my main intent was to start a farm, to become a substantial landowner with the land grant Bushrode had transferred to me.

"That, too, Johnny. With Kate and David arriving early next year, I expect them to partner with us to find the land, confirm ownership with the Governor, build that farm, and to work it. I'm not sure whether David will ever go back to sea after being so badly injured during the pirate attack on *Rosie*. Kate is determined to farm and David, I'm sure, will happily support her. Annie, too, loved the life we had at Barrow Farm and had become a farmer, herself. She realizes that I am at heart a seafarer and a trader and is supportive of my longer term intentions. As for you and Jeannie, what would you like to do? Where would you like to be?"

"Isaac, where you go, I will follow. Jeannie wants to continue to be a part of your family. She is devoted to Annie and adores James and Abigail."

That settled and after a walk round the garden, careful to avoid stepping on the plants in the darkness that had settled quickly, we returned to the house. Over a supper of venison stew, potatoes, and cabbage from the garden, William questioned me further about my plans. I said that we had arranged temporary housing with the Gardner family in Naumkeag. Because of a significant difference of opinion with the new Governor, John Endecott, I wanted to move my family as far as conveniently away from his immediate jurisdiction as possible. I would also like to build a sturdy dwelling to accommodate Johnny, Jeannie, and my family securely over the winter and give us time to find the best location to build a permanent home and farm.

William asked, "How does that objective translate into your plans to be a ship owner and trader?"

"I have a close friend and his wife arriving early next year who I expect will, with my wife, Annie, assume development and management of the farm. We hope to have more children in our respective families. They will need a nourishing environment to grow. A working farm will provide that. Plans are in place to bring many, many hundreds of settlers to New England. Trade, therefore, will become a vital resource to supply provisions and ship produce."

William sat silently with a wry smile on his face. Then he said sadly,

"I found, with your help, Isaac, a peaceful haven to pursue my own interests without having to deal with the noisy outside world. I have found the most soul-satisfying tranquility here. What you tell me is a warning that this happy solitude cannot last. Unhappy though that makes me, I do understand that I have been given the gift of a perfect existence that God has allowed me to appreciate in gentle solitude. However, God did not intend for me to have it all to myself."

Johnny and I commiserated with him. William continued,

"Enough of that. I am minded to help you with your first objective. I have land here beyond anything I can use myself. I would be pleased if you would find a suitable location here on Shawmut for your sturdy homestead. I will introduce you to my Indian friends so they can assist you as they have me. Also, having friendly neighbors will reintroduce me to a social order I thought I had escaped, which I must now learn to reenter."

We thanked him for his wonderful generosity. Johnny asked him about the Indians. He told us that the Shawmut, a segment of the Massachusetts tribe, had been almost completely wiped out by the plague of 1618. The few that survived had moved on, although some came by on hunting trips and became his friends and helped him find water. There were five natural springs, as well as Mill Creek and the Charles River to support life. He cultivated six acres of land to support himself, sharing his produce with the Shawmut over the winter. William said he has the resources to feed us all over the winter, as well, with help from his Indian friends and the expectation that Johnny and I would hunt for meat and provide fish in addition.

He also said that Shawmut, the place, offered so much more than Naumkeag. Fat, black earth around the Charles River, while there was clay soil, graveled and sandy, around Naumkeag. Gentle rolling landscape, fit for pasture, plough, or meadow. There were thick woods with much ground that had been cleared by Indians. There were many hundreds of acres available if we wanted to settle close by. We would need to explore it, which we could do on foot and by boat. William told us that he had been able to become self-supporting quickly. His cows' milk quickly became abundant. Harvests were extraordinary, one gallon of seed produced 28 bushels of corn. Vegetables, all bigger and sweeter—turnips, carrots pumpkins, cucumbers. Wild fruit grew in abundance; strawberries, mayberries, raspberries, cranberries, crabapples, cherries, and currants. He had planted two apple and two plum trees which appeared healthy and were producing more fruit every year. Then there were acorns, chestnuts, hazelnuts, and walnuts. Four kinds of oak, ash, elm, willow, birch, beech, sassafras, juniper, cypress, cedar, spruce, pine and fir—producing turpentine, pitch, tar, masts for building ships and houses. The Indians had also showed William the roots and berries they used to make permanent dyes, soap ash (potash and lard), and salt peter.

"What about the wild animals?" Johnny asked.

"Large animals such as bear and moose, predatory animals that will take your livestock like wolves, fox, martins, wild cats, and—" William laughed, "garden vegetable eaters like deer, muskrats, and squirrels. All of which are useful for their meat and pelts, in addition to the beaver. And while we are about it, the fish. There is an incredible amount available as soon as you throw a baited hook into the water. Bass, skate, lobsters that can be too heavy to land with vicious claws, herring, turbot, sturgeon, cusks, haddock, mullet, eels, crabs, clams, mussels and oysters."

By now it was getting late. We thanked William for the meal, conversation, education, and his hospitality and went to our beds in the hay loft, cows settling for the night below us.

Next morning, refreshed from sluicing ourselves in a nearby stream, we returned to the house to find William making us breakfast. Johnny, ever curious, asked whether he ever became lonely. William said he was a solitary person who was happy in his own company. On occasion he had visitors, Thomas Walford and Samuel Maverick—very different people, Walford and his wife, private people who minded their own business and didn't like society. Maverick, gregarious and a sharp businessman. People were either attracted to him or found him overpowering. I was surprised to hear the gentle Blackstone speak with such vehemence about a man. I assumed he had the latter opinion. I asked about David and Amyse Thomson.

"Ah, I remember you knew them."

"Yes, I have known them for fifteen years, since I first started working for Sir Ferdinando Gorges in England. Good friends, David and I came to New England together in 1616 when we stayed the winter in Saco, then again a few years later when he built Pannaway, his home at Piscataqua. I was greatly saddened to hear he had died. What happened?"

"No one really knows. Mrs. Thomson said that he liked to visit Indian tribes in a light sailing shallop. Normally, he would leave with a companion, an Indian friend, and be gone several days. He used to say he was always looking for trading opportunities. I think he just enjoyed being with Indians. Anyway, he didn't return from one of his trips. None of his Indian friends knew what had happened to him. I asked my Shawmut friends to see if they could find out anything, but they were unsuccessful. His shallop was found some time later, waterlogged and damaged on a rocky ledge south of here. When the Thomsons moved from Piscataqua down to their island near the entrance to the harbor here in 1626, they had become friendly with Maverick. After it was accepted that Thomson had died, Maverick took Mrs. Thomson back to Winnisimmet and they married."

There were obvious questions to be asked. William had become tightlipped, clearly unwilling to discuss the subject further. I had the feeling that he had questions of his own which he had decided to keep to himself. I felt I needed to pursue this at another time, perhaps with Mr. Maverick and his new bride. We left William Blackstone after breakfast saying we hoped to return soon to begin the work of building ourselves a home.

CHAPTER 9

Journal entry – *October 1628*

When we arrived back at the Gardner house we were met by a distraught Jeannie, clutching a crying Abigail to her breast.

"Oh! Mr. Stanfield, someone tried to take James. He is being cared for by Mistress Gardner in the kitchen. She sent one of her boys to fetch Annie from Mistress Endecott."

I left Johnny to comfort Jeannie and went into the kitchen. James was sitting on a stool with a huge grin on his face, his right arm bandaged and in a sling. I looked at Margaret Gardner. She shook her head and grimaced.

"No serious harm done albeit frightening for the poor boy, a superficial knife wound in the right forearm and a wrenched left shoulder."

I turned to James who did not appear frightened, in fact rather pleased with himself. I asked him what had happened.

"Oh! Daddy! That was an adventure. I was damming a brook in the woods with Tom and we ran out of large stones near us so I went looking for more further away. Suddenly, I was grabbed by a man."

"Was he armed?"

"Yes, Daddy, a knife. He was behind me."

"James, how do you know he had a knife?"

"He had it pressed against my throat."

"Jesus save you, what did you do?"

"I shouted in surprise. Tom saw what was going on and ran for help."

"I bet he did. Then what happened?"

"The man started pulling me into the woods."

Margaret and I looked at each other, horrified.

"What did you do?"

"He didn't know I had a big stone in my hand. He stumbled over a root, and I hit his knee as hard as I could. He fell down still holding on to me. As he did he wrenched my arm. I hit him again as he tried to defend himself with his knife and it cut my other arm. He let go and I ran away."

Margaret's and my mouths were open with amazement, mingled with the shock of what might have happened. After a moment to calm myself, I was able to say, "Well done, James. You were splendid. I'm proud of you. Did you recognize the man? Did he say anything?"

"Daddy, he said some naughty words when I hit him. He had a hood over his head so I couldn't get a good look at his face. I think he was from *Abigail*."

"How so?"

"What I saw made me think I had seen someone like him on the voyage."

"Do you remember whether he was passenger or crew?"

"No, Daddy, sorry."

Tom, Georgie and Tim were watching this from a corner of the room. At that moment, Annie arrived. Margaret shooed the boys out of the kitchen. James jumped off the stool and with a wave of his right arm to me then a hug for a perplexed Annie, followed them out. Margaret picked up the crying baby Samuel, disturbed by all the bustle, who was soon comforted. We sat down round the kitchen table and after I had told a shocked Annie what James had said, Margaret told us that when Tom had come running back to the house, her husband, Thomas, was ploughing the far field. Tom went to fetch him and by the time they had gone to where James was attacked there was no sign of the attacker. Nothing more to be done, Thomas had gone back to his ploughing. Margaret was clearly upset and couldn't understand why anyone would try to harm a young boy.

Annie, still shocked and worried, told Margaret about the incidents on the boat on our voyage from England. This latest attack proved there was a continuing serious danger not only to me but, as I had feared, to my family. Margaret's immediate reaction was to fetch Thomas back. He needed to be part of any further discussion. So saying, she went outside to tell one of her sons to go for his father. Annie followed her to check on James. I remained at the table pondering my next steps. It was clear that the family could not be left unprotected, which meant that until the attacker was caught, Johnny and I needed to stay close by.

We all gathered at the table. After providing Thomas with the full story, we then discussed our options. We agreed that James' attacker was likely to have been acting for someone else and was probably the same person who had attacked me on *Abigail*. We needed to find and confront him to learn who he was working for. It also seemed highly probable that person, or persons, was among the new settlers. Thomas said that he would organize a party of Old Planters to search Naumkeag for the sailor. They weren't complicit in that possible conspiracy of new settlers, and they knew Naumkeag, every bush, tree and hiding place.

"Wait, Thomas," "You don't know who you are looking for."

"If we find someone running from us or hiding, we can bring him in for questioning."

"What if our assailant isn't hiding? He could be an indentured servant or a sailor masquerading as one. He might even be one of the other passengers. All we know is that it is almost certain he came over on *Abigail*."

Johnny suggested he participate in that search in case they did find someone behaving suspiciously, as he would most likely recognize the man, passenger or crewman. I needed to meet with the new Governor and attempt to determine whether or not he was the instigator, intentionally or otherwise. I was of the firm opinion that he had not wanted me harmed and would like the matter resolved. Meantime, a watch would be mounted that Thomas would organize to guard the Stanfield family. Until the attacker was found, Annie, Jeannie, James, and Abigail would need to stay on the Gardner property.

After the meeting when Annie and I were alone together, she put her arms round me and her head on my shoulder.

"Isaac, the attack on James brought back the horrors of when he was taken away from us."

"Annie, love, that was so long ago."

"My dear, you don't understand. I lost a part of me then. The seemingly endless time he was gone, not knowing if he was alive. When you brought him back, I rejoiced. But those precious months of his life were lost to me. That void is still there."

I hugged her.

"Isaac, my love, I'm frightened. We are in an unsafe place. Any one of us could be attacked." "I know, my dear. It is worrying. I feel that the only way we will find him is if we actually catch him in the act."

"What do you mean? Lay a trap for him with you the bait? No, absolutely not. Over my dead body!"

I laughed and Annie admitted she could have used different words. I said we had to reduce the unknowns. We needed to eliminate Endecott as a suspect and convince him to help us find the instigator if there was one. So, with a further hug and a plea for me to be careful, I left Annie to meet Endecott, while Johnny watched over my family until I got back.

I found Endecott at the Conant house with his wife. Apologizing for the intrusion, I told him I needed to have a private word with him. Somewhat ungraciously he took me to a bench a little way from the house. I reminded him of the three incidents on the boat. He was dismissive, saying he was convinced they were accidents. I then told him about the attack on James. He was silent. I waited.

"Mr. Stanfield, I am truly sorry. I am horrified that your son was subject to such a frightening experience. I don't understand what that has to do with the incidents on *Abigail*?"

"Governor, do you think it was a coincidence?

A further long pause.

"No, Mr. Stanfield, I don't believe it was. In which case I need to amend my opinion of those earlier incidents, or should I say attacks on you."

"Governor, please forgive me if I seem impertinent. I am concerned for the safety of my family."

He nodded for me to continue.

"We have not had an amicable relationship. I know you are frustrated at my unwillingness to join your staff. You view me as being insubordinate, which I have never had any intention of being. Have you expressed your displeasure of me to any of your entourage?"

He shifted uncomfortably and said he hadn't, as far as he could remember. I reminded him of King Henry's frustration with Archbishop Thomas Beckett which resulted in his unfortunate and unintended murder. The Governor bent his head and slowly admitted he had said harsh words about me. He was convinced they had not been acted upon by any of his people. He certainly, as God was his witness, never wished me any harm. There was no point, he still saw me as a valuable contributor to the ultimate success of the settlement.

"Governor, if there is the slightest chance that your words might have been acted upon, we need to explore that possibility. Would you instigate a confidential enquiry and attempt to find out if there is any suspicion, however unsubstantiated, that one of the passengers might have persuaded one of the crewmen to attack me, or worse, one of my family."

"Mr. Stanfield, when it is learnt that your son was attacked, my people will be as horrified as I am and will do everything possible to find the man responsible."

I thanked him and advised him that two crewmen, Spiggott and Hendry had deserted *Abigail* and might be passing themselves off as indentured servants or otherwise trying to hide among the throng of new settlers. Could he let it be known that if they are found they should be held for questioning. He agreed. I told him that my wife had been keeping me abreast of Mistress Endecott's condition and I wanted to express my sympathies to him and wish her a speedy recovery. He thanked me and we parted company. I felt comfortable he had not intended me any harm. I also believed he would do whatever he could to find out if there was some kind of nefarious connection between one of the passengers and a crewman. I returned to my family and told Annie of my meeting.

Annie was thoughtful.

"Do you really believe the Governor?" she asked.

"Yes. I really believe he is now supportive, which is a major change and helpful both now and for the longer term."

"So, my sweet, out of the bad comes the good."

I laughed and we hugged.

CHAPTER 10

Journal entry – *October 1628*

For the most part, we all stayed close to the Gardner property. Johnny helped Thomas with ploughing and harvesting. Annie, Jeannie, and Margaret settled into a close, friendly and mutually supportive relationship. The children, when not doing their schoolwork, were given household and garden duties to keep them out of mischief. They were told to keep away from the woods, be within calling distance, and Tom or James must always be with the others. I kept abreast of the search for possible clues and spoke regularly to the Governor or Mr. Gott, who appeared to have taken on the role of his assistant.

At one meeting with Mr. Gott, I mentioned that some of the more enjoyable activities on *Abigail* were the duets sung by Johnny Dawkins and Mistress Gott's maid. Gott laughed and said it had been a surprise to him and his wife. They too found it delightful. He sighed and said Agatha, the maid, had always been bright, smart, and cheerful. Now she had sickened, and they didn't know how to treat her. I commiserated and asked what her symptoms were. I was told that she had lost all her energy, burst into tears when questioned, couldn't eat or sleep. I laughed. She sounds like she has fallen for someone who doesn't reciprocate. Gott looked startled and said he would mention it to his wife. I wished him luck as I left.

A day later, I was sent a message from the Governor requesting my presence. When I met with him, he told me that they had captured one of the runaway sailors, were holding him in a hut under guard, and would I like to interrogate him. Apparently, Gott's wife's maid had been hiding him. I went immediately.

His name was Hendry, a Scotsman. He had left *Abigail*, he said, in a moment of madness, because he had fallen for Agatha on the voyage, a love returned by Agatha. He had been seduced by her lovely voice. Because he had deserted, he was frightened of being caught and punished. So Agatha had helped him to hide in the woods close to the shore near the South River. She brought him food and they spent time together, the little she had available. They had been close on board. Now, he realized his mistake and wanted to escape. He was not set for the marriage that Agatha wanted. She, of course, was upset. I would need to talk to her to confirm Hendry's story, but first I needed to ask him some more questions.

"You left *Abigail* with another member of the crew?"

"Yes, Spiggott. He was the one who persuaded me to desert with him. He said it would be easy, as long as I stayed hidden till *Abigail* had left."

"Why did Spiggott want to desert?"

"He said he had been looking for an easy way to get to America. He wanted to go to Jamestown. *Abigail* was the best chance he had to cross the Atlantic. He said he could find another boat once in New England for him to complete his journey. So, he signed on as a seaman with every intention of jumping ship when he got to Naumkeag."

"Did you believe him?"

"At the time there was no reason not to. I started having some doubts when he persuaded me to exchange favors."

"What were the favors?"

"He knew I had taken up with Agatha. He offered to cover for me if I needed to spend some time with her. In exchange he wanted me to cover for him occasionally. I asked him why and he said he had an eye on another passenger and wanted time alone with her, too."

"So, what caused you to have doubts?"

"The attacks on you seemed to coincide with his absences. Something I only realized after the third incident. I questioned him. He refused to answer and told me to keep quiet. He said that I had already covered for him and, as a result, if he was caught, he would be believed if he admitted that I was his accomplice."

"Where is Spiggott now?"

"I don't rightly know. He was around till a short time ago. He stayed with me one or two nights in my hideaway. After your son was attacked, he told me it was time for him to leave. He had a bag and some food with him, and he slipped away during the night. He told me to keep my mouth shut."

It all sounded plausible. The problem was that I liked Hendry. I wanted to believe his story. I asked him what he intended to do, assuming he was free to go. He said he wanted to leave Naumkeag, whether he was under suspicion or not. He found Agatha too difficult to deal with. Anyway, she wouldn't recover as long as he was around. I asked him about his background. He said he was a ship's carpenter. I questioned that, as I had met *Abigail's* carpenter. He said he had been the carpenter on another boat and had been laid off with the crew when the owner went into serious debt. He signed on as *Abigail's* assistant carpenter because Captain Gauden knew that the carpenter would be retiring after this voyage and wanted to make sure he had a good replacement. I told him I needed to confirm the story he had told me. If I was satisfied, I would arrange to have him released. I suggested he think about his future while I was away.

I went to see the Gott family and asked to speak with the lovelorn Agatha. Mistress Gott called her to attend us both. We sat in chairs outside the house that the Gotts had been given as temporary accommodation. Agatha stood before us.

"Agatha, I have been to see Mr. Hendry. Tell me what you know about him."

Poor Agatha, at the mention of his name she burst into tears. Mistress Gott was impatient with her, and Agatha stopped crying, just the occasional sniff.

"I met him on the boat, sir. We began courting. He said he loved me so much he was going to leave *Abigail* to be with me. Only now he says he doesn't love me anymore."

At which point, she broke down entirely. Mistress Gott stood up and clasped the sobbing Agatha to her matronly bosom and patted her back. She looked at me with raised eyebrows, a clear message, did I have any other questions. I shook my head and left the two of them.

I went to see the Governor. Mr. Gott was with him. Although they were busy, I was given a minute or two. I told them about Agatha and Hendry. I was comfortable that Hendry was not my attacker, rather I believed Spiggott was and that he seemed to have left Naumkeag. I had no idea what his motivation was. God knows when if ever I would find out. I told them I had decided to take care of Hendry. He would be removed from Naumkeag and Agatha would be able to regain her equilibrium. Gott sighed with relief. The Governor thanked me, he would cancel the watch he had placed on the Gardner property and told me he was happy to release Hendry into my custody until such time as his innocence could be confirmed and, as an afterthought, until Captain Gauden informs us that he will not be pressing charges for desertion. Those could be a long time coming as Gauden and *Abigail* had departed. It seemed I had acquired an indentured servant. I was dismissed.

I returned to Hendry and told him what the Governor had said, asked him to gather what possessions he had and to come with me. I had a job for him elsewhere and away from Agatha. He thanked me, shook my hand and I took him back to the Gardners' house. While I felt comfortable that Hendry was not my assailant, I was sure Annie would need some further convincing. It would help if James was able to confirm he was not the man who had tried to snatch him.

While walking back, I explained to Hendry that I was moving my family to Shawmut, a hill on the Charles River. To do so, I had first to build a home large enough to house several families, together with outbuildings for animals and storage. I said I would like him to help us design and build the house. There were two people he needed to deal with besides myself, my wife Annie, who would be the principal designer and Johnny Dawkins who would, with me, be the heavy labor. Hendry nodded, smiled and said he would be delighted to help. He asked whether we had the tools. Probably, I replied, as I had brought plenty from England, and would make sure we acquired more as needed.

Back at the Gardners' I introduced Hendry to Annie and Johnny. I explained that Hendry was one of the two sailors we had been searching for who had left *Abigail*. I stated that I was comfortable that he was not in any way involved with the attacks on us and had been released into my custody pending final confirmation. I told them he would be working for us to build our house on Shawmut. Johnny shook his hand and said he remembered him from *Abigail*. Annie looked startled then asked him his given name. Gavan was the reply.

"Welcome, Gavan Hendry. Come, let me introduce you to our hosts, the Gardners, Jeannie, Johnny's wife, and our children, who you will probably recognize from the boat."

After they had left, I told Johnny that the other sailor, Spiggott, was our likely culprit and had left the area, possibly bound for Jamestown. However, I wanted to make sure Hendry was not involved.

"It seems that as we are no longer being guarded and have freedom of movement, we can start the design and building of our house on Shawmut. We need to complete the house by the end of November. I would like you to work with Gavan to plan the construction. I will get Annie to work with him on the design. We need to know what materials and tools we need, as well as collect what we currently have available."

Johnny was doubtful.

"Isaac, are you really certain that the impetus for the attacks did not come from someone close to Endecott? I know he has told you that none of his people had anything to do with it. Spiggott, if it was him, seems to have no reason himself, and he told Gavan that he had a job to do at the time James was attacked. Someone from the boat has reason to do you harm. I have to believe that person is still around. If it wasn't an overreaction to a remark made by Endecott, then it seems that person has a personal grudge."

I admitted to Johnny that the thought had been circling in my mind for some time. I hadn't wanted to express it and cause worries for my family. I had made a mental note of all the people I had come across who might harbor such deep animosity, from Tred Gunt on. He was long dead, as were others that would otherwise have been happy to see the end of me. I told Johnny that while we needed to be careful, we had to get on with our lives. It remained a small irritant, a horsefly that buzzed around my head occasionally. Johnny said he was glad that James had put into practice some of the defensive skills we had been teaching him. He was determined to continue his teaching. James was an apt and receptive student.

Later, James and I found a quiet corner and I asked him what he thought of Gavan. James told me he remembered him from the *Abigail*. He had noticed Gavan and Agatha together. Gavan had seen James and put his finger to his lips. James was delighted to share their secret, grinned and turned away. Gavan had been friendly thereafter on the rare occasion they crossed paths.

"The man who attacked you, could it have been Gavan."

James was shocked.

"No, Gavan is big and strong. The man was thin. Anyway, Gavan is my friend."

I reported James' observations back to Annie and Johnny. Annie relaxed. She had been concerned that I had made a too hasty decision.

CHAPTER 11

Journal entry – *October 1628*

Johnny was keen to return to Shawmut.

"Isaac, I think we need to visit Reverend Blackstone as soon as possible. No point designing a building till we know the location. We also should choose a location acceptable to him. He has established a solitary place to live. I would hate to crowd him."

I was aware that Blackstone liked his privacy, but I needed to provide Johnny with some perspective.

"Johnny, over the next few years there will be waves of new settlers coming to Massachusetts Bay. I know, for a fact, that there are five or more ships coming early next year with about 300 settlers, including the Tremaines, with many more thereafter. It will become increasingly crowded. I want to make sure we have a snug and comfortable home to protect us this coming winter away from the confusion and politics of Naumkeag. I know that we need to be looking for a permanent location for our farm within a couple of years. However, when David Tremaine, Kate and daughter Beth arrive, remember they are, or at least Kate is, instrumental to our plans to build a substantial farm. They will need to be housed, so the house needs to be big enough for them, as well. The other thing that we need to be careful of, the Governor needs carpenters. If he had known Gavan was one, he would not have let the man come with us. I can't help feeling a little guilty about it but we need Gavan on Shawmut as soon as possible."

Johnny nodded his understanding.

"Right, first thing to do is build Gavan a wetu on site. Actually, I should be there, too. Jeannie will stay with Annie to look after the children."

Annie was relieved that we no longer had to guard ourselves from unexpected attacks. She was excited to start the process of building our new home, temporary though it might be. She hadn't experienced the cold New England Winter. She had heard enough stories from me to know we had to work quickly to build a house in which we could all survive. We had been so busy since our arrival, sorting out ourselves and our family, as well as dealing with Endecott and his wife. We had hardly spent the time alone together we both treasured. Back in England, we'd achieve this by slipping away on our dear horses, Maddie and Tess, for a night or two at an inn or just clearing space for ourselves amid the family noise and action. *Abigail's* crampted space had not been conducive to that end either. I told Johnny that Annie and I wanted some time to ourselves before I became embroiled in the house-building on Shawmut.

"Right, leave it to me."

Johnny organized an overnight camping trip on Shawmut for the family and Gavan in the Gardners' shallop. Secretly, he and Gavan packed the equipment they needed into the shallop, together with an ample supply of food that Jeannie had prepared. The following morning after breakfast, the children were informed that a mystery sailing adventure was to begin that very morning. They were told that Annie and I had duties that prevented us from joining them and off they all went, with an excited James and apprehensive Abigail.

Annie was unaware of Johnny's plan and had left early to check on Mistress Endecott. When she returned an hour later, she was surprised to find the children gone. I explained what had happened. Surprise turned to concern, then realizing the reason, put her arms round my neck, pulled my face down to hers and we kissed. I looked into her wide blue eyes, gazing up at me, a few remaining freckles on her nose burnished by the sun, and the hardworking mistress of the Stanfield family dissolved into the free-spirited loving woman I adored beyond all things. I slipped the coif off her head and untying the bun, let her long auburn hair cascade down over her shoulders and back. She held me tight, closed her eyes and buried her head in my shoulder. I felt her trembling and then a whispered,

"Oh Isaac, my dear sweet man. It had been so long since we were truly alone together."

We walked back to our little house and, once inside and door closed, slowly removed each other's clothes until, naked, we stood pressing ourselves to each other. Her eyes opened then narrowed, a wicked smile on her face as she felt my arousal and moved her soft belly to hasten the process. She then turned pushed her bum into my stomach and continued to excite me rocking her firm cheeks while my hands moved down over her full breasts, stroking and squeezing her nipples as they hardened. She gasped, lifted and turned her head, and kissed me hard, her tongue seeking mine, exploring and teasing. One of my hands slipped down over her belly and into the bush of hair between her legs, slowly stroking her. She moved in time with my stroking, and I felt the wetness of her own arousal, matching mine. Annie sank to her knees then down on her back onto the bed, her legs wide and pulled me down and into her. We tried to enjoy a slow ride. Our mutual desire was too much to hold back and the walk became a canter and then a full and glorious gallop driven by sheer physical compulsion to our blissful completion. I attempted to slide off her delicious body. I was held captive. Annie refused to let go, staring up at me with a wonder on her face I had not seen since England, many, many months ago.

"Isaac Stanfield, I do love you. The wait, as long and unsatisfying as it has to be, was oh so worth it. This lovemaking was beautiful. Thank you."

She released me. I lay beside her holding her in my arms and we slept. Several hours later, I woke with the gentle, soft Annie asleep in my arms, her lovely butt pushed into my belly. I lay content and full of memories; how terribly I had treated Annie after Aby had died, how loyal and faithful she had been to me, since she had first seduced me—could it really be fifteen years ago?—then our mutual love for each other despite the long absences. The sadness of the loss of baby Miranda. All the memories, good and bad, flowing, mixing together and separating until I was left dreaming and content with my wife in my arms.

I was woken a short time later by my soft bundle of a wife turning towards me a hand tousling my hair and pressing my head towards her, to start kissing me with a probing tongue while another hand slide slowly down my chest, over my stomach and started tugging my hair until the hand tiring of that unproductive exercise, reached further down, clasped and played with me as I hardened until she was happy with the result. With a quick, decisive movement she rolled me on my back and with her straddled above me she pushed me into her and we began our ride again, only this time it was a gentle walk. This was a long, tender expression of our devotion for each other. Annie's fingers explored my face, my eyes and ears, tracing the outline of the cropped ear and scar from a pirate's sword, then the thin trace of the attempted flaying by Epinow's sister on Capawak. She sighed. I reached to her breasts, full and proud tracing their outline, wondering how after feeding two children they could still be so young and firm. The walk became a trot and remained so until we dismounted spent and happy. We slept again until I was awakened by Annie leaving us to prepare a meal.

The afternoon we spent hand in hand, exploring the parts of Naumkeag we had missed, along the water's edge by the South River, which was more of an inlet than a river. We walked west through trees where the undergrowth had been cleared by the Indian inhabitants, although we saw none, for a mile or less until the river turned south, to open land, on a cove, where Governor Endecott had decided to build the new settlement. Little activity seemed underway, and with the winter looming we wondered how sufficient shelter could be built in time. I was also worried by the new settlers' apparent indifference to the approaching danger, the lack of the food they would need to survive. Endecott was governor. It was his responsibility. He had his entourage as well as Roger Conant and his experienced Old Planters to advise and assist him. It made me all the more determined to be housed in Shawmut as soon as possible. I said so to Annie. Her reaction was to feel sorry for the people who might not be ready to deal with the harsh winter to come.

"Isaac, my husband. It sounds like you are torn. You seem to be feeling guilty that you are leaving them to deal with this issue. You shouldn't. Your priority is the wellbeing of your family. You have always insisted that you are not nor will ever be a part of the Governor's entourage. The experiences you have had of the New England winter makes you feel you should help the settlers prepare. But, the more recent experiences of Mr. Conant and his planters will surely provide the Governor with the help he needs ."

That night we ate a good meal, cooked for us by Margaret Gardner. She had asked us if we had taken advantage of the day without family and smiled conspiratorially. Annie caught the smile, blushed, thanked her for the meal and changed the subject. I was unaware of the implication until Annie told me later. We went to bed early, loved, slept, and loved again as the sun rose. Later that day our family returned, the children full of excitement with stories to tell.

Gavan, Johnny, and I met with Thomas Gardner to discuss what we would need to build our house. Thomas had built his house himself, as well as assisted in the building of Roger Conant's house on Cape Ann, so was informative. If we wanted a permanent two story home, he advised us to build a solid stone foundation with a cellar, frame the house and side it with overlapping planking or clapboard. We should also have a brick fireplace in the center of the house to warm every room, together with a shingle roof. I remembered the house that David Thomson built, Pannaway at Piscataqua. He had brought brick and a number of skilled builders with him and had the time to build a large, fortified house. We would have to make do with what we had in the short time we had available before the onset of winter.

On our next trip to Shawmut, we squeezed everyone into the shallop. James told us all how he had sailed a small boat in Bermuda with his friend Anthony. It had been a few years back and I was surprised that James remembered his name. After a five-hour sail, beaching the boat, we climbed the hill to William Blackstone's house. He heard the excited chatter and came to the door to greet us. After introductions, he accompanied us to a location about a half mile southeast from his house close to a thick stand of trees with open ground further to the southeast with a view of the sea, a large bay, coves, islands, forests and rivers stretching away into the distance. Anywhere around here, he said, and left us to our own devices.

We needed a location that sheltered us from the winter nor'easterly gales and close to a spring or brook with good water. We walked on from where William had left us and followed the land which dropped down towards the water with thick woods at the top of the slope. It was an ideal place for our house. James, who had gone to explore came back in great excitement. Just a little way off, there was a brook running down the hill from out of the woods. On a level piece of ground, Annie began pacing the outline of the house she imagined. For the Stanfield, Dawkins, and Tremaine families, we needed four separate bedrooms, a separate living room and kitchen, she said. Gavan pursed his lips and shook his head.

"Too big, in the time we have. Might I suggest a simple two-story house, a loft that can be divided by a canvas screen to use as bedrooms and two bedrooms and living room on the ground floor. The rooms should be built around a central fireplace and chimney. We don't have brick, so we need to build the hearth with river and field stone, and line the wooden chimney with clay. The walls of the chimney would be warmed from the fire and provide heat throughout the house."

I asked about a foundation.

"Not a foundation, no time. We need to have post holes dug deep. Then a buried layer of gravel between the posts. I didn't see much on the walk here but there will be plenty close to the water. Then we place a timber footing on the gravel. Rather than a cellar, I suggest you build a cold store into the hill behind the house where the slope is steepest."

Annie had revised the outline of the house, so we had an area of about ten paces (30 feet) wide and seven paces (20 feet) deep. With a knife, Gavan cut stakes from some dead branches on the edge of the wood and pushed them into the ground at each corner of the area. Now, he explained, we need to draw some plans so we can work out what materials we need. I suggested we should return to Naumkeag and do just that.

Johnny was insistent that we not waste time, especially as the weather was fine. He said he would stay and start work on a wetu. He knew the design. By the time we returned, tomorrow or the day after, he would have set up temporary accommodation for him and Gavan. William said he had an axe, saw, spade and mattock which he would be happy to lend us. Gavan said he would make a list of the additional tools needed. Thanking William and wishing Johnny a productive day or two before we were back, with a long hug from Jeannie, we returned to the shallop and sailed back to Naumkeag.

It took several days for us to organize ourselves, for Annie to draw the designs for the house, front, back, side, and interior views with approximate measurements, together with constructive commentary and advice from Gavan, and for me to complete the reorganization of all we had brought over from England so that we could take what we needed to Shawmut. We had been advised to bring glass for windows, iron and steel to fashion the required metal pieces. I would enlist Thomas Walford, with his metal working skills, to help us produce what we needed.

I also barely escaped becoming involved with Endecott's first attempts at governing. There were serious disagreements with the Old Planters. He, and they separately, had written to Matthew Craddock at the New England Company in London complaining about each other. Endecott had been advised about the large house on Cape Ann built for Roger Conant and had sent the Old Planters to dismantle it and bring it back to Naumkeag for his use as the Governor's mansion. He was also aggravated by Thomas Morton, whom I had last heard of in 1624, when he was planning to move to New England with a large party of settlers.

I was told that he had, in fact, come to New England later that year with a Captain Wollaston, at a location close to Wessagusset, which they called Wollaston. They built a house there and started trading with the Indians. Captain Wollaston left in 1626 for Virginia leaving Morton in charge. Morton changed the name to Merrymount and, remembering his liberal views, I was not surprised that Merrymount became a source of serious concern for the scandalous behavior that was purported to be carrying on there. Bradford in New Plimouth was certainly scandalized and sent Captain Standish to arrest Morton. He was sent back to England, at about the time we were travelling over here. Although Morton was no longer present, his followers were, and Morton's absence had not calmed things down. The new Governor determined that as, in his opinion, his jurisdiction included Merrymount, he decided to go there to see for himself and instill discipline under threats of the most dire punishment. Because I had known Morton, he pressed me to join him. I politely refused. I was pressed for time, trying to get everything ready to build the house on Shawmut. More important, I didn't want to set any precedent that had me working with or for Endecott.

Endecott's visit to Merrymount resulted in a large maypole being upended. It was deemed by the Puritan governor to be the focus of deviant behavior. Endecott delivered a stern lecture to those of Morton's followers who had decided to stay.

Gavan and I returned to Shawmut with a shallop load of food, spare clothing, and provisions for a lengthy stay. We transported tools and building materials, as well as a detailed plan of the house. We met up with Johnny, who had been busy. A wetu had been built at the building site. There were large piles of gravel, fieldstones for the hearth, and a stack of cut and stripped lengths of locust, pine, and oak trees. I was amazed at how much he had been able to accomplish. Johnny laughed and admitted that Reverend Blackstone had organized two of his Indian friends who had helped collect the gravel and stones, cut the wood, and dragged them to the site, with the additional help of Blackstone's two oxen.

Gavan had cut stakes and brought them with a large roll of twine with which we helped him mark the perimeter of the house, the long front and back walls facing north and south respectively, squaring each corner with a bevel. We then marked the center load bearing dividing wall from front wall to back in the same way. Finally, the outline of the central hearth was laid bisecting the center line. We could now dig a trench round the house outside the perimeter twine. Gavan suggested a one foot wide trench, one foot deep. We had a quantity of spades and several mattocks so began work immediately. By the end of the next day, we had cut the trench and dug deep post holes at each corner of the house using a special narrow, long bladed spade and crowbar to loosen the soil as we dug, with a further post hole every ten feet. Gavan said we needed to dig down at least four feet to avoid frost heave during the winter which might otherwise dislodge the posts, with a flat stone placed at the bottom of each hole. The timber footing in the trench would be beams attached to the posts. Joining the top of each post would be a heavy horizontal beam he called a plate. Each post needed to be notched to take the plate. Then each plate and the footing beam had to be notched to take vertical pine studs placed every two feet to form the frame of the wall. We needed a large number of ten-foot lengths of oak for posts, plates and beams.

While the weather stayed pleasant, the three of us worked hard, cut and notched the posts, charred the bottom ends, sunk and packed them in the holes. Wind and rain came as we were finishing attaching the plates to the posts. We had been working for three days. Gavan drew the design of the chimney, a square latticed funnel wide at the bottom where it would rest on the two sides and back stone walls of the fireplace and a heavy oak lintel across the front. All this would sit on a wide stone hearth. The funnel would have its insides coated with a thick clay slurry that would form the lining of the chimney.

He also drew his design for the steep roof, pitched from the front to the back. Beams from each post on the outer wall angled upward to connect to the long ridge beams that ran the length of the house. We would surely need help to set those roof beams in place.

We built the hearth and fireplace while Gavan started cutting the studs from the pine logs. He split each log along its length with hammer and wedges and then sawed the lumber on sawhorses he had made. I left Johnny working on the fireplace and went to help Gavan. With two of us, we could use a pit saw with me working in the pit below Gavan as he worked from above. I had not had the dubious pleasure of working a saw pit before. Gavan gave me words of caution. Go slowly, pace yourself. It is hard, tedious, and prolonged work. How true. I used muscles I didn't know I had. I developed blisters that were quickly rubbed raw and bled profusely. Gavan said to ignore the pain, it would become less after a few days. At night, Johnny massaged my aching back with some foul-smelling ointment, which diminished the discomfort, but not by much. Then there was the irritation from the sawdust smeared into and around my eyes, mouth, and nose from my tears and attempts to wipe it away. Damned if I was going to give up. I gritted my sawdust-caked teeth and kept going, driven by the methodical and seemingly inexhaustible Gavan above me. Thank God the flies and mosquitos had gone with the approaching winter.

—— CHAPTER 12 ——

Journal entry – *November - December 1628*

The three of us worked through November to complete the house, with occasional help from William Blackstone, when he could tear himself away from his books. He had built his house from logs and was keenly interested in our frame house and in our progress. He fed us well on a regular basis. We had constructed another two wetus, for storage and to make living conditions easier. We also had the occasional Indian visit us and show friendly interest in what we were doing with the material they had collected for us. At opportune moments they helped us with some heavy lifting. In the evenings around a campfire, we might be visited by one or two of them, who spoke a little English and would join us at our invitation. Johnny became quite friendly with them.

One morning, Johnny had been out with his bow looking for game to add to our larder, and that of Willam Blackstone. He had returned with a small buck when one of our Indian friends appeared. He was interested in Johnny's bow and by word and gesture the conversation became quite engaged. Johnny said the Indian wanted to test his skill against Johnny's. I remembered well the Indians' love of competition. A target was set up at fifty paces and a few arrows were loosed. The Indian was impressed by Johnny's accuracy.

Johnny or I would return to Naumkeag regularly to make sure that all were safe and to keep Jeannie and Annie abreast of our progress. Occasionally, they would all come and visit us. The weather was turning cold, wet and windy, so there were few days that provided comfortable sailing. We would also bring supplies of food back to support the game and fish we had caught.

More concerning was the lack of progress in the settlers attempts to build sufficient housing for themselves. Another disturbing factor was the indifference being shown by the young men, brought over as indentured servants, to working hard. The food and alcohol that had been brought over were being consumed at an unsustainable rate. Thomas Gardner said a disaster was looming. Roger Conant had a continuing fractious working relationship with the Governor. Letter responses had been received from London, counselling cooperation and patience, which had caused Endecott to be less truculent and more accommodating. Roger Conant and the Old Planters, including the Gardner family, had thoughts to leave the Naumkeag peninsula and move across the North River to what they called the Bass River side. There was good arable land there, and the river would be a useful barrier.

Our house was finished at the end of November, and we began the task of moving the family and all our possessions to Shawmut. Cold and wet winds from the northeast whipped up the water along the coast. We sought the lee as much as we could. Where there was open water we had to sail through it with reefed mainsail, shipping water that had to be baled. Our possessions, where not covered with oilskins, became soaked, as we were. All was accomplished by early December. The one sadness was the leave taking of the children. James had become great friends with the Gardner boys and Abigail was smitten by young Tim. They promised to stay in touch. On the last trip, carrying the goats in a large wooden cage, Thomas Gardner sailed us over. We entertained him and showed him round our house and barn. He was suitably impressed. We thanked him for his and Margaret's kind hospitality. He thanked us for being such good neighbors and leaving him a comfortable house where an incomplete storage shed had once been. A valuable asset when he came to sell his property and move over the river.

Gavan approached me and asked what he should now do, since the house was finished and his job was done. I had paid him for his excellent work. I had no intention of him being indentured to me. He was free to go and seek employment as a skilled carpenter.

"Mr. Stanfield, you have paid me well and been a kind and thoughtful employer. I am loathe to part from you. As the winter sets in, construction work will become increasingly difficult so I doubt I will find suitable employment."

I had hoped Gavan would stay. I was certain we would have need of an extra pair of hands, if nothing else, to ensure the house remained weatherproof.

"Gavan, I would be pleased if you would stay with us. You will receive room and board and I will pay the same daily rate, should I have need of your services. We also need furniture. If you care to make it here, of course we will pay you. I also suspect that Reverend Blackstone might need your services over the winter."

"Thank you, sir. While I did not presume to believe I would be living here, when I designed the barn, the hay loft, or what will be the hay loft when the hay is harvested next year, can be easily amended to include a room for myself. If that would be permissible? I have already had conversations with Mistress Stanfield about the furniture she requires—beds, table, chairs, benches, cupboards, chests, and shelves. However, she had not given me cause to think she wanted me to make them."

I laughed. Clever, he had thought through his continued value to us but had allowed me to make the offer. I said he was going to be busy this winter. Thankfully, the barn, apart from an indoor pen for the goats, would be little used so he could set it up as his carpenter's shop. I also gave him leave to modify the hay loft, insulated with hay, to provide him with a comfortable place to sleep over the winter. If it became too cold, I told him to join us in the house for the night. He laughed. He was young, had thick clothes and blankets. He could make a good nest for himself in the hay.

Meantime, I believed our home needed work to reduce drafts and provide us with added insulation from the winter blasts.

The house had been designed to protect us from the Winter. A large fireplace, open to the west in the spacious parlor. The door, on the south side, which had now become the front of the house, led into a hallway with a doorway to the left into the living room and to the right to the first bedroom. There were two small windows, one on each side of the door on the south side. There were two other small ground floor windows, one at each end of the house on the east and west walls, with no openings on the north facing wall. At the north end of the living room behind the fireplace was a doorway into the second bedroom. By the doorway, a ladder through a trapdoor into the loft, where there were two additional bedrooms, with a canvas screen between. The chimney was designed to provide heat to both rooms. The roof was thatched with reeds cut from the marshland at the bottom of the hill. We needed to have doors for each of the doorways. We had used the two hinges we brought with us for the front door. We would ask Thomas Walford to make us more.

The external walls were covered in clapboards. These were riven from squared white oak logs which had been cut into quarters in Gavan's saw pit. The inside walls would be daubed with straw and clay, a job still to be done. However, we had fixed narrow, riven pine strips horizontally to the vertical studs between the posts. To make the daub we had to collect clay and the straw stubble left over in the hay field from the Blackstone harvesting, after which the whole family were then employed in the game of wall daubing, mixing the clay and straw together in a large barrel and the carrying it in a bucket to each of the daubers. It was cheerful, messy work. James and Abigail loved it. Encouraged by their parents to spuddle in the mud, hopefully transferring enough mixed daub to the wall. At the end of each day, while daylight faded, they were sent to the brook to rinse the mud off and run back before they froze to warm and dry themselves with towels in front of a roaring fire.

The children continued the responsibility they had at Naumkeag, looking after the goats, Amos, Nanna, and Beatrice. James had become an excellent milker and was patiently training his assistant Abigail to do the same. Another job for the children, together with Jeannie, was to collect firewood. They went to the woods with a large canvas cloth, two corners of which had lines tied to them which they used to pull the canvas behind them. In the woods they collected deadwood lying on the ground until they had a full load and dragged it back to the house. By the front door there was a covered wood store. Johnny and Gavan had produced a winter's load of timber off-cuts which they chopped up and added to the store. Prior to the snow they had also cut and stacked logs, the piles circular in shape, tightly stacked, the hole in the center filled with kindling. They were left to weather.

The first snow fell in mid-December, and I decided to return to Naumkeag to find out what progress had been made in the town's preparation for the winter. Johnny came with me and we borrowed the Blackstone shallop. I had apologized to William and promised to acquire another one, or better still, have Gavan make one for us. He told me that he was glad it was being sailed as he had only used it in the finest weather and rarely at that. We could treat it as our own. After a brisk sail, passing Noddle's Island, we approached Naumkeag. I told Johnny that I realized we had been so busy I had not had the courtesy to call on Mr. and Mistress Maverick. I was more concerned that I had not been to greet Amyse and offer my condolences to her on the death of my old friend David Thomson. He reminded me that they had done nothing to make any contact themselves. Something, he observed, one would have expected someone to do to welcome a new neighbor.

When we landed at Naumkeag, we found the situation to be grim. On the positive side, the large house I remembered from Cape Ann had been disassembled, brought down by boat to the South River and unloaded at the open clearing Annie and I had stumbled across on our walk. It was reassembled and a dozen or so other small houses and, in some cases, huts had been hastily built around the main house. There was insufficient food and inadequate housing. In a decisive moment, Endecott showed his worth as a leader, if not as a compassionate man, by ordering a number of the indentured workers to leave the settlement and make their way elsewhere. The choice was theirs, to return to England or find shelter at another settlement, of which there several in Massachusetts Bay and north of Cape Ann. He had also sent back some settlers for disciplinary reasons. It seemed that for any serious misdemeanor, the Governor did not have the means to incarcerate them and was cautious about administering corporal, let alone capital, punishment. More to the point, he had not had the opportunity to establish a functioning administration with the necessary governing infrastructure.

Later, Johnny asked if the banished indentured servants had all left. I asked why.

"Isaac, there is a young man that I met on the boat coming over, Giles Burden, indentured by the company. Nice lad, it would a pity for him to be sent into the wilderness. He is a farmer's son, strong. Might I check to see if he has gone? If not, may I bring him to you?"

I was not sure I wanted another mouth to feed, and I was sure Annie would roll her eyes, but sending a young lad out into the wilderness wasn't right. A while later Johnny returned with Giles, a mop of curly blonde hair, a wide-open face, tanned a deep brown, broken nose and ears that stood from under his hair. He had an infectious grin. Cap in hand, he bowed and waited.

"Giles, Johnny says he knows you from the boat and speaks well of you. Why are you being sent away from the settlement?"

"I'm sorry, sir. Lack of discipline. To be fair there was no leadership to begin with. We arrived and were largely left to our own devices. One or two of the older workers were quick to take on that role and we followed them. We worked a little and relaxed a lot."

"Doesn't sound like the sort of worker that could be trusted. Why should I take you on?"

I was surprised and impressed by his honesty.

"Under the right master, sir, I would be as hard a worker as any man. I'm a farmer since I was ten years old. I want to continue to farm, eventually have my own. That's why I came to New England."

I smiled and turned to Johnny.

"Johnny, it looks like you have yourself an assistant. Make sure Giles has his possessions and is at our boat ready to sail with us back to Shawmut. I have a need to visit Mr. Gardner."

I wanted to talk to Thomas Gardner. There were signs of scurvy and other sicknesses, evidence of malnutrition, and I worried about the exposure to the cold. Thomas was worried too. They needed a doctor, more and better accommodation for the newcomers, and food. Roger Conant was working with the Governor and had persuaded the Old Planters to support the newcomers. To build cooperation, Endecott had wanted the Old Planters to move to the new location. There weren't enough houses so there remained two camps separated by a wood and when the heavy snow and ice arrived there would not be much contact. I asked about the plan to move across the North River. He said it made little sense for the foreseeable future, they had adequate homes where they were, the new settlers were attempting to establish themselves elsewhere. The Old Planters had food and were prepared to give what they could. It was not enough. The now banished workers had consumed much of the supplies Endecott had brought over. The local Indians could help a little, though there were now few of them and they needed what they had for themselves.

"So, Thomas, things look dire. I don't see what I can do to help."

"You can't, Isaac. Poor planning and poor, thoughtless leadership. I believe Endecott is a strong, determined man, although he needs a steadying hand and direction. He has the tendency to act before thinking things through. This winter will make or break him."

Clearly, we thought alike. Then there was the worry about Endecott's wife.

"What about Mistress Endecott?"

"Very unwell. She lies abed in the new governor's house being administered to by the ladies. Mistress Conant spends much time with her, but soon it will be difficult for her to travel as frequently as she now does. I pray that Mistress Endecott will survive the winter. I do have serious doubts."

"Poor Endecott, with all the other problems he is facing he has a sick wife to deal with."

It was well after mid-day, and I wanted to be back on Shawmut by nightfall, so I bade farewell to the Gardners and Johnny, Giles, and I sailed the five hours it took us to get home. I feared what disasters could occur in Naumkeag over the winter.

CHAPTER 13

Journal entry – *December 1628 – February 1629*

The Twelve Days of Christmas were fast approaching. A white Christmas was assured with heavy snowfalls producing deep snow around the house. The daily chore of fetching fresh water from the spring was eased by the use of a sled that Johnny had built. It contained supports for two water buckets each with a lid and was pulled by rope. Now the children could handle the weight and have fun. After trying to use the sled for their wood gathering, they found the canvas to be better, being easily pulled over the snow.

Giles had been welcomed without outward reservation by Annie. I was able to resolve her concerns about an extra mouth to feed, once we were abed and comfortably entwined. In winter he was an additional hunter/gatherer, in the spring he would be helping Johnny with our little farm growing the food we needed. To the delight of the children, he helped them with their water carrying duties. He and Gavan had known each other on *Abigail* and were friendly. They would share the loft in the stable. The children had also introduced him to the goats. He immediately went into their pen and felt Nanna and Beatrice, despite the aggressive tendencies of Amos. He came out of the pen and asked James to fetch Annie, who came immediately with a worried look on her face. James had obviously raised the alarm.

"Mistress Stanfield, your two nannies are pregnant."

Annie was startled. She had left James and Abigail in charge of the goats. Abigail admitted she had seen them get fat over the last month or so but had put it down to their healthy appetites and good food.

"Giles, when do you think they will produce?"

"I would say in perhaps two or so months. You will know for sure because they stop producing milk about two months before they drop them."

"James, what about the milking? Have you noticed anything?"

"Yes, Mummy, now you mention it, Nanna has been producing less milk than normal. In fact, today hardly anything. Beatrice is still going well."

Annie became quite excited and told James and Abigail they should set up separate calendars on the wall of the stable for Nanna and Beatrice, then tick off the days until each is due, Nanna first as her two months has started. As soon as Beatrice stops producing, do the same for her. Any problems they should talk to Giles. Both children, wide-eyed with excitement, hugged each other, then Giles over this new and important responsibility.

Gavan had set to with a will, making furniture to Annie's specifications and order. The barn had been enclosed and, though cold, was weatherproof. He had become a favorite of the children who would sit on piles of wood to watch him work while he told them stories about his childhood in Scotland. I noticed James beginning to develop a Scottish burr to his voice, rolling his 'rrrs'.

Christmas was a redemption for us, heralded by James' 9th birthday on the 6th day of December. After the trials we had gone through, the brightly decorated house, the spirit of Christmas with the Twelve Days was an extraordinary deliverance for us. We had regained the close, happy family household we had had back at Barrow Farm in England. We welcomed Giles as our newest member. His gratitude was profoundly moving.

While we enjoyed the festivities, we were mindful of Reverend William Blackstone and he had an open invitation to share our table whenever he liked, something he was pleased to accept. Annie had asked him if he would be willing to provide us with a service every Sunday, which he graciously agreed to do. At our house he offered us prayers from the Book of Common Prayer followed by readings from the King James bible. He also provided short, amusing homilies. He then stayed for lunch. Over Christmas, we pressed him to hold services on Christmas Eve, matins and evensong on Christmas Day. We sang carols, music being provided by Gavan on the recorder, Johnny on the flute. The food seemed never ending with Annie and Jeannie producing a constant stream of delicious dishes. By Twelfth Night we were spent, happy, complete. Annie and I retired early to our bedroom, now replete with a large oak bedstead and feather mattress with quilted blankets. We celebrated my 31st birthday on Twelfth Night under the covers with Annie at her most inventive.

The winter was cold and long. We were supplied with food from William's stores. The dried apples from his orchard being especially welcomed. Johnny with his bow and hunting skills kept us well stocked with meat. He started taking James with him. A secret they shared was that Johnny had been giving James lessons. Gavan had made James a bow that fit him and Johnny had fashioned and fletched some arrows. I only heard about the secret when James proudly showed me a duck he had brought down. The sea had frozen for a hundred paces or more out from the shore as well as the whole of the Charles River. On the Charles the ice was thick enough to walk on. Gavan cut a hole with an auger then opened it a little and we were able to catch bass. He advised us to keep quiet, no stamping of frozen feet or the fish would hear us. He told us he used to fish the frozen lochs back home.

We remained isolated throughout January and February. The major excitement was the arrival of four kids, Nanna producing two in mid-February and Beatrice another two a week later. Giles had made sure, with help from the children, that the pen in the stable was as warm and comfortable as possible, with a protesting Amos kept out of the way in a separate pen. With each birthing, the children wanted to be present as Giles stood by to help the mother if she got into trouble, which neither of them did. The days thereafter Abigail took great pride in announcing at the breakfast table every morning the state of the health of all the goats. Names had been discussed but the ever sensible James had started calling them by number as they appeared, so we had One, Two, Three, and Four.

Late February, with the snow starting to melt, we were able to prepare the shallop for use. We had overturned it before Christmas with the sails rolled round the mast stored underneath. I took the opportunity to sail with Johnny to Winnesimmet, where the Mavericks lived. We sailed to a landing stage, mooring our boat we went ashore. The house was large in the form of a palisade, with thick walls made from vertical tree trunks, much as you would see a stockade built. He had some cannon as well, their noses sticking from embrasures. We wondered who he was defending himself against. We followed the path around to the back of the building to be greeted by a servant who, having seen us approach, was waiting for us by an open door. He asked our names, taking our hats and coats, then led us up a wide staircase to a light-filled room looking south over the water. Amyse was waiting for us by a large welcoming fire. The servant announced our names before leaving us.

"Isaac, is it you? It has been so, so long since we were last together! Forgive me, it must have been at about the time dear Aby died."

She came to me, an elegant, mature woman, holding my arms looked up at me, marking the aging in the face she remembered.

"You've changed. David used to talk about you so often. It is sad he is no longer here to be with you. He cherished your friendship, always wondering if you would ever move to New England. I understand you married again. I remember young James. Do you have other children?"

I smiled down at her earnest face. I, too, thought back seeing the changes. Amyse was older. She had suffered. I answered her questions, then said how shocked and sorry I was to hear about David's disappearance. Amyse was quick to change the subject. Apologizing to Johnny, she went to him and took his hand.

"Forgive me my rudeness. Isaac distracted me. Tell me your name again, please."

Johnny bowed over her hand. "Johnny Dawkins, ma'am."

Amyse looked puzzled. "I seem to remember that name. If I'm not mistaken, you were a friend of Isaac's many years ago."

I congratulated her on her prodigious memory. She invited us to sit in chairs around the fire, then waited for me to explain my visit. I told her about Annie and my family, how we had decided to move to New England, accompanying the new Governor on *Abigail*, although not part of his entourage. She smiled and acknowledged she knew something of the new Governor's reputation from remarks Maverick had made. I said that I had met Reverend Blackstone and become friendly with him on my last voyage over here. When we arrived at Naumkeag last September, we wanted to move away, to put it bluntly, from direct engagement with Endecott. Blackstone kindly offered us some land on Shawmut, on which we have built a house and in which we have had a comfortable winter. Unlike the poor souls at Naumkeag, she whispered. I asked her what she meant.

"They have had a bad winter, many have died of cold, sickness and, I suspect, even malnutrition. Poor organization, lack of housing and qualified builders, food wasted and inadequate. Sickness from scurvy and fever. We have tried to help with provisions. Our needs are few, so we have insufficient stored to give away much. We offered shelter to a few. They have recently returned to Naumkeag. Simply put, like trying to put a quart of water into a pint pot."

I asked her about David.

She sat back and sighed. She said that he had liked to go on trips, many times alone, visiting his Indian friends and bartering with them for produce, pelts, and the like. One day, about a year ago, he left and never returned. I said I understood she had remarried.

"Yes, a fine young man, Samuel Maverick. David had become friends with him when Samuel moved here from England in 1624. He landed at Pannaway on the Piscataqua River, where you know we lived before moving to our island down here in 1626. When Samuel wanted to buy land and build the house here, David helped him. He became a regular visitor and was a great comfort to me when David used to go off on his trips. After David died, it seemed logical that when Samuel proposed to me, I accepted. And here we are."

I congratulated her. I was puzzled, keeping my thoughts to myself. I asked her where Mr. Maverick was now. He was away on business. The thawing ice had made it possible for him to sail down to New Plimouth, from whence he would be sailing to Jamestown. From what she said he is a trader, seemingly hard working and successful. After further conversation, I expressed the desire for us to meet again with our respective spouses and regretted we had to leave. We needed to sail back to Shawmut before the weather and the light worsened. Amyse held both my hands and thanked me with much emotion for coming to see her. It reminded her of England and happier times. She looked forward to meeting Annie in the near future.

After we had left and as we walked back to our boat, I asked Johnny what he thought about the conversation with Amyse.

"I'm not sure what your reasons are for asking, and of course I have never met the lady before. Having said that, Mistress Maverick did not appear to be comfortable talking about Mr. Maverick. She also used her words rather oddly, especially the tone of her voice. Why would she say Maverick was a great comfort to her while her husband was away? She sounded dismissive, almost embarrassed. Why did she say it was logical for them to marry? She seemed to be implying, accidentally or otherwise, that they were so intimate that her husband's death removed the obstacle to their marriage, yet I got the impression she was not altogether happy about the marriage."

"Perhaps. We might be reading much more into her remarks than we should. However, I come away from that meeting with an impression that Maverick might have set his sights on Amyse and courted her before David died. David was quite wealthy with land, house, and a successful trading business. Those assets would pass to Amyse on David's death. It seems fortuitous from Maverick's perspective that David died when he did. It would be interesting to meet Samuel Maverick and get a sense of how he views things."

We sailed back to our family with a strong northeast wind pushing us through the choppy seas. Over the next few days, Annie and

I discussed the meeting with Amyse. Annie provided an interesting perspective.

"Wasn't David much older than Amyse? He seems to have left her alone a great deal of the time. I even wonder whether the passion had left their marriage. To be stuck in a strange new land, a woman needs security, reassurance, and companionship, preferably from her husband. Loneliness is a terrible thing, made worse by memories, longing for home and family. Maverick supplied those needs. It seems logical that she should want to validate that relationship both in the sight of God and the society, small as it might be, that she moved in. I think she was prepared to recognize that Maverick's interest in her was in part due to her wealth as a fair exchange for security and companionship."

—— CHAPTER 14 ——

Journal entry - *March 1629*

A week or so later, on a clear day with a gentle wind from the south, I sailed to Naumkeag, accompanied by Johnny. I was dreading what we would find. We sailed around the headland into the North River. After beaching the shallop, we walked up through the trees to the Gardner house. Young Tom was the first to see us. He and Charlie were throwing snowballs at each other, not too successfully as the snow was largely melted. Just as we appeared, Tom was hit with a projectile containing more mud than snow. He, displeased, turned away holding his arm, to see us watching him. Forgetting the pain, he shouted a greeting before coming up to us to shake our hands, followed by a grinning Charlie.

"Mr. Stanfield, Mr. Dawkins, it's so good to see you. How has your winter been? Did you have a good Christmas?"

"Good day to you both. Yes, we are all well. Christmas was exceedingly good. I trust yours was, too. We are here to see your father. Is he about?"

Tom told us his parents were in the house so we walked there, saying we would leave them with their snowballs. Johnny couldn't resist throwing a couple of snowballs before following me, pursued by a couple in return. Hearing the noise, Thomas Gardner came to the door and welcomed us into his house.

We sat before the fire listening to the sorry recounting of the past winter by Thomas, with the occasional interruption from Margaret, his wife. It had been miserable, indeed. The loss of life had been crushing. Endecott had pleaded with Governor Bradford in New Plimouth for medical assistance. In response to the plea, Dr. Samuel Fuller was expected to arrive at any moment. I asked about Mistress Endecott. Margaret shook her head. She said it was a miracle that she still lived. She hoped the doctor would arrive in time to save her. The Old Planters, by staying where they were, had been able to remain isolated from the sickness. They tried to help but there was little they could do. They asked us about our winter. After hearing about the horrors in Naumkeag, we were loathe to sound too enthusiastic. We just said we had survived our first winter as a family in New England.

I wanted to meet with Roger Conant, then go to the new settlement further down the Naumkeag peninsula to meet the new Governor and others of his entourage. We left the Gardners, wishing them well. We looked forward to our families getting together again in the Spring.

We were welcomed kindly by Roger and Sarah Conant. They looked unwell, malnourished, tired. Their story was much the same as we had already heard. I asked about his relationship with Endecott. He smiled.

"Could be better, could most certainly be a lot worse. He came in like a raging bull, but the circumstances forced him to temper his fiery approach. He has made some difficult decisions. He has also learnt to listen to the advice of us old settlers. Sadly, too late for many of his unfortunate followers. The winter has been hard, but no harder than normal. I'm sure you found the same." I nodded. He continued, "It has been tough, especially as they insisted on learning through the hard experience of their first winter rather than benefiting from the previous experiences of others. The one thing none of them has had the experience or skills to deal with has been the extent of the sickness and the high mortality. Yes, we are all malnourished. Too many people, not enough food. They were poorly advised about the scurvy and the ways to prevent it."

I interrupted him.

"We had no incidence, perhaps one, of scurvy on *Abigail* and that was towards the end of the voyage. With fresh fruit and vegetables, once we all landed that should have been dealt with. Certainly, my family was not affected."

"The biggest problem was Endecott's inability to control the workmen he brought over. They refused to work, consumed the food that should have been sufficient for all for the winter, became drunk and disorderly. The beer and hard alcohol were not secured. He had no option but to drive them out. Too late, the damage was done. The cold, the lack of food, the inadequate shelter exacerbated the sickness, the fever."

I asked him what he thought was going to happen to Naumkeag. He didn't know. He was aware that many more people were coming later in the year, perhaps 350 more settlers. He shook his head.

"There is no room for them here. They will need to move further west. I hear that the political and economic, as much as religious strife back in England will open the flood gates. I feel sorry for those of you who have escaped the immediate press of civilization. I fear that places like Shawmut, Winnisimmet, and Mishawum are going to be overwhelmed as we are finding here in Naumkeag. You will see the names changing, no longer honoring the Indian tribes that used to live here. For example, there is a new name already beginning to be used in place of Naumkeag."

I said it was inevitable. It had happened everywhere else. A reminder of home. I asked him the name being used for Naumkeag.

"No reminder of home, I assure you. Peacemakers want to show the world that the differences of opinion that threatened to destroy Naumkeag have been resolved. Salem, from the Hebrew for peace."

"Are you content with that change?"

"Isaac, I am a peaceful man. I have worked hard to fulfill my obligations to the Reverend John White, in Dorchester, when he appointed me to manage the Cape Ann settlement. I worked even harder to ensure the settlement survived, although reduced in number, by moving it here. Despite what I consider, in confidence, a lack of loyalty and support for what I've being attempting to do, by the people back in

Dorchester with the appointment of Governor Endecott, and by the lack of consideration for what we have accomplished, how we have managed to keep body and soul together, I have striven to accommodate the Governor's directives. Where I have disagreed, I have referred those disagreements back to the new company and Mr. Craddock for resolution. I will abide by their ruling."

"Are you comfortable with the religious differences which appear to be surfacing here?"

"I am a confessed Puritan, wishing for changes within the Church of England, Isaac. I was disappointed with the intolerance shown to those who were not comfortable with the dogma of Separatism when I was in New Plimouth. By leaving there, I hoped to move, to become part of a more tolerant society. I now see that Mr. Endecott is exhibiting a strong attraction to the Separatist way of thinking. I fear that for what he wants he demands the obedience of everyone. It troubles me. Perhaps more disconcerting are the arrivals of committed Anglicans who do not want any changes made. This does not bode well for a peaceful society."

I suggested that by calling Naumkeag, Salem, it could be the banner under which everyone strives for peace. Roger laughed and agreed. I wanted to visit the new settlement location and attempt to meet with the Governor. Wishing Roger well, I left with Johnny, who had been a silent witness to the conversation. I asked him what he thought.

"A good man, harshly treated. He would have made a good governor of the settlement. I hope he is not driven away. He is a good leavener."

We walked down to the South River and followed the track that Annie and I had walked along several months ago. We came to the cove where the river bend turned south. Since we were last there, perhaps a dozen houses had been built clustered round the reassembled Governor's house, brought from Cape Ann. In contrast to the crude houses around it, it seemed immense. Many people milled about, looking gaunt and unhappy. They had lost loved ones and barely survived, themselves. The Governor was present in his house, and invited us into his office. We sat in front of his worktable, covered in documents. He was a busy man and I thanked him for sparing the time.

He asked me how the family was and how we had survived the winter. I said passing well, thank you. I commiserated with him about the hard winter he and the settlement had suffered. He nodded and leant back, folding his arms. He frowned at me. He had aged, lines on his grey face, his moustache and beard were untidy, his clothes rumpled, as if he had been wearing them for many days. Above all, with deep, dark, sunken eyes he looked exhausted.

"I believe, Mr. Stanfield, your presence at my side would have been of great benefit."

I felt sorry for the man. He had been unprepared. He had been arrogant enough to believe he had the skills and temperament to deal with establishing a new settlement in a hostile country. He had wanted me to make life simpler for him. Instead, I believe he had been given an effective and critically important lesson. I told him so. With what he had gone through, he was more equipped to govern a settlement that would be growing quickly. He accepted my comments with some grace. He admitted that the learning process had been savage, unlike anything he had ever dealt with before. As he sat, ruminating over the lessons learned, I asked him about his wife, saying that Annie was most concerned and eager to visit her.

"Mr. Stanfield, I say again, how grateful we are for the support Mistress Stanfield provided my wife. Mistress Conant has taken on that role. Sadly, I believe her time is short. She hangs on to life by barely a thread. Governor Bradford has promised to send a doctor, Mr. Fuller, who is due here today or tomorrow. I fear he will be too late."

I commiserated with him. Johnny nodded his agreement.

"Mr. Stanfield, before you go. I have something to tell you. A short time ago, two of my settlers were out hunting some miles from here. They came across a body, or the remains of one. It was a man and he had been dead some time. The wild animals had found him. Before burying him, they went through his pockets and a bag he had with him. They found the remains of letter which they brought back. I have it here."

He produced a soiled and stained scrap of an envelope and handed it to me. I was surprised and looked questioningly at him. He told me to read it, which I did with some difficulty.

On it I could decipher

"*S…ott?*"

"Scott", I said. The governor shook his head. I handed it to Johnny who studied it.

"Spiggott?"

The governor then handed me a scrap of paper.

"*…I trust you will have completed the job I gave you by the time I come over in '29. If you can't deal with the man, take the boy.*"

The rest was illegible. So Spiggott was dead, and the instigator was due to arrive this year sometime. It also meant that no member of Endecott's entourage was any longer a suspect—something he was quick to point out. However, it left us with a king-sized problem. The governor shrugged. He regretted having to say so, but it was now our problem, not his. While I digested this, Johnny asked whether there was anything we could do to help him.

"Yes, we need able bodied men to help build the additional houses we need for the summer arrivals. We also need meat. We use fowling pieces which are too long and too unwieldy to be effective. Solve those problems for me."

Johnny looked puzzled.

"Surely, you have carpenters. I was aware of several on *Abigail*."

"We need fishing boats. We must have fish to improve our diet. They have been put to building them, as a matter of utmost priority."

He thanked us and said he must end the meeting. There was much to do, not least to build the additional housing with the largely unskilled and weakened people he had available. He hoped to leave the sick to the ministration of Dr. Fuller. In leaving, I promised him to send men to help with both the hunting and house building. He again thanked us. We left him, returned to our boat and sailed for home. It had not been an ideal moment to broach my land grant.

—— CHAPTER 15 ——

Journal entry *March – May 1629*

I sent Johnny, with his bow, Giles, and Gavan back to Naumkeag. They hunted and constructed houses three days a week from March through April. Four days a week they were back at Shawmut working the farm. Gavan had a hard time avoiding Agatha, but when he was cornered, they came to an understanding. Thereafter, he was left alone. With his skills and setting an example by his hard work, ably assisted by Giles, the construction proceeded quickly. The housing was simple, designed for the summer. Johnny was successful initially, but his success meant he had to work harder and go further afield to find game.

Johnny and Jeannie slept in one of the loft bedrooms, next to the children's bedroom. By March, he told me that while they would forever be thankful for being such intimate members of the Stanfield family, would it be possible if I would grant them two small favors. Of course, I said.

"We need a window in our bedroom. The children do, too. The sun rises earlier and stays later. We could use some natural light up there. Could we have a gable window at each side of the house?"

I agreed. A good idea.

"We need stairs, not a ladder to the loft. A ladder makes carrying things so much more difficult."

We consulted with Gavan, who had no issue with providing both.

He also had some glass left over. On a fine day, the windows were cut and framed. The next day glass was mounted. The stairs took a little longer, with Gavan spending half the week in Naumkeag. By mid-March the children were reveling in their newfound freedom and had now made the loft their preferred place to be, especially as the days grew warmer.

I had told Annie about Spiggott's body being found and the contents of the letter I had read. We realized that there was nothing we could do until the boats arrived from England. I was certain it was someone I knew. Our advantage was that whoever it was had no idea we had been warned. Annie remained worried. We had received a letter, a while back, from David Tremaine. He said they were planning to sail over on the *Lion's Whelp* with the Sprague family. They were due to leave in April this year, one of a number of boats sailing over together. I wondered if Spiggott's sinister associate might be on the same boat.

With the ground no longer frozen, by March we needed to prepare our land for growing the food we needed. We could no longer depend on William's generosity. We also had to plan for the Tremaine arrival in July or thereabouts. I wanted to wait until they arrived before making serious plans to build a farm. We needed hay and vegetables, irrespective of their intentions. We also had to prepare for the arrival of, hopefully, both our cows in July. Altogether, William had offered us about five acres of land, separate from the six he had cultivated for himself, together with the use of his oxen and plough. While the land was clear of trees, there were too many large stones, boulders even, for us to be able to plough it. The stones had to be cleared, set to the side of the field in piles from which we could build walls. All of this was very time consuming and we didn't have the labor available to us, with Johnny, Giles and Gavan otherwise occupied in Naumkeag. We had paced out four acres to be cleared, ploughed, and seeded. We fenced another acre, closer to the water, where the soil was fertile with few stones, to be our vegetable plot. We had brought seeds with us from England, which together with the seeds William had given us, provided all we required.

We had planned for rows of corn to be planted in April, little mounds, each to contain a seed and buried rotten fish as nutrient, along with potatoes, turnips, carrots, parsnips, parsley, lettuce, spinach, and cucumbers. We made room for pumpkins which would be planted in May. We wanted to produce our own beer, so hops were also planted. Until we could plough our four-acre field, the hay, barley, oats, and wheat would have to wait to be sown. In March, the whole family began to clear the field of stones and boulders. It was tough work. Johnny, Giles, and Gavan joined us on the days they were back from Salem. William Blackstone's oxen were hitched to two large wooden platforms with sides. Stones and boulders were placed on the platforms, when full they were dragged to the perimeter of the field, dumped, and the empty platforms dragged back for the next load. We all worked on this back-breaking task, even James and little Abigail, every day from sun-up to sunset, with breaks for meals. Luckily the weather stayed cool and dry. We eventually had cleared enough to un-hitch the platforms and hitch up William's plough. Johnny and Giles took turns driving the oxen to turn the soil. Occasionally rocks were struck by the plough. They had to be quick to halt the oxen before serious damage was done to the ploughshare. Gavan had had enough of dragging the platforms and made some wheels, iron shod, and an axle, thanks to Mr. Walford. He converted one of the platforms into a cart. Life became much easier.

By the end of April, the four-acre field had been planted. Now we had to learn how to keep the birds from stealing our seeds. Thinking ahead, a worse problem, according to William, was to keep the wild animals from eating the seedlings as they sprouted.

With the production of our own food, we would be able to barter the excess for the produce we needed. I had brought a large chest filled with English currency, but while the Old Planters preferred selling their produce for coins, I restricted, as much as possible, the depletion of my reserves. I knew I would need money later for items I doubted I would be able to obtain through barter. The food we had was insufficient. We had not yet started to develop new produce to sell here or elsewhere.

I took the opportunity to take Annie with me to meet with our neighbors, prompted by a note received from Amyse, inviting us to visit, saying that Samuel Maverick was in residence. We first met with Jane and Thomas Walford. It was a brief but pleasant visit. They were pleased to see us. Mistress Walford took Annie on a tour of inspection. I asked Thomas whether it was possible for me to buy hinges and door latches from him. He told me he would be happy to supply whatever hardware we wanted. In fact, he showed me an array of hinges and latches he had made for me to choose from. I had nothing to barter that he did not already have. He asked me what currency I wished to use, which surprised me. He told me that there were four types of currency in circulation: tobacco, wampum, Spanish silver dollars, and English pounds, shillings, and pence. I had English money, so he quoted me the fair price of a few shillings, which I happily accepted. I knew about the wampum belts, white beads valued at one penny per bead, purple beads twice that, offered in strings of eight, twenty-four or longer. He told me that Spanish dollars were otherwise known as pieces of eight. One dollar was cut into eight pieces and each piece used as currency. A dollar was worth about four shillings.

Annie returned with Mistress Walford. In further conversation, it became clear that Annie and Mistress Walford had struck up a friendship. We were pressed to visit them again. Annie, in return, invited them to visit us on Shawmut. Thomas said he was a regular visitor with William Blackstone. I said, in that case we should arrange for us all to meet in the near future.

The boat trip across the Mystic was short enough for me to row rather than sail. I asked Annie what she thought about our visit.

"I think Jane is lonely. Thomas is a bit of a recluse and has isolated the two of them from active contact with other settlers. When Thomas visits Blackstone, he goes by himself. I like her. She has learned to live over here with a host of stories to tell, both funny and frightening. From what she told me of their earlier life, I think they are about our age. I hope to see more of her."

Arriving at Winnesimmet, we moored the boat and walked up to the house. Again, we were greeted by the servant and escorted up the stairs where Samuel and Amyse were waiting for us. They had been alerted to our arrival. Introductions were made and Amyse was quick to embrace Annie, insisting they use each other's given name. Amyse wanted to know everything about England, Annie's background, how she met me, and did she know Aby. Annie laughed.

"Gracious, Amyse, let's leave the men to get acquainted while I try to answer all your questions."

Amyse tucked her arm inside Annie's as they moved to sit in two chairs looking out over the water. Mr. Maverick "Please call me Samuel", bade me sit with him by the fire. He said I was known to him and asked whether I remembered him, a member of Robert Gorges' expedition to Wessagusset. He had sailed over on the *Prophet Daniel*. I said I had been on the *Katherine* and admitted I didn't. Reasonable, because shortly after arriving, he had decided that Wessagusset was not to his liking and decided to go to Nantasket. He said he had followed the hapless Robert's dismal efforts from afar to build a government. He shook his head.

"I had assumed, Isaac, that the debacle was due as much to you wrongly advising him. I found out subsequently that Robert was the one responsible for all that happened, in spite of everyone's efforts to steer him in the right direction. I thought, mistakenly, you were his chief of staff. I have to say, you must have had a time of it."

That set me back a little. I had never spent any time wondering what Robert Gorges' men had thought about what my role was or the extent to which I was held to blame for that fiasco. Interesting. I said I was impressed at how he had been able to become so successful in the five years or so since he had arrived in New England. Trade, he said. Initially, David Thomson had helped him by engaging him as a junior partner in David's own trading business.

"Samuel, David didn't come down to Massachusetts Bay until 1626. What were you doing until then?"

"I moved on from Nantasket later in 1624 and joined David and Amyse in Pannaway, after you had gone back to England. He told me that having a trading post at the mouth of the Piscataqua had been a bad decision. The Hilton brothers had established a site six or seven miles upriver, much closer to Indian villages. He said he was planning to move down to Massachusetts Bay. He suggested that if I wanted to go into business with him, it would be better if I established a post there. He said he had contacts among the local Indians that he would pass on to me and when he and Amyse came down, he would be pleased to go into business with me. He lent me the means to build a small house. I immediately returned to Massachusetts Bay and began looking for a good site. I quickly found Winnesimmet and, with David's help, was able to build a house, on the site of the much larger house you see here."

I congratulated him and asked how he had prospered with the local Indians. He shook his head. It had been difficult but not impossible. By working hard, he had begun to trade with a number of Indian villages. When David and Amyse arrived, things became easier. David's workers had spent the previous six months building a substantial house and out-buildings on his island, with David a regular visitor. Once they had settled in, David spent much time away in his boat, exploring the rivers and seeking trading relationships with new villages. Samuel was responsible for further developing those relationships.

"Amyse must have welcomed your presence with David away so much."

He looked at me with a slight frown. I tried to appear guileless. After a pause he said that she was welcoming. In fact, he was able to provide the hard labor that would have been David's responsibility had he been there. While Amyse tended the livestock, collecting eggs, milking cows, and tending the vegetable garden, Samuel cut the trees for firewood and used the saw pit to cut lumber for the repairs that were constantly needed, which he was pleased to handle. I laughed, saying that he made it sound like a full-time occupation, but I was puzzled. I wondered why he did that? David had his workmen. For that matter, Amyse had a number of servants and maids.

I remarked as off-handedly as I could, that he must have come to know the best routes to take, depending on time, weather, and tide, between Thomson Island and Winnesimmet. He admitted that while David was away, he found it easier to stay. Realizing what he had just admitted to, he insisted that he lived in the loft of the stable whenever he stayed on the Island. I smiled. He laughed and acknowledged that Amyse had suggested he would be more comfortable in a bedroom in the house, which he was grateful to accept.

I apologized for all my questions, but David was a friend of long standing. I had been shocked to hear of his death. I wanted to know how David had died, but I also needed Samuel to tell me how he had become so successful.

"When David disappeared and was believed dead, I moved in permanently with Amyse. We married and through that marriage I gained access to David's wealth."

I thought it was convenient. I asked him how he believed David had died.

"I really don't know for sure. His boat was found but not his body. I don't believe he was attacked and killed. His boat would have been taken."

"Could he have taken his own life? Out in the bay a long way from shore, he could have jumped overboard. The boat, driven by wind and currents, eventually cast up on one of the islands."

He acknowledged that could be true. The obvious next question was why? Samuel looked a little uncomfortable. I could understand his reaction. The answer was equally obvious to me. David could have become distraught over what he believed to be Samuel's relationship with his wife. There was another possibility. Perhaps, Samuel became so tempted by David's wealth that he wanted to get rid of him. After which, by marrying Amyse, he would gain access to David's estate, through his widow. I decided to end the conversation. It was time to join the ladies.

Notwithstanding my doubts, we spent a pleasant few hours together, while refreshments were served, talking about the flow of settlers coming here and what effect that would have on the development of New England, especially around Massachusetts Bay. Samuel was worried about the intolerance of the Separatists, the threat they made to old church adherents. Samuel and Amyse were Church of England. Governor Endecott was strongly attracted towards Bradford and his Separatism, in New Plimouth. With it likely, therefore, that a Separatist minister would soon be appointed, it would be difficult for Anglicans to follow their faith unchallenged. We bid our farewells and promised to meet regularly. Samuel said he was often away and it would be of great benefit to Amyse to have a friendly neighbor close by.

On our return boat ride to Shawmut, I asked Annie how her conversation with Amyse had gone.

"I don't believe Amyse is happy, the marriage to Samuel was not her idea. She feels she was pressured. David's death had drawn a number of suitors, according to Amyse, attracted by David's wealth. So, when Samuel kept proposing, increasingly forcefully, it became a matter of accepting the hand of someone she knew over dealing with the constant attention from relative strangers. It seems the warmth Samuel showed to Amyse cooled markedly once they were married. I asked her about David's health, mental and physical. She said she had become saddened by David's detachment. She feared that he was depressed about Samuel's attention towards her, despite insisting that there was nothing between them."

She thought for a while, the breeze from the northeast pushing us gently towards home. I took the moment to recount the conversation Samuel and I had and my possible conclusions. Annie discounted the possibility that Samuel had killed David.

"Why, my love, would Samuel want to do that? He had access to everything he needed while David was alive, possibly even his wife. Not only would he have lost a key trading partner, he risked alienating Amyse, if she found out. More than alienating, she would want him to be punished for what he had done."

We received a note from Thomas Gardner that Doctor Fuller had come to Naumkeag and had been unable to help poor Anne Endecott, who had died shortly after his arrival. However, he continued to work to help the sick there. They now had their doctor. It seemed that he had become close to the Governor. Fuller's committed Separatism was having a marked influence on him.

Strange how the world turns. Twenty or so years ago, the Separatists fled to Holland in the face of persecution for the manner in which they worshipped God and their desire to separate religion from the civil authority vested in the King. Roger Conant's concerns about the intolerant constraints of Separatism restricting the freedom of worship should also include the usurpation of the independence of civil authority in Salem.

—— CHAPTER 16 ——

Journal entry - *June 1629*

The whole of June, Giles, Johnny, and I worked the field, while Annie and Jeannie tended the garden, to bring to harvest the vegetables and crops we would need not only to cover our existing requirements but to store for the winter. We expanded the acreage we had, clearing the land, ploughing, and planting. Giles was a godsend. It was clear that he was a much more experienced farmer than Johnny. I made Giles responsible for all farming matters with Johnny his thankful and willing helper.

Gavan and I had had long discussions about the need for our own transport. We had been given unlimited use of the Blackstone shallop, but I wanted my own, bigger one. Gavan said he would be pleased to design one to meet our needs and on approval he would build it. Once the house was built, he had felled a number of locust, oak, and pine trees, some already dead, trimmed and split the trunks before stacking them to dry over the winter. Not long enough to dry, he said, but needs must. He preferred black locust to white oak for boat building as it was harder and longer lasting, if he had enough of it. He had stacked the dead locust, pine, and oak by the saw pit and spent the winter months hard at work cutting additional timber in preparation for boat building. I said we also needed something light, rowable, and sailable. Eventually we would need a larger vessel than the shallop, a pinnace capable of carrying large loads. I had been developing plans that I would discuss with David Tremaine when he arrived.

I saw the need approaching for the local movement of produce between the settlements already existing in Massachusetts Bay, as well as beyond Cape Ann. The expected influx of settlers would result in the propagation of new settlements both along the shoreline and spreading up the many rivers. Large merchantmen would come to drop their freight in ports like Salem, for onward distribution. Local settlements would want their produce taken to these ports for consolidation and shipment back to England. I doubted that even a large shallop would be big enough, but it would have to do. A pinnace with crew would be better. As the business grew, we could move up to a small barque (fond memories of the *Sweet Rose)*, and begin to think of trade between England and the West Indies. One step at a time.

By the end of May, Gavan began to build the new shallop with help from me, Johnny, and Giles, when they could be spared from their farming,. He produced the drawings he had made in anticipation, recommending an overall length of twenty-four feet, including rudder, with frames and stem of locust and planking of pine. Given the go ahead, he cleared a large flat space, close by the water's edge and constructed a rectangular wooden bed, pegged together and laid on the ground, upon which he would build the shallop, upside down. James became fascinated. When schoolwork and duties allowed, he spent much time watching and learning from Gavan. They soon became inseparable. Listening to James in the evenings before bedtime, he sounded like he was becoming an expert builder. He talked knowledgably about the locust frames being cut, shaped, glued together, and fixed on the bed to form the hull, in specific order, height and width of each frame different conforming to the graceful lines of the hull shape Gavan had drawn, the stem, also of locust, holding the first frame in place and how he, James, was given the important task of keeping vertical each frame as it was fixed in position. The transom was added, supporting the final frame. Then the pine planking, each plank pegged to the frames they covered. By the end of June, the hull was finished, and we were all enlisted to roll it over, to excited celebrations. The next stage was to complete the interior, with supports for the floorboards, mast support, thwarts for seating, and most importantly, the rudder.

Gavan had discussed with me the need for ironwork, sailcloth, and cordage. We made a list and I was able to get everything he needed. The particular pieces of ironwork—nails, brackets and pinions, oarlocks, stay and shroud blocks, and fittings for the mast and boom, as well as anchor, I had made by Thomas Walford. It provided opportunities for me to take Annie with me so that she could spend time with Jane. The sailcloth and cordage I bought from fishing boats that were regular visitors to Salem. With everything to hand by mid-June, Gavan estimated that the boat would be ready for sea trial by mid-July.

Annie and I were eagerly anticipating the arrival of the Tremaine family. We knew that the *Lion's Whelp* was scheduled to depart England with the *Talbot,* a much larger vessel which we assumed would arrive earlier. Her arrival would probably alert us to the imminent arrival of her smaller companion. Our assumptions were not correct— they arrived together. Luckily for us, they were spotted off Cape Ann on 27 June. The 28th being Sunday they would wait in order to arrive at Salem on the Monday. Given the bustle of so many arriving settlers, we all decided to sail the Blackstone shallop over to Salem, leaving at dawn on the 30th.

When we rounded the headland protecting Salem Bay and looked across to Salem, the South River was crowded with shipping. Numerous boats ferrying passengers and stores, like water beetles, to the landing stage built for the new settlement. Already, many passengers were on the shore milling about, confused, excited, thankful to be on dry land and unsteady on their feet. We beached our boat down river from the landing stage and walked up looking for a sign of the Tremaines. It was a deafening madhouse, mothers calling for children, fathers shouting for directions and demanding access to their possessions, children out of control for the sheer excitement of it all. Everyone talking at the top of their lungs to make themselves heard. We needed to find David, Kate, and Beth as soon as possible and escape with them back to Shawmut. I said, knowing David, he would expect us to be there to meet him, so would have positioned his family in an open spot and waited for us. I suggested we walk around the perimeter of the mass of people. We agreed to split up and meet back at the spot we were at in thirty minutes or sooner if we found them. James insisted on doing his own search. I went one way, Annie with Abigail in her arms went another. James had already disappeared into the throng, to work his way to the far side.

James found them and proudly led them back to our meeting spot. He told me later that it was Beth who spotted him and had run to meet him. Face to face, Beth had suddenly become shy, but pulled him by the arm back to her family. They were waiting for us with happy smiles on their faces when we returned from our search. It was a joyous meeting. Beth with her cornflower blue eyes under a thicket of golden curls, had grown and was the image of her mother. While they had the possessions that they had kept with them during the voyage, it would be a day or so before the ships could complete unloading, especially as there was little room ashore to pile the stowed baggage and freight from the holds, let alone the livestock. David said, thanks to God his two cows, both Devon reds, had miraculously survived. Kate pulled a face and said they were North Devon, much better than the South Devon, and it was due to her constant and tender nursing as much as the hand of God. We agreed to sail back to Shawmut immediately. David and I would return the following morning to retrieve the rest of their things. I would arrange with Thomas Gardner to look after the cows until we could arrange transport for them back to Shawmut.

The sail back had the passengers quickly rearrange themselves, David and me in the stern, Kate, Annie, and Abigail amidships, Beth, shyness gone, and James in the bows. The wind was kind, the seas calm, only the occasional spray dousing the bowmen, to squeals and laughter. There was much catching up on all that had happened in the five hours it took us to reach Shawmut.

I told David about Spiggott and the attempts on my life and James', together with the note found by his body. I said that we had intended to watch the passengers coming ashore from the recent boat arrivals, but I realized we didn't know who we were looking for. It would have been pointless. David grimaced and thought for a moment.

"That is interesting. When we were all assembled on the dock in Gravesend waiting to board, Kate said she noticed someone behaving oddly. Apparently, a man approached through the crowd. Kate happened to glance in his direction. He looked at me, stopped, turned, and disappeared back into the throng. She described him as being of medium height, slim, and bearded. He seemed well dressed, not a servant, certainly. Kate said it looked as if he was shocked when he saw me and didn't want to be recognized. Later when we were under sail, I asked Kate to let me know if she saw him again, it would be difficult for him to avoid being seen in the close confines of the passenger deck. Kate kept a look out over the next few days, to no avail. She stated that he could not be aboard. I was intrigued and sought out the skipper, John Gibbs, an old acquaintance. I asked him if he had a full complement of passengers aboard. He checked with the second mate who said that according to the manifest, one passenger failed to board in time before departure. The name on the manifest was Septimus Grindle. A merchant. A name not known to me. In light of your tale, presumably not his real name. Anyway, I thought no more of it. Then, after we landed in Salem and just before James appeared, Kate suddenly pointed and exclaimed that it was the same person she had seen on the dockside in Gravesend. By the time I looked up, he had slipped away. He must have come on one of the other boats."

So, Spiggott's sinister associate had landed. It was as well we have removed ourselves from Salem. A stranger would soon be spotted on Shawmut. Grindle would be looking for Spiggott. David suggested that Grindle would need to ask around. I didn't think so. not at first, anyway. Grindle and Spiggott would be looking for each other. If Spiggott didn't make contact, Grindle could reasonably assume he wasn't there. I said it was more likely that Grindle would want to know if Spiggott had been successful in eliminating me. We knew he wouldn't find Spiggott so we needed to find out if a stranger off the boats was asking about me. Unless, of course, he had already spotted me looking for the Tremaines.

David gave news from home during the rest of the trip to Shawmut. The Patriarch sent best wishes and a bulky letter which David would give me when we arrived home. He said that Richard Bushrode had died suddenly, no more than a week after we had left on *Abigail*. Very sad. He had been a supportive business partner and generous in his dealings with me. I reminded David that Richard had left his New England land grant to me which I needed to have the new Governor ratify. I had paperwork from Sir Walter Erle, of the Dorchester Company, acknowledging the Bushrode grant and a letter from Richard to me confirming his transfer of all rights to the grant to me. But with the demise of the Dorchester Company, superseded by the New England Company, I was concerned whether that transfer had survived. My relationship with Governor Endecott was not the best, though slightly better than it had been on *Abigail*. I would need to choose an appropriate time to press my claim with him.

There was much chatter in the bows, where Beth and James had become friendly. Deep, head-to-head conversations amidships came to a halt as we entered the Charles River and approached our landing place. We had been sighted and a welcome party was awaiting us. Quickly ashore, we hurried our newly arrived settlers up to the house to clean up and relax for the first time in many months. Abigail showed Beth and her mother their favorite water hole on the Charles River, leaving them to bathe away the memories of their journey and return refreshed, hungry, and tired. Jeannie and Johnny had prepared a welcome meal for us all. After which Kate and Beth retired to their bedroom and slept.

David had retrieved the bundle of papers he brought over for me which I scanned quickly. We then went for a walk. With respect to each letter, he gave me some background information. He had been handed each or otherwise had them delivered to him shortly before they had left England. A letter from the Patriarch, Rev. John White. David said he had been to see him at P.'s request, to bid David and his family farewell. They had sat in his study for an hour or two. David said that P. was concerned about the rising tide of settlers planning to come over. John Winthrop was expected to lead what P. thought would be an invasion that would swamp the small settlement of Naumkeag. That advice he did not want to commit to paper in case his implied criticism might be picked up by the wrong eyes. It seemed that P. was sensitive to the animosities that appeared to exist over the demise of the Dorchester Company. He told David that I should plan to move away to a more remote place and claim the land that should come with Bushrode grant. The contents of the letter were a report on the activities of the New England Company. David had also met with Will Whiteway while in Dorchester, who gave him a package to give me. There was a sealed letter from Sir Ferdinando Gorges which was delivered to the *Lion's Whelp* by courier from Sir Ferdinando's house in Clerkenwell, with the stricture to David that it be delivered directly into my hands. The sun was long gone, the night illuminated by a heaven of stars. We walked back to a slumbering house. David to Kate and me to my sleepy wife. We had much to talk about, but it would need to wait till morning.

—— CHAPTER 17 ——

Journal entry - *July 1629*

The next morning, David suggested that Kate should come with us. She was the only one who had seen my presumed adversary. Her job was to act as lookout with Johnny as her guardian while David and I gathered the Tremaine possessions. We sailed back to Salem leaving at first light. We planned to stay there until we could claim everything. We had supplies to keep us for a few days.

The situation was even more dire than that we had left yesterday. Too many people, not enough space. We met up with the three Sprague brothers, old friends from my school days in Dorchester, who were lively and pleased to see me. Joanna, Ralph's wife, and their three young sons, had been found temporary accommodation in the old village away from the confusion and disorder of the new village being built further down the peninsula under the Governor's direction. They had become firm friends with David and Kate. Kate said that friendship had kept them sane amidst the desperate conditions on the voyage over. Apparently, there was an engineer on board, Thomas Graves, who had something of a name for himself as a surveyor. As soon as he arrived, Endecott, anxious to move people out of Salem, asked him if he would move down to Thomas Walford's home at Mishawum where there was much land and draw up plans for a new settlement, called Charlestown. The Spragues and many others were keen to accompany him. I felt sorry for Graves.

While David went in search of the Tremaine possessions, I went to visit Thomas Gardner, shadowed by Kate and Johnny. He had kept himself and his family well away from the mass of newcomers milling around, waiting for directions. I told him I had two cows on the *Lion's Whelp* and asked him if he could look after them until I could obtain transport to move them to Shawmut. He said he was happy to do so, but I should move quickly. He feared the relative isolation he and his family enjoyed could not last. I also asked him if he could spread the word, quietly, that someone with ill intent might be looking for me. I needed to know who that man was. He said he would inform the Old Planters. I then went to the Governor's house to see if I could have a word. Not possible, but I did bump into Mr. Gott. I repeated what I had said to Thomas Gardner and Gott said he would let it be known and would keep me informed.

Back at the landing stage, David's personal possessions had been offloaded but he had also shipped crates of provisions, including wine and beer, winter clothing, farm equipment, and seeds which would not be offloaded till the next day. What he found he collected and took down to our shallop. The cows were brought ashore early and were in a collecting pen. While Johnny stood guard over the shallop, David and I, with Kate keeping an eye out for any new arrival we might recognize, went to extract his two cows and herd them to the Gardner's property. Each had David's identifying mark and he had the papers to prove his ownership. Each of us, leading a cow on a halter worked our way back through the crowds, now thinning quickly, and left them with Thomas. When we got back to Johnny, he said he had noticed that the livestock were being transported by a barge from the boats to the shore. He suggested we find out how we might make use of it to transport our cows to Shawmut. I delegated him for that job which he went off to do immediately, leaving us to load the shallop. Johnny came back, shaking his head. The barge was a flat-bottomed raft, poled in. No good for us. Our shallop wasn't designed to carry large livestock, even one at a time, unless we removed the mast and sail. Then we would have to row the twenty miles back to Shawmut. There had to be a better way.

We decided our short-term solution to moving our cows was to find a pinnace we could borrow. There were several I knew of, including one based in New Plimouth that made regular trips to Salem. I would send a note to my friend Isaac Allerton to see if we might make use of it.

We made camp, lit a fire, and settled for the night. The next morning, back at the landing area, I was surprised to see a pinnace dropping anchor. A ship's boat being towed astern was brought alongside and the skipper was rowed ashore. I went to find him and introduced myself.

"Ah! Mr. Stanfield. I am Stephen Hopkins. I know your name and I believe have seen you before, a few years back when you visited us in New Plimouth. I understand that you have become a settler in New England, yourself. We were made aware of your arrival at Naumkeag last year. I'm sure you would be most welcome if you were to visit us again."

I was surprised and gratified at Hopkins' reaction. I had no idea that Governor Bradford and his people were keeping such a close eye on what was happening and who was arriving in Salem. I explained my cattle predicament. He laughed.

"I have business to attend to with Mr. Endecott which will take much of the day. I plan to return to Plimouth tomorrow. I believe I can make a stop at Shawmut on my way."

I was grateful, showed him where our camp was located, and invited him to visit with us at the conclusion of his business with the Governor. He said he would be pleased to do so. True to his word, later that evening, Hopkins joined us for a beaker of ale and some stew we had simmering on our fire. It seemed that Johnny and he had some mutual acquaintances, their memories eliciting much amusement. I am not one for coincidences but as we talked about our respective lives, I was astonished to learn that Hopkins had lived in Bermuda, albeit for a short while, in 1609 when the *Sea Venture* carrying Sir George Somers to Jamestown was shipwrecked on Bermuda. He had gone on to Jamestown before returning to England in 1616. He was on the *Mayflower* in 1620. What was even more amazing was that in Plimouth he became friendly with my old Indian friends Samoset and Tisquantum. When

I expressed my surprise, he said he had been with them when they had come to see me after I had barely escaped with my life from Epenow. The sight I presented had been memorable and was still fresh in the memories of many who had witnessed it.

He returned to his ship after telling us we should bring the cows to the landing place tomorrow morning by 10:00, when the tide would allow the transfer of the cows. The next morning, we led the cows back as requested where Hopkins had organized a raft onto which we were able to walk both animals. The raft was poled out to the pinnace and Hopkins supervised the hoisting of the animals onto the foredeck where a temporary pen had been built with a straw covered canvas to protect the deck from manure. Meanwhile, David had retrieved his now unloaded crates. A cart was borrowed, the crates were moved to our shallop, those that fit, stowed into the boat, the rest Hopkins was happy to take. David and Johnny set off immediately for Shawmut. Having seen no one resembling my adversary, Kate and I waited until Hopkins and the pinnace were ready then sailed with them, directing them to our landing area on the Charles. Hopkins said that we would probably be able to offload the cows into the water, close to shore, depending on the tide, and walk them ashore. We passed the laden shallop which was making heavy weather of the trip, overloaded as it was. Hopkins asked me why I hadn't asked him to carry all the crates. I said I was already amply beholden to him. He was concerned that the shallop might not make it. I said David was an experienced ex-cox'n in the English navy. He would manage.

We arrived off our beach on the Charles River. The tide was up. We had been seen. Gavan and Giles came down. The boat was positioned bows pointing towards the beach and held by a stern anchor. A crew man had gone ashore with a line and tied it to a tree to keep the bows steady. The first cow, in its sling and blindfolded, was swung over the side and gently lowered into the water. Kate had jumped overboard, the water up to her waist with the halter rein in her hand. She took the blindfold off the cow and led it gently to the shore, where Giles took it. I led the second ashore and Gavan led it away back up the hill, following Giles to the stable. I waded back to the boat and helped off-load the Tremaine crates and take them ashore. After which, I shook Hopkins' hand and paid him for his services, thanking him. He said he was delighted to help and told me I was now obligated to come to Plimouth and meet my old friends, once more. I promised I would. I returned to the water and waded ashore. When I turned to wave, sails had been set and they were moving down the Charles and away. It was two hours later that the shallop arrived. It had been quite a journey, overloaded, low in the water with Johnny bailing most of the way. We were there to meet them, except Beth and Abigail who had immediately been captivated by and remained with the cows. I sent James to fetch Giles and the cart. Between us, we loaded the cart and three journeys later David had everything back at the house and stowed.

That night, after a happy, thankful family meal and not long after the three children had gone to their bed, we all agreed it had been a long day and we retired. I was more than keen to have Annie to my-self, warm and intimate in our bed. I had been away two nights, it had seemed longer. There was a gentle urgency about our lovemaking. Aware we now had an occupied bedroom next door, we were quiet. It was a reaffirmation of our love. It also cleared our minds so that happy in body and spirit we lay with dear, sweet Annie's head on my shoulder, whispering to each other.

Annie shook her head. She couldn't quite grasp that we were not only settled into a substantial house of our own, we had four bedrooms full of people and two further members of our extended family in a sta-ble that also boarded seven goats, Amos, Nanna, Beatrice, One, Two, Three and Four, as well as two cows. Kate had named them Ruth and Naomi. How was all that possible? We hugged and kissed, as I shared Annie's happy amazement. We slept.

Early the next morning, Annie and I rose before anyone else and, while she prepared a meal, I described our trip to Salem and the prob-lems there, too many people, not sufficient accommodation, or space. I told her what Ralph Sprague was doing, that Thomas Walford was in for a rude shock when a hundred settlers descended on him, and how concerned I was that we were also in danger of being overwhelmed. The hundreds that had just arrived were to be followed, in the coming years, by thousands more. Blackstone would not be able to keep that multitude from his land. We needed to move on. Annie sighed. She understood and said she shouldn't have been so thankful that we had settled so quickly. Foolish. She knew about Richard Bushrode's land grant and that we had to get it ratified by the Governor, which was not necessarily a simple process. I needed to sort my papers out so that when the time was right, I could present to him the written confirmation I had received from Sir Walter and Richard. However, Endecott reported back to the Governor in England of the New England Company, Matthew Craddock. Sir Walter was no longer directly involved.

Changing the subject, I mentioned that Gavan's new shallop would be ready soon. I would take David and Gavan on a proving sail. I wanted to round Cape Ann and sail along the shoreline exploring the rivers there, as far as the Piscataqua. We needed a home and farm removed from Massachusetts Bay. I wanted us to be on a river for ease of transport, fresh water, and fishing, as well as a base to reestablish my trading career. Annie asked how long we would be away. I thought about a week and mentioned that Johnny and Giles had plenty to do on the farm.

Annie responded,

"Remember, Kate is the farmer here. If you are thinking of taking David on maritime adventures, Kate must be given responsibilities in keeping with her skills and experience.

"Annie, my dear, we are a little ahead of ourselves here. We don't yet know what David and Kate's plans are.

"No, Isaac. Kate and I have had long, deep conversations about her relationship with David and what they have or have not planned for themselves. Kate has come to the conclusion that David is not a farmer, nor does he want to be one. If you tell her that you have David earmarked for maritime activities and you want Kate to run the farm with Giles, plus others as necessary, I'm sure she will be delighted.

There was much to do before I set off with David and Gavan. Not only to advise Johnny and Giles of Kate's responsibilities, I needed to introduce Kate to William Blackstone. He had mentioned some time previously that he had had difficulty when he first brought his oxen to Shawmut. There were local plants that seemed poisonous to cattle. Our goats hadn't seemed too worried. Perhaps we were lucky. I wanted Kate to learn as much as she could as quickly as possible. At the moment, the cows were still recovering from their long journey in the stable and their fodder was the hay we had grown. I also needed to take the time to study all the papers brought over by David.

The meeting with Johnny and Giles went well. I told them that Kate had successfully run a substantial farm in England for many years as a tenant farmer. She had come to New England to establish her own farm with me as a silent partner. My intention was to establish that farm north of here within a year and move the family there as soon as accommodation was built. They were excited at the prospect and admitted their experience was limited to being farm laborers. After Giles had left us, I told Johnny that once the farm was established, I planned to restart my trading activities and understood that he would want to participate. Johnny's eyes lit up at the prospect. I asked him how he and Jeannie were coping with all the changes that were happening to their lives. He paused before responding.

"Isaac, Jeannie loves the activity, but she worries about me leaving her. Farming is something she is comfortable with because I would be there with her. She frets at the thought of me sailing away from her. Isaac, I have to admit we are in a bit of a tussle. She wants a child of her own. The years she has lived with you and Annie looking after your children has made her yearn for one."

"Johnny, understandable. I think Jeannie would be a wonderful mother. You are so good with children I'm surprised you and Jeannie haven't produced a nest-full already."

Johnny went quiet, then, sadly he said, "You never met my first wife, Rebecca. She is a deep, aching memory."

I remembered, Rebecca had died in childbirth; the baby was

stillborn.

"Isaac, I can't bear to think that I could lose Jeannie the same way."

"Oh, Johnny. What a terrible thought. Is that why you are in a tussle with Jeannie?"

"No, no, no! I would never tell Jeannie that. Nor must anyone else. I tell her I don't want children. She asks why and I am unable to give her a good reason. Quite rightly, that upsets her."

I shook my head in commiseration. What a desperate quandary. We moved on to other matters.

Later, I introduced Kate to William. She quickly charmed the reticent minister, and I left them deep in conversation. I then settled down to read my correspondence. Will's letter was full of his news starting with the political convulsions caused by Buckingham's assassination and the sad death of Richard Bushrode on 1 July, 1628, a few days after we left Weymouth. I had no idea he was so unwell. He gave me family news as well as his duties as a senior member of the Dorchester community and his activities representing Dorchester in Parliament. He ended with a grateful tribute to my latest journal entries that had found their way to him, and a plea for more.

The letter from the Patriarch, John White, was a long one, describing the politics and economics around the continuing instability of the New England Company. He recounted what he described as the Lincolnshire and East Anglia influence, under the benign leadership of John Winthrop, beginning to assert itself with an enormous number of people, mostly Puritan, wanting to move to New England. He told me that both he and Richard Bushrode's investment in the New England Company had been written into the record and that he and Bushrode had written to Craddock that they had delegated their benefits to me, with respect to land grants, and all proceeds that might accrue in perpetuity. They had received written confirmation of this from Craddock, a copy of which he enclosed.

P. warned there was likely to be a successor organization to the New England Company, called the Massachusetts Bay Company. All rights would be subsumed within that new company, so I needed to be watchful. There was talk that once the new organization was in place there might be a reassessment of all property granted or otherwise within the new company's domain to ensure proper control and management. An ominous warning. I needed to talk to Endecott as soon as possible.

Finally, a short letter from Sir Ferdinando Gorges, wishing me well and happily settled but asking me to help him. He said he was being undermined and the property he owned on Massachusetts Bay was being illegally taken from him. He needed to reclaim my eyes, ears, and loyalty to him for action on his behalf, as yet unspecified. No wonder he wanted this letter delivered to me personally. It would be incendiary if it got into the wrong hands, destroying my credibility and eliminating any chance of my family being able to settle in New England. I burnt the letter and waited for a time I could send a sealed note back to Sir F. by a reliable courier to be placed into his hands.

I also needed to find out what had happened to my adversary. It had been a month since he had landed. No word had come back that any enquiries had been made about me. I needed to talk to the Governor and John Gardner. I also needed to talk to Johnny about defensive measures at Shawmut while we were away. We were isolated but decreasingly so as tracks and roads were being cleared in the land between Salem and Charlestown and the shoreline around the harbor. Annie and I should go to Charlestown to meet with Ralph and Joanna Sprague to find out how they were coping with the creation of a new settlement. For that matter, to visit the Walfords, as well. From being happily alone for so many years, the changes must be mind-numbing for them. It was quite possible that my adversary had moved to Charlestown. He had had the time to explore Salem. I needed to tell Thomas Walford and Ralph about the threat to me and my family. I had been remiss in leaving it so late.

—— CHAPTER 18 ——

Journal entry - *July 1629*

By mid-July, Gavan had his shallop ready and in the water, fully caulked with no leaks. We had a ceremony where Annie named her *Rosie*, in fond memory. With a pot of paint and extremely steady hand, Giles emblazoned her name on the transom. Paint barely dry, I took the opportunity to sail with Gavan, the Tremaines, and Annie to Charlestown, an easy and short first trip.

On the hill behind Walford's house, it had become a wasteland, trees had been cut down, stumps dotting the landscape, logs stacked to be turned to lumber, branches scattered in heaps ready for firing. Amongst the debris was an encampment of tents and huts, in the wetu style. Pegs had been placed marking roads showing that Mr. Graves' town planning was well underway. David, Kate, Annie, and I went in search of the Spragues, among the hundred or so settlers crammed into the space allotted to them by Graves in his zeal. I wanted Kate to keep a sharp eye out for the person she had seen in Salem. The man, if he was there, stayed out of sight. While the others met up with the Spragues, I left them to visit Thomas Walford. He was sitting at the back of his house watching the bedlam of the new town's birthing pains. He rose to greet me, shaking his head. The situation was not a good one for him and his wife, noise and lack of courtesy was wearing. His prior possession of the land was not a consideration among most of the newcomers. Much worse was the lack of clean drinking water. A small brook had been sufficient for the Walfords' needs but totally inadequate for everyone else. One bright spark was the need for his metal working services. His forge was kept permanently active. I asked him if anyone had been enquiring about me. I told him the background. No one had asked him, but he would keep his ears open. The description Kate had provided I passed on to him. He promised he would let me know if he found out anything. I wished him well and returned to the others.

Ralph remained enthusiastic about the new settlement, his brothers less so. Ralph saw the future. They, unhappy, only saw the present. Kate had provided them with a description of the man we were seeking, and Annie had impressed on them the concerns we had and by the time I came back had provided a somewhat lurid description of the attempts on my and James' lives. They were horrified and promised to keep their eyes open. I told Ralph what Walford had said about the lack of water. Ralph was unconcerned. God will provide, he said. He certainly was imbued with religious fervor. Annie was worried and said so as we sailed home on *Rosie*.

"We have someone we don't know, who hired an assassin, thankfully presumed dead, and who we believe is now here in New England wanting to kill you, Isaac, and, failing that, kill James. He has been here a month and seems to have disappeared. You don't seem concerned. It is clear he knows David, since he recognized him at Gravesend. Have you really thought together about who you both know who might want revenge for something you did? And why would he target James?"

David and I looked at each other. David after a moment of thought said he could think of two people and they were both dead—Tred Gunt and Seth Tremont.

Annie then asked,

"How can we be certain they are dead?"

David said that he was certain that Gunt had been executed at Plymouth Fort, fifteen years ago. As for Seth, all he knew was that he had been taken away by the authorities to face capital charges. Annie shuddered at the thought of her despised cousin and the grief he had caused with the kidnapping of James.

Once ashore, I congratulated Gavan on the fine, seaworthy boat he had built and with everyone back at the house David and I went for a walk.

"David, if it is Seth, I cannot believe he was able to escape being hanged or to have constructed such an elaborate means of exacting vengeance without the help of an influential and/or wealthy confederate. To be convicted on lesser charges, he must have had a competent advocate. Expensive, as well. Why would such a person invest so much for such a worthless individual? That person would also have had to react quickly to save Seth's neck, which meant he knew and was in some ways beholden to Seth when Seth returned to England."

We both stopped and turned to each other—Hook!

Hook had left *Swallow* as soon as we had docked on our return from Bermuda. We heard nothing more from him. Seth had been recruited to go to Bermuda to be his agent.

"David, I doubt Hook had any interest in seeking retribution. He would have been grateful to us for enabling him to escape with his skin, even if it meant him losing a considerable amount of money to his smuggler friend."

"No, Isaac. It was knowledge that Seth had. If he went on trial facing the death penalty, he might have spilled the beans about something nefarious that Hook had done. So, Hook gets him off to serve a lesser sentence. Seth leaves prison and demands a further payment. The means to avenge himself on the Stanfields. Hook has no morality about that if it meant Seth would be gone from England. Otherwise, Hook would eliminate Seth."

"David, Seth was a miserable little man. A coward. It would have been like him to pay someone like Spiggott to kill me. It would be a different matter for him to attempt the same. Could it be that he was certain that Spiggott would do the deed and his coming here was to escape Hook and start a new life with the money Hook gave him. When he arrived and found out that I was alive and Spiggott dead, he would want to make himself scarce as quickly as possible. He had places to go, even Jamestown or down to the islands, Barbados, or some such. We need to go back to Salem and see what we can find out."

Very early, next morning David and I sailed to Salem with Gavan. We no longer felt that Kate was needed. If the culprit was indeed Seth, we would recognize him immediately. A longer trip, all the better to further test *Rosie*. When we arrived, while Gavan minded *Rosie*, David and I went in search of the Governor. Bad timing on our part. As part of the company of 350 settlers that had arrived were three men of God, ministers, Reverends Higginson, Skelton, and Bright. Endecott was engaged in establishing precedence among those ministers, Skelton, being a Separatist had preference over Higginson, a Puritan, although older and wiser. Bright, being an Anglican, didn't have a chance. I managed to have a moment with Endecott and told him that I had plans to move further north. I reminded him that signatories to the New England Company charter included not only himself, but John White and Richard Bushrode, who had both assigned their property rights in the land grants to me that would ensue from their investments in the company. He said he was aware and that he understood that 200 acres had been assigned in my name. However, he said the New England Company had been subsumed into the Massachusetts Bay Company, the charter of which he had just received. Until Winthrop arrived next year, that assignment could not be confirmed. While I was free to explore and lay claim to a suitable plot of land within the remit of the new company, which included land up to three miles to the north of the Merrimack River, I would be at risk of losing that land. I was then dismissed. I craved his indulgence for one further matter. He, with considerable impatience, asked what I wanted.

I reminded him about the attempt on my life and the finding of Spiggott's body. He remembered. He also remembered my being concerned about a newcomer seeking my whereabouts. He had delegated my request for any information about that to Mr. Trask. I should see him.

We left in search of Mr. Trask. He was an Old Planter, therefore would be back in the old village. We went first to John Gardner. He said he and Trask had discussed my concerns and decided the best thing to do was to alert all their colleagues, including Conant. With a wide net cast, they should be able to catch their fish. "And did you?" I asked. He smiled and said they had. About two weeks after the settlers had arrived, a man had approached young Woodbury saying he had been looking for a friend who had arrived the previous year, a crewman on *Abigail*. Woodbury suggested that perhaps he had continued on *Abigail* back to England. No, his friend had planned to leave *Abigail* as soon as it arrived in Salem. Woodbury was well aware of the desertion of the two crewmen from *Abigail* and their names. He asked the man for the name of his friend. Spiggott, was the answer. I'm sorry to have to tell you, sir, but Spiggott died last winter. The man asked how. Difficult to say, was the answer. His body, or what was left of it after the wild animals had been at it, was found in the woods outside the settlement. The man was shocked. After a minute, he asked Woodbury if he knew another friend of his, Isaac Stanfield. Woodbury said he didn't. Then, with great presence of mind, he said if it was important, he would find someone who might know Mr. Stanfield. If the man would like to return tomorrow at the same time, Woodbury might have news for him. The man nodded and walked away, towards the new settlement. Woodbury wrote down a detailed description of the man and it was circulated in both the old village and the new. He hasn't been seen since.

I thanked John and we walked to Trask's house. On the way we noticed two men engaged in what appeared to be a friendly duel. We stopped to watch them, neither a very proficient swordsman. One of them noticed us and stopped. The other had his back to us. He turned to face us. It was the young man I had had problems with on the *Abigail*, Richard Darnell. He recognized me, lowered his sword and approached.

"Ah! Stanfield. What are you doing here?"

"Just passing", I said.

His tone became angry.

"You've not lost your impertinence. I'm surprised. I would have thought you would show more respect."

Intrigued at his arrogance, I couldn't help but ask what he meant. I could see David was becoming a little agitated. Darnell bristled.

"I still believe you are a self-aggrandizing charlatan. You interrupt your betters engaged in a practice with which someone such as yourself will have had little engagement. Go away."

I laughed and turned to David. "What a puppy."

Darnell lost his temper. "You deserve a thrashing" and attempted to strike me with the flat of his blade. I crowded him and blocked his arm. David quickly turned to Darnell's companion and asked to borrow his sword. The man, bemused, surrendered it.

Darnell stepped back, furious. David handed me the sword. Darnell smiled.

"Now, Stanfield, I will teach you a lesson."

He immediately attacked, which was met with simple parries. I did no more than defend myself. He was a very poor swordsman. This foolishness needed to be stopped before Darnell hurt himself. A quick flick of my wrist and his sword was sent flying several yards away.

"Mr. Darnell, you have an ungoverned temper, an overweened sense of your own importance and you are reckless. Good day to you."

I handed the sword back to its still bemused owner and with David turned to continue on our way, to find it blocked by Mr. Trask.

"Mr. Stanfield, I must thank you for treating the foolish Darnell kindly. I will have words with him anon."

David's look of puzzlement was alleviated by my description of Darnell's behavior towards me on the *Abigail* in 1628. We accompanied Mr. Trask back to his house. We told him of our meeting with the Governor and John Gardner. He promised to keep us informed of anything he might uncover. We thanked him and left to go back to Gavan and *Rosie.* Sailing back, David felt we had fairly convincing evidence that our surmises about Seth were correct. He had been suspicious of Woodbury's offer. With Spiggott dead, possibly killed by me, and the settlement alerted, he fled for his life. I was less certain, and I was sure Annie would not be satisfied.

—— CHAPTER 19 ——

Journal entry - *August 1629*

It was a week before we were able to set off on our exploratory trip around Cape Ann. Annie remained concerned about the possibility that Seth was lurking in the bushes. I had planned to take Johnny with me, but he also voiced his misgivings. He thought we had come to a too convenient, even if plausible, explanation. He said he would prefer to stay with Gavan and Giles to ensure there would be no intruders, or if there were to deal with them. He had contacted his Indian friends who said they would keep a watch as well. With those assurances and protection Annie was happy to see David and me leave. She did recognize the importance of our finding a new home and ensured we had supplies and provisions for two weeks, more than enough.

We sailed east, along the Massachusetts Bay shoreline of Cape Ann, passing numerous islands and entrances to natural harbors and bays. We did a quick tour of Beauport Harbor. I told David about my earlier visits over the years and the attempt to establish a settlement there six years previously. We sailed on around the end of Cape Ann heading north, then west as we skirted the northern shoreline. We passed a river mouth which seemed to be flowing directly southwards back to Beauport Harbor. We continued past a long sandy beach to another narrow entrance to what looked like a large bay guarded by huge sandbars. There was an ebbing tidal flow out of the entrance close to slack water, so we sailed into the bay and beached *Rosie* to the west sheltered by a high sand dune. We climbed to the top of the dune for a better view of the bay which was surrounded by a heavily wooded shoreline receding into the distance with a hilly landscape to our right. What looked like a river meandered its way around the far side of the bay, the view blocked in part by a mass of marsh grass growing in in the middle of the bay. It was entrancing. Evening was drawing in with the sinking sun making the distant land indistinct. The water was calm with wild fowl in abundance.

The next morning we caught the tide before it turned to flood. We made it safely out of the entrance to the bay and continued our journey westward, following a sandy beach for several miles. The land behind the beach gained in elevation and was heavily wooded. The current swept us into a channel between a long, low, sandy island to starboard and a large, hilly island to larboard. We were carried into a large marshy bay continuing north with the marsh grass closing in on us on either side. The channel opened up before we entered the Merrimack River. We headed northwest upriver, keeping close by the larboard shore out of the strong current. After about four miles we came to an opening on the left bank with marsh grass on either side. The shoreline had risen to form a high cliff surmounted by trees then dropped to a low bank behind the marsh, overhung with tree branches. We turned the boat up into a narrow stream some twenty paces wide, tree-banked on either side. To larboard we saw in the dusk an opening in the trees and a place we could ground *Rosie* with the bow out of the water. Tying *Rosie* to a tree we unloaded our camping supplies and started a fire, reheating the stew Annie had made for us. We ate and slept, ready for an early exploration the following morning.

We were woken early by the sound of muttered voices. Two young Indians had come down to the river and stood a short distance away from us. They appeared to be wondering who we were and what they should do about it. Curious rather than frightened, I thought inclined to be friendly. They looked to be about fifteen years old, tall and lean, well-formed with large chests and slim waists. The taller one had his long black hair tied behind him, the other's loose and flowing. They were naked apart from a cloth between their legs secured by a snake-skin belt round their waists. The cloth folded over the belt and hung down over their loins and buttocks. They reminded me of the young Kitchi and Mingan, my friends from Saco over ten years ago.

I waved to the two Indians and added some kindling to the embers of the previous night's fire. David put a pot on the fire containing the remains of our stew and two ears of maize to bake in the embers. I again waved to them, beckoning for them to join us. They slowly approached to within a few paces and squatted. I moved to one side, making room for them by the fire, gesturing for them to come closer. They looked at each other. After a moment they both came and sat with us. One of them asked "English?" I nodded. I patted my chest, "Isaac." David did the same, "David". They nodded, repeating our names. I looked at them and opened my hand to them. "Nootau" said the taller, "Ahanu" the other. David and I repeated their names and smiled. We offered them the maize which they accepted. Nootau spoke a few words of English, enough together with signs and drawing diagrams on the sand for us to be able to communicate while we ate. They said their village was nearby, further up the stream. They had seen our boat last night. The villagers had watched from the cliffs. Their chief had sent them to meet us this morning. They invited us to return with them to their village. We agreed and set off as soon as we had tidied up our camp and doused the fire.

We followed our new friends along a path that followed the stream, through cultivated fields bright with yellow sunflowers on long stems and tobacco plants with their large green leaves, all growing in profusion. The path then turned away from the river up to higher ground. It stretched away before us. Tall trees with little undergrowth. Beyond, more cultivated fields were scattered among the woodland, also cleared of undergrowth in many areas, leaving berried thickets for birds and small animals. The village was on open land and surrounded by a stockade, similar to the villages at Saco and Winnipesaukee, with wetus dotted around the outside the stockade, each with fenced vegetable plots. The stockade meant that they had enemies, presumably the Mohawk. It was clear that what had been a populous village was now much smaller. The open land had been cleared to meet the needs of many more people.

We entered the village. The Sagamore's dwelling was a large house raised on posts, with steps that led up to a platform, on which an imposing figure waited for us. Later, I found out that he wasn't the Sagamore, he was the local village leader. We introduced ourselves. His name was Chogan. He welcomed us with good English. I complimented him.

"English fishermen would come in their long boats, rowing up the river. They were friendly and taught me some English words. I was pleased, in return, to show them where the best fish were and how to catch them, as the fish were clever. I spent much time with them. They caught many fish and I learned English. Their favorite fish was the sturgeon. I knew where to catch the really big ones. They called me Mr. Sturgeon."

"How big?"

He stretched his arms wide. I said I would like him to show us, too. He grinned and nodded. I asked him to tell us about his people.

"My people, here, are a part of a larger tribe. Our Sagamore is Masconomet and his village is Agawam, several miles south of here, where he lives during the summer. Masconomet's people are Pawtuckets, part of the Pennacook confederacy, whose Sachem is Passaconaway. The leader of the Pawtuckets is the Squaw Sachem, the widow of Nanepashemet, who died ten years ago."

It was Masconomet who had established such good relations with the Old Planters. The land under his control appears to be the territory between the Charles and the Merrimack Rivers, including Cape Ann. It seemed clear to me that any land the settlers might wish to acquire or otherwise make use of could only happen with his blessings. This all brought back memories of Askuwheteau, the Sagamore in Saco, whose tribe was decimated by the sickness. They joined up with the Winnipesaukee where Askuwheteau was subsequently elected Sagamore. The Winnipesaukee are also part of the Pennacook. I wondered if my old Indian name Machk was still remembered.

Chogan asked us what our business was on the Merrimack River. I told him that I had recently brought my family to his beautiful country, from England. My friend David and his family were here for the first time, but I had been coming over here for many years, since I was a boy. I had met and befriended many of his people, both here and back in England. It was because of my many experiences that I was determined to return to live here permanently. He asked me who I knew. I mentioned my old friend Samoset. He knew him as an occasional visitor, who was well known to the English, remarking that Samoset is well named, 'He who travels far'. I told him about my winter spent in Saco where Askuwheteau was the sagamore at the time of the great sickness when his tribe was almost wiped out. That was when he moved his people to Winnipesaukee where I met with him again. Chogan knew him. They were part of the same confederacy. I asked him if he knew about the man called Machk. He sat back and considered me, thoughtfully.

"Yes, Isaac, the story of Machk is legend. The Englishman who killed a huge bear. The skin still hangs in Askuwheteau's lodge. You are Machk? How am I to know this is true? Legend has it that Machk was sorely wounded, close to death. "

I nodded, slowly opened and discarded my shirt, then turned to show Chogan the faint but unmistakable claw marks on my back.

While we had been talking, the villagers had gathered in a circle round us on the platform and down the steps. Chogan stood and with his arms raised he loudly proclaimed that a legend, Machk, had come to them. Everyone laughed and cried out greetings, wishing to shake our hands. It was a happy moment. Once peace and quiet were restored Chogan asked me what it was that we wanted. I told him we would like to build a house here for my family and to farm the land. He nodded.

"Isaac, we would like that, too. We would both benefit from your being here. You will give us access to the produce that comes from England. You will also help us defend our village from the Mohawk. You will have rich land to farm and us as friendly neighbors. However, you will need to go to discuss this with our sagamore, Masconomet. I would be happy to accompany you. Masconomet speaks no English."

All this while David had stayed silent, listening in some amazement to the effect my past experiences were having on Chogan and his villagers. He now asked whether it would be possible for us to walk around the area and enjoy its beauty. If we went to Masconomet without a clear idea of what we wanted and where we might want to build, we would look foolish and be wasting his time. Chogan agreed and told our two young friends, Nootau and Ahanu to guide us. With Chogan's blessing we left to explore. Beyond the village, the land rose steeply to form a plateau which had a most pleasant English feel and appearance. Rolling grassland with hills and coombs, ponds and woods, sometimes too dense for us to easily walk through, containing oak, elm, ash, beech, birch, locust, pine, spruce, walnut, and many other types of tree, mature, tall and straight, with no low branches. We dug into the grassland with our knives finding good soil underneath. Occasional stone ledges and large outcrops would appear. We found a flat and open area about 100 paces from the edge of the cliff overlooking the Merrimack and the stream where we had moored *Rosie*. Including the walk to the village, we had walked about a half mile from there but if it weren't for the densely packed trees I'm sure we would be able to see her below us, a short distance away. It would be a steep path down through the trees to the river. The open area where we were was sided by woods with an open stretch of grassland to the northeast of perhaps five acres. The trees and further woods to the east could be cleared for additional pasture and plantings. We both felt we had found the spot to build our house.

Then I came to my senses. I had been overwhelmed by beauty of the location. There was no water close to hand. I asked Nootau. He smiled and pointed downstream along the cliff above the Merrimack. We followed him for about a half mile through the trees until we came to a wooded coomb, a deep hollow through the middle of which ran a brook that emptied into the Merrimack. A small pond had collected in the coomb where the brook had widened. It could be easily dammed to make a larger pond if need be. We walked up the course of the brook and found it came from a spring some distance away. With the wood cleared, we would have an ideal sheltered location close by running water.

We returned with our guides to the village. A meal had been prepared for us in which the whole village participated. It was a hot August day, but a fire had been prepared for the ceremony that preceded the meal, as well as to cook the meats and vegetables we would be consuming, tubers from the sunflowers we passed, which tasted like artichoke, maize, squash, and beans. All the villagers, apart from two on drums, formed a circle round the fire and with Chogun leading began a lively dance to shouts and clapping of hands. At one stage, David and I were pulled into the circle and became a part of the village. It was a happy occasion.

After the meal, Chogan suggested we should go with them in their canoes to Agawam, as it would be much quicker than walking or using our boat. He said watching us rowing on the river yesterday told them how heavy and slow our boat was. We walked down to the stream. Two canoes appeared as if by magic from the surrounding brush each to be paddled by four Indians. We were invited to board different canoes. I had had much experience in my earlier trips to New England and was quick to regain my balance. Poor David was less fortunate and to the delight of the villagers who had come to watch us leave, he capsized his canoe twice before grimly holding himself steady in the middle of the canoe. We left the stream and paddled swiftly down the Merrimack. Leaving the river we retraced the route we had taken behind the sandy island that acted as a barrier to the sea beyond. Past the hilly island we had passed yesterday, we entered a river that took us west and then southwest. It quickly narrowed through marsh land. The rolling, open, and forested lands beyond reminded me of England. There was some evidence of a settlement, one or two small houses on cultivated plots. At a certain point we turned off the river into a creek, heading south. Shortly thereafter we reached our destination and Chogan led us ashore. We were then escorted to meet Masconomet.

I presumed we were in his village of Agawam. Chogan went before us to meet with his chief and explain who we were and why we had come to see him.

Chogan returned and invited us to accompany him into the Chief's long house. Seated at one end was a most impressive man. When he rose to greet us, he was well over six feet tall, with broad shoulders covered by a woven cloth of many colors. Dark, angular, smooth face, with black penetrating eyes. Black hair pulled back and held with a colored headband of small beads. Large, well-proportioned chest and strongly muscled legs. He wore short, deerskin breeches. Chogan acted as interpreter. Masconomet welcomed us to his village. Chogan had spoken about our coming to his village and had told him of my past visits to his people. The Chief looked at us both, standing respectfully before him. "Machk?" he asked. I raised my hand. He smiled. He patted his chest and said "Machk" and spoke a few words. Chogan explained that Masconomet had become famous as a young man for killing a great bear. He said that we were bear brothers and extended his hand which I shook. We both laughed. He asked a question which Chogan translating asked me if I had had injuries from my adventure with the bear. I took my shirt off and showed him the marks on my back. He laughed again, turned his back and showed me similar marks.

We sat and through Chogan we explained what we wanted and where we would like to build a house and start a farm. He told us that he had already been pleased to offer other English people land on which they could settle. What we wanted seemed good to him. He had become familiar with Mr. Conant when he lived on the harbor at the eastern end of his land and moreso when they moved to Naumkeag. However, he said he felt with Isaac he had a more intimate relationship—bear brothers! He would be happy to share his land with me where we had indicated. In exchange we would help him and his people deal with the terrible Mohawk and even worse Tarrantines, also called Micmacs. We thanked him. After more pleasantries were exchanged and an invitation to return whenever we wished, we took our leave to return to our canoes for the paddle home, quietly elated.

I was with Chogan on the return journey and asked him what formal process existed to confirm we had been given approval to build a house and farm on his land. He said it was not the land they owned, only what they produced on the land. They were happy to share the land and for us to make the land productive. From an Englishman's perspective that arrangement sounded somewhat nebulous. I would need to talk to Roger Conant and the Governor about the process currently in place to deal with the acquisition of Indian lands.

When we arrived back to the landing spot where we had left *Rosie*, we thanked Chogan and his paddlers. I told him we needed to return to Shawmut as soon as possible, but we would like to return in the near future to show him what we intended to build. I wanted to ensure he was comfortable with our plans. He said he would welcome our next visit. We parted as friends. It was late afternoon, the tide was at full ebb, so we hurriedly packed our belongings in *Rosie* and launched ourselves back onto the river and in the calm of the early evening, rowed downstream to the Merrimack River, where we raised the sail. Nootau and Ahanu watched us from the shore where the stream joined the Merrimack. We waved to each other as we passed.

—— CHAPTER 20 ——

Journal entry - *August 1629*

Back at Shawmut, Annie told me that all was quiet, no intrusions, we were barely missed, but it was said with a welcoming kiss and hug. I brought everyone together to hear about the journey of discovery we had just made. I left it to David to provide the account. He had been an acute observer and would provide an objective assessment of what we had accomplished. At the end of which there was a long silence. Annie was the first to speak.

"Do we have the land, or not? You say Masconomet has given us the go ahead to share his land. What does that really mean?"

A general discussion took place with everyone invited to contribute. It was a lively meeting and brought us all together. At the end of which I provided a summary of what we all appeared to agree.

We needed to be away from Shawmut by the time Winthrop and his invasion arrived and had begun to fill all available living space. He was due to arrive in the middle of next year, give or take a month. Within a few months of his arrival, he and his staff would have determined where they needed to settle everyone. Therefore, at the latest by October 1630, we had to be elsewhere. Based on our glowing reports and the welcome shown us by Chogan and Masconomet, we should plan to move to the site we had identified on the Merrimack River. However, there were unknowns which could, at worst, prevent us from doing that or take the land from us after we had moved. We also agreed that it would be illogical for Winthrop to deny us land. We had the grant of land documented. We had the approval of Masconomet. We even had the acknowledgement of the current Governor, Endecott, that we had the right to the land, subject to approval by his successor. It was, therefore, worth the risk to build a house similar to our house on Shawmut and take residence before Winthrop focused on land ownership. He would most likely consider it a *fait accompli*. At worst we could barter with him, using our house here on Shawmut. With that understood the meeting ended and we went about our separate tasks. I asked Gavan to stay.

"Gavan, we have come to consider you a much-cherished part of our family. But I also recognize your extraordinary worth and would not wish to take advantage of you if you see your future elsewhere."

"Mr. Stanfield, I feel I have been adopted into a loving family. I have no wish to change my good fortune. I am extremely grateful. You ask me to do what I love, working with wood, building houses, boats, or anything else you might want. I see another exciting project ahead. I am ready to start."

We shook hands and we discussed payment for the services he rendered. I had taken him on unofficially as a sort of indentured servant, to help him escape from being held as a deserter. Now, I needed to make sure he saw himself as a freeman. He said that he received room and full board and was part of a family he had never had. That was payment enough. I assured him I would ensure that an amount was set aside on a regular basis for him to access whenever he felt the need. With that cleared, we started planning the project. I told him of the wealth of timber available that would need to be cut down and turned into lumber, which meant construction of a saw pit and heavy labor between now and next spring. Gavan said that he was sure Giles would be pleased to go with him to the Merrimack site and spend a couple of months before the winter preparing the wood needed for construction of the house. I responded that we would share that effort with regular trips by me, David, and Johnny between helping Kate with the harvesting and laying up what we had managed to produce for the winter. Kate asked me to meet her at the stable. She had her proverbial farmer's hat on.

"Isaac, how much do you know about cows?"

"Not a lot, truth be told."

"Cows can produce milk for about ten months after calving, then they start to dry up. Ruth and Naomi had their calves in February, two months before we left England. That means by January next year we would need to find our milk from elsewhere, hopefully Mr. Blackstone. Also, he has a bull. Our cows have been ready to be served for the past several months."

"Presumably not possible on the *Lion's Whelp*?"

"Very funny, Isaac. My point is that it's time for the cows to get pregnant again. Apart from the milk, we want to build a herd. It takes about nine months for a cow to produce a calf, hopefully more than one."

"An interesting dilemma. We want to be resettled in Merrimack within a year. Do we want the calves born here or there?"

Kate thought about that.

"I wouldn't want to ship two heavily pregnant cows; the stress might cause them to lose the calves. We need to wait to have them served until shortly before we leave or serve them as soon as possible, so the calves can be born in plenty of time before we go. I recommend the latter."

"Sounds good to me. What needs to be done?"

"Cows come on heat every three weeks for about 24 hours or less. I can work out when we need Blackstone's bull for each cow. On the right day, I can take each cow to its appointment with the bull. I will let Mr. Blackstone know. He'll be pleased. He has already suggested that his bull is ready and eager. Oh! And by the way, Nanna and Beatrice are pregnant again. We can sell One to Four or slaughter them to eat ourselves over the winter. Otherwise, we could become overrun with goats."

I suggested she come up with a plan for how we manage our goat production business. Kate grinned. Her farm was becoming an enterprise.

A week later, we loaded up *Rosie* with essential supplies for Gavan and Giles for a month. Johnny and I had a pleasant two-day sail, taking them to the Merrimack River, camping overnight where David Tremaine and I had stopped on our first voyage there. Johnny suggested we give a name to the new homestead and suggested we name it after the house we left at Bincombe in Dorset—Barrow Farm. How about New Barrow Farm, I said. And so it was.

Our friends Nootau and Ahanu were quick to notice our approach and arrival. I introduced them to my companions and they helped us carry our supplies, saws, axes, maul hammers, and wedges. They were fascinated having never seen the like. If Chogan allowed them I imagined they would quickly become observers and even apprentices to Gavan and Giles, at least until the novelty wore off and they realized how tiring the work was. When we arrived at the site of our New Barrow Farm, I left the others and asked Nootau and Ahanu to take me to meet Chogan. He was pleased to see me. He was also happy to be able to practice his English. I told him what we wished to do. Our plan was to cut and store the wood we needed to build our house where we had indicated on our last visit. We wanted to cut the wood before the Winter set in and to build a shelter for the wood to start the drying process before we returned in the Spring to build the house. I would be leaving two of my men to begin the cutting but would return regularly until the work was completed. He thanked me for keeping him informed and would keep a friendly eye on their progress.

Johnny and I stayed a few days to help establish a campsite. We built two wetus for accommodation and storage. Nootau and Ahanu, who had managed to persuade Chogan that they should become the on-site observers, were impressed with the skills we used to build them. We also helped dig a saw pit while Gavan cut wood to build the frame upon which the logs would rest. Gavan and Giles marked the trees to be cut, oak and pine. There were a significant number of dead trees both standing and lying on the ground. I asked him how he proposed to move the trees to the saw pit once he had cut up those in its immediate vicinity. Mauls and wedges to split the trunks, then crosscut to the sizes needed. Two men should be sufficient to shift the wood. He said he might even persuade our young Indians to help.

The land would have to be cleared of the stumps of the trees where we planned to build the house. Gavan showed us how by digging down to expose and cut the roots. The larger stumps were levered out of the ground. We had to move the site slightly to avoid one very large stump. It would need to be cut to below ground level, the stump split, covered in soil and left to rot, an additional heavy labor that needed to be accomplished before winter.

Before we left, Johnny had gone hunting with his bow, accompanied by Ahanu. They returned with a young buck, enthusiastically dragged by Ahanu, which was then butchered with choice cuts provided for Gavan and Giles. The remains of the deer were given to Nootau and Ahanu to take back to their village as a present from us.

We left Gavan and Giles hard at work and returned to Shawmut. First, we stopped at Salem. I wanted to inform the Governor's office about what we had been doing on the Merrimack. I was told he was too busy to see me. Apparently, he was meeting with his newly formed advisory council. I thought back to my time in Bermuda where it had taken them over twenty-five years to establish a Governor's council. I was gratified that they appeared to be learning from Bermuda's example. I was told it consisted of twelve men, seven elected by the New England Company, five by Endecott, and two by the Old Planters. I made my report in writing. I was leaving the office when I bumped into my old acquaintance Thomas Morton. He was in a hurry but said we should meet to catch up. I said come to Shawmut. He agreed and said he was back in town making a nuisance of himself. Funny thing, the last I had heard was that he had been arrested at Merrymount, before we had arrived, by Captain Myles Standish, the militia commander from New Plimouth. After exile on Smith's Isles Morton had been sent back to England. He told me with some satisfaction that his return to New England meant the authorities in England had not seen fit to charge him with anything to keep him from coming back here. I returned to *Rosie* where Johnny was waiting for me.

We had brought *Rosie* to the beach on the South River, along which Annie and I used to walk. It was between the old village and the new settlement further down the peninsula, where I had gone to try to meet the Governor. On my way back, I was troubled about Morton's predicament. I felt he was as much an enemy to himself as the enemy of others. Distracted by my thoughts, I was barely aware of the path I followed into the wooded area that separated the new settlement from the old village. The people that I passed seemed similarly distracted, borne down with their own challenges. We paid little heed to each other. I left them behind, the trees closed in, the path narrowed. Suddenly, a deafening explosion, a cloud of smoke, and the snap of something slapping into a tree trunk next to my head. A gunshot! I dropped and crawled behind the tree. I heard some rustling, a shout from Johnny and then silence. A minute later Johnny came running up to me. I told him what had happened and where I thought the shot had come from. I said I thought the assailant had gone but with great care we separated and worked our way through the trees, approaching the spot where I thought the shot had been fired. We came to another path. No one there but evidence that someone had been, the smoke from the discharge still evident. People began to gather, attracted by the gunshot. We asked them whether they had seen anyone running from where we all stood. No one had seen anything. We returned to *Rosie*, each silent with our thoughts. Once we were out on the water, Johnny gave voice.

"Is this the same assailant or someone else? We assumed the original assailant had left Salem. Isaac, I have the gravest concerns that you and David Tremaine concocted a plausible culprit and built a neat solution, on the basis that somehow this character Seth had escaped capital punishment and was so obsessed with revenge he would risk his neck sailing to New England just to confirm his accessory Spiggott had killed you. I think we need to think again about who might want you dead."

These words echoed my thoughts. I admitted so to Johnny, which set us thinking again. Johnny couldn't help with any alternatives. I was left to delve deep into my past to try and find a reason. Nothing came to mind. However, now we had an active assassin to contend with, we needed to decide what we had to do about it. Back home we held a council of war.

Annie was horrified, even though I played down the incident. David was concerned. There were too many unknowns. Was Seth hanged, as we thought? No way of knowing in the near future. A request for confirmation sent by us today could take up to six months to come back to us. But it should be sent, anyway. Who else? David wondered whether this was somehow tied up with the political intrigue we had left behind in England. I asked him what he meant.

"We know that the West Country interests centered on Sir Ferdinando Gorges in Plymouth allied to some degree with the Reverend John White's interests in Dorchester could be seen as having been usurped by Matthew Craddock in London. The Earl of Warwick is the power behind Craddock and he has blessed if not encouraged the Lincolnshire and East Anglian involvement to the extent that the greater majority of the settlers planning to come over next year, led by John Winthrop, are from there.

Annie interrupted by asking who the Earl of Warwick was. I told her that he is an important and powerful political figure in London with an aggressive reputation and a major investor in the Virginia Company and the Somers Isles Company governing Bermuda. David continued.

"Sir F. had granted himself and his family substantial land holdings on Massachusetts Bay which have been regranted or, if not regranted, the rights to grant have been given to the Massachusetts Bay Company. Warwick used to be a business associate of Sir F. and now seems to have betrayed his old partner. Could it be that a guilty Warwick thinks that Sir F. will fight to retain the land he considers his? If so, how would Warwick see that threat being carried out? You, Isaac, have a considerable reputation as a key Gorges supporter and former employee. The Bushrode land grant, the rights to which you hold, are tied up with Sir F.'s land grants. Perhaps Warwick sees you as a troublemaker, seeking to disrupt the function of the Massachusetts Bay Company on Sir F.'s behalf."

Around the table, we nodded as we considered the possibility.

"One further thought," David added, "when we were in Bermuda, your dealings with Captain Tucker and his involvement in privateering and smuggling, were a real concern because of the Earl of Warwick's possible participation. Could an outcome of our successfully rescuing James and your close engagement with Tucker have caused problems for Warwick? Remember that Tucker has a secret that he didn't want exposed. Could that secret have something to do with Warwick? Might Warwick think that Tucker might have disclosed all or part of that secret to you?"

Annie asked me if we had ever found out what that secret was.

I responded, "No, we never did. Also, I haven't been in the employ of Sir F. for over five years. Sir F. told me he had given up on the land grant he gave to his son Robert, which was all the land he had on Massachusetts Bay. I do admit that his letter you gave me belied that statement because in it he did ask me to help him with respect to that land grant. He had previously told me his New England interests were confined to Maine and I wrote back and told him that the Massachusetts land was lost to him and he should focus on Maine. Despite that, I really do not see any conflict with Warwick. My dealings with Matthew Craddock were amicable. He was aware that I was not impressed with Endecott but I did nothing to oppose his selection as the Governor. As for Tucker, you know we tiptoed round the wider implications of our involvement with him. The Bermuda Governor's displeasure with us if we stirred up trouble with Tucker made sure we behaved ourselves, as far as was possible."

Annie was more thoughtful.

"I think David has a point. Isaac. You used to tell me how difficult Sir F.'s attempts were to settle New England. The passions of all the parties involved were intense. I can well believe that once Sir F.'s disappointment over Robert's failure to set up a government over here had eased, he started thinking about how much he had invested in establishing New England and how crushing it must be to have all that effort ignored or entirely discounted. If I was Warwick, especially given the reputation you say he has, I would be extremely worried that Sir F. might attempt something. Nothing better than to use someone already in New England who had already served Sir F. so well."

"Annie, my love, if I had been sent or agreed to come to New England to make mischief for Sir F. I would have grabbed the opportunity to come as Endecott's chief of staff, which is what he and everyone else wanted me to do. I have done nothing since to show the slightest interest in undermining Endecott's position."

Johnny, who had been listening to all this with rapt attention, offered a thought.

"Isaac, you said at one point that Endecott might have suggested something to one of his entourage on *Abigail*, which had been incorrectly interpreted as a desire for you to be dealt with. This seems to have been proved an incorrect assumption. However, is it possible that Warwick was overheard saying something about you, which was also wrongly interpreted? If that is the case, that person, a Warwick supporter, would now probably be fairly close to Endecott in Salem. While I'm speculating, I suggest it would probably be someone young and foolish, hoping to win glory by removing such a threat."

The others looked at me.

"I suppose it's no more far-fetched than thinking Seth is alive and after my blood. So, let's decide how we deal with this one."

It was agreed that I needed to go back to Salem to talk to the Governor. I should also send a letter to Will Whiteway and explain the attempts on my life and our predicament. He would need to find out via the Patriarch whether there is any overt or covert antagonism between Sir F. and the Earl of Warwick or any other reason that would cause someone to want to have me killed. We also need to know if Seth was executed or otherwise a prisoner somewhere.

—— CHAPTER 21 ——

Journal entry – *September 1629*

Johnny and I returned to Salem. We discussed the shooting while we sailed and how the Governor might react. We agreed we needed someone to speak for us, perhaps Roger Conant. I also wanted to send off my latest journal entries to Will. The boats, fishermen, and merchantmen arriving from and departing to England were frequent at this time of year. David stayed to help Kate with the harvest gathering and to watch over the family. We beached *Rosie* close to the old village in the open with plenty of people around. I went to see Roger Conant, who fortunately was available. Now a member of the Governor's Council, he had been in meetings since early morning. He was home for a break before they resumed later in the day. I told him what had happened. He was aware of the previous attempts and thought the problem had been dealt with, so this latest incident shocked him. He found it difficult to believe it had been instigated, even unwittingly by the Earl of Warwick. He accepted that, however unlikely, it had to be investigated. He suggested that we walk back to the Governor's house where the council meetings were taking place and attempt to meet with the Governor.

At the Governor's house, Roger told me to wait while he went in to find Endecott. A few minutes later, he came out and beckoned me to follow him. Endecott was sitting behind a large table, strewn with papers. He looked harried.

"Ah! Mr. Stanfield, Mr. Conant tells me you've been attacked again. I'm sorry to hear that. I'm afraid I do not have the time to deal with this myself, but I want it resolved. I will not have violence here. Matters are tricky enough without someone taking such outrageous matters into their own hands."

He called for his assistant and told him to fetch Mr. Gott. While we were waiting, he told me that Gott was well aware of the previous attempts and he would delegate Gott to work with me to resolve this latest attempt. Gott entered, was told that I had a problem which the Governor wanted sorting out and he, Gott, should set aside his current duties to work with me. I would explain everything. We were dismissed. I was pleased to see Endecott capably decisive and in charge. As his true colors began to show, so my respect for him rose.

Roger said he had to go to a meeting but would catch up with Gott later. Gott led me to a quiet spot and we sat and I told him what had happened and the possibility that it was a new assailant. After voicing his thoughts on the unlikelihood of it being other than the continuation of the earlier attempts, he agreed that something should be done.

"Mr. Stanfield, if the man shot at you from the thicket on your return from attempting to see the Governor we can agree that the man saw you arrive, from whence you had come, where you were going and the likelihood of whither you would be going afterwards. So, he was of the new settlement. Second, he would not have been aware of your intentions beforehand. So, this must have been a spontaneous reaction upon his seeing you. He did not know how long you would be. You say you were only a few minutes. The assailant had the briefest time, therefore, to grab a gun, load it, and find a place from which to shoot you. It would be difficult for anyone to do all that, in a great hurry, unseen."

Gott had covered the ground that we had discussed on our sail from Shawmut, so I could only agree. I was happy for Gott to take the lead. By owning his conclusions, I thought he was that much more engaged in finding our assassin. I asked him if he had any ideas as to the sort of person who might behave in such an uncontrolled manner.

He responded,

"A young man, quick of action, slow of thought. He hadn't thought through the consequences. What if he had been seen? He missed, fortunately. What would have happened if he hadn't?"

I said I would be dead. Gott laughed.

"I mean the consequences to the assailant. Of less immediate concern because no one was hurt, but if he had been successful the Governor would have torn the place apart looking for him."

I asked why would a young man take it on himself to attempt to do such a thing? Gott thought about it.

"Interesting question. You say you know of no one apart from the person who had instigated the attacks on you on *Abigail*. It makes more sense that this latest attempt is a continuation. On the other hand, Mr. Stanfield, I don't think that instigator was a young and thoughtless man. He had found his accomplice and planned the attacks to ensure for whatever reason he was not directly involved. The man had a deep personal grudge and was prepared to wait. Also, I understand that if he was the instigator, you believe he left the settlement or at least has gone missing for two months. If he was still here, he would have been able to plan his attempt with much more care. So, on reflection I do agree with you this does look like a new assailant."

I was relieved that he had reached the same conclusion that Johnny and I had come to. Mr. Gott was pleased with himself and fully engaged. I asked him what was next. He said there weren't that many guns around, the militia only in the planning stage. The man must have had immediate access to one. His house must have been close by for him to grab the gun. He would need to be competent with it, to be able to load it so quickly. It was even possible that his having a gun was not an unusual sight. Perhaps he had been hunting and seized the opportunity. Mr. Gott said he had more than enough information to find the person. He said I should leave. I would be a distraction if I stayed in the village. I would be informed when the man was found and detained.

Before I left, I asked him if a package of papers was being prepared to be sent back to England. He said there was a bag prepared and a ship expected to leave Salem in the next day or so. I asked that my package for Will be included. He offered to put it in the bag, himself. I gave it to him with thanks. Johnny and I returned to Shawmut. It was a cold, wet and tiring ride. That evening over a late supper, in front of a warming fire, we agreed that Mr. Gott would create enough disturbance to keep our assailant quiet with his head down until, hopefully, he was caught.

We spent the following three weeks completing our harvesting and produce gathering. We dug into the side of the hill behind the house to build a stone-lined root cellar with wooden posts holding a timbered roof. Shelves were added and the whole completed with a stout wooden door. We then covered the exposed portion of the roof with heavy grass turves. Annie and Jeannie had large earthenware pots which they had filled with blanched and salted runner beans, the seeds of which we had brought from England and which Annie had grown in abundance in her kitchen garden. We also had cabbages, carrots, potatoes, turnips, onions, and parsnips. William Blackstone had invited us to gather as many apples, strawberries, raspberries, and plums as we wanted. Annie and Jeannie preserved as much fruit as possible by stewing them and putting them into sealed pots. They wanted to find wild cranberries, crabapples, and cherries, as well. The children had been given the task of collecting the berries, walnuts, and hazelnuts from the woods around us. Annie said the nuts would last the longest, unshelled in cold storage. Then there were the wheat, the maize, oats, and hay. We had grown them sparsely with the small acreage we had but the harvest had been as bountiful as Blackstone had told us, the soil rich and fertile. The maize we would await until early October when the ears were dried and had turned different shades of brown and red. But the hay was needed for our livestock for the winter. We had already stored the early summer cut in the hayloft, now we needed to add the autumn cut. With Giles away with Gavan at New Barrow, David and I set to with scythes, Johnny and James following with rakes.

It had been a month since we had left Gavan and Giles and it was time to return to check their progress and allow Giles to return. David said he would gladly replace him at the saw pit. I had not asked David before about his old shoulder injury, a cutlass slash at the time we lost the *Sweet Rose*, three years ago. To all appearances he had fully recovered, and Annie had told me that Kate thought he had, too. However, a saw pit was another matter. He told me that Kate's cruel persistence had forced him to take the exercises necessary to restore full function. It almost caused an irretrievable rift between them but David said he was so thankful afterwards. He owed a huge debt to his wife and her incredible strength to deal with his irascibility. He insisted that they were much the better couple as a result.

We loaded *Rosie* with provisions and returned to New Barrow Farm. The two days it took us to sail there enabled David and me to cover old and new ground in great depth. We talked about what was happening in England, King Charles was attempting to maintain absolute control while the House of Commons was fighting him at every turn. It could only end up badly for the country. Religious intolerance had increased, whence the increasing flood of settlers fleeing persecution. The economic situation had worsened. Whole villages with their landowners were planning to come over. It really was a mess.

I asked him about his plans for farming with Kate. Most emphatically he stated he wanted to return to the sea. He missed it. On the trip over on the *Lion's Whelp* he asked the skipper John Gibbs whether he could serve in some supernumerary manner as an officer. He explained to Gibbs that after the loss of *Rosie*, which Gibbs remembered well, he had spent several years recuperating. This was the first time he had been on an extended sailing trip since then. Gibbs had welcomed him, introducing David to the ship's officers as an experienced skipper and one time bosun in the English navy. He was well received being treated with great respect. Gibbs made the quarterdeck available to him whenever he wanted and occasionally had him stand as watch officer. How did Kate view his determination to return to the sea? She wants to farm more than anything, with or without David, as long as she has the help, companionship, and the support of friends that she needed. We discussed my plans for the farm and the subsequent trading enterprise. He saw the need to set priorities and committed himself to both the move and the establishment of the farm before focusing on what happened next.

At our Merrimack landing spot, we were greeted by Nootau and Ahanu, as ever watchful. They accompanied us to the building site and we were greeted by Gavan and Giles, both pleased to see us. We were amazed at the work they had accomplished. Stacks of lumber, oak, and pine, under shelter, each plank separated by spacers. Posts and beams also stacked and under shelter. Piles of off-cuts, used for firewood both by our sawmen as well as the village. I asked Gavan how much more work was needed. He felt that two weeks would suffice. I asked him if he was in need of a break. I wanted Giles back and would be leaving David to replace him. Gavan assured me he was doing what he liked best, working with wood, living outside in a beautiful location. He would be happy to introduce David to the life of a woodsman.

We had a most companionable two days together. The evening before Giles and I left to return to Shawmut, Gavan raised the subject of harvesting timber to sell. He had been thinking about it for a while. We could build a loading dock on the river for boats to come alongside to load the timber. The timber was of such high quality he felt it could be sent back to England. There was less need to ship it within New England, as the local settlements had enough standing woods and forests of their own. I was enthused. I immediately thought of Bermuda. They had a constant need for timber for boatbuilding and construction. We could bring back cedar, sugar cane, rum.

CHAPTER 22

Journal entry – *September 1629*

Giles and I sailed back via Salem. I had heard nothing from Mr. Gott. Upon landing I went to find him. In the weeks since I was last there, much progress had been made in building housing and cleaning the whole settlement. There was now a functioning governing infrastructure in place, with rules, regulations, law and order. It looked promising. I couldn't help thinking about a thousand new settlers bearing down on this little village next year. God knows what Winthrop was expecting when he arrived. Setting aside my fears, I was directed to Mr. Gott. He didn't seem particularly happy to see me. I took his demeanor to mean he hadn't found my assailant and asked him if that was the case.

"Mr. Stanfield, we found the gentleman who shot at you without too much difficulty. He was brought before the Governor for questioning. The intent was to charge him with intended murder."

"What do you mean by the intent was to charge him? Are you saying no charge has been laid?"

"It seems the gentleman insists that what he attempted to do was entirely justified."

"How so?"

"He claims that you are a threat to the existence of Salem and, indeed, the future of the Massachusetts Bay Company, a spy for Sir

Ferdinando Gorges, and, therefore, a traitor, to be tried and hanged."

I was shocked into silence. Gott looked uncomfortable. I suppressed the desire to expostulate. Gott was just the messenger. Eventually, I asked the inevitable question.

"Mr. Gott, you look uncomfortable. Why?"

"It is a strong accusation and puts the Governor in a difficult position."

"Mr. Gott, anyone with a grudge can make the wildest of accusations. Does this man have any evidence to support his claim?"

"No direct evidence, but he says he represents the beliefs of the office of the Earl of Warwick and has given us names of people who will confirm his claims and provide the necessary evidence. More to the point, one or more of those people is coming to New England with Governor Winthrop."

"Have you received any correspondence from England that corroborates the claim, on any basis?"

"No."

"Has Governor Endecott received any indication since he arrived that I have acted or spoken in anyway detrimental to him, his office, Salem, or the Massachusetts Bay Company?"

"Mr. Stanfield, you can't have forgotten the unfortunate circumstances on our journey over here on *Abigail*."

"Mr. Gott, you know, as well as I, that certain of the Governor's entourage took issue with me for not agreeing to be his chief of staff. That did not in any way suggest I was trying to undermine him. In fact, if I had wanted to create mischief what better place to cause that mischief than holding that position? Also, you haven't answered my question."

"No, the Governor is not aware of anything detrimental that you might have done or said."

"Mr. Gott, are you perhaps implying that the attempts on my life on the journey over here were somehow further evidence of attempts to remove a traitorous threat to the settlement? The man who makes this claim, was he on *Abigail*?"

"No, he came over this year."

"Could he have been the instigator of Spiggott's attacks on me and the attempted seizure of my son?"

"That we don't know. We haven't asked him, as yet."

"I would like to see this man. I have questions to ask him."

"Mr. Stanfield. The Governor will not allow it. Nor will he allow us to tell you anything about him. The man has been ordered to avoid you at all costs, on penalty of being arrested and confined. The Governor has also asked me to tell you that he can do nothing more to resolve this problem until the arrival of Governor Winthrop."

"So, where does that leave me? It would appear I am under suspicion."

"Governor Endecott requests that you do not return to Salem until Winthrop arrives and judgement can then be passed. He also advises me to warn you that there can be no further consideration of your land grant until then. He suggests that you do not continue to invest time and money in the property in which you have interest on the Merrimack River. You might never be granted land there."

Mr. Gott by now was acutely embarrassed. After the early misunderstanding on *Abigail*, we had been on cordial terms.

"Mr. Stanfield, for what it is worth, I am deeply sorry for what has occurred. I'm sure it will be resolved to your satisfaction next year."

"Two questions. No matter the reason, I was shot at and nearly killed. That surely is a crime, a possible capital crime, regardless of his apparent motivation. Has this man been charged? Secondly, if this man was sure of his ground, why did he try to kill me himself, rather than alert the Governor to deal with it through the courts?"

"Mr. Stanfield, you ask interesting questions. I will pass them both on to the Governor. Good day to you."

At that moment, I was hailed with a "Why Mr. Stanfield!" I turned and Thomas Morton approached me with hand outstretched. "Mr. Morton," I responded as we shook hands. Mr. Gott frowned. Clearly, Mr. Morton was not a popular man. Morton nodded to Gott, unconcerned.

"Mr. Stanfield, I hear you are in a spot of bother. A spy for Sir

Ferdinando, I hear." He laughed. "Ridiculous, of course. They accused me of the same thing. Expelled me back to England on some pretext with charges that were dismissed, so back I came."

"But why are you not being constrained, now you are back?"

"Isaac, if I might be so bold, I am a known quantity, a thorny irritant. You, however, are an unknown quantity and, therefore, dangerous. Rather than use his brains, the Governor prefers to sweep the problem you present into a distant corner and leave it for others to deal with."

Mr. Gott, torn between wanting to leave us, clearly unwelcome company in the circumstances, but also anxious to witness any relevant remark that he might report back, could only indicate his discomfort by an occasional grunt. Morton grinned at him.

"Mr. Gott, here, is a fine fellow, a heart of gold, sensible but conflicted. He is loyal, an admirable quality, sad though it is, to the Governor. I would suggest that of the many obvious questions that I'm sure you've raised there is one you, Mr. Gott, might want to take back to the Governor. If Mr. Stanfield was a spy, why would he bring his family over to settle on land for which he has been given a sizeable grant which he knows you or Winthrop has to ratify, so I understand?"

With that, Morton shook my hand again, wishing me well with the hope of seeing me soon, and walked away. I caught a disgruntled Gott's eye, shook my head and left him.

I returned to Giles, and we sailed back to Shawmut. My evident anger silenced Giles' normal chatter. He focused his whole attention on sailing *Rosie*. I told him I would prefer to wait on further conversation until we returned home. I needed a strong drink and a comfortable seat in the bosom of my family before I was ready to calm down. As it turned out, conversation wasn't possible anyway. The wind had risen and filled from the South. We were on a beam reach, with our wash and the spray down our leeside ever threatening to swamp us. It became exhilarating and my anger abated. I played the mainsheet and bailed. Giles hung on to the tiller, fighting the weather-helm that was trying to make us broach. I eventually took pity on him and eased the mainsheet and we completed our journey without incident, both of us soaked to the bone, me happy and poor Giles, inexperienced helmsman that he was, terrified.

With the children in bed, supper cleared away, and Giles returned to his stable quarters, Annie, Jeannie, Johnny, and I sat round the table with filled beakers of wine or ale, and I told them exactly what had occurred in Salem. There was a long silence then the questions flowed from Annie.

"What is the worst thing that could happen?"

"Annie my love, if this situation can't be resolved before Winthrop arrives and we don't take any risks, New Barrow Farm won't be built in time for us to move there."

"You are assuming that Winthrop will find you innocent. What happens if you are deemed a Gorges spy?"

"I imagine I will be confined and returned to England. Where I will most certainly be able to clear my name and return to New England, much as Morton has. If Winthrop clears me and my land grant is confirmed, we will have lost maybe six months. If I am sent back to England, perhaps a year."

"What happens to us? Do we go back to England with you or stay here?"

"If I am sent back, I would like to think that you, my love, and the children will return, while everyone else stays here and runs the Shawmut farm. There are a number of different possible outcomes, each of which has a whole host of details to be resolved. We will work on the outcome that occurs, when it occurs."

"What about New Barrow Farm?"

"Luckily, the lumber we need to build is almost complete. We must go back and fetch David and Gavan. We also should make arrangements with Chogan and his people to guard that lumber over the winter. If we are delayed further or even if, heaven forbid, we lose New Barrow, that lumber has considerable value. Depending on the outcome, I'm hopeful we will begin building in the Spring, or later, if need be. What is important is that we do not become overburdened with fear. We all know that the accusation is false and comes from a most unreliable source without evidence to hand. Over the winter, we must work out a plan to overturn that accusation and, at a minimum, restore our standing with the Governor and his recognition of our land grant, subject of course to final ratification by the new Governor. With that restored, I am happy to take the risk and resume building New Barrow."

Johnny suggested we start with the unexplained action of the man who shot at me. Why was he in such a hurry to kill me? It made no sense and was unjustifiable in any court proceeding. A question, I hope, that is weighing on the Governor's mind. However, we do need to add weight to those scales.

—— CHAPTER 23 ——

Journal entry – *October 1629*

Early October, I sailed with Annie and James back to the Merrimack River. Abigail, after her first trip on *Rosie* from Salem to Shawmut, was happy to stay home with Beth. Beth had taken over from James and had joined Abigail in goat management duties. Three of the four kids had been sold and we were down to one doe, Two. Kate had set up an arrangement whereby she took them to William Blackstone, who sent his young goats to Salem. There they were added to existing flocks or sold for meat. Kate had kept us, especially the children, aware of the states of both Nanna's and Beatrice's pregnancies. They were due late January. For James and Annie, this excursion was an opportunity to see the property we hoped to get with our land grant. In addition, James was happiest in a boat, especially if he had the helm.

Arriving back at our landing spot, once again, Nootau and Ahanu were there to greet us. I introduced them to Annie and James, both of them greeting us in English, a pleasant surprise. Annie smiled and nodded to them. James bowed and shook hands with them to their delight. The three of them led the way up the track and we followed, increasingly distant, as James set the pace and his new Indian friends glad to accommodate him, seemingly in happy conversation. Annie stopped and looked about her in wonder at the open green grassland surrounded by thick, lush woods. She turned and hugged me. Then a brief shadow. "How awful, if this does not happen," she whispered. Then, tucking her arm through mine, she and I followed the disappearing James and his companions.

At the site, James had interrupted the workers. He was in deep conversation with Gavan while David sat by a fire that looked like it was a permanent fixture, around which the camp's activities revolved, with a large beaker of ale in his hand, happy to see us. It was an opportune visit. They had completed sawing the lumber and were adding the final pieces of roof planking to the shelter. A large pile of fieldstones had been gathered, as well. Annie had brought some fresh provisions, a large pot of stew with a secure cover, several loaves of bread, homemade goats' cheese, and flagons of ale. The contents of the pot were poured into a large metal pan, much blackened and probably not too clean, and placed over the fire. Nootau and Ahanu had faded into the background while the rest of us sat around the fire and had a most satisfying meal.

I told David all that had transpired and answered his many questions. At the end of which, he asked what my next steps were. I told him that we needed to secure the store of lumber over the winter. I would visit Chogan to make the necessary arrangements. I said it likely he would allow us to employ Nootau and Ahanu for the job. David responded that they would be ideal. They had been helpful and been rewarded with a number of spare tools, which overwhelmed them. They had also taught Gavan and David a few words of their Abenaki language. As important, they had learned a great deal of English, of which James had obviously taken immediate advantage. Next, I said that I needed an ally in Salem, someone to take on some discrete investigations for me. David asked did I remember that Thomas Morton was an experienced and highly skilled lawyer. I said that that was back in England, and he is now barely tolerated in Salem. David thought that might not be too bad a handicap. If Morton could find out more about my attempted assassin and even, most discreetly, question him, we would be in a much better position with the information he gathered, irrespective of his standing in the community. I also wanted to build on the friendships we had developed among the Old Planters. If I could get word to Thomas Gardner for him to meet me, possibly in Charlestown, which was as yet not denied to me, I would be able to recruit him to help us.

The week after we returned to Shawmut, David and I sailed across to Charlestown. Mr. Graves, the Surveyor, had been busy in the three months since we were last there. Houses had been built, with the frames for many more already erected and waiting completion. While David went exploring, I sought out Ralph Sprague. The whole Sprague brood had built a house big enough for all of them, Ralph, Joanna, their three children and Ralph's two brothers. I told Ralph about my problem with the Governor. He was shocked at Endecott's inaction, especially as he was known for his decisiveness. I suggested that the inaction might not be such a bad thing. It will give him time to think before making a rash decision.

Ralph asked me what he could do to help. I told him about Morton and Gardner—the former to gather information on my assailant and the latter to build support for me in Salem. Would Ralph provide a courier facility for me so that I could get messages to them both and, hopefully, their responses? He said, of course he would. He already had such a facility in place. His youngest brother, Will, had his eye on a girl in Salem and was always keen to go visit her. I gave him notes for Morton and Gardner, asking them for an opportunity for me to meet with them in Charlestown. I pressed Ralph and Joanna to visit us on Shawmut. Very much less crowded. In fact, downright rural, compared to the noise, crowds, smells, and filth of an emerging town. Ralph said he would let us know when he had the responses from Morton and Gardner. I thanked him, wished them all well and left to find David.

He had met up with a harassed Mr. Graves who was somewhat subdued. Graves had leapt at the chance to design a whole town but hadn't understood that the design and construction would be impeded by over 100 settlers camping and defecating on the space he needed. The other critical problem that Walford had raised at the start was the lack of drinking water. With so many people due to arrive next year, all the land round the harbor and up the Charles and Mystic Rivers would have to be turned to housing. In fact, some families were already migrating away from the mess of Charlestown.

From there, we went to see Thomas Walford. He was secure in his home and busy, so busy he had taken on an apprentice to deal with the continuing flow of orders for metal work of all kinds. He was becoming worried about his stock of raw metal. He had sent word back to England for more supplies. We left him and returned to Shawmut.

Two days later, Ralph came to visit. He apologized to Annie that Joanna hadn't come. She was tied to their house looking after the three boys. They hadn't yet found a suitable housekeeper. He was amazed at the space, the quiet, the country setting of our house and how we had established a small farm so quickly. He recognized the incredible opportunities that New England offered to the enterprising settler. What we had accomplished so far was a good example of that. He passed on to me responses from both Morton and Gardner. They said they were happy to meet with me. Morton said he planned to be in Charlestown on Friday, in two days. He suggested we meet at the boat landing at midday. Thomas Gardner asked me to suggest a day and he would be happy to meet me then. I sent a note back with Ralph, suggesting a meeting at 4:00pm on Friday at the Walford house. I knew they were well acquainted.

Friday morning, I went with Gavan to Charlestown. He had a long list of items he wanted from Walford before Winter set in. Morton was waiting for me at the boat landing. We walked along the shoreline while I explained what I would like him to do, if he had the time and inclination.

"Isaac, I would be happy to. Not only will it give me something to do, intellectually satisfying, it will also give me much pleasure if I can stir the Governor into taking action against his will on a matter he would much rather delegate to his successor."

"Thank you, Thomas. How do you plan to proceed?"

"Our young friend, your assailant, is free to wander. I have seen him although not talked to him. I know where he lives. From what I have seen he seems to be living with an older couple who have servants. He might be related to them, in some way. Now that I have cause, I will investigate that household, followed by a chance meeting and an opportunity to become acquainted with the young man. His behavior has been strange, even illogical based on the information we have. I will be most interested to understand his motivation. Leave it with me for the next week or so. I must move carefully."

I thanked him and asked him what his current situation was. He laughed.

"Isaac, in the years since we met in London, I established the settlement that Sir Ferdinando required of me. I successfully built a profitable trade in beaver with my Indian friends, to the chagrin of the Separatists in New Plimouth. I also supported said Indians in their perpetual fights with their bloodthirsty neighboring tribes, the Mohawk and the Tarrantines, by supplementing the firearms they already had from elsewhere."

"You've been busy." Morton ignored my remark and continued,

"I was kidnapped by my Separatist friends on false charges, in order to remove me as their prime competitor in the beaver trade. They exiled me and then sent me back to England, where the charges were laughed out of court, thereby allowing me to return to New England, which I have just accomplished with many thanks to an old friend of yours, Isaac Allerton. He accompanied me back from England to lodge with him in New Plimouth, to the fury of Bradford, Standish and the rest.

My current situation, you ask. I wish to re-establish my settlement and my business in trade. However, I am frustrated by ineptitude, religious intolerance, and bureaucracy, the things I wished to escape from in England. I am attempting to become a law-abiding citizen here in Salem. My long legal career, unfortunately, causes me to take issue with Endecott's attempts to create law and order. I raise points of order, I question, I suggest changes based on sound legal practice. The result is I am seen as a pernicious irritant. Not only do I fail to change anything, I am also making it almost impossible for me to achieve my own objectives."

Poor Morton. From what I remembered from conversations with Sir F., Morton had always enjoyed fighting against the establishment, championing lost causes. He had made a superb Lord of Misrule at the Inns of Court. I recall a drunken night when David Tremaine and I enjoyed some of the excessive revelry of that occasion.

We parted friends with his promise to help my cause. I hoped it wasn't a lost one. I met Gardner at Walford's house. Gavan and Walford were there having completed their business. Walford introduced Gavan to Gardner, who remembered Gavan's name but couldn't remember why. Gavan did not remind him. I told Walford that I would be pleased if he and Gavan would join us in conversation. Walford invited us into the house for an ale and a comfortable place to meet. After I explained my problem, there was general debate about what my best course of action should be. My hope was that by establishing a base of support, a group of allies among the Old Planters, that support would help in any discussions that might take place in the Governor's Council, two of the twelve councilors being the Old Planters, William Trask and Roger Conant, both well known to me.

Gardner was quick to point out that I would have no problem with the Old Planters, since even those that did not know me personally were well aware of my history. I was seen much as a supporter of the Reverend John White in Dorchester. Endecott was not particularly enamored of Old Planters, however. We needed to build support among the newcomers. Gardner observed that Trask had told him he and John Woodbury had become close to several on the voyage over on *Abigail*. Gardner took it on himself to enlist Trask and Woodbury to help us. As an afterthought he mentioned Humphrey, John's son. I said I had known him on *Abigail*. Gardner continued. This man who attempted to kill you, is it possible Humphrey knows him, presumably of similar age? They might have become known to each other after he arrived here. It was certainly worth checking. Walford was listening to the conversation, smoking his pipe. Then he spoke.

"Gentlemen, you look to build support for Mr. Stanfield among the old and new settlers. For what purpose? What might be the unintended consequence of attempting to sway Endecott through public opinion? Why not focus on destroying the young man's credibility with Endecott? I believe it would be better to gather as much information as possible about that man, befriend him, and find out why he did it."

I agreed and said that my friend Thomas Morton would be doing that, but a pincer movement on the young man might be a grand idea, my attempted assassin being approached from different quarters. Gardner said he would talk to Trask and both Woodburys, reporting back to me if he learned anything of value. I was grateful and we parted. Gavan and I returned to Shawmut.

—— CHAPTER 24 ——

Journal entry – *November - December 1629*

It was early November before I heard back from Morton and Gardner. The three of us arranged to meet again in Charlestown at Ralph Sprague's house. Ralph was away but Joanna made us welcome and left us to our meeting. I brought David Tremaine with me. Morton told us he had managed to corner the young man. His name is Arthur Beamish. He had been sent to New England by his father, a Suffolk landowner. It had taken some penetrating questions from Morton to uncover the reason why he had been sent. Arthur was the third son of a widower who had little time for him. He would not inherit the family estate, he was too profane to enter the church, and the military would not accept him other than as a trooper. His only apparent accomplishment was that he could ride a horse. Morton had gained the confidence of the young man who was happy to recount his youthful adventures. Morton's assessment of those adventures was that they came from a recklessness and the limited intelligence of a feckless child. The father was happy to banish him from the family hearth. Beamish senior knew the Winthrop family and was sympathetic to the Puritan cause. Visitors to the Beamish house included those who espoused many shades of Puritan and Separatist opinions, some radical. Arthur was attracted to the more radical ones. They excited him, especially if couched in simple terms. It seems that Sir Ferdinando Gorges' name came up, a West

Country man, beyond the pale to the Suffolk community. Arthur embraced the idea that Gorges was a dangerous foe. A simple concept that incubated in his mind. Morton felt that the simple Arthur, banished to New England, thought he could regain the respect of his father and return to England a hero, if he struck down that foe. So I became his target. Gardner had spent time with Trask and John Woodbury. They had done some digging and found that because of the relationship that exists between the Winthrop and Beamish families, Endecott doesn't want to have anything to do with Arthur, stating it was Winthrop's problem to deal with. Humphrey Woodbury had had some contact with Arthur but found he was immature and untrustworthy.

I thanked them both for their efforts, but I was still perplexed.

"Where does that leave me? I am constrained by a foolish boy, fixated on a delusion."

Morton thought that Arthur was so unpredictable that Endecott would not be able to ignore him for long. Endecott needs to be awakened to the potential danger of having a loose cannon, possibly ready to explode over some imagined slight or in pursuit of his foe. He was prepared to shoot me, spontaneously without a second thought. David, who had been quiet all the while, asked whether it was possible that Arthur might react as spontaneously if he saw someone he thought was an ally of mine. Might he see a nest of vipers, to be exterminated? Morton slowly nodded.

"I believe he might. He is irrational enough. It is possible he sees the minimal constraints placed on him as being an attempt to mitigate the danger that you, Isaac, present to the community. That could inflame him, especially if he feels he is not being taken seriously, or worse, being patronized."

Gardner, shocked at the potential for mayhem, said he needed to talk to Trask and Conant. They were in a position to raise the danger of doing nothing about Arthur Beamish. He should be put on a boat and returned to England, just like the five dissolute youths that Endecott had recently sent back. Morton commented that Endecott needs to be made aware that. Much better to have the boy returned to

England ahead of time. We all agreed with Morton's assessment and Gardner said he would pass it on. It would be for Endecott to decide.

Ralph saw me just before we left and passed on a word from Mr. Graves asking me if they could hire Gavan. They desperately needed carpenters to build houses before the winter set in. I told him I would have a word with Gavan. David and I returned to Shawmut. On the way, I asked David what he thought about it all.

"I think Thomas Morton has it absolutely right. Young Arthur is a danger to himself and others. He needs to be removed, quickly and quietly. Endecott should see too, that by sending him back without formal action and a note to his father the whole incident can be expunged from the record. On the other hand, we still haven't resolved the problem we have with your original assailant. Young Arthur is a separate happening, hopefully resolvable without further action on our part—loathe as I am to let a young criminal off the hook."

I said we would have to wait and see. Firstly, whether Endecott responds, secondly, if nothing breaks beforehand, what I get back from Will Whiteway. I then asked him how he and Kate were getting on. David looked at me.

"Isaac, you keep asking me about Kate. What are you worried about? Kate is doing exactly what she wants to do. Beth and she are part of a loving family, something they have not had since her first husband died and that is a long time ago. The grief she bore after Davey died has only recently been shed. That's because she enjoys seeing Beth adopted by James and Abigail. Beth has regained her love of life. She has transferred her devotion for Davey, her lost brother, to James. In Abigail, she has a younger sister now, who adore each other."

"Sorry, David. I care about you all. I am driving everyone towards goals I have set for myself. I want to make sure I'm not taking you all for granted."

"Don't worry, my dear friend, drive on, we are willing and supportive followers."

I talked to Gavan on our return. He asked whether I had something I would like him to do at Shawmut. I said nothing that was urgent and that he should contract with Graves at a favorable rate. I was a bit worried that the experience might convince Gavan he would be better off becoming a permanent contractor. It did mean that I needed to pay him his worth, going forward. He would have more than enough to do when we moved to New Barrow farm. Johnny sailed him over a few days later, staying until Gavan confirmed with him he was gainfully employed with Graves.

We settled in, warm, comfortable, and well provisioned. Snow and wind kept us busy at our little farm. We enjoyed our second Christmas at Shawmut, with the added pleasure of having the Tremaines here. Gavan took a break from his building to spend Christmas with us. He told us the conditions were stark at Charlestown, apparently even worse in Salem. Too many people, insufficient planning to deal with the influx, lack of food and sickness. Annie was determined to take Jeannie with her to Salem, with as many provisions as we can spare, to offer their help with the sick. I would have gone as well, if I had been allowed to. Johnny volunteered to go. We loaded up *Rosie*, and the three of them went to Salem, leaving the day after Boxing Day, when the weather had turned benign for the first time in the month. They promised to return before Twelfth Night, depending on the weather.

I borrowed the Blackstone shallop to take Gavan back to Charlestown, leaving David and Kate to look after everything at home. We further depleted our winter supplies with provisions that we gave to the grateful Spragues, who would share them with their neighbors. I said I would be back in a couple of days. I wanted to find out for myself the state that the Charlestown settlers were in. The weather reverted the following day, cold and a blizzard blowing. I stayed with Gavan in the rough shelter he had been sharing with other construction workers. It was bleak. The benefits of being working carpenters, there was plenty of wood to burn. While I was there, little work could be undertaken, except for houses that had a roof and walls where inside finishing work was needed. But if a house had a roof and walls, it was quickly taken over by a desperate family. Food was rationed. Snow and ice were used for water. It was a lot more wholesome than the normal supply which, anyway, had frozen over. Gavan had brought provisions for his colleagues, but they didn't last long. For them it was Christmas fare and pleasing to them.

The weather grew steadily worse the last few days of December. The builders struggled to assemble some kinds of shelter with the wind and snow swirling about them. It reached a point when it became too cold to hold a hammer or saw. I was aware of a brief window in the stormy weather. I asked Gavan if he would like to attempt the crossing back to Shawmut. He had had enough and was happy to take a break. The shallop had been hauled up onto the shore and contained a thick layer of snow which we shoveled out as best we could. It was too windy to sail so we would have to row. The water was ice fringed which helped us initially as we pushed the boat into the water, then caught on the ice broken by the weight of the boat. By the time it was floating, we had wet and unbelievably cold feet, legs, and hands. Luckily the wind was from the northeast and would help to push us in the direction of the Charles River and Shawmut. Rowing warmed us up. While we were in the lee of the Charlestown landmass and the Mystic River we made steady progress. The brief window in the weather slammed shut when we were out in the open water, halfway back to Shawmut. Then the wind really hit us, blowing the snow horizontally into our faces, the waves increased causing the boat to pitch up over a wave and risk being buried in the following trough. Again, we were thankful that the wind was with us, otherwise it would have been impossible and even more dangerous than it was. We made it into the Charles River with the bilge water halfway to our knees. We both had to row, no capability to bale any of the water out of the boat. We drove the boat through then over the shore ice which we beached, tied to a tree, and fled for the shelter of home. We would summon help later to empty and overturn the boat safely above the high watermark.

We realized that Annie, Jeannie, and Johnny would not be coming back to us by Twelfth Night. The winter weather continued at its most ferocious for another two weeks. We were warm, staying fed and healthy. The animals were well looked after and Kate oversaw the arrival of four more goat kids, aided by the children. James suggested they be named Five, Six, Seven, and Eight, all does. Beth argued that they should be given nice names. James said Beth and Abigail would be much more unhappy to see a favorite goat with a nice name being shipped off to slaughter. Beth was still inclined to argue. OK, said James, how would she feel if Nanna or Beatrice was sent away? Nothing further was said on the subject.

—— CHAPTER 25 ——

Journal entry – *January - February 1630*

It was mid-January before Johnny was able to sail *Rosie* back to Shaw-mut, Annie on the mainsheet and Jeannie baling. It was a bright sunny afternoon, a gentle breeze and bitterly cold. The first sun we had seen since before Christmas. Jeannie, poor love, was in a state of nervous exhaustion and almost prostrate. She looked thin and unwell. Johnny said the conditions in Salem were simply terrible. They had had little sleep, were constantly cold with less than adequate food. The provisions they had taken with them did not last much beyond Christmas. People, shocked into a numbed disbelief at their first experience of a New England winter, were suffering from ill-health, even scurvy, in addition to the malnutrition and the cold.

Kate had a stew pot simmering on the fire. After Jeannie had time to warm up in front of the fire, Johnny took her to her bed with a bowl of stew and a beaker of hot mulled wine. A wrapped hot stone was put into her bed to keep her feet warm. Johnny stayed with her, wrapping himself round her for comfort and warmth. With a roaring fire, hot stew, warm bread, and mulled wine the rest of us had an early sup-per with so much to tell and talk about. I wanted to hear all about the happenings in Salem.

Annie expanded on Johnny's account. There were not many peo-ple in the new settlement that had remained healthy. Those able to stand looked after those bed-ridden. Annie and Jeannie had gone to the houses with the sickest, mostly women and children, and cared for them, as well as cleaning, keeping fires going, fetching wood, cooking what provisions were available. Johnny chopping wood, fetching water, helping the men continue to add to the shelters they had, blocking windows, even making wetus, until the weather forced them inside. I asked where they stayed. Johnny and Jeannie were given space with the Gardners in the old village. Annie was invited to stay with Governor Endecott. I was shocked and speechless. Annie smiled at me and kissed me, my mouth still wide open. My expression asked all the questions. Annie took the time to enjoy answering them all.

"Isaac my sweet, you must remember that the Governor was most grateful to me for looking after Mistress Endecott before she died. I was visiting Mistress Trask, who was unwell and in bed, when the Governor came by. He greeted me most cordially and asked how we were all coping at Shawmut. He also thanked you for the provisions we had brought with us and for letting me come to help his people. He asked how long I would be staying to help. I told him I was with Johnny and Jeannie Dawkins and we expected to sail back to Shawmut by Twelfth Night. Where were we staying? I said that the Gardners had offered us space. He replied, "But that's in the old village. I need you here to help us. You should come and stay at the Governor's house. It's full of people, but I will make a bed available for you, if you don't mind sharing with another lady."

"Isaac, my immediate reaction was that here was a golden opportunity to warm Endecott's heart to our predicament. So, I gracefully accepted his kind invitation. How was he to know that the two or three days he thought I would be with him would stretch to nearly three weeks? It did mean, however, that we had plenty of opportunity to talk and get to know each other better. It helped by having those conversations over a dinner table, albeit sparsely filled with food, the Governor on the same rations as everyone else. Endecott was hospitable with many guests, men and women, who participated in the conversations. One evening, a few days before we came back here, the subject of young Arthur Beamish arose. What should be done with him? It seemed that word had come back to the Governor, presumably through Mr. Conant or Mr. Trask, that, might I say, you were somewhat more than seriously inconvenienced. I was ready make our position clear but felt it much more politic to keep my mouth shut and listen. It was made plain quickly that young Arthur was an embarrassment. Not only for what he done, trying to kill you, but his irrational behavior since. He was now confined to the house he was living in, forbidden to leave it unaccompanied, under threat of being locked up."

I started to interrupt, but Annie put her finger to my mouth and continued.

"The Governor was asked whether he thought Arthur's accusations about Mr. Stanfield were rational. That created a moment of discomfort as the questioner had forgotten, or perhaps in hindsight he hadn't, that I was present. However, the wine obviously helping, the Governor admitted that it was not rational. He had had a full report and drawn the conclusion that young Arthur was not to be believed and needed to be dealt with. 'How so?' the questioner asked. "Is he to be left for Mr. Winthrop to deal with?' The Governor had not, to that moment, seemed to have considered that question. He hesitated. The guests round the table waited, me with bated breath. 'No. He needs to be sent back to England on the next boat out of Salem with a letter to his father to take care of him. I want all evidence of his having come here expunged. Mr. Winthrop should not be embarrassed by being made aware of the behavior of this son of a friend of his.' He then turned to me, 'Mistress Stanfield, I would like to apologize to you and for you to take these apologies back to your husband. I have been less that courteous. I have also been advised by Mr. Conant that your husband has become close with our good friend Masconomet. How so?'

"Isaac, my love, I had to laugh. I said that my husband and Masconomet were bear brothers. The guests round the table responded with various versions of 'Bear brothers, what in heaven's name are they?' I had to explain about your adventure with your bear in Saco, being given the name Machk, the Bear, to become legend among the

Indians. Masconomet had had a similar adventure many years ago and he, too, had been given that name and become a legend. I couldn't resist saying 'Killing large bears, single-handedly is not the sort of thing most people do.' Everyone laughed and cheered, even the Governor. He leant back in his chair and raised a toast to the two bear brothers. He then said that Mr. Conant had told him that Masconomet was anxious to have Mr. Stanfield move to the location he chose on the Merrimack. Good for trade but also important as a protection for his people against the Mohawk. The Governor then said he would like me to advise my husband that in the circumstances he would be pleased to have the Stanfield family relocate at our convenience. He would be grateful therefore if Mr. Stanfield would come to Salem and he, as Governor, would confirm the grant of land in writing."

Stunned silence after Annie stopped speaking. Having described the scene and conversation at the Governor's table with a look of heavy concentration, Annie relaxed and, a slow grin spreading across her face, looked at us all staring at her. I reached over and hugged her. Only then did the others react with cheers and laughter.

The next few weeks, outside our normal chores and the settling in of Five, Six, Seven, and Eight, were spent planning our move to New Barrow Farm. Gavan and Annie spent hours drawing and redrawing the dimensions of the house in great detail, but in the end, Gavan managed to persuade her that she needed to keep it simple, and all the many ambitious designs Annie had produced were discarded and our Shawmut house was used as the model. Kate then joined them to make sure the stabling and paddock fencing were planned to her satisfaction. David and I talked to Gavan about the possibilities for a sawmill on or near the property. If we were to build a trade in lumber, we would need a more efficient way of producing it. Gavan said we needed running water to drive the mill to saw the wood. The typical sawmill was sited below but close to a weir or dam, which created a body of water behind it. A conduit was dug to direct a fast flow of water, bypassing the weir, down to the mill that drove the wheel which powered the saw. Perhaps our stream might suit. It had a narrow mouth and was quite fast flowing. Perhaps we didn't need to build a conduit. We might be able to narrow the stream still further to increase the flow. We should be able to build the sawmill by the water. We would need to survey our stream when we were next there.

By the end of January, the weather had relented sufficiently for us to be able to use *Rosie* on occasion. Johnny took Gavan and Giles to help the building of Charlestown. I sailed with Annie, Johnny, and the fully recovered Jeannie back to Salem for them to continue to help the settlers there. I also took the opportunity to go with Annie to meet with the Governor. He looked haggard, thin, unwell, exhausted. The same visage on everyone I saw. They continued barely capable of enduring the appalling winter. He welcomed Annie and offered her the same accommodation for as long as she wished to stay. Annie was pleased to accept, once more. He greeted me warmly. He had come a long way in his development as a leader. I said as much, as tactfully as I could. He smiled ruefully and agreed that it had been a horrible but necessary learning experience. He thanked the good Lord and the spiritual strength he took from the Reverends Skelton and Higginson, for his survival. He looked forward to the end of the winter affliction and the promise of a new beginning with the arrival of Winthrop and his armada.

Endecott took me aside and expressed his regret for his past indifference to my situation. I said I understood he had been preoccupied with his duties as Governor. I told him that Annie had returned to Shawmut, grateful for his kind and generous hospitality. I, too, was grateful for the decision he had made to allow us to move to the Merrimack and to confirm our land grant. He handed me a document which was his official ratification of the grant and the approximate location of the land. He asked that I confirm in writing the precise location and boundaries with a map, as soon as possible. He also asked me to put the incident with Arthur Beamish behind me. He apologized and said he must leave me as he had many duties still to perform that day. We shook hands. I left Annie to continue her good work and went in search of Thomas Morton.

He had not borne the winter well, either. He said that he felt in his bones that he would not be in New England much longer. He was being tolerated, barely. With the arrival of Winthrop, he felt that tolerance would be gone. I asked him why he bothered coming back at all. He replied that he had people here who depended on him. He saw the potential for good things to happen here, but the increasing Separatism irked him. He wanted to fight the personal restrictions being placed on the lives of ordinary people. Changing the subject, I thanked him for his investigation of Arthur Beamish. He waved my thanks away. He took it as an interesting challenge but quickly realized there was little to do. Arthur was a poor young third son, intellectually challenged and thrown to the wolves by an uncaring father. God knows what would happen to him when he was returned to his father's care. Morton wandered off, an unhappy, unfulfilled man.

I went to visit the Gardners. Thomas was pleased that everything had been resolved satisfactorily, although he did ask about the original set of attempts on my life which he worried, on my behalf, had not been resolved. I suggested that it sounded like he had been talking to Johnny while he and Jeannie were staying with him. He admitted so. We talked further about the effect this winter was having, by far the worst since he first came to New England. Many people had died and he felt certain many more would succumb before Spring came. He and his family were healthier than most, for which he was thankful. The Old Planters were more experienced with the cold and had time to build their resources to withstand the winter. They had reached out to the new settlers to the extent possible, but food was scarce, accommodation lacking, and many people appeared to have lost the will to survive. I thanked him for sheltering Johnny and Jeannie. He replied that he and his family were happy to have them. Johnny had become a firm favorite of his sons.

The following morning, the weather stayed calm but promised a change for the worse, so I took my chances, said my farewells to Johnny, Jeannie, and Annie, telling them I would return in a week. I sailed for Shawmut. The wild winter weather closed in again and I wasn't able to return to Salem for several weeks. On my return, Annie had been confined to her bed at the Endecott house suffering from a debilitating cold and exhaustion, being cared for by Jeannie. She was now up and feeling better, anxious to release the Governor from any further responsibility for her. Endecott, looking slightly better from when I last saw him, was most courteous. Annie thanked him, he kissed her hand. With a "God speed, my dear" he waved us away.

Johnny and Jeannie had gone ahead to the boat, both looking much improved. There was a suppressed excitement about them, which I took to come from the desire to leave Salem. I caught Annie's eye. She whispered, "Wait till we get home." Most mysterious. Back home, everyone happy to see the wanderers returned, Abigail, most of all. The evening meal was prepared and everyone sat. After grace was said, Annie said that Jeannie had something to say. All eyes turned to a blushing Jeannie. She grabbed Johnny's arm and buried her face in his shoulder. Johnny, hugging her, announced that they were expecting a baby. They weren't sure when the baby might be due, but the signs were unmistakable. There was much joy at the announcement. I was happy but surprised. His memories of Rebecca and her desperately sad death seemed to have been put to rest. I looked at Johnny. He caught my glance. A brief shadow flickered across his face. Then he smiled and I smiled with him. I had not mentioned to Annie Johnny's heartfelt disclosure about his memory of Rebecca dying in childbirth. I had obeyed Johnny's plea and left it unsaid. Now, I wasn't so sure.

On the last day of February Thomas Morton appeared at Shawmut. He was sailing back to Merrymount and needed to speak to me. He told me that Arthur Beamish was on his way back to England. Before he boarded the fishing boat taking him back, Morton had met with him. Reason being, he had had a nagging doubt about the circumstances of Arthur's attempt on my life.

"Isaac, had you ever met Arthur before?"

I said I hadn't, with no knowledge of him. Morton explained his question.

"When I had first interrogated him, I asked him where he had been before he saw you. Out hunting, he said, which was why he had the gun with him. By yourself. Yes, he replied. I then asked him if he had ever met you before. He hadn't. I asked him how he knew it was at you he was shooting, from the trees at some distance away. He said you had been pointed out to him. I didn't pursue it then, but it has worried me since. It seemed altogether too spontaneous an action, given the circumstances. When I saw him this time, he was much more subdued. He was apprehensive about returning to the wrath of his father. I asked him if he was allowed to hunt on his father's property in England? Yes, he said cheering up, fox hunting. No other hunting? Occasionally, fowling, rabbits. Not so much fun. Did you bring many kills back to the table? He laughed. No, he wasn't a good shot. So, I said, no fox hunting over here for you then. He sighed, no, but it was one thing he looked forward to when he got back to England. Did you hunt much over here? Not really. Did you ever go hunting by yourself? No, he replied. Not much point, he wasn't likely to hit much. So, why you did go hunting at all? Some man I met persuaded me to go with him. Did he have a gun? Of course. Was he a good shot? Yes, very good."

I was startled and asked Thomas what he was inferring.

"Isaac, I infer nothing, hear me out. I took Arthur by the shoulders and pointedly asked him why he admitted to trying to shoot Stanfield? Arthur sagged and I let him go. He sat in a dejected heap with his head in his hands. I reminded him of our initial conversation about the shooting and that he admitted never having met Stanfield before. How was it you were so certain the distant figure you saw was Stanfield that you tried to kill him? He repeated Stanfield had been pointed out to him. When? I asked. He was vague in his response. Where? In the new settlement. How often did you see Stanfield? Many times, he said. Isaac, how often did you go to Salem?""Rarely, even less to the new settlement."

"So I thought. I then suggested to Arthur that Stanfield hadn't been often to Salem, and he must have been damn certain to react so quickly. I asked him was anyone with him when he went hunting this time. Yes, he admitted. With the man that had pointed Stanfield out to him?

Yes. Was he the one who actually shot at Stanfield? Yes. I asked again, why did you admit to the shooting? Arthur said he was threatened by the man to say nothing, admit to nothing. If Arthur told the authorities what had really happened, he would be killed. The man concocted the story about Stanfield being a traitor and had to be dealt with. I asked Arthur what the man's name was. Septimus Grindle. Where did he go? Arthur had no idea. He never saw him again."

It made so much sense. I thanked Morton. My adversary, Septimus Grindle, had reappeared. Morton nodded. His ride to Merrymount was waiting. We shook hands and he left. I was still awaiting a response from Will about Seth.

—— CHAPTER 26 ——

Journal entry - *March 1630*

Having an unknown assailant hunting me down was disconcerting. Somehow, it was less so when the assailant had a name. It became more personal. If it did turn out to be Seth, it was an even more tangible threat since he was the man who kidnapped James and taken him to Bermuda. If Seth had managed to escape his deserved retribution, he needed to be recaptured and returned to England. Thomas Morton sent me a note from Merrymount. Apparently, Septimus Grindle had been there. He was in Salem at the time of the shooting. Thereafter, he had returned to Merrymount and then found a local trader going to Jamestown, where presumably he is now.

I talked to Johnny and David about the problem. David said this was too serious to be left to chance. By doing nothing, Grindle or whoever he was, was in control of the situation. He could continue to bide his time, to take advantage of any opportunity that might arise. We need to go after him. Johnny agreed but said we still don't know who this man was for certain. He might have changed his name again. While I agreed with the sentiment, I suggested we wait to hear from Will. If Seth was on the loose, we could assume he and Grindle are the same person. Then we could take action. David said, in that case, he proposed going down to Jamestown himself. He knows Seth and whatever he might call himself, David would recognize him. I thanked him for his sentiment but said we should wait for the Whiteway letter then decide what to do. There might be a better way of flushing him out without the possibly fruitless long voyage. I noticed that David was showing signs of wanting to grab any opportunity to get back to sea.

We needed to focus on New Barrow Farm. The weather was still cold, windy, and snowy. Gavan and Giles had returned from Charlestown, happy to be home. Conditions there were bad, many dead, but, although no consolation, not as bad as in the new settlement at Salem. Giles keen to work with Kate preparing for Spring farming, Gavan anxious to start building our new home. We prepared *Rosie* after her winter layup and put together supplies from our now depleted stores, thankfully bolstered by contributions from William Blackstone, for two people for a month. We would replenish those supplies before the month was done. David volunteered to take the first month with Gavan. It would take his mind off the sea, I thought. A break in the weather and *Rosie* was quickly loaded. Johnny and I would go with them and bring *Rosie* back. James considered himself the man of the house and said he would take care of the women and children—I had to remind myself that one of the 'children' was actually older than the young man who had declared himself to be in charge. Annie grinned at me over the serious looking James. We hugged, kissed and the four older men sailed into a boisterous sea, wind from the North. We would have a time of it rounding Cape Ann and out of the lee.

David was increasingly in his element the more the weather deteriorated. Cape Ann was a worse trial than I had envisioned. Wind on the nose, we tacked under the shelter of the large, flat and rocky island off the eastern shore of the Cape, then had a wild ride back towards the shore before tacking again for another equally wild ride back out to sea. Gavan and Johnny acted as moveable ballast, risking life and frostbite perched precariously against the windward rail while I baled. We alternated regularly, baling was sheltered and warm work, the other was not. Once round Cape Ann we had the wind on our starboard beam and both *Rosie* and her crew were much happier.

When we made the Merrimack River, our thoughts turned from

survival to the work we had ahead. Gavan was anxious to explore the mouth of our stream, which he had taken to calling Erichuck. Why, I asked? It is an approximation of the name the Indians call it, he answered. So Erichuck it was. He wanted to see if it was possible to build a sawmill, not so much for our immediate needs, but it would be necessary to have one conveniently situated if we were to harvest and trade lumber. We rowed *Rosie* into the mouth of the Erichuck, the narrow entrance bordered by marsh grass and reeds. The banks on either side were high, then on the northern side dropping to some six to eight feet above the water, the water flow was steady. We took some soundings, the water had a depth of between one and two fathoms. If the channel could be restricted the flow would increase sufficiently to drive a wheel. I asked about blocking Erichuck, preventing our Indian friends from easy access to the Merrimack. He said he would have to think about that once the house was built.

Up to the building site, remains of the snow still covering the ground, with green patches showing through. The lumber store looked in good condition. Nootau and Ahanu had been diligent guardians and were there to greet us. We set up camp. Johnny and I set to building two wetus, one for equipment and supplies, the other accommodation for the builders. Gavan and David set up a covered work space while Johnny and I fetched the rest of the equipment from the boat. What we had taken away with us when we left the site last year had now been brought back with full sets of building tools: axes, saws, hammers, mallets, chisels, mauls, wedges, line and reel, and a canvas bag full of smaller instruments, vital to the proficient builder. While Johnny and I were there, we helped Gavan establish the outline of the house, copying the external outline of the house at Shawmut, with a few minor changes agreed to by Gavan and Annie, marked by pegs. We also helped dig the trench. At Shawmut we had dug a trench one foot deep by one foot wide. Gavan said that if we had the time and the manpower, we should build a foundation four feet deep, so we didn't get frost heave in the winter. With the constraints we had, we decided to repeat what we had done at Shawmut. Perhaps at some time in the future, a more substantial house might be built. When Johnny and I left them two days later, Gavan and David were already beginning to sink corner posts.

Back at Shawmut, settled in for the evening, and alone together, Annie brought me a package of correspondence newly arrived from England. The first letter was from Will, full of news from home. He reported that a gentleman had made serious inquiries about acquiring Barrow Farm and was prepared to pay a substantial amount. While he had been happy to act as our agent while we rented the property, he felt the time was propitious for me to take advantage of the opportunity presented. It would also relieve him of the continuing obligation, albeit with the income from the rental that I had so kindly provided as more than fair recompense. He then turned his attention to what might have happened to Seth. He wrote that he had had some difficulty tracking down exactly where Seth might be. He found that when we had brought Seth back from Bermuda to Plymouth, the authorities had been alerted and Seth was detained and taken away from *Swallow*. He had been charged previously with various serious felonies and had escaped with James, a captive, to Bermuda. Those charges were still outstanding. Will said further that we had detailed the additional felonies of child kidnapping and mistreatment. They were added to the charges leveled against Seth. He was then remanded in custody awaiting trial. Due to a backlog in cases before the court he was tried on his original charges only and received a four-year prison sentence. The later charges were held over. When that case came before the court, through some administrative error, Seth had completed his sentence and been released under custody with the instructions that he was still on remand and would have to await the court case. The penalty for those charges if found guilty would almost certainly be death. Unfortunately, the two people needed to be called as witnesses for the prosecution were me and David Tremaine, both now in New England. In our absence, the charges could not be brought and Seth was released.

Will puzzled over the timing. The attempts on my life on *Abigail* were made when Seth was still in prison, which meant, if Seth had been the instigator, he must have had an accomplice sign on as a crewman on *Abigail*. Of course, Will added, those early attempts might have had nothing to do with Seth at all, or for that matter the last attempt. Will said he did try to trace the man called Spiggott to see if he appeared on any crew manifests in 1628, with some success. A seaman called Spiggott had been remanded for a short time in Plymouth for a minor infraction at about the time Seth was in remand. Spiggott had been fined and released. Nothing more was known other than he was on the crew manifest for *Abigail*.

After reflection, Annie asked, "Where does that leave us?"

"I think, considerably further ahead. Seth is alive and free, but we don't know where. He could be Grindle, but how the hell was he able to transform himself and pay for a trip over here? He must have had significant assistance. Which means yet another person involved in this enterprise to kill me. Anyway, while it isn't definite, what Will describes fits what we know. What we need to do is track down Grindle. I think we need to reengage Thomas Morton in Merrymount."

I then turned to my next letter, from my English business manager Mr. Ebenezer Scroud. He was pleased to inform me that my investments were doing well and that he had taken the liberty to send additional funds, suitably buried in a large chest of supplies he felt I might need, so far from civilization. The chest was to be delivered to Mr. Roger Conant in my name with the instructions to forward it, or otherwise provide information as to its whereabouts, to me. He also said that the Admiralty Court had at long last reached a verdict on the claim the owners of the *Argossy* had made demanding compensation for the loss of business due to the sinking of the the *Sweet Rose*, with the countersuit Mr. Scroud had made stating the loss of *Sweet Rose* was due to the non-appearance of the *Argossy*. Scroud had represented the owners' interests in the court proceedings. Tiny Hadfield, on his return from dropping us off in New England, had made contact with Scroud as he had promised me, which was opportune. Scroud was able to use him as an expert witness in the court case.

It turned out that the owners of the *Argossy* had instructed the

Captain not to rendezvous with the *Sweet Rose*, in spite of being contractually obligated to do so. The court had ordered the owners of the *Argossy* to recompense the owners of the *Sweet Rose* for the cost of replacement of their ship and the full price of the freight contained therein as itemized in her manifest. *Argossy's* owners had refused to pay, so the *Argossy* was impounded with per diem fines until the payment was made. After a month, and no fine paid, the *Argossy* was expropriated and a hefty penalty levied on pain of imprisonment if not paid, with ownership transferred to the owners of the *Sweet Rose* in full compensation, with costs of ongoing maintenance partially covered by the penalty payment. Mr. Scroud further went on to say that Mr. Richard Bushrode, co-owner of the *Sweet Rose*, had, before he died, and aware of the possible outcome of the Admiralty Court case, renounced ownership of all assets and liabilities associated with *Sweet Rose* and returned his part-ownership to the previous owner, Isaac Stanfield. Mr. Scroud had written to the other co-owner and previous Captain, Mr. Isaiah Brown, now retired, to inform him of the findings of the court. Mr. Brown had written back saying, all benefits accruing from the unfortunate sinking of the *Sweet Rose* due to him as part owner, he wished to have transferred to the rightful owner, Isaac Stanfield, in abiding gratitude for saving the lives of himself, his officers, and crew from capture and ultimate death at the hands of the Barbary pirates. Therefore, concluded Mr. Scroud in his letter, Mr. Stanfield, welcome back to your career as a ship owner and merchant trader. He also said that he had retained Mr. Hadfield, currently without a ship, to assume temporary command of the idle *Argossy* until such time as I provide him with instructions.

Having read Mr. Scroud's letter, I sat stunned. Annie, concerned, reached over and took my arm.

"My love, what's wrong? What's happened?"

I shook my head and told Annie to sit down with a full glass of wine and listen while I read her the letter. After which, we just stared at each other. Now what do we do? I broke the silence by telling Annie what Will had said about someone wanting to buy Barrow Farm. Eventually someone had to go back to England to sort all this out. Annie suggested that it should be me. I thought it ought to be David.

"Why?" asked Annie. "Do you want to keep the boat?"

"Of course. It is an unbelievable turn of events. As you know, I had planned to acquire a pinnace for local trading and then move up to a merchantman to trade with England, Bermuda, Barbados, and the Islands. Now, I can skip the local trading. What is needed, is someone to organize a full survey of *Argossy*, and if sound to find a crew, gather a freight, and sail it back to Salem. That would be David."

Annie shook her head.

"I didn't mean to bring this up with you, because I hoped it was just a passing storm, but I have to tell you that if David does go back to England, to be gone for, how long, six months to a year?" I nodded. "Then it does not bode well for the Tremaine marriage."

I thought back to seeing David's eagerness to get back to sea. Perhaps it was a desire to get away from Kate. I asked Annie what she thought about their relationship.

"Not good. We all know Kate wants to farm. She wants a husband who shares her life as a farmer, not someone who thinks of nothing but sailing and adventure. They have not been arguing, at least publicly, but their relationship is at best civil. Between you and me, having Giles here isn't helping the situation. He is young, fit, and a dedicated farmer. He also has great difficulty disguising his attraction for Kate."

We talked about the projects we had on, the priorities and the resources we had at our disposal. David and Gavan were at the Merrimack site building New Barrow Farm. If David goes to England, he must be replaced. In fact, I was worried that just two men working there was not enough. Perhaps we should all go and camp there. Annie didn't like the idea of leaving Kate and Giles alone together. On the other hand, we could not leave the livestock untended. Does needed to be milked, their kids kept safe from wild animals. The cows had stopped producing milk, so they weren't a problem, but we couldn't leave our growing agricultural small-holding untended for more than a week. Annie suggested Johnny stay with Kate, Jeannie,

Beth, and Abigail while she and James travel with Giles and me to the Merrimack.

It was a good solution, but now the immediate excitement of being a ship owner once more had settled, I realized that there was no immediate hurry sending David back. I needed to write back to Scroud and advise him what to do. It would be several months before we came to claim *Argossy*. Meantime, he was needed to find a care-taker crew with acting skipper and bosun. He also should have *Argossy* thoroughly surveyed. That message should be sent as soon as possible. I would leave tomorrow for Salem, taking the letter to Scroud and one to Will to be put on the next boat out, as well as fetch Mr. Scroud's chest from Roger Conant. Annie and I agreed Barrow Farm should be sold and the proceeds forwarded to Scroud. After dropping off the letter I needed to go to the Merrimack and tell David what was going on. Then I needed to go to Merrymount to talk to Morton. Annie said I should take Johnny with me, *Rosie* was too big for one man to handle on long journeys with the changeable spring weather. She would keep an eye on things and she had James and Giles to take care of "manly" challenges.

It had been many months since Annie and I had had a peaceful evening alone together. We were happy with our home, but it housed a lot of people. Something we needed to rectify when we built New Barrow Farm. While I was there, I would discuss it with David and Gavan. After the shock of the news from England, we settled in the big chair by the fire, Annie on my lap with her arms round my neck. We kissed and she rested her head on my shoulder, looked up at me with her big blue eyes wide, and slipped her hand inside my shirt, gently tugging the hairs on my chest. Her arm pushed her lovely breasts up and filled the top of her dress. I freed one of those lovely breasts and felt the soft warmth in my hand as I gently stroked it. Annie closed her eyes, seemingly relaxed, then sat up, released her dress from both shoulders and leaned back, her hands round my neck, and pulled my head down to caress her breasts with my lips. She smiled as she felt my loins react and moved her sweet bum to speed the process. Standing, her dress slipped to the floor, her hand now inside my breeches and, holding me hard, pulled me to the bedroom. I undid and discarded my clothes as we went. I was pushed onto the bed and Annie straddled me still holding and stroking her precious (and mine) prize, while I reached between her legs, teasing till she was moist and ready before she settled and guided me into her. As she moved gently rocking backwards and forwards, I put my arms around her and rolled her over onto her back and took up the motion with increasing urgency, Annie responding. We climaxed together and lay still, the pounding of our hearts easing and our fierce holding of each other turned to gentle stroking. No words had been spoken, just the gentle cries of release then silence as we absorbed the warmth and love we had for each other.

CHAPTER 27

Journal entry – *April 1630*

I went to Merrymount with Johnny to meet with Thomas Morton. He told me the people still there were dispirited, and many had moved elsewhere, some returning to England, others to Jamestown. They were under continuous threat by Myles Standish from New Plimouth. They no longer had their maypole to dance round. Their Indian friends had been chased away. But the remnants had hung together. They had welcomed back their once exiled leader and hoped for better days to return. Morton was not able to give them that assurance. Still, he was there providing some semblance of the leadership they had lacked.

Morton had made inquiries about Septimus Grindle, who had been there but had moved on, it was thought to New Plimouth. He had been passing himself off as a merchant and was a not too pleasant character. No one had bothered much to get to know him. He had the appearance of being gentry, as they called it, but his behavior belied that appearance. He was coarse, inarticulate, and his professed background as a merchant was just not believable. The general opinion was that he was some kind of fugitive from England. As there were no saints in Merrymount, he was left to his own devices and soon left on a trading ship heading initially to New Plimouth but the ship was subsequently heading away from the Massachusetts Bay and sailing south to Jamestown.

Johnny and I sailed on down to New Plimouth. I was greeted by

Isaac Atherton and accompanied him to pay my respects to Governor Bradford. I was greeted cordially. They had heard I had come with family to settle and they were gratifyingly pleased. While I was no Separatist, they acknowledged the work I had done to help the settlement process in New England. They counted me as a friend. They asked why I was visiting. I replied that I wanted to come down out of common courtesy but I did have an ulterior motive. I was looking for someone by name Septimus Grindle. They didn't know the name, but so many people were now using New Plimouth as a pass-through location for other final destinations, it was quite possible he might be there.

After pleasant conversation with them both, I left to seek out Stephen Hopkins. I found him down at the landing stage. I imagined he would be as likely to know of itinerant passersby as anyone. He greeted me by wanting to know if I needed more cows moving. I laughed and said, not at the moment, although by July, I would have need of help. He told me to let him know and he would be happy to assist. I asked him if he had come across a Septimus Grindle and described him as best as I could, adding the not respectful description I was given by Morton. Hopkins observed that it was apparent from the way I described him the man was not a particular friend. He thought for a minute. He was aware of such a person. He had met him. A shifty individual he thought. Surprisingly, he had not gone to Jamestown but to the Dutchmen at New Amsterdam at the mouth of the Hudson River. Stephen knew that because they had a discussion about how Grindle could best get there. There was a businessman he had to meet, he said. Stephen told him he could walk, not advised, or get a boat of which there were many. When he had last seen Grindle, he was talking to the skipper of a small fishing boat. We returned to Shawmut.

As Annie had suggested, she, James, Giles and I were at Merrimack from the first week in April. When we arrived, we were again amazed at how much work had been accomplished. Gavan had decided to dig a four-foot-deep trench for the foundations and had used the fieldstone collected the previous year to build them. They had also created a large fieldstone platform for the hearth, bigger than the one we had at Shawmut, and all vertical posts had been sunk. James had imme-diately gone to find Nootau and Ahanu who were sorting out lumber from the store. James wanted to explore the brook so off the three of them went, chattering away. James was becoming quite proficient in the local Abenaki dialect.

Annie scrutinized the work already completed, delighted with the progress. She and Gavan had a long and earnest discussion about the work to be done. She had some ideas about the fireplace and chimney. How could they be modified to generate more heat on both floors and to reduce the chance of the chimney catching fire? Something Annie had worried about all last winter. The only real protection was to make the chimney from brick or fieldstone. With no brick available, Gavan said he planned to have the three walls of the fireplace lined in field-stone to about four feet high. The back wall would have a cast iron reflector plate. The front of the fireplace would have a long oak lintel resting on the side walls. The chimney, narrowing as it rose through upper floor and roof, made of clay on a wooden frame. Unfortunately, the upper floor would remain cold, with only some warmth seeping through the chimney wall and up the stairs. As had happened fre-quently on cold winter nights at Shawmut, everyone slept in the main room round the fire with the table pushed against the far wall. Giles set up our camp near the existing fire pit, a temporary shelter for Annie, James, and me. He would settle in Gavan and David's shelter as David would be returning with us to Shawmut.

I gave David a full account of the letters I had received. He was overjoyed at the thought of returning to England to take command of a ship once more. He was delighted to think that Tiny Hadfield was currently in charge. He would make an excellent officer. I also told him to seek out J.B. Braddock and Obi Burch, one time skipper and bosun of the *Swallow* that had been sold to new owners in Barbados, which J.B. and Obi had delivered to them. They would have complet-ed the delivery sometime last year. I had told them to maintain contact when they returned, which they should do via Mr. Scroud in Plym-outh. David laughed in sheer pleasure at the thought of the officers he knew so well being a part of the *Argossy*. I asked him about Kate and Beth, whether being away for a year would be a problem for them, and him for that matter.

"Isaac, I think you must know or at least suspect that my marriage to Kate is a trial for both of us. We have tried to keep everything civilized but I'm sure Annie is fully aware of the situation. Kate does not wish to discuss it, even with Annie, but Annie is an astute and caring woman. Nothing gets by her. I am also aware that Giles is sniffing around Annie like a tom cat. I hope they can control themselves. My going to England is fortunate, if for no other reason. I have had a private word with Reverend Blackstone. He says that getting a divorce in the Puritan faith is, at least in theory, straightforward, as they consider it a civil contract that may be terminated for cause. But he advised me to make myself scarce when the marriage is declared void. As punishment, if I was deemed the cause, I could be beaten or put in the stocks if the authorities have a mind to. So, I will tell Kate before I leave that she should make a request to authorities in Salem that she be allowed to divorce me on the grounds of my desertion."

"What about Beth?" I asked. David was silent while he considered how to respond.

"Poor Beth is confused. Despite our attempts at civility, she is aware that things aren't right between Kate and me. Sadly, Kate has distanced herself from Beth. She says to protect Beth from the sadness and irritation she feels towards me and the situation. Luckily, Annie is there and provides her with maternal comfort. Beth felt discarded but Annie told her that Abigail adores and looks up to her. She said that Beth has a huge responsibility to guide Abigail, advise and protect her as the elder sister."

"What does Beth think about such a responsibility? I thought she was devoted to James."

David laughed. "I think Beth realizes that James is in a world of his own. Exceedingly polite but distant. Another sadness for Beth now alleviated, thanks to Annie."

I shook my head. So much goes on without me being aware. We

reverted to discussing David's departure. I told him that he should sail back to England on a boat that we knew would be leaving at the end of the month, by which time he would have put in six weeks hard work with Gavan building New Barrow Farm.

I let Annie know what he had said about Kate getting a divorce. She said she had guessed as much, and that Kate should stay with us until she decided what she wanted to do. However, Annie felt that Johnny and Jeannie, expecting as they were, should really have a place of their own. Therefore, an additional smaller house needed be built for them. Back at Shawmut, I saw Kate leading one of our cows, Ruth, back from the Blackstone bull. I imagined Ruth's normally placid demeanor hid a sense of satisfaction from the service provided. Kate said the event went well. Naomi's turn would come next week. That meant we should expect calves in January next year. Kate seemed content. I didn't ask about her and David. I would leave that to Annie. Nor did I have words with Giles. They were adults. They would sort their own lives into whatever order worked for them.

David and I spent the weeks before he left discussing what he needed to do and what I hoped he would be able to accomplish while in England. I wanted him to spend some time in Dorchester. He needed to find out from P. what he understood the plans to be for New England and what participation he retained with all the changes to the governing structure. I gave him a bundle of my journal entries to give to Will. The sale of Barrow Farm should have been completed but I told David I would be grateful if he could help Will resolve any outstanding issues there might be. He should also visit Mr. Scroud in Plymouth. I needed to know if he had made or planned to make arrangements to work with a correspondent business agent in New England. If I was to build a business here, I would need access to credit facilities. Regarding Sir F., David should find out what his intentions were with respect to New England. I saw no possible advantage to Sir F. in his attempts to overturn or influence the inevitable success of the Massachusetts Bay Company. What future he had in New England could only be in Maine.

Then there was the *Argossy*. After the first excitement of being offered ownership, some doubts had started to prick my enthusiasm. She was a large merchantman of some 350 tons, capable of carrying three times the freight of the *Sweet Rose*, with a related increase in crew, armaments, and running costs. I talked to David about what we needed and what we would find most cost effective. I argued that something similar to the *Sweet Rose* would be ideal. David thought otherwise.

"Isaac, I have some questions. What freight do you plan to ship from here? My understanding is that your primary interest is in lumber. The more lumber you can ship at a time the more profitable it will be."

"Lumber, yes, but also dried fish and fur pelts."

"And what do you expect to import?"

"Good question. Over the next few years there will be a huge increase in the number of settlers. The natural resources here are unlimited except for one thing, livestock. Cattle, horses, pigs, goats, and sheep will all be needed in large numbers to feed the settlers and to build self-sustainability. Then there are the manufactured tools that will be needed, domestic and farm. Eventually, the quantity of livestock brought in will enable farmers to continue to build their herds from their own breeding animals, local manufacturing of essential tools, with locally mined raw materials. Our imports will transition from these basic commodities to meet the needs of a thriving population, looking for improvement in their quality of life."

"Isaac, everything you say points to a need for a boat with large carrying capacity."

"That's debatable. For the next few years, we will be trading with different settlements along the New England coastline, even down as far as Jamestown, as well as to Bermuda and the islands of the Caribbean. We have to be flexible and responsive to ever-changing opportunities. It takes longer to fill a large boat and restricts our freedom to follow the trade. I also think you rather like the idea of commanding a larger boat."

David laughed.

"You're right. I will look for another *Rosie*. I take it, you want me to ship a hold-full of livestock as soon as we have the right boat?"

"Yes. Before you leave, I will have talked to Kate and produced a shopping list for you. She has kept a close eye on livestock shipments and sales. She will know what is needed."

Having agreed to look for a buyer for the *Argossy* and use the proceeds to find a more suitable alternative, once the right boat was found, surveyed, acquired, and fitted out for transatlantic trade, David should rebuild his relations with local traders and ask Mr. Scroud to explore further business opportunities for trade with New England. I felt certain there were good prospects with Bermuda. They needed lumber of all kinds for construction and ship building. David said he might return to New England via Bermuda with freight for Bermuda and to load up with cedar, sugar, rum, and whatever else they were exporting.

"No," I told him.

"I want you to send back by another boat, as much livestock as you can put together. You need to buy and arrange shipment as soon as you arrive in England. We need cattle to sell over here. We also need more cows, as well as a couple of oxen and horses of our own, which are in short supply. The extra items, you should bring back with you. We can't wait for you with all that you have to do before you return, but we want you back as soon as possible. Again, I will defer to Kate to provide a detailed list for you."

I met with Kate and we discussed what cattle were good for the import trade. She said the North Devon breed was by far the best for New England. Smaller, more placid, disease resistant, fodder tolerant, producing excellent meat and rich milk. We should be importing heifers and bullocks, easier to ship across, more likely to survive the crossing. The bullocks were good for meat, could be castrated for oxen, while they were still young, or they could be used for breeding. Pigs, she thought we should stay clear of, they were destructive and needed too much foraging space. If our goats were anything to go by, the numbers already imported would suffice, expanding through reproduction. She felt we should concentrate on the cows. With respect to our own needs; three oxen, North Devon, allowing for one loss on the voyage. Horses, depending on what I wanted them for, should be young, well-gaited if they were to be ridden, or bulky if they were to be worked. I thought the former, as we would have oxen for the latter. I suggested that she needed a large dog to help protect the livestock from wolves. Kate said it would need to be a mastiff, All this I passed on to David before he left for England. I also gave him letters for the Patriarch, Mr. Scroud, and Will Whiteway.

CHAPTER 28

Journal entry – *May – June 1630*

By mid-May Gavan, with help from Johnny and me, had built the chimney, completed the walls, floors and shingled roof of New Barrow Farm and had begun to plaster the inside walls, lathing splints covered in a clay and straw mix. We had spent the previous winter under thatch, which became a sodden mess by Spring. Gavan agreed that a shingled roof was the only way to go.

We were spending most of our time there. Annie and the three children planned to stay permanently. Johnny had moved the heavily pregnant Jeannie to New Barrow. Annie was comfortably predicting an August birth. She and Jeannie had started a new vegetable garden and a small orchard of apple and plum saplings that William Blackstone had given her with comprehensive instructions about starting an orchard—pollination and good soil being the keys. He had also advised us to build a secure chicken house inside the orchard with a sturdy fence around the whole orchard. He would supply us with some chickens.

Annie had also made herself known to Chogan's squaw, who was called Kimi. After a shy start the relationship had blossomed. Kimi and other women would come to New Barrow Farm and help Annie and Jeannie develop their garden. I was sure their primary interest was to see the tools we used and to learn about the seeds Annie was planting. James offered his services as translator. By so doing his Abenaki vocabulary continued to increase. The women were amazed and pleased. Kimi asked if James would visit her back in her village on a regular basis so he could teach her English. Surely, Annie suggested, her husband Chogan spoke good English, could he not teach her. He's too busy, was her reply. Perhaps Chogan was proud of the English he had and did not want to share it with her. Kimi also confirmed that Jeannie was due in August and the baby was well. Jeannie was comfortable enough to allow Kimi to examine her.

Gavan said the house and stable would be finished by the beginning of June. I needed to return to Shawmut. We needed to plan for our departure. Kate was not prepared to move until the weather improved and the conditions were right to transport the animals. I needed to contact Stephen Hopkins to hire his pinnace. We would use it to transport all our belongings as well. The land on which we had built our house at Shawmut belonged to William Blackstone. However, the house and stables were ours. I needed to sell or rent them to another settler, approved, of course, by William. I would talk to Governor Endecott. I also wanted to find out what was happening in Salem ahead of the expected arrival of the Winthrop fleet.

A few nights before I left for Salem and Shawmut, Annie and I moved our palliasses from our camp site into our new unfinished bedroom for a last night alone before I left her for what was likely to be several weeks. Our lovemaking was gentle and prolonged. Afterwards, nestled in my arms, Annie whispered.

"My love. I'm pregnant."

I gave a long sigh. Annie raised herself on an elbow and with a look of consternation asked me what was wrong. I pulled her back down and kissed her.

"Annie, my dearest love, it was a sigh of happiness. It will be wonderful to be able to grow our family in our new home. A new chapter in our lives with so much to look forward to."

Annie relaxed and said she was about three months gone. My calculations pointed to our memorable and celebratory night after we received the news from England. Annie smiled and said something had happened that night, different and more profound. She felt it deep down and had thought on what it meant.

I told Annie I would take Johnny and James with me. James loved sailing, a born sailor. I wanted him to have as much experience as possible. It won't be too long and he will want to go to sea. Annie and I had often talked about James' future. It seemed inevitable that once we had our own merchant ship under David Tremaine's command, James would want to enlist as a cabin boy. Annie had always demurred, saying he was too young. I reminded her that James was a mature ten-year-old, eleven in December. Cabin boys started when they were between ten and twelve, as Johnny Dawkins did. Annie changed the subject by asking me why I didn't walk to Salem, twenty-five miles at most. A day's walk with a good Indian trail to follow. I had always wanted to explore that trail. The time would come when I would want a more convenient and quicker route to Salem than by boat. But now I needed *Rosie* to get to Shawmut. I also had other ports of call to make.

On a late May clear and warm morning, Johnny, James, and I sailed down the Merrimack River out into the bay and headed southeast for Cape Ann with a steadily increasing on-shore breeze as the land warmed under the sun. By late afternoon we had reached the inlet to the bay where David and I had camped on our first trip to explore the Merrimack River, and spent the night. By late the following day we were close to Salem, mooring off an island in the bay and making another camp. James had manned the helm regularly throughout the two days sail. Determined as he was, tiredness, flagging concentration and a young body meant I kept him to thirty minute spells with a two hour rest in between. Father and son had two days of close companionship—no distractions other than sailing *Rosie*. James described his days with Nootau and Ahanu. They had explored the whole area around New Barrow, as well as spending time with the Indians in their village. James had been teaching English to Kimi. Other villagers had joined them. James said he was learning more than he was teaching, but everyone seemed to enjoy the experience. We also talked about his schooling. Johnny and Annie had been conscientious about teaching the children to read, write, and do their sums. James said that Abigail was much smarter than him or Beth. He admitted that competition not to be bested by his young sister spurred him on. He asked about David's absence. I told him what we had planned and that we expected to start trading in our own merchant ship by next year.

"Daddy, you and Johnny went to sea when you were young, didn't you? Johnny, you said that that Daddy even saved your life?"

Johnny nodded, but stayed out of the conversation.

"I want to go to sea too. Uncle David has told me so many stories about his life sailing that I can't wait."

I smiled and said we needed to wait until Uncle David returned before making such an important decision.

Next morning. we sailed to Salem and beached Rosie at our favorite spot on the South River. Johnny stayed with *Rosie*, while I took James to the Gardner house, where Tom and Charlie were playing. They ran to greet us and were quick to take James away. Thomas Gardner was mending a fishing net and offered me a log to sit on as he continued mending. He told me it had been a rough winter at the new settlement. The Old Planters had survived but had been worn down in their attempts to help the new settlers. Over eighty people had died, the bodies stacked in huts until the ground was soft enough to dig graves. There was little food, everything edible had been eaten, perhaps one unintended outcome was that with so many deaths the survivors were all housed adequately. When the new Governor arrived, he was going to be in for a shock. Charlestown was in the same sorry state. I asked him how Governor Endecott was managing.

"I think the Governor has learnt a great deal this winter and is much the better for it. He has been humbled and acknowledges the fact. However, with the Reverend Skelton at his elbow he seems to have become a firm Separatist. Dr. Fuller, whenever he comes up from Plimouth, pushes the Separatist's creed, as well."

After exchanging accounts of our respective families' activities and our housebuilding on the Merrimack, I asked if I could leave James with them while I went to see the state of the new settlement for myself. I was horrified at what I saw. So much worse than when I was last back in February. The people looked as if they were starving, thin and wretched. Every household had lost members to sickness, the cold, and malnutrition. There had been scant time and few resources to repair and clean the settlement. With the warmer weather, efforts were beginning to be made. I sought a meeting with the Governor, but he was away at Charlestown. I did meet William Trask, thinner and greyer, who welcomed me. He had little further to tell me beyond what I had already heard. Endecott had been a revelation during this troubled winter. Whatever his shortcomings, he had been an inspirational leader. He had shown how much he cared for his community and they, in turn, respected him. Trask did tell me that he was aware that my colleague, David Tremaine, had been cited in a divorce petition made by his wife, which had caused quite a stir, more so from the Anglican community than from the Puritans, it must be said. I asked what the process was to obtain a divorce. Trask didn't know. While he understood the Puritan view was that marriage was a civil not a religious contract, no formal process had yet been put in place. Bradford had ruled that divorces should be determined by the court. But that would need to be confirmed by the Governor's Council. Given the weight of business before the council and the general distaste for divorces anyway, he doubted the rules would be established and confirmed for some time. It seemed that Kate was in for a long wait. I told Trask about our move to the Merrimack. He had been aware that we had been planning the move. I asked him to pass on to the Governor that we would be completing the move, hopefully, before the end of June. I also said we had a house and stable to dispose of, sited on Rev. William Blackstone's land. I would welcome a reasonable offer to purchase the dwelling. He said he would pass the information on.

I returned to the Gardners', collected a now muddy and tattered James—his tree climbing had resulted in torn clothes and scraped hands but oh! so happy and we sailed to Shawmut. I told him to jump into the water when we got there, clothes and all, so he could arrive back at the house clean, if wet. Kate was waiting for us when we returned. Giles had told her he had recognized *Rosie* approaching. She asked how everything was proceeding at New Barrow. I gave her a full description. She asked about Beth. She was wistful, perhaps remembering the years gone by when she and her daughter were so close. I comforted her and told them how excited Beth was about all the new experiences. She had sent her love and hoped to see Kate soon. I gave her a short, laboriously written note that Beth had written to her Mum just before we left her.

Kate had heard from Blackstone that the Winthrop fleet was expected to arrive within a few weeks. She was concerned, knowing my desire to be away from Shawmut before they arrived. The animals were ready to be moved. I needed to obtain transport as soon as possible. The next day, James and I sailed down to Plimouth. Stephen Hopkins was found and, after some negotiation and confirmation from Governor Bradford, agreed to bring his pinnace to Shawmut the following week to help us move. James and I spent the night as guests of Isaac Allerton. We paid our respects to the Governor thanking him for helping us. He wished us well and we sailed back to Shawmut. Kate was alerted. She, Giles and Johnny would start the process of preparing to move animals and our belongings to New Barrow. I needed to get back to New Barrow and make sure Annie and Gavan were prepared for our arrival. Johnny sailed me to Salem, dropping me off on the northern bank of the North River. I told him I would be back in three days. I found the Indian trail that would take me north towards Agawam before branching off towards the Indian village by New Barrow. I was in a hurry to reach home. I did not pay sufficient attention to my surroundings, bedeviled by flies and mosquitos, I was distracted as I strode through the sometimes wild, sometimes marshy countryside. I wanted to spend more time exploring this land of opportunity, but the time to dawdle was when the insects had gone.

At New Barrow, I found Gavan had been true to his word. House and stable ready. He had begun to build a small house for the Dawkinses. I told Annie and Gavan that animals and belongings were being shipped next week. Gavan and Giles had built a paddock, close to the stable, in a corner of a large meadow of about five acres. He needed to complete the fencing before the animals arrived. There was plenty of grass available, both close to the stable, in the meadow, and down on the marsh. Annie had the time to determine how everything would be placed and stored once it arrived. We could land everything on the Erichuck stream and use the pregnant cows to haul the cart we brought with us, fully loaded, up to New Barrow. I went with Gavan down to the mouth of the Erichuck, along the northern bank. Where the bank dropped to about six feet, I suggested a landing stage there would help us offload the cattle. We had taken soundings previously and knew the water was deep enough for the pinnace. Gavan agreed. The rest of the day, we cleared the trees, cut the suitable ones to size and sunk them into the water close to the bank. Gavan said that by the time we got back with the pinnace he would have the posts braced, framed and deck added. The following morning, happy that everything was in hand, I hugged Annie and strode back the way I had come, arriving back at the North River, opposite Salem, late afternoon. Johnny was waiting for me. He said he had been there since noon and had walked among the cultivated fields the Old Planters had established there. It was clear that they were moving away from Salem to avoid the crush of the new arrivals.

Johnny, Kate, Giles, and James had been busy. A pile of our furniture, boxes, crates, and bags had been started near the beach. More piles had been put together ready to be carted down from the house. Stephen would be there in two days. I went to visit with William Blackstone. He had been a most obliging and generous host. We had reciprocated regular supper gatherings. While he preferred his solitude, he enjoyed the occasional sound of happy children, if they were distant. Now it was time to say farewell. He was charming but I felt relieved his idyllic space would return to its previous peace, if only for a short time. He hoped he would have a month or so to recover but was certain he would not be allowed to continue his isolation. He admitted that it would be wrong, given the obvious needs of the gathering settlers. Rather than wait for the inevitable, he said that at a convenient time he would meet with the new Governor and offer him Shawmut. While he hoped to retain the acreage he had cultivated, he was realistic about the possibility that he would have to move on, moving south and away from the Puritan crowds in search of the peace he craved. I told him that the house and stables we had built were to be sold or rented out. He said he would help that process. He had no interest in them, himself. I thanked him and wished him well, hoping we would meet up again. A gentle man, I was fond of him and his unworldliness.

Stephen Hopkins arrived with crew on his pinnace. The cows were persuaded to wade out into the water till just their heads were showing, close to the side of the pinnace. They were hoisted aboard, heads covered by sacks, lowered, and tethered in the hold with ample bedding and fodder for the journey. The goats, Amos, Nanna, and Beatrice with the kids, Two and Eight, (Five, Six, and Seven had been sold), and our pile of belongings were ferried on *Rosie* to the pinnace and stowed in the hold and when full wrapped and tied in a tarpaulin and secured on deck. The last item aboard was our cart. With waves to the solitary figure of William watching us from the top of the hill, we turned and began our journey and the start of the next chapter of our life in New England.

CHAPTER 29

Journal entry – *June 1630*

We left Shawmut in the early afternoon and five hours later anchored in Beauport Harbor for the night. It gave us a chance to settle the animals in the hold. We all slept on deck under a star filled heaven. We weighed anchor with the dawn and worked our way out of the harbor under an early morning mist with a southerly breeze, the indistinct glow of the sun in our eyes as we turned east to round the Cape and its attendant islands. Bread, cheese, and a beaker of ale were served to each of us, watered down for the children. By midday we were entering the Merrimack River at slack tide, the day now warm, the sea calm with the darker patches of ripples disturbed by the occasional passing southerly breeze. It took us two hours to make our way to the Erichuck. Turning into the stream, we saw Gavan, Annie, Jeannie, Beth, and Abigail waiting for us on the completed landing stage. The pinnace made fast, greetings exchanged, our freight was unloaded. Our belongings were moved away from the landing stage to allow the animals to be hoisted and cleared away from the boat. We cleared the bedding and remaining fodder from the hold and Stephen, anxious to return to Plimouth, was quick to wish us well and ready the pinnace for departure. I thanked him and paid him our agreed amount. As I disembarked, Stephen called out to me.

"Isaac, sorry I forgot. Your man Grindle has turned up again in

Plimouth. Only, he has changed his name to Carson. Someone had told him that I was leaving for Salem to do a job for you. He came up to the boat just as we were casting off and asked me if that was true. I told him I didn't know what he was talking about and left him standing there. So, you might be seeing him."

The pinnace was poled out of the stream and catching the breeze and the current turned and disappeared downstream. Damn, I thought. We needed to prepare.

Gavan had fashioned a yoke with leather harnesses which we used to hitch the uncomplaining cows to our cart. Kate was less than happy that her pregnant cows were being treated as dumb oxen. But Giles stilled the complaint with a quiet word. Startled, Annie and I looked at each other with raised eyebrows. Now that was an interesting development in their relationship. The cart couldn't fit all our belongings so leaving the remainder for a second trip we led our goats up the path and along the trail to New Barrow Farm with the temporary oxen plodding along behind, a solicitous Kate and Giles at their heads. A pen had been prepared for the goats and while the children fussed over them, we unloaded the cart and carried each item to the house where Annie directed us where to place it. The empty cart, with oxen, was then sent back to fetch the remainder of the load, led by Kate and Giles. Gavan followed behind to help load the cart.

I took Annie and Johnny aside at a convenient moment and told them what Stephen had said. They both looked serious. Johnny's immediate reaction was to want to find and deal with the threat, head on. No, I said. We need to set a trap and entice him into it. Annie wondered who the businessman was that Grindle was meant to be meeting in New Amsterdam. Could it be Hook, she pondered, aloud.

"Johnny, I want you to get to Salem as soon as you can—take the Indian trail, find a boat to take you to Plimouth. Grindle has no idea of who you are. Find him and gain his interest, even confidence, that you are a disgruntled former acquaintance of mine. I don't believe he knows we are on to him being Seth, so we have an advantage. Use your initiative to lure him to Salem. Prior to going to Plimouth, see if you can assemble a welcome for Grindle, ready to apprehend him for my attempted murder. I'm not sure Endecott would want anything to do with it, but I need him detained for as long as possible, so we have time to discover who is behind his attempts to kill me. It will allow us to put the fear of God into him against any further attempts to do me damage."

Annie was concerned I was putting Johnny in danger. Johnny was quick to ease her fears.

"I'm an actor, Annie. In my role as Isaac's foe, I will pose no threat to Grindle. I aim to make him want my reluctant friendship to help him gain access to Isaac. This is a task I will relish."

Before dawn the next day Johnny, having promised the pregnant Jeannie he would be back in a week and been bid a fond and tearful farewell, disappeared down the trail to walk the twenty-five miles to Salem. A light rain would keep him cool on what promised to be a warm early summer's day.

On his return four days later, he told me what had happened.

Upon arrival that same evening in Salem he sought out Thomas Gardner and begged the stable loft for the night. Johnny had a long conversation with Thomas covering all that we had discussed about Grindle before Johnny left for Salem and asked whether there was any way that Grindle could be detained without Endecott being informed. After all, he would be so distracted by the imminent arrival of Winthrop that he would pay little heed to someone arrested and kept in a cell for a few days. Thomas said he would talk to Trask and Conant. Boats were sailing between Salem and Plimouth on a regular basis. Johnny was quick to obtain a ride the following morning. Arriving in Plimouth in the late afternoon, he sought out Stephen Hopkins, who was pleased to see him again. Johnny told him his tale and Stephen said he would be happy to help. Grindle was in Plimouth and clearly anxious about something, presumably to do with Isaac Stanfield. Johnny explained that it was important for Grindle to seek Johnny's reluctant help in finding Stanfield, so Stephen needed to tell Grindle that Johnny was the man he needed to speak to. Stephen offered Johnny accommodation for the night. The next morning Johnny wandered down to the landing stage and found a fishing boat that agreed to take him back to Salem. It would be leaving later that morning. He then waited, watching the activity in the harbor. A little later, he was approached by a stranger.

"Are you Dawkins?"

A thin, clean-shaved, angular-faced man stood a few paces off, examining Johnny. He was curt, unfriendly, awkward. Johnny turned and asked who wanted to know with casual disdain. Without waiting for an answer, he turned back to look out over the harbor.

"My name's Carson. I understand you know a man called Stanfield."

Johnny turned slowly back to Carson. He looked like the description he had of Grindle but without the beard. Johnny said he had no interest in talking about that bastard, Stanfield, and walked away. After a moment, Carson followed.

"Why don't you like him? What's he done to you?"

Johnny didn't answer.

"Do you know where he is?"

Johnny asked why he wanted to know. Carson said he had an important message to give him. Johnny shrugged and said that it was no concern of his or reason to stir himself, especially if it meant being of service to Stanfield.

"It's not of service to Stanfield."

"What do you mean?"

"It's a threatening message."

"Threatening! That sounds more interesting. Are you threatening him?"

"No. I have to deliver the message."

"Do you know what the message says?"

"Yes. It isn't written. I have it memorized."

"What's the threat?"

"I can't tell you, but it is dire."

"What does that mean?"

"I can't tell you."

Johnny shook his head. He made it plain he wasn't interested. Carson saw his chance of getting to me was fading. He pleaded.

"Can you at least tell me how to reach him?"

"What are you going to do if you do find him?"

"Give him the message."

"And if he rejects the message?"

Carson shrugged. Johnny stared at him in disbelief.

"You go through all that effort to find Stanfield. You deliver a threatening message and when he throws it back in your face, as he is sure to, you do nothing? What! you walk away? You just go back to the man who sent you and tell him? Ridiculous. You're wasting my time. Go away."

"I've been told to kill him."

"Kill him! Who the hell has such a hold over you that you are prepared to kill on command and probably be caught and hung for it? Who sent you?"

"I can't tell you."

"If you say those words one more time, I will have nothing further to do with you. What's in it for me if I help you? I have no time for Stanfield, but don't fancy being hung as an accomplice to his murder. More to the point what's in it for you?"

"I will be rewarded."

"How much?"

"Enough. If you help me and I'm paid, I'll give you £10."

Johnny laughed. He said it wasn't enough. He told Carson he didn't believe him, anyway. His story was a fable. A mysterious man promises to pay Carson for the highly risky action of killing someone. Why would he agree to do such a thing? Johnny told him he didn't believe the man existed.

"The man's name is Doncker, a Dutchman in New Amsterdam. Stanfield owes him a great deal of money. I agreed to help Doncker in payment of a debt I have."

"What debt?"

"My life was saved."

Johnny turned and looked back across the harbor as if in deep thought, then said,

"For £20, I will take the risk of helping you but only so far. I am about to leave for Salem. Once there, I will find out where Stanfield is and tell you. How do I get word to you?"

"I'll come with you."

Johnny had guessed right. Carson or Grindle or Seth, whatever his name was, wasn't going to let Johnny out of his sight. The fishing boat that Johnny had organized was waiting and sailed shortly after the two of them were aboard, Carson carrying a heavy canvas bag. Johnny realized that Grindle had changed his name, aware that his name was probably known in Salem, thanks to Beamish.

Approaching Salem, there was much activity on the water. Small boats, lighters, shallops filled with people were scurrying about the bay and harbor. It seemed the arrival of the Winthrop fleet was expected. The fishing boat took Johnny and Carson to the town dock on the South River, where they disembarked and walked into town, Carson nervous, with a large cavalier hat pulled down on his head covering much of his face. Johnny said nothing but thought he looked suspiciously like someone who did not want to be recognized. Carson asked where they were going. "To find out where Stanfield might be", was the reply. Johnny hoped to see Trask or Gardner. Trask found them first.

"Ah! Mr. Dawkins. What are you doing here? With the expected arrival of the new Governor, we are restricting access to the town. Anyone not known to us will be asked to leave, on pain of being detained until they can be vouched for. Who's this with you? I don't know him."

Johnny looked at Carson and said he had shared a boat ride with him from Plimouth. Trask waited for the man to speak.

"I'm Carson."

"Where do you come from? Why are you in Salem?"

"I'm travelling from New Amsterdam. I'm going to Charlestown."

"What's in your bag?"

Carson looked increasingly uncomfortable. Personal effects, he said. Trask took the bag; Carson was loathe to let it go.

"Heavy, open it."

Carson opened the bag. Trask looked inside, put his hand in the bag and lifted out a flintlock pistol. He looked at Johnny who appeared bewildered at the sight. He turned to a burly man behind him and said, "Seize him". Before Carson could react, his arms were pinned behind him. Trask told Johnny to remove himself from Salem and informed Carson he was being detained in the town gaol until he could prove his innocent intent. The protesting Carson was led away. So much for the £20. After he was gone, Johnny shook Trask's hand and thanked him. Trask grinned and said it was a pleasure and to wish Stanfield well, after which Johnny left Salem immediately and made his way back to New Barrow Farm, arriving in the late evening, when we had settled in for the night.

── CHAPTER 30 ──

Journal entry – *June 1630*

After he finished telling us his story, Johnny leaned back and quenched his thirst from a refilled tankard of ale I had thrust into his hand. I congratulated him, Annie gave him a hug, and Jeannie kissed him, still in tears of relief at his safe return. It was late, Annie shooed Jeannie off to bed and with a kiss told me she was retiring too. Johnny, still exhilarated from his adventure, wanted to talk about the ramifications of what he had learnt.

What struck me was the way Grindle had described the debts. He didn't say he or I owed Doncker the debts. Johnny agreed. He realized immediately that Doncker was an intermediary. Someone else thinks I owe him some enormous debt and had saved Grindle's life. I needed to go and see Grindle and find out if he's Seth. He would certainly be motivated to hunt me down and would have grabbed the chance to kill me. Johnny said there was something that puzzled him. Assuming Grindle was Seth, he could understand his past attempts to kill me. But if he was delivering a message, demanding a pay-back on behalf of someone else, why would he have made the earlier attempts? Perhaps, I said, he met up with Doncker only after he had escaped from Salem to New Amsterdam following his attempt with Beamish.

I asked Johnny how Jeannie was. He was surprised at my question, he had been away, then realized what I was alluding to.

"I'm terrified, quite honestly. I try to stay busy, keep my mind occupied on something, anything else. I dread the birthing process but am longing for a healthy wife and baby at the end of it."

What a frightening burden. He was carrying it alone. I was of no help. I longed to confide in Annie but Johnny was still adamant that no one should know of his fears.

The next morning, I left for Salem. Winthrop had arrived earlier that day. Late evening the crowds were still milling about and the noise was deafening, largely confined to the new town. I went to see Gardner at his home in the old settlement. He was pleased to see me. Trask had told him what had happened. He said I would find it difficult to fight my way through the crowds to get to the gaol. Best to wait till morning. I agreed and we spent a pleasant evening together. He had plans to move his family across the North River to join the exodus of Old Planters away from Salem. He had fields there which he and the other Old Planters had been allotted by Endecott. His wife and the boys had already gone a few days earlier to avoid the expected chaos of the Winthrop arrival but would be back later when everything had calmed down.

Early next morning, Sunday, 13 June, I walked to the new town and made my way to the gaol. I was met by a warder who asked me my business. I told him I was aware that a stranger by the name of Carson had been detained. I believed I knew the man and had come to identify him. "That would have been useful," the warder replied. I looked surprised.

"Carson is no longer here," he explained. "He was released, yesterday, into the hands of Mr. Maverick, who vouched for him. He said he was taking him back to his property and would ensure he was kept secure. We were pleased to see the back of him. An unpleasant whining sod. It also meant our holding cell was vacated."

"Maverick?"

I wandered off into the gathering crowd. Everyone wanted to catch a glimpse of the new Governor. I bumped into Mr. Trask. He and I apologized before we recognized each other. He said that the crowds were going to be disappointed. Mr. Winthrop and his party had been ashore the previous evening but were back on board the *Arabella*, anchored out in the bay in the lee of an island, where he planned to celebrate the Sabbath on board. He was not expected back ashore till the next day. Trask said he had helped Mr. Dawkins a few days previously, detaining the man Grindle, although he gave his name as Carson. I said I had just been to the gaol to talk to him but was advised that Mr. Maverick had taken him away, yesterday. Trask was surprised too. He hadn't heard. He knew that Maverick had been invited to attend the welcoming meal for the Governor yesterday evening, so it must have been earlier in the day. Trask was looking over my shoulder while he spoke and suddenly stopped talking. He caught my arm and said, "There's Maverick now."

I said,

"Attract his attention and ask him why he had taken Carson. I do not want to participate in the conversation, I want to find out what Maverick knew without me appearing to have any interest."

Trask nodded and called out to Maverick.

"Mr. Maverick, good morning to you. I believe you know Mr. Stanfield."

We greeted each other civilly, although I thought Maverick was somewhat cold. Trask said he had heard the stranger, Carson, that he, Trask, had detained, had been released into Maverick's hands. Maverick replied that Trask's action was unfortunate, as Carson was a business acquaintance of his. Trask bridled at the criticism and said Carson had behaved suspiciously and did not explain himself other than saying he was travelling from New Amsterdam to Charlestown. He also had a pistol in his baggage. Armed strangers in Salem on the eve of the arrival of the new Governor were a possible threat and needed to be dealt with. Maverick apologized and mollified Trask by agreeing he had done the right thing in the circumstances. Trask then said that when Carson was apprehended, he had been accompanied by Mr. Dawkins who had met Carson in Plimouth. It seemed Dawkins was surprised when Carson said he was going to Charlestown. He thought he was going elsewhere. Maverick shrugged. He turned to me, "Dawkins works for you, doesn't he?" I said he did although not now. We have a difference of opinion which needs to be resolved. He asked whether I had talked to Dawkins about Carson. I replied that if I do talk to Dawkins, sometime in the future, I didn't see why I should want to talk about this Carson person. He seems to be an acquaintance of Dawkins. I changed the subject by asking Maverick if he did business in New Amsterdam.

"Why?" he asked. "I'm building a business and looking for trading contacts," I said.

Maverick said he had and gave me the name of a trader called Anton Hoekstra. He asked what my business was.

"Lumber. I plan to build a sawmill on my property which has extensive coverage of oak, pine, and locust."

Maverick looked interested.

"How much property do you have?" he asked.

"Two hundred acres."

"How did you come by that amount?"

I thought the question impertinent and said so. Maverick looked angry. Trask, to ease the tension, asked what had happened to Carson. Maverick said he had gone back to New Amsterdam. With that and a nod to Trask, a dismissive wave of his hand in my direction, he disappeared into the crowd.

Trask grimaced.

"Do I get the impression that Mr. Maverick is not disposed to be friendly with you?"

"It certainly seems that way. Which is a pity. I wonder why?"

Trask thought for a moment.

"I think he is aware that Carson is Grindle and knows where he was going. I'm sure Carson told him that Dawkins was helping him and possibly gave Dawkins more information than he should have. Maverick has to assume that no matter what your relationship with Dawkins is, some of that information might have been passed on to you. In which case, Mr. Stanfield, you need to be vigilant. Because, if what I surmise is true, Maverick might be behind the attempts on your life. He also suspects we know or think Carson is Grindle and has whisked him away before he is interrogated and reveals all."

I thanked Trask for his advice and help, thinking there were wider ramifications that I needed to deal with. I could do nothing more in Salem. Time to go home.

I arrived back at New Barrow late. After a hot meal and nursing a second glass of wine, I sat with Annie. I had covered my visit to Salem during the meal. I was interested in hearing her thoughts. Annie's first reaction was that Maverick was still upset with us from when we met him and Amyse with our questioning about David Thomson's death and their relationship prior to that. It seemed he had covered his tracks well and was worried we might be uncovering them. At the time, I thought Maverick was an opportunist, not a murderer. I still thought so. He might not have liked our prying into his private affairs which would have been enough to cool his relationship with us. It seemed that something else was driving him. Annie then commented on the fact that Maverick had been invited to Winthrop's welcoming banquet. It implied he was well in with the new Governor or was attempting to be so. Grindle had convinced Beamish that I was a threat to the new settlement. We thought Grindle was Seth and, out for revenge, acted alone. Had Grindle been influenced by others? Could he have persuaded Maverick likewise? If so, what might such a malign influence have on Winthrop? I reminded her that Grindle had told Johnny about the debt he owed. Wasn't it possible that it was Maverick to whom the debt was owed?

While I saw the problem as a challenge to be dealt with, Annie found it overwhelming. That night in bed, nestled in each other's arms she whispered:

"My dear wonderful man, ever since we started on this new journey two years ago, I have been torn between the thrill of a new adventure, shared with the man I love above all things, and the fear that you might be taken from me. With every unsuccessful attempt on your life, I become more terrified that the next one will kill you. An unknown assailant somehow seems manageable, especially as his obsession is matched by his incompetence. Now we seem to have a more sinister threat, involving more people. It feels as if it is closing in on us."

"Sweet Annie, we must not subside under the weight of an ill-defined threat. We must break that threat down into manageable pieces. We have identified a number of players, each of whom we can deal with. What we don't know is what's driving them. Each player might have their own reason for participating in these attempts. In fact, we can already guess what some of them might be but there has to be an overriding motivation that binds them together. My first task is to find out what is collectively driving them, then we can deal with each of the players separately."

"How do you propose to do that?"

"With Johnny's help, another attempt appears to have been thwarted, we know more about Grindle, we have learned about Maverick's involvement and Doncker, in New Amsterdam, is somehow involved. Yet, there appears to be a malign influence, a driving force behind all this. I need to think deeply and carefully about what I might have done or presumed to have done that could be the cause. Meanwhile, we have work to do at New Barrow Farm. We can't become paralyzed; we have our lives to live."

Annie sighed, we loved and slept.

—— CHAPTER 31 ——

Journal entry – *July 1630*

Gavan had started work on designing his sawmill on the Erichuck River. He had sunk two posts a pace apart, in the river near to the bank. He had then dropped rocks between and in front of the posts, creating a weir, to understand better the effect a wider barrier would have on the water flow. What he wanted to do was build a weir across the river that would raise the height of the river by a foot or so, leaving a channel by the bank unencumbered where the water would be free to flow more strongly and, hopefully, drive a millwheel. He had talked to Chogan about the barrier the weir might have on the freedom of movement of the Indians up and down river. When Gavan had explained what he was attempting to do and that the weir would be no more than a foot high, Chogan was delighted at such an English invention coming to his river and saw no problem moving downstream, with the canoes able to sweep over the weir. Moving upstream, they could slide their canoes by hand round the weir on the bank. However, Gavan realized that by restricting the depth of the river at the site of the sawmill, the flow of water would increase to allow the same quantity of water to flow over the obstacle under the water. If the depth of the river was ten feet, a barrier of rocks on the riverbed just five feet high would double the water flow. If he also narrowed the river at the sawmill by half, the flow would be doubled again. The benefit was that there wouldn't be any surface barrier for the Indians to deal with. With the water flow problem solved, he proceeded to draw the design of his sawmill. It looked complicated, but he told me to think of the design of a capstan on a boat. All he was doing was using water to replace manpower to turn a capstan.

Annie had been keeping an eye on Kate and Giles. They worked well together. The early sign that Giles had assumed a more dominant role in the relationship had become more evident and it seemed to be working well. Kate respected Giles' knowledge and was, clearly, comfortable with him. Annie didn't want to think about their intimacy. They were adults, presumably comfortable in their adultery. Kate had filed for divorce and had told Annie that in her mind she was, as a result, no longer married to the absent David. While their bedroom had been left for Kate to use, it was used by her infrequently. Accommodation had been built above the stable for both Giles and Gavan. For whatever reason, Gavan had built himself a small hut down near the Erichuck River.

The animals seemed to be thriving. Naomi and Ruth, no longer oxen, at least for the time being, had grown fat and happy with the grass in the field at New Barrow. Railings had been installed which could be moved so the cows would not overgraze. The goats were confined to a separate pen.

Johnny was much distracted and distressed by the pregnant Jeannie. Kimi had examined her on an increasingly frequent basis. She was concerned. The baby was big, and Jeannie was small. Jeannie was uncomfortable. Annie and Kate were advised to help Jeannie as much as possible. Massaging her, keeping her cool and confined to her bed. Johnny was frantic and needed to be given a job to do to take his feverish mind off his adored wife. I needed to find out what was going on in Salem. I also wanted to check on Maverick's movements.

I asked Johnny to make the trip. He was assured that Jeannie wasn't due to give birth for at least a month. I wanted Johnny back within a week. I told him that he should maintain the guise that he and I were estranged. He should meet with Trask and advise him accordingly.

Trask was a useful ally for us. He was in a perfect position to watch and report back any adverse comments or actions concerning Stanfield. I told Johnny to tell Trask not to attempt to move to defend me at any time. We needed him to be an impartial observer. It would be easier to gather information from people like Maverick, who would be more likely to let slip something of value if they believed Trask, one of Endecott's council members after all, was indifferent to my fate. I was worried about Maverick and the influence he might have on Winthrop. Johnny should use his natural initiative to track his movements and get a better feel for his apparent negative attitude towards me.

Johnny should also ensure Stephen Hopkins remains an ally. He is similarly well placed to help us in Plimouth. If possible, Johnny should make contact with Morton, give him my regards and ask him to keep in touch with us. Finally, if he has the time, Johnny should visit Charlestown and find out how the Spragues and Walfords are doing. With such a full load, Johnny was able to leave Jeannie and set off for Salem with a semblance of enthusiasm.

I took James with me to visit Chogan. After James bowed to him, he left to meet with his young friends. Chogan greeted me with affection. He said he was pleased that my wife had developed a close friendship with Kimi, his squaw. He also thanked me for allowing James to come to his village. He has taught Kimi English. I said that Kimi and the villagers had also taught him to speak the Abenaki language. Chogan laughed.

"James understands our dialect of the Abenaki language. He must not be discouraged when he finds other Abenaki that he does not understand so well. James is in danger of being adopted. He has a wide circle of friends among our children. He amazes them at how proficient he is with his archery. Even the older villagers are amazed at how mature he is for his age. Are all young Englishmen like him?"

I bowed my head in acknowledgement of his compliments. He asked me what he could do for me.

"Nothing, I came to pay my respects to you and to thank you for all you and your villagers have done to make us so welcome. In fact, I ask whether there is anything you might need from us?"

"No, Isaac. We are happy you are here. We learn as much from you as you do from us."

We talked about the arrival of the new Governor in Salem. Chogan called him the big chief. He said that his Chief, Masconomet, had met with Winthrop on Winthrop's boat when he first arrived before Winthrop moved on to Salem. Chogan reported that the meeting had been a good one and Masconomet stayed with Winthrop for most of the day. I was pleased and said so. Chogan said that Masconomet was pleased that he had been welcomed and was able to spend time with such an important Englishman before he went to his own people to be welcomed. A sign of great respect which was much appreciated.

"For the two chiefs to meet and become friends is important for both our peoples."

The week went quickly, then Johnny was back with us with a story to tell. He first broke the news that Winthrop's son Henry had drowned the day after his arrival from England, which had shocked everyone. Governor Winthrop, apparently, had been most stoic about his loss.

Johnny's last meeting before returning to New Barrow Farm was to have been with Thomas Morton, who was in serious trouble with the new Governor. Seems he has been detained. Winthrop's first court session is planned for late August. Morton will be held until his case can be heard. No one seems to know what he is actually being accused of. Johnny didn't have a chance to see him. He did talk to Trask, who promised to keep his ears and eyes open, and his mouth shut. Johnny said that Trask seemed to relish the idea of being a spy. Trask did say that the new Governor was currently on a tour of the area looking for a better place to establish his base and build a new town for all his settlers. He doesn't like Salem. Maverick is showing him around and will be entertaining him overnight at the end of the tour at his house at Winnesimmet. Trask also said he understood that Maverick is planning to make an overseas trip soon and expects to be away for several months. Johnny was able to see Stephen Hopkins when Stephen was making one of his regular trips to Salem. He told Johnny that he would keep an eye out for Grindle and anyone he was seen associating with. He confirmed that Grindle had returned to Plimouth from Salem and was quick to leave on a boat for New Amsterdam. Stephen said it almost looked like the boat was waiting for him, because it left as soon as Grindle was aboard.

Johnny did get to Charlestown. What a mess, he reported. Winthrop had been there. Didn't like it. Walford told Johnny that they had gone on to Shawmut then explore the coast further south, with the plan to explore up the Charles River as well. Walford was well. Being the resident blacksmith in a town under construction, he remained busy. His Anglican views were causing problems with the authorities, as was his demand that his right to the land granted him by the Council for New England back in 1623 be recognized. Thomas Walford was not one to compromise. However, the need for his skills kept him out of trouble, Johnny wondered for how long. The Spragues were well set in their substantial house. It was a two-acre property at the top of the hill on which Charlestown was located, next to other houses on similar lots, the row of houses in the shape of a crescent looking south, fenced off from the rest of the town. The town had suffered grievously over the past winter with over eighty people dying. They looked over a sprawling town under delayed construction, their houses belying the poor state of the rest of the town with encampments scattered through building sites, tree stumps, dirt, and squalor—no wonder Winthrop looked elsewhere.

Ralph Sprague asked how our search for my assailant was proceeding. Johnny said it was increasingly complicated as there appeared to be levels of intrigue which we were trying to uncover. He asked what he could do to help. Johnny said to be aware of any talk that might hint of participation in a conspiracy against the Stanfields. Ralph remarked that seemed a little overblown and suggested we were being irrationally anxious. Johnny said it was better to be careful than complacent. He asked Ralph whether he knew Maverick. He didn't; but had heard positive things about him. He was well liked. Ralph looked puzzled and asked if Maverick was part of our conspiracy. Johnny realized he had made a mistake and sought to undo any damage he might have done. "No," he said. "Isaac is looking for a trading partner and thought Maverick someone he should approach." Johnny admitted to me that it was a clumsy attempt which seemed to satisfy Ralph. They talked about the business I was establishing, initially lumber. Ralph laughed and said he knew Isaac Stanfield would be back in business before long.

He told Johnny he had just been appointed to be the Charlestown Constable, charged with ensuring the good behavior of the townspeople. Johnny congratulated him. His appointment seemed most opportune. Johnny explained that the mysterious Grindle, a person of interest to Isaac as the probable assailant, while thought to be in New Amsterdam is known to appear locally from time to time. He had possible accomplices. Grindle believed Johnny and Isaac were now enemies and believed Johnny to be an ally. Ralph was quick to recognize what Johnny was saying. "Ah!" he said, "the conspiracy." He promised he would act as if that were the case and would report back anything suspicious. He wished Annie and me well and they parted. Ralph, as an ally, was well placed, especially as he was now rising through the ranks of officialdom.

I would need to meet with him to satisfy myself he would be an effective and loyal ally. With all the changes in the governing structure of the Massachusetts Bay Company and the establishment of many separate towns, there would a myriad allegiances formed and broken until everything settled down.

Johnny had the time to visit William Blackstone and he walked over our old property. Settlers were moving to Shawmut. Our house was being lived in, with rent being paid to Blackstone, who was keeping an account of what needed to be passed on to us. He felt he was likely to be seriously constrained. Land was needed. Shawmut, he felt, was of serious interest to Winthrop as a possible site for his government. In his remarks to Blackstone, when he came to inspect Shawmut, he made it plain that the Shawmut peninsula was much too important a location for Blackstone to claim rights to purely because he happened to be the first to arrive. Johnny said that Blackstone, fully aware of the awful conditions in Charlestown, had already suggested that settlers should come to Shawmut. Unlike Walford, Blackstone was amenable and happy to work for the common good. But he was also much a solitary person, who loved his peace and his books. Therein lay the conflict which Blackstone recognized would probably drive him away from the home he had established and loved since he settled there in 1624.

—— CHAPTER 32 ——

Journal entry – *August 1630*

Johnny was back at New Barrow in five days. Jeannie was overjoyed to see him. She had found his absence stressful. Johnny looked calmer than when he left her. The break from being the expectant father had been good for him. His being calmer also had a soothing effect on Jeannie. Without us having to point that out to him, he realized that his demeanor was an important contributor to Jeannie's well-being.

By early August, we were preparing for what Chogan told us would be a cruel winter. "Worse than last winter?" I asked. "Yes." I didn't ask how he knew. His quiet certainty brooked no questions. I worried about Annie, due in December. Although herself obviously pregnant, she continued to watch over Jeannie, as well as look after all of us. I also worried about the new settlers scattered around what Winthrop was beginning to call Boston and its harbor, from his Lincolnshire connections, presumably. They had not recovered from the horrors and loss of life of that last winter, nor had the time to build substantial housing for everyone. Food was also going to be scarce. Winthrop was well aware and had ordered supplies from England to arrive before winter set in. He was also building his administration and establishing a working government. I was impressed with his energy and diligence. He had created a name for himself as a disciplinarian, fair but occasionally harsh. Winthrop was less impetuous than Endecott, who had decided to stay in Salem among the people he knew. Winthrop gave him the respect and title due to a former governor, which Endecott appreciated.

Jeannie was an increasing cause for concern. Even Kimi was worried. Johnny outwardly stayed calm but when away from Jeannie, which was rarely, he was distraught. "So many babies and their mothers die," he kept repeating. Annie and Kate tried to soothe him, telling him of their own experiences and to look, rather, to the many, many more that survive the experience and go on to have more children, as they both did. The week leading up to Jeannie's confinement became an enclosed space, in which we were all held captive. Our focus was all centered on the bedroom where Jeannie lay, in terrible pain, unable to move. Kimi came every day and brought herbal remedies to ease the pain and to loosen the muscles that seemed to bind her abdomen. Annie and Kate were in constant attendance. I persuaded Johnny, now a wreck, to escape for hours every day. He took James on hunting expeditions, went fishing with Giles, helped Gavan with his building of the sawmill. At night, he lay with Jeannie, with a damp cloth to cool her and wipe the sweat from her body, whispering words of love and comfort.

Early one morning, Kimi arrived with a new herbal remedy. Annie explained it was to help induce labor. The baby needed to be born, Jeannie would not survive otherwise. The men were banished, including Johnny. It might take several days. We left the women and began to scythe the long grass in our meadow to make hay for the winter. The first evening, Kimi, who had come with a woman skilled in medicine and childbirth, left us saying nothing should happen that night, but if it did word should be sent for them to return immediately. The men were told to stay away, so we made camp with the children by the stables. Early next morning, Kate came and told us Kimi was needed. James left immediately to run to the village. It was a long morning. We went back out to the meadow, but we found it difficult to concentrate. Johnny just sat on a pile of hay with his head in his hands, the children sitting with him occasionally touching him to let him know they were there for him. He would look up with tears in his eyes and smile his thanks for their caring. Annie brought out a basket of food and pitchers of water. She had not slept, looked dreadful with red eyes. I took her aside out of Johnny's hearing and asked her what was happening, how was Jeannie? She shook her head. "Not good," was all she said and left. Johnny looked up and saw Annie going back to the house. I went over to him and told him that the women were still working with Jeannie to bring the baby into the world, but it was difficult. "God willing, you will soon have your wife back with a healthy baby."

But it was not to be. The baby was stillborn. Jeannie died an hour later, Kimi and her medicine woman unable to staunch the flow of blood.

—— CHAPTER 33 ——

Journal entry – *September 1630*

We buried Jeannie and her baby in a grove looking over the Merrimack River. A simple ceremony. I read from the Book of Common Prayer. Many villagers came with Chogan and Kimi to pay their respects. They were puzzled by the simplicity of the service but accepted our way. However, Kimi stood over the grave as Jeannie's body, wrapped in a white cloth, with the baby in her arms, was lowered. She held a small bundle of dried tobacco leaves in her hand which she lit and waved the sweet smoke over the grave. Chogan led the villagers in a short, mournful chant accompanied by someone playing a musical pipe. Poor Johnny, who had stood manfully by the grave as his beloved wife and son were laid to rest, responded to the chant by breaking down, sobbing. Annie and Kate put their arms round him, also in tears. The children, wide eyed and holding hands, remained mute and still. James and Abigail were still in shock, unable to comprehend their beloved Jeannie had left them. Beth moved to Abigail and folded her into her arms and they wept together.

Johnny told me he needed some time on his own, packed a shoulder bag, with bow and a quiver of arrows, and walked away heading west. He did not know when he would return and we should not worry about him. I said that when he came back, I had a job for him which would mean him leaving New Barrow for a while. He nodded.

"That would be good."

Johnny returned two weeks later, dirty, tired, and now bearded. He had aged as well. He didn't talk about his journey other than it was his way of sharing the remaining moments of his life with Jeannie before he let her go on her own journey. Over the days following, it was clear Johnny had changed, more introspective, quieter. He seemed to be gathering himself, a different Johnny, to begin a new life. Kate observed that the new Johnny showed a depth to him, previously hidden. He would have no trouble finding his way, especially with women, who would be drawn by the signs of his suffering. Annie thought Johnny was all that a woman might wish for already, but she told me she understood what Kate was saying. It was then I told Annie of Johnny's terror stemming from the loss of his first wife and baby in childbirth, which had long dissuaded him from agreeing to Jeannie's desire for a child. Annie laid her head on my shoulder, sobbing and whispering her grief and compassion.

When Johnny was ready, he approached me about the job I had mentioned to him. He said he was ready to move on. New Barrow had too many memories of Jeannie for him right now. He needed to be elsewhere. I asked him if he would be prepared to move to Salem for an extended period of time, find a job, and join that community. I wanted him to be my eyes and ears, covering the development of Winthrop's administration. It would help if the job he found enabled him to go to the other towns being established around Massachusetts Bay. There were business opportunities that I would normally be pursuing but until Grindle and his backers were dealt with, I wanted to stay clear of any possible entanglement, personal, commercial, or political, which might be damaging. Johnny understood. He said it was an extension of what he had done previously. He would be more than happy to do it. He would use Trask, Gardner, and Sprague as his contacts. I said it would be best not to let anyone else know that we were not in fact estranged. He asked, "What about Walford?" I said that Walford, Blackstone, and Maverick had known each other since they came to New England with Robert Gorges in 1623. They had been friendly with David and Amyse Thomson. I didn't want word to get back to Maverick that Johnny was not what he seemed. He agreed.

With Johnny gone, a few days later, Annie and I had a long discussion. The situation had changed. The house being built for Johnny and Jeannie had been completed. It would now be empty. Giles and Kate were comfortably settled in their relationship. While we had turned a blind eye, the authorities would be disconcerted. Kate had heard nothing back from the Governor's office about her divorce petition. The first court sessions were due to be held this month. What would happen if the petition was denied? Annie said she had asked Kate that. Kate and Giles had discussed that possibility. They would want to stay as long as it was tenable. If the worst came to the worst, they would move further away from authority. They would most certainly not separate. That means they would head north or west, into the wilderness and build a farm for themselves. It also meant we would need to rethink about our plans for a substantial farm here at New Barrow.

Annie frowned and was silent. After a few moments she said, "I think Gavan might want to have better access to other people."

"What do you mean?" I asked.

"He wants a wife. Isaac, my love. Your plans need to be rethought. We have come to this beautiful but isolated spot. We have built a new home. You have been granted 200 acres which you want to farm. You plan to acquire a sizeable sailing ship and become a trader again. You expect to build a lumber exporting business. Am I right?"

I agreed. She continued.

"At the moment, you are being pursued by someone who wants to kill you, seemingly working for someone or more, unknown, who wants you killed. You are worried that Governor Winthrop might be persuaded that you are someone not to be trusted or even worse a traitor. Either way, he could arrest you and if nothing else take your land grant away. David has gone to England, hopefully, coming back with a sailing ship for you. Perhaps, perhaps not. He and Kate were meant to take over and run your farm for you. Now it's Kate and Giles living in adultery and quite possibly, escaping retribution to disappear into the wilderness. Would they take Beth with them? I doubt it. She is now part of our family to all intents. Finally, your lumber man, Gavan, is getting restless and might move on."

"Interesting challenges," I said and laughed. Annie said, "I haven't finished."

"Isaac, we have three children including Beth, another on the way. With dear Jeannie gone and with no community on which we can depend, like we had back in England, we are isolated. Yes, I know we are wonderfully supported by our Indian friends, but it's not the same. We came to New England knowing we were coming with friends. In Salem we were beginning to make more friends. They now have a church, a community to be a part of, something I cherished both in Plymouth and in Bincombe."

I was silent. What Annie said was right. I had been too focused on what I saw as opportunity. Annie, my loving and loyal wife, had followed me, uncomplaining. I needed to keep us in step with each other, not just for me to push ahead and expect her to follow dutifully behind. She was my love, lover, companion and partner in everything. She was there to rein me in. I needed to get her to slow down, too. She should be focusing on her own health and that of the baby she carried. Easier said than done, she was our mother hen.

I asked about the children. With Jeannie gone and Johnny absent, how were they coping, how should their schooling continue? How is Beth? Would they be better off living in a community with other children their age and going to school? Annie said that she had talked to Kate months ago when she saw how Beth was reacting to what she saw as her mother's rejection. Kate was angry but admitted that Beth was much happier enveloped, as she now was, in the Stanfield family. Annie felt the children had been well cared for by Jeannie and Johnny. They enjoyed playing with the Indian children, but they needed proper schooling, mixing and developing friendships with English children. The Indians taught them valuable lessons, but they would be growing up in world that was predominantly English. They should not grow apart from that cultural heritage.

I pointed out that there were new towns being established around Massachusetts Bay and up the many rivers that flowed into the Bay.

"Those towns will eventually have their own churches, schools, and governing structure. Only Salem currently has these. It won't be long before settlers will spread to locations north of Cape Ann, following the same compulsion that drove us here. They too will establish towns that have churches and schools over the next few years."

Annie whispered that it would still be a long time for the children to wait. I went on,

"Beth is now eleven years old, James ten, and Abigail seven. With Johnny back with us in a month or two, schooling can continue as before until such time as Johnny moves on. At that time, we can decide what we should do. The circumstances could be different. Impossible to plan for. The children had already been taught to read and write. Beth and Abigail were probably well in advance in their education of any the other girls they might school with in the future, if, in fact, girls were even being schooled to the same extent as the boys. As for James, it won't be long before he wants to go to sea. I'm most concerned that he learns to fend for himself. I will continue to teach him defensive skills and Johnny's made a fine bowman out of him, which he continues to practice with his Indian friends."

Annie grimaced at the thought of James leaving, then nodded and agreed with me, sadly. I looked at this wonderful, supportive, caring and giving woman. She needed the support that Jeannie had provided.

"We should look for someone who could come and live with us to help you with the house and the children. We have another mouth to feed in the New Year, you will need help with the new baby."

Annie sighed, "I can't imagine anyone coming here to replace dear Jeannie. It makes me weep just to think of it. But you're right. I need to go to Salem and find someone to help me. I must be careful with Johnny, though. Jeannie will always be family, but a young woman starting with us as a hired help should not upset him."

I told Annie that I shared her concerns about the challenges we faced.

"We are taking risks, but those risks are a part of coming to a new country and not just surviving but succeeding. We have managed to avoid the horrors that our fellow settlers have suffered these last two years. We are now working to establish ourselves. Kate and Giles are still committed to farm with us. Time will tell what will eventually happen with them. It is possible that Kate's divorce will be granted in the next month or so. Gavan should be given every opportunity to seek a wife. Perhaps you should take him with you to Salem, as your escort. Anyway, he is totally absorbed with building his sawmill. It is a new challenge for him."

"Isaac, what about your life? I feel we are on a knife edge. Someone standing behind a tree ready to shoot you. Winthrop having you arrested for treason and possibly taking away your land grand? We must organize ourselves to deal with those threats."

"Annie, dear lovely lady, Johnny is in Salem now working with reliable contacts to keep us alerted to specific threats. Someone, presumably the same person or persons pushing Grindle, is using my past employment with Sir Ferdinando Gorges to create a mirage that I constitute a danger to the Massachusetts Bay Company. This is not true and easily shown to be so in a Court of Law if it should ever come to that. I have strong backing from important allies and basic logic argues against any such accusation."

"What about David? He has gone to England. He feels freed from a loveless marriage. He is back sailing, expecting to command a ship, returning to what he loves. When can we expect him back?"

"He left us in April. Assuming it takes about twenty weeks to sail a round trip to England from here and another two weeks minimum to find out enough to send a report back to us, we should plan to hear from him within the next few weeks. That will give us a good idea of what we can expect going forward. I think it will take at least six months for him to complete the tasks I've set him. So, I don't expect him back in New England until April, at the earliest."

—— CHAPTER 34 ——

Journal entry – *September 1630*

Johnny arrived back late one evening less than a week after he had left us. He had gone to see Thomas Gardner as soon as he got to Salem. Margaret Gardner and their five boys were back from their summer at the Gardner property over the North River. Johnny was welcomed and invited to stay in the accommodation he had helped build when we first arrived. Gentle questioning by Margaret had Johnny telling them about his losses. Tears were shed and a strong drink was handed him by Thomas. Johnny told them why he had come to Salem. Thomas asked what they could do to help. First thing, Johnny said, was that he needed a job that would enable him to become a recognized member of the community. Preferably a job that would enable him to visit the towns being established around Massachusetts Bay. Margaret said Johnny should work for a trader, buying and selling produce being shipped to Salem for onward distribution to the settlements springing up. Thomas agreed. He said that John Woodbury's son Humphrey was getting involved in something similar. He would find out and let Johnny know.

Next morning, Johnny went to see William Trask, who was eating his breakfast with his family. Johnny was invited to join them, after which Trask took him aside and told him he had as yet not uncovered any rumor or commentary about Mr. Stanfield or heard anything of Mr. Grindle. There had been a meeting of the court. Mr. Morton was in deep trouble, but judgement had been deferred until the end of this month. It was expected that he would be sent back to England, after suitable punishment. It seems his offenses were many but providing firearms to the Indians and teaching them how to use them was considered the most serious. Johnny thought that he might need to talk to Morton and obtain a written statement from him about what he had found out about Grindle rather than Beamish being the person who shot at me. If Morton was sent back, that information, useful or not, would be lost.

Trask said that the new Governor had been busy. Shawmut, or Boston as he was calling it, would likely be the seat of Government. Salem and Charlestown would definitely not be. Winthrop had been unsettled by the high mortality among the new arrivals, a much higher ratio than among the Old Planters. Sadly Lady Arabella, daughter of the Earl of Lincoln had died, and Mr. Johnson, her husband, a close ally of Governor Winthrop, was mortally sick. The women were saying it was a broken heart. Johnny said he could well believe it. He told Trask that, as part of his subterfuge to be seen as separating himself from Mr. Stanfield, he was planning to stay as a guest of Mr. Gardner and become a Salem citizen. He told Trask the type of job he was looking for. Trask said he would see what he could do to help. Johnny warned Trask that only he, Mr. Gardner, and Ralph Sprague knew of Johnny's subterfuge. Trask promised to keep the secret. Before leaving, Johnny asked if it was possible to visit Morton. Trask said that as he had not been sequestered it should not be a problem.

A forlorn Morton was sitting in his cell. He had paper and quill, plus books to read. He seemed to be being fed well and was not bothered by anyone. Friends were allowed to visit, few though there were given his reputation. He seemed mildly interested in Johnny's visit but brooded over the sentence he was expecting, without proper trial he said. Nor could there be one, he admitted. They wanted him removed from the country. Endecott had already tried that for the same reasons. It had failed then and would fail again. Such a waste of time and energy. Johnny commiserated and said the reason for his visit was to make sure there was a record kept of what Morton had discovered from Beamish before Beamish was sent back to England. Morton laughed.

"Do you honestly believe they will accept evidence from a convicted felon? I am happy to scribble a note and sign it but doubt it will do much good, unless they are already inclined to believe it."

Johnny thanked him and waited till Morton had written and signed the note. Morton handed it to him and with a casual "good luck," dismissed Johnny with a wave of his hand, and went back to his brooding. Returning to the Gardner house, Thomas told him he had talked to Humphrey Woodbury. Best thing to do was for Johnny to go and see him down at the town's landing stage straight away, which Johnny did.

"Hello, Johnny, what are you doing here? I heard you had moved with Mr. Stanfield to the Merrimack. Mr. Gardner told me about Jeannie and the baby. I'm so sorry."

Changing the subject, Johnny told him that he was estranged from the Stanfields and was looking for a job. Humphrey replied that he had been told to get a crew together to man a coastal trading pinnace working out of Salem. Was Johnny interested? "Very," said Johnny. "When can you start?" Johnny replied, "As soon as you want."

"Right, get your gear together. You will be living aboard. I know you have had experience at sea. You'll be one of three seamen, together with a bosun, mate and skipper. Come to the landing stage on Monday, 13 September, the boat is *Marie*. You will meet the crew then and the skipper will sign you on."

"Aren't you a member of the crew?"

"No, I'm not a sailor. I was told to muster a crew. I was missing one man, so it was most opportune you appeared. You've enabled me to complete my task several days early."

It was now Friday. Johnny realized that by leaving first thing Saturday, he had time to report back to me at New Barrow and get back to Salem Sunday night.

I congratulated Johnny for all he had accomplished in such a short time. I told him he had been sorely missed by the whole family and what a pleasure it was for us all to see him again. I was pleased he had brought back Morton's description of what he had extracted from Beamish. It was useful evidence that I had hoped Morton would have been around to describe in person, should the need arise. Johnny had shown great presence of mind when he realized Morton would probably not be able to do so. I was sorry to hear about Lady Arabella. Her sister was married to John Gorges. I had been surprised that such a gracious and important person had undertaken to come to the squalor of New England, to live in conditions no better than those of the farm workers on her father's estate. When I mentioned it to Annie, she smiled and said, "The love of a woman for her man is exceedingly strong." With that she gave me a kiss. Johnny returned to Salem, leaving before dawn on Sunday. Before he left, he also let drop the news that Endecott had married again, a widow, Elizabeth Gibson.

With Johnny gone, now light by one man, we had necessarily begun to gather provisions for the winter. We had two months before the frosts came. If the winter was going to be as bad as Chogan had predicted, we needed to work hard. A cold store had been dug into the hill behind the house in our sheltered coomb. The stream flowing through the coomb had been dammed to create a pond about five feet deep, which would provide water below any freezing that would occur. We had the grass hay, marsh hay and corn husks ready to finish gathering, to be stored in the stable loft. Jeannie and Annie's garden had produced a first harvest and continued to produce vegetables, which Annie was beginning to conserve. Our Indian friends had promised to provide us with a stock of maize to store for the winter. We needed fruit. The children were detailed to go with Nootau and Ahanu to find berries, nuts, and mushrooms that could be dried and stored, while they were abundant. Annie wanted to go to Salem in a few days. It might be the last time for her before her confinement. She suggested Gavan should go too, in his quest for a wife. While there she would visit William Blackstone and buy some bushels of his fruit and vegetables. I suggested we all go in *Rosie*. Safety in numbers, I said. But Kate said she preferred to stay at New Barrow with her animals. She said Giles should go without her as they needed another buck goat for breeding purposes. She also wanted to spend time with Kimi and her villagers. She wanted to fully understand how the women prepared for and lived through tough winters. That knowledge would help us all.

—— CHAPTER 35 ——

Journal entry – *October 1630*

We dropped Gavan and Giles off in Salem, telling them we would use the Gardners' house as a meeting point in a few days, and sailed on to Boston. Annie and I, with the children, beached *Rosie* in our old landing spot and climbed the hill to visit William Blackstone. He was pleased to see us. He blessed Annie and, especially, the child she so obviously was carrying inside her. He hadn't established any relationship with the people renting our old house, but they did pay William the monthly charge in Wampum shells, which he kept in a sack, and handed to us. Annie gave it back saying it would pay for provisions he might be able to spare ahead of the coming winter. Annie went to his extensive larder with him and returned with all she could possibly want. The children had gone to explore their old favorite haunts. William offered us accommodation for the night in the loft of his stable, it being a warm evening. We had planned to camp but gratefully accepted his invitation. He made us an evening meal and after the children went to sleep in the hayloft, we talked about Winthrop's arrival and what it meant for the future.

William said it was extraordinary how quickly the settlers had spread round the harbor and up the various rivers to establish settlements of their own. It seemed like an incoming tide filling all the inlets and bays, covering the beaches, and eroding all opposition—except the tide never ebbed. Winthrop had assured him he could keep the five or so acres that he had cultivated but the rest of Boston (William had difficulty using the name) was an ideal peninsula on which to build his city on a hill. I asked him what he meant. Evidently Winthrop had delivered a sermon before he arrived, wherein he defined Christian charity as a reality that must be followed by all the settlers arriving here, He had ended his sermon with the admonition:

"For we must consider that we shall be as a city upon a hill. The eyes of all people are upon us."

William said it was similar to the Covenant the Separatists had all signed on the *Mayflower*, ten years earlier. He agreed wholeheartedly with the sentiment but the discipline and rigorous enforcement that would be required would make the effort onerous for people such as himself. He saw his Anglican ways being inimical to the new order. He loved his prayer book and the services he recited every day. The influence of Separatism over Puritanism would be difficult to resist. Endecott had already shown the way, Winthrop would surely follow. The conversation continued late into the night. Annie excused herself and went to join the children.

William said that he had been visited by Maverick a little while back and my name had come up. Maverick asked whether I was still working for Sir Ferdinando Gorges. Rumors are going around, Maverick said, and if true might be a cause for concern, because Gorges is known to be trying to subvert the properly constituted government under Winthrop's leadership. William suggested to Maverick that I had shown no interest, as far as he knew, in such political intrigue. Maverick admitted it could be so but asked that William let him know if he hears anything to the contrary. William asked me if the rumors were true. I said not at all. I was happy the way things were. I wanted to make my life and that of my family here in New England.

Next morning, laden with barrels, baskets, and sacks of provisions from the most generous William, we bid farewell and sailed to Charlestown to find Ralph and Joanna Sprague. Forewarned by Johnny, we were still surprised and dismayed at the disheveled state of Charlestown. The weather had turned. It was colder and had been raining overnight. We trudged up the hill through the mud and the remains of the forest that had been cut down to make space for the new town. We passed by half-built houses, tents, and the smell of squalor and open cesspits. At the summit there was a row of completed houses including the Spragues' home. They welcomed us. Joanna was excited to see Annie's condition, taking her and the children on a tour of the house, while Ralph and I sat and chatted. I congratulated him on his appointment as Constable of Charlestown. He grimaced. It was a grand title but meant unremitting work, little financial recompense, and no gratitude from his fellow citizens. However, he considered it his duty to serve his community in any way he could. Ralph had seen Maverick at a town meeting and been introduced to him. In the course of conversation, Maverick learned that Ralph and I knew each other well from our Dorchester days in England. He had asked Ralph some rather pointed questions about me and my relationship with Sir Ferdinando Gorges. He had told Maverick that he was unaware of any current association.

Then Ralph said to me,

"Prior to my meeting with Maverick, Johnny Dawkins came to see me and was talking about the conspiracy against you and then apropos of nothing asked me if I knew Maverick. I asked Johnny if Maverick was a part of the conspiracy and he made some offhand remark about you looking for trading partners. I was left with the distinct impression that you think Maverick is at least under suspicion."

"Ralph, you make an excellent constable. We don't know for certain, but he does seem to be making enquiries about me and had extracted Grindle, my assailant, from the Salem gaol."

Ralph nodded and continued.

"Definitely circumstantial. Well, with that impression firmly implanted in my mind, I decided to try and tease some more information out of Maverick. I asked him why he seemed concerned about you and Sir Ferdinando. He told me that the Governor had expressed some concern about Gorges being a possible threat to him. Maverick told me that, subsequently, he had heard that Isaac Stanfield was an active agent of Gorges. I asked him where he had heard that and how reliable was that source. He said that he had been told by someone he knew in New Amsterdam. He didn't know how reliable the information or the informant was, which was why he needed to be certain before he said anything to the Governor. I mentioned the name Grindle, a man seemingly known to Maverick, whom I had heard was involved in an attempt on Stanfield's life. He said that wasn't possible. As far as he knew, Grindle was detained by an overzealous official in Salem as an unknown, armed person who, Maverick insisted, happened to be passing through Salem on his way to Charlestown. While he didn't know Grindle, he had been advised by a business acquaintance of the incident and was asked to go and extract him, then send him back to New Amsterdam, which is what he did. I asked Maverick if this was something I, as the Constable, should be concerned about. If he comes to Charlestown should I arrest Stanfield on suspicion of being a threat to the Governor? Maverick said no, he was trying to find out whether there was any truth to what he had heard. I asked him why he didn't just pass on the information he had to the proper authorities for them to investigate. He replied that if he did that and the information he had proved to be false, he would both have imputed blame on an innocent person and damaged his own reputation. He felt he owed it to both Stanfield, whom he respected, and the Governor, who was a friend of his, not to start a hare unnecessarily."

I thanked Ralph and he promised to let me know if he heard anything germane. Annie and Joanna came back to us. The children were left to explore the garden. Joanna told Ralph that Annie was looking for a young woman to enter service in the Stanfield home and wasn't there a maid servant working for a family close by that was relocating to Watertown up the Charles River and was dispensing with her services? Ralph said her name was Patience Milsted, she was eighteen years old and had come from a village in Kent, Horsmonden, he recalled. She was well liked and had looked after two small boys with considerable skill and tact. Joanna said she would find out more. If we would stay to lunch, she should have an answer by afternoon. "Better still," Joanna said, "stay the night. We have plenty of room, Ralph's brothers are away at the moment." Thanks to Joanna, Annie was able to meet Patience that afternoon. She made an immediate, favorable impression. Patience was tall and slim, with light brown hair, tied in a bun under a bonnet. Clear, brown eyes in a friendly open face. She spoke well when asked questions and seemed quietly self-assured. Her current service was due to end at the end of October. She had not yet found another position. She had worked for her current family back in Kent and come with them to New England as a paid employee, not an indentured servant. When asked why she wasn't staying with the family she smiled sadly. "There was an elder son," was all she said. Joanna explained later that the son's behavior had become an embarrassment to both Patience and the family as he had grown to manhood. Annie was so taken with her that she offered Patience the position to start 1 November. Patience was pleased to accept.

On to Salem, the following morning, A northwest wind was raising whitecaps on the water. *Rosie* responded well with the wind abeam but the spray soaked us all and kept James and Beth bailing. Abigail huddled under Annie's cloak, she said to keep the baby warm. We sailed into the South River and beached *Rosie* on our favorite beach, down river from the crowded pool off the town dock and the crowds of people in the new town of Salem. I found a couple of youngsters and negotiated an acceptable fee for them to look after *Rosie* and her contents while we walked to the Gardners' house. The Gardner boys were happy to see James again and they soon disappeared. They had built a hideaway up a tall tree which was their special place. Giles was at the house. He had acquired a buckling goat of about six months. Beth and Abigail decided to call him Jethro. No packages had arrived for me from England, but a number of ships were due to dock in the next week.

Gavan was still out and about looking for a prospective wife. He arrived back later that afternoon, frustrated. He told us he had talked to many people over the days he had been in Salem. He had even visited Agatha who had fallen for him on *Abigail*, on the journey from

England in 1628. Agatha was now married with a child. Gavan said it had been a difficult meeting. Agatha was rightly inconvenienced by Gavan's search for a wife after he had rejected her in such a painful way. Being a kind-hearted soul, she relented and was able to tell him who among the indentured women servants were still unattached.

Giles and Gavan returned to *Rosie* with Jethro, where they camped on the beach. We joined them the next morning. The return to New Barrow was a rough one. Gavan rigged a cuddy in the bow, a wooden frame covered by canvas which protected Beth and Abigail. Jethro was induced to join them with the help of a tether. James indignantly declined a similar offer. He was there as crew, not a passenger. With a balanced helm, he was able to take his turn at the tiller.

CHAPTER 36

Journal entry – November 1630

Annie had arranged with Joanna to have Patience taken to Salem at the end of her employment on Monday, 1 November, where someone would be there to walk with her back to New Barrow, weather permitting. Gavan volunteered to walk to Salem to fetch her. He left the day before with an admonition from Annie, that Patience was coming to work for the Stanfields. He was there to escort Patience back here, that was all. Gavan grinned and said he would be the epitome of discretion. I asked him to check for any packages that might have been sent to me from England. I was concerned I hadn't heard from David Tremaine.

Johnny appeared out of nowhere. He had been away six weeks. He told us he had persuaded the skipper of the pinnace, *Marie*, to drop him off at our landing stage. *Marie* was on her way to the Piscataqua to deliver some merchandise and pick up a consignment of beaver pelts. They would return in 24 hours to collect Johnny. He looked fit and well, the pall that had lain over him when we last saw him had lifted. He was much more like his old self. We welcomed him warmly, the children most of all. They had missed him, a much more forgiving teacher than Annie.

By a warming fire, Johnny sat with me and Annie to tell us his news. I told him that we had heard from Ralph Sprague that he was now a crewman on *Marie*. Old news he replied. The trading business was so brisk, the owners had made Johnny quartermaster, in charge of all direct interactions with the clients at each port of call. He worked directly under *Marie's* skipper but reported to the owners. It paid well, it suited Johnny's organizational skills, and he was meeting a wide range of clients in an increasing number of settlements and trading posts. We congratulated him. He thanked us and admitted it was a job he was really enjoying. It had taken his mind off the loss of Jeannie and he had accepted that she had now gone on her own journey, unencumbered by Johnny's desperate attempts to hold on to her.

He had been keeping his ears open for any mention of the Stanfields, retaining his perceived antagonism toward me. There had been little to report other than I was respected for the reputation I had regarding my support for the early efforts to settle New England. However, there were pockets of resistance that seemed to come from one or two of the settlers who had come over with the Robert Gorges expedition. The failure of that enterprise, while being blamed on Robert Gorges' incompetence, was also attributed to the people who had appointed him in the first place. Johnny said that as Sir Ferdinando's agent, I shared the blame. Little else to report, that is until the recent *Marie* trip to New Amsterdam.

It had been a long trip down, about 250 miles, almost like a sea voyage except they were in sight of land for most of the journey. It had taken them nearly three days. They arrived in the large bay into which the Hudson and the East Rivers flow. Between the two rivers there is a peninsula, at the tip of which is the town of New Amsterdam, guarded by a fort. There is a town landing stage on the south bank at the mouth of the East River, tricky to come alongside in all but slack tide, otherwise a fierce tidal current. There is a mooring field a bit further to the north, out of the current. The town has a number of houses clustered round the fort, some tightly packed together, others with open land round them inside perimeter fencing. Near the landing stage are numerous warehouses. Johnny said *Marie* was delivering household goods and grain, while taking delivery of beaver pelts, barrels of wine and spirits, as well as heavy Dutch woolens.

Grindle had mentioned a merchant called Doncker. Johnny went looking for him. The name was known and he was shown, through a bustling crowd, to where Doncker's office was located. He knocked and was bidden to enter. Johnny introduced himself as the quartermaster of the pinnace *Marie* looking for opportunities to ship freight to settlements within New England. He said that he had heard that Mr. Doncker was a successful and important businessman, the first man to approach for advice. Doncker nodded at the inflated compliments and preened like an overstuffed, florid, and rotund peacock, brushing ash and tobacco flakes off his full white beard. He told Johnny, in a thick accent, that he should see the agents that acted for the more important businessmen. He would be happy to give the name and address of his. A servant came in bearing a tray carrying a tall thin metal pot with spout and a lid. Steam was coming out of the spout. On the tray were two small cups. Doncker poured a black liquid into the cups and offered one to Johnny. Doncker said, proudly, it was expensive coffee, just arrived from England. Johnny politely sipped and barely caught himself from spitting out the bitter, hot liquid. He coughed and Doncker laughed, offering some sugar. Johnny thanked him but said the coffee was a little too refined for someone of his lowly station, which relaxed Doncker. He became quite affable, sipping his coffee. He asked about Johnny's background and how he came to New England. Johnny mentioned that at one time he had worked for Isaac Stanfield back in England and when they first came over two years ago but had since left the bastard to do what he was doing now. At the mention of my name, Doncker reacted sharply. Johnny asked him if he knew me.

"No, but I have heard bad things about him. It seems you aren't too happy about him, either. Wait a minute, you say your name is Dawkins. That's the name that Carson mentioned to me."

"Mr. Doncker, a while back while in New Plimouth Carson was told I was on my way back to Salem and introduced himself to me. He asked me to help him reach Mr. Stanfield. He told me you had a message to give him."

"No Mr. Dawkins, I was told Carson was going to Salem and I asked him to deliver a package to someone in Charlestown. I have no reason to have any contact with Stanfield."

"You said earlier that you have heard bad things about Stanfield. What were they?"

"I heard that he is a secret agent in a conspiracy to overthrow the Winthrop government."

"That sounds serious. I'm prepared to believe Stanfield is engaged in something nefarious, but I'm surprised that this is not more generally known. Perhaps this needs to be reported to Winthrop."

"Maybe," said Doncker, "but certainly not by me. This is a problem for the English."

"I understand, but if I'm to do it, I'll need a little more information. Who did you hear this from? I will need to talk to him."

"A colleague of mine, Mr. Anton Hoekstra. You will find him at this address," he said as he scribbled on a piece of paper, handing it to Johnny.

With that he abruptly ended the meeting and Johnny left, thinking that Doncker wanted nothing more to do with English conspiracies. He went to find Mr. Hoekstra. An assistant told Johnny that Hoekstra was not available. Johnny asked the assistant if a Mr. Carson works for Hoekstra. Occasionally, was the reply. Johnny asked whether there was any way he could contact Carson. He was told that Carson could normally be found at a tavern called *De Druif,* on the waterfront. He would recognize it by a sign with a bunch of grapes on it.

Carson was in a corner with a tankard of ale in front of him. He looked the worse for wear. It seemed he lived a sordid, drunken life. In his bleary state it took him a while to recognize Johnny who had sat on a bench next to him. Johnny leaned over him.

"You owe me £20."

"Like hell I do. Wait a minute, you're Dawkins. What are you doing here? You didn't come all this way for that, did you?"

"Do I call you Carson or Grindle?"

Grindle slouched down, his head almost resting on his tankard. He took a pull of beer then admitted that he was known as Carson in New Amsterdam.

"How did you know I was Grindle?"

"A friend of mine who had met you as Septimus Grindle subsequently saw you using the name Carson. Why did you change your name?"

"The name Grindle is known in Salem."

"So?"

"You still prepared to get me to Stanfield?"

"Maybe?"

"What do you know about me?"

"Well, Septimus, very little. The name is associated with a shooting in Salem for which a young man Arthur Beamish was sent back to England. Thereafter, it seems you went to Merrymount, on to New Plimouth, and ended up in here in New Amsterdam. Oh! and for some reason you want to kill Stanfield. Why do you want to kill him? It would need to be a good reason for me to even consider helping you."

"I never said I wanted to kill Stanfield."

"You told me when we first met that Doncker had sent you with a message to deliver to Stanfield and if he didn't cooperate you would kill him. I've just been with Doncker, looking for you. He told me he used you only to deliver a package to Charlestown. I think you used that as an excuse to get to Stanfield. So, I ask again. Why do you want to kill Stanfield?"

Grindle refused to answer. Johnny changed tack.

"One thing Doncker did tell me was that Stanfield is believed to be a traitor to the English. He is said to be part of a conspiracy to bring down Winthrop. Did you tell him this?"

"Why do you want to know?"

"If Stanfield really is a traitor and if I can prove it, I can tell the relevant authorities. I get rewarded and I get the pleasure of bringing him down."

"No, I didn't. But I know who did and I can't tell you. More than my life's worth."

"Was it Hoekstra?"

Grindle refused to answer. Johnny then told Grindle that if it was Hoekstra, he could only have heard it from someone else, an

Englishman. Either way, an Englishman must be spreading the word. Why, Johnny asked Grindle, would anyone spread these rumors and not go straight to the authorities, unless the man was uncertain of his facts and couldn't prove anything? Johnny changed direction, again.

"When I left you with Mr. Trask in Salem, I thought you would be detained for some time. I also thought you would have some difficulty convincing anyone of your innocent intent. How did you get out of gaol so quickly? When I went to see you the next day, you had gone."

Grindle ignored the questions. He asked, "What did you come to see me at the gaol for?"

"I wanted to find out if there was a way to free you and get my £20."

"A man called Maverick came and convinced the gaoler that I was legitimate. He escorted me down to the harbor and told me to go back to New Amsterdam, by any means as quickly as possible. I didn't ask questions but did as he said."

"Who is Maverick?"

"I don't know. He said he had been asked by someone to rescue me."

"Did he say who? Maybe Maverick or this friend of his knows more about this conspiracy."

Grindle just shook his head. Johnny told him that if he wanted his help he would need to come up with some good reasons. He would be returning to Salem the next morning. If Grindle came up with a credible source that Johnny could use and if Grindle wanted a lift back to Salem, he should meet him at the loading dock first thing in the morning.

The next morning, Grindle failed to appear, and *Marie* left for Salem. A few days later *Marie* brought Johnny to New Barrow.

Annie and I sat in silence after Johnny finished, digesting the information he gave us. An unknown Englishman was spreading rumors about me. Annie thought it didn't preclude the mysterious Englishman from being involved with Spiggott and Grindle. Also, who told Maverick to rescue Carson? How was it that Maverick was alerted so quickly to Grindle's detainment that he was able to extract him within two days?

—— CHAPTER 37 ——

Journal entry – *November 1630*

Johnny was picked up by *Marie* and at dusk Gavan, carrying Patience's belongings in a bag, appeared with the weary Patience. Luckily the weather, while cold, had stayed dry. The children were introduced, James, matter of fact, shook her hand, Beth and Abigail nodded shyly. Patience, obviously well practiced with children, greeted them each warmly. Annie relaxed, assured they would become friends in no time. Annie, accompanied by Beth and Abigail, then took Patience off to show her Johnny and Jeannie's old room, where she would be sleeping, and the rest of the house and stables. Gavan with a mug of beer sat at the kitchen table and handed me a packet that had just arrived for me from England. We talked until Patience, Annie, and the children returned, together with Giles and Kate. We all had supper together before Annie ushered the half-asleep Patience to bed. The children followed and were told not to disturb her.

Later, in the stillness of the late hour, Annie and I nestled together in our favorite settle in front of the fire, opened and read the package from David Tremaine. He apologized for the delay in writing to us. He had arrived in Weymouth, after a quick crossing, in June. He met with the Patriarch in Dorchester who gave him a letter for me, which he enclosed. He met with Will Whiteway who was delighted to receive the latest installment of my journal. He also gave David a letter for me. He then went to Plymouth to see Mr. Scroud.

Mr. Scroud reported that a problem had arisen, recently, with respect to the *Argossy*. The original owners had appealed the decision of the Admiralty Court, stating that the case should have been brought before the Common Law Courts of England. While the appeal was being heard and adjudged, the ownership of the *Argossy* remained undecided. The owners were still funding the maintenance and had agreed that Mr. Hadfield could remain nominally in command until the ownership was decided. Mr. Scroud opined that the appeal was a desperate attempt by the previous owners and had no legal merit, but it did cause a delay. David wrote that while dismayed, he took heart from Mr. Scroud's assertions. He gave him my letter to him wherein I confirmed that David be given the wherewithal to purchase the animals and provisions we wanted shipped back to New England. Mr. Scroud gave David the credit facilities that would enable him to buy whatever he needed. David then returned to Weymouth and began assembling what he had to send over. Kate had given him a detailed list, a mastiff dog, three north Devon bullocks, three gaited horses being two fillies and a colt, and five Dorset sheep, three ewes and two rams. Kate was assuming there would be attrition on the voyage over.

David arranged to have prepared the provisions Annie had listed for him: household utensils such as pots, pans, spoons, ladles, jugs and goblets, crates of apparel, such as woolens, flax, hemp, linen, calico, canvas, leather, hose and stockings, aprons, hats and boots, soap and candles; as well as dried food such as prunes, raisins, currants, nutmeg and cloves, jars of honey, with a colony of bees. David added a list of ironware of his own, hammers, axes, saws, hoes, spades, augers, barrels of nails and spikes. These and more provisions were all brought together to be shipped over.

All this took time to gather and to find a ship to transport together with the animals. The merchantman David found, the *Mary & John*, was due to make a return trip to Salem in September, to arrive in early December. I looked at Annie. We have a month to prepare. Annie said she would alert Kate and Giles first thing in the morning. We should try and book *Marie* to bring everything on to us once landed.

We read the letters from P. and Will. They were full of local news which made us nostalgic. Mr. Scroud's letter went into great detail about the legal situation with the *Argossy*. We needed to be patient. However, Mr. Scroud did warn us that the political situation being what it was in England, the rule of law can sometimes be subverted. On a brighter note he gave us the details of a Boston correspondent agent with whom he had established credit facilities for me. The agent was due to arrive in Boston to take up his position in early 1631. The agent would be in touch with me when he arrived. Scroud also was pleased to report that my financial affairs, *Argossy* excepted, were in excellent shape. Barrow Farm had been sold as I had instructed. The capital released from the sale was immediately reinvested, producing good returns.

As soon as Kate had been alerted to the impending arrival of the animals, she, Giles, and Gavan met in the stables to decide what additions were needed to house the new livestock. Not knowing how many would survive it was deemed best to assume all would. The fenced fields needed to be extended and inside stabling built to shelter them through the winter. Kate was also concerned about whether they had harvested enough feed. Marsh grass had to be gathered. It was too late for the uncut hay, already flattened by the weather or ploughed under ready for the winter, using Kate's poor cows again. The month was spent getting ready.

Patience had worked her magic and become a firm favorite with the children. She and Annie had become close, almost immediately. It turned out that, like Annie, she had been brought up in an inn, the Gun at Horsmonden, where her father was the landlord, and had been a barmaid before going into service with the family that eventually brought her to New England. She told Annie that she had participated in a number of births. Although not a midwife, she felt comfortable with the process and would be pleased to help Annie. She had also persuaded Annie to slow down and allow her to take responsibility for all the housekeeping. Annie was grateful and took to her bed with a couple of warm, wrapped river stones for a rest every afternoon. Kimi became a regular visitor to oil and massage Annie and check the baby. At one point, she said she was now convinced about something she had suspected a while back. She could feel two babies in Annie's womb, which explained why Annie was so large. Annie was surprised, worried, and then delighted. I was confused. Having settled my mind on the imminent arrival of one new child, I was unsettled to learn we would be having two. I was also concerned that having twins further complicated the birth with greater risk to the mother and babies. My confusion turned to fear, which I tried to keep to myself.

Gavan had behaved himself bringing Patience back to New Barrow. He was attracted to her but Patience less so to him. I asked Gavan to take a message to Salem for Johnny, saying we needed *Marie* to move a shipment of livestock and freight to New Barrow as soon as the *Mary & John* arrived from England, due in early December. Gavan saw the opportunity to look again for a wife and left to walk to Salem, saying he would be away for a few days. He returned four days later, subdued. He had delivered the message to Johnny. He had also found someone he thought would make a splendid wife, but she would require courting. He told me that he had been offered an important position at a new boatyard close to Salem, building pinnaces and planning to build a barque of up to 100 tons. They wanted him to start as soon as possible, before the winter set in. I asked him about the additional stabling. He said the lumber had been cut, the addition framed and roofed. He suggested that Giles and I would be able to complete it. I also questioned his intent to build a sawmill and help me develop a lumber business. He shrugged. He was a boat-builder not a lumberman. I gave him my blessing. He had worked for room and board and had asked for little more. He had been an immense help to us, for which we would be forever grateful. We gave him £20 which he found difficult to accept. Annie, the bookkeeper, was pleased to insist he should, with our gratitude and continuing friendship.

—— CHAPTER 38 ——

Journal entry – *December 1630 – February 1631*

The second week in December we were informed that the *Mary &
John* had arrived off Salem and was waiting, sheltered in the lee of an
island in the bay while a nor'easter blew through, before she was able
to work her way to the loading dock on the South River. Kate and Giles
immediately set off walking to Salem to oversee the transfer of animals
and freight to New Barrow. A week later, James on watch, from his
perch up a tree on the clifftop overlooking the Merrimack River, ran
to tell us that a pinnace was approaching our landing stage. We went
down to meet it, with our cows harnessed to the cart, leaving Annie
with Patience.

Johnny greeted us from *Marie*, tied up at the landing stage. On deck,
were a colt and filly, two young bullocks, a ram and two ewes and a
large puppy mastiff. Kate was delighted that so many animals had survived the crossing. If the third bullock had survived, one would have
been kept for breeding. The two that arrived would both be castrated and used as oxen. One of the fillies had died, two out of the three
horses surviving the crossing was considered remarkable. Three out of
five sheep arriving was also met with satisfaction. Kate and Giles, with
help from the children, entranced by the young mastiff, led the hal-
tered animals up the path and onward to their new home, while Johnny, the crew and I offloaded the freight David had sent us and piled it

on the stage. Lots of honey but no bees, all had perished. We used the cows to pull the loaded cart on several journeys until everything had been stored in a corner of the stables. David had ensured that each of the horses came with a saddle and full set of tack. Johnny had sold the spare tack in Salem.

Johnny handed me a letter from David and I paid him for services rendered. He apologized for leaving us with the winter on us and Gavan having left us undermanned. I told him what he was doing to help us find out who was behind the threats was much more important. I also told him he had fallen into a new line of work which he seemed to be enjoying. He admitted that was so, but he also said being with Annie so close to her time was too much for him to bear with Jeannie still so fresh in his mind. Annie, who had joined us, overhearing his last remark, hugged him and said that dear Jeannie was constantly on her mind too.

Before he left, he took me aside out of Annie's hearing and said trouble was brewing. He asked me, "Do you remember Richard Darnell on *Abigail*?"

"Yes, he was that insolent young man who accused me of disloyalty to Governor Endecott. Why, what's he done?

"He has become a member of Winthrop's staff and according to Trask he has been telling the Governor that you are not to be trusted. He claims that you are in touch with Sir Ferdinando Gorges, and have been seen with the traitor Thomas Morton, another Gorges spy, before he was expelled. He also passed on to the Governor information about your evident disloyalty to Endecott. God knows what else he has been saying, but Trask says Winthrop is seeking advice from Endecott."

With that Johnny left. He said a storm was on its way, snow was expected, and *Marie* had to get back to Salem.

Johnny was right. The storm arrived a day later. We hoped to God *Marie* and her crew were safe. The snow came and with it the start of a harsh and cold winter. New Barrow was cut off from the outside world for the next three months. Sadly, most of our Indian friends had moved to their winter quarters further west.

In the middle of the snowstorm, Kimi arrived. She said simply that the time had come for Annie to drop her babies. I was startled both at her premonition and the term she used. But I remembered that tended to be the actual Indian practice. Squat, drop the baby, and continue working. Kimi recognized that the English were not so practical or prepared for such natural actions. She went to see Annie in the bedroom, returning shortly thereafter. Patience was told to bring the birthing stool and come with her to prepare the bedroom for the birth, which Kimi said should be a simple birth that would start to happen within the next hour or so. I was told to absent myself and with the children went to see Kate and Giles at the stables to help clear snow, muck out and groom the animals, in fact anything to take my mind off what was happening back at the house. Kate left us to go to Annie.

The mastiff, a bitch, Kate named Belle. Kate was pleased as she would be able to breed more dogs from Belle, both to meet her expanding needs and to sell. The children had named the additions to our stable. The sheep were Joseph, Dorcas and Mary; the bullocks, Gog and Magog; and the horses Samson and Penelope, shortened to Penny. James admitted that the girls had come up with the names, except for the bullocks which he had insisted on naming. He remembered his times playing on Plymouth Hoe and the enormous chalk figures cut into the turf. I now set them to thinking about names for the two babies. There could be two boys, two girls or one of each. Leaving the children to it, I went outside to shovel snow, clearing the path to the house, which proved fruitless. The snow seemed to gather faster than I could shovel. So, I went to spend time becoming better acquainted with Samson and Penny. Samson, just under fourteen hands, was a sturdy bay with a white blaze and two front white stockings, curious and friendly. Penny, barely thirteen hands, piebald, huge eyelashes and coy.

Kate came running down the path through the driving snow to fetch me. Happy and excited she led me by the hand back to the house, saying not a word. I went to the bedroom; Kimi had gone, leaving Patience to tend and tidy. My adored wife, with the happiest of smiles, was sitting up in bed with two bundles at her breasts, feeding already.

Patience told me it had been the simplest birthing process she had ever witnessed. Kimi seemed to weave a magic spell and everything just happened. I knelt down beside Annie and the babes and kissed her.

"Isaac, my dear, clever father, your seed has produced two healthy children. Meet Nathaniel and Hannah."

I rolled the names round my tongue. I liked them. When Hannah had finished, Annie passed her over to me and I held the sweet bundle, instantly fast asleep. What a joy. Then Nathaniel, or Nat as I immediately called him. Awake and staring up at me with Annie's blue eyes. Time froze. It seemed I was in a picture alone with Annie and our two babies. It was a serene moment, shattered by the arrival of three noisy, excited children. They climbed onto the bed and surrounded Annie. I gave her back Nat and she introduced them to their new brother and sister.

Life quickly returned to normal. Annie was back on her feet and fully mobile within a few days. No wet nurse, Annie was responsible for the continuous feeding of two insatiable babies. Patience earned her name every day, dealing with house-bound children as the snowstorm continued to howl outside. We were snug, well provisioned, and happy.

Christmas came and was celebrated in the true Stanford manner. It was only after Twelfth Night and my 34th birthday, 6 January, I told Annie about the threat that Johnny had passed on to me before he last left us, a month earlier.

Annie was silent for a long time. Then she sighed, "My sweet, we both knew that this might happen. We still don't know who is behind all this. Until we do, we cannot combat it. You and Johnny are doing everything you can but right now we can't move from here. What is the most likely thing to happen?"

"Assuming that no evidence is uncovered to disprove what is being said about me, in the meantime, I imagine Winthrop will summon me to appear before his court to answer the charges, as soon as the roads are clear enough for travel. Probably not before the end of February, if Chogon is to be believed."

Chogon had paid us a brief visit before he and his tribe had moved to their winter quarters to the west. Kimi had stayed, with some of the villagers, to help with the birth before joining them. He warned us again that the winter would be long and hard.

Annie continued,

"That means in two months, give or take, you might be taken to Boston and tried for treason. If found guilty you will be executed."

Annie couldn't believe what she had just said and burst into tears. I held her and she clung to me.

"My love, that is an extreme and most unlikely outcome. We know the accusations are false. We have many allies who will be able to show them to be so before any trial, and, if not, make sure that whoever is making the accusations will be made to present themselves in court to defend their accusations. By so doing, he will be shown to be lying."

"But you did work for Sir F. You did come to New England with Robert. You do know Morton. You did refuse to work for Endecott."

"All circumstantial, Annie. Please don't worry. We will deal with this, if and when it happens. Now let's enjoy our splendid isolation in this beautiful spot. By the way, James and I should go hunting as soon as the snow stops. We also need to go fishing."

The months of January and February went quickly. The livestock needed constant attention. Ruth and Naomi each produced two healthy calves, despite what Kate called our extreme abuse of them so late in their pregnancies by using them as oxen. I suggested the exercise was obviously good for them. Three heifers and a bullock. Until Kate had decided what to do with them, they were left unnamed. We were now beginning to fill the stable and the extension that Gavan had built. We had separate stalls for Samson and Penny, a pen for the six goats, Giles' buckling, Jethro, a happy member of the herd, and another pen for the two sheep. The extension became the cattle barn where the cows were kept and milked, with an attached yard and feeding bin. The children wanted Belle to be their pet, but Kate insisted she was to be a working dog and should have her kennel in the stable, close to the animals she was to guard. Anyway, she would soon be too big to be allowed into the house. For the most part the oxen were kept outside with a lean-to shelter on the lee side of the stable. A heavy labor but a delight for Annie was the increasing size of the manure heap which promised a rich source to fertilize her vegetable garden and the fields in the early spring.

—— CHAPTER 39 ——

Journal entry - *March 1631*

Johnny appeared on 1 March. The first significant break in the weather. He was on his way elsewhere on *Marie*. He said that an escort had been detailed to come and fetch me to answer several charges that had been laid against me. He understood they would be arriving by horse within a couple of days. He had no further information. He promised he would be in touch with me later. He thought I would be detained in Salem. He also told me that it had been a terrible winter for the new settlers that had come with the new Governor. As many as two hundred people had died because of the cold and lack of food, the second year in succession that so many had perished. The Governor had settled on a place to live and work after surveying a number of sites. The place was Watertown, up the Charles a short distance. Towns were springing up to the north, south, and west of Boston. There appears to be some dissension among the senior members of Winthop's administration. Dudley, his deputy, having built a house in Charlestown, refuses to join Winthrop in Watertown. Endecott will not leave Salem. Johnny observed that the Governor has his hands full. He didn't think Winthrop would have the time or inclination to deal with me, other than to find a way to keep a watch on me. With that he wished me luck and left.

The two days' notice gave me time to alert Annie and plan for an indefinite time I would be away. Giles was given additional responsibilities in my absence. Annie, Kate, and Patience would share the workload to keep home and farm safe and working. If I found that I was to be away for an extended period I would arrange for a man to come to help. We were so busy re-organizing ourselves that the escort surprised us when they arrived. It was led by Richard Darnell with two burly guards, leading a spare horse. Darnell was rude and peremptory. He declared that he had been authorized to take me to Salem to face serious charges and showed me a warrant to that effect. He was barely civil to Annie who bristled at his bad manners. I calmed Annie down and said he was clearly unused to this role and was hiding his nervousness by being ungentlemanly. Darnell glared at me and one of the two guards laughed. I turned and studied the guard.

"Good day to you. May I ask why you have come with Mr. Darnell?"

"Good day to you, sir. We've come to make sure you get to Salem safely."

"Safely?" I queried. He grinned and jerked his head towards Darnell. I laughed.

"You look familiar. What's your name?"

"Sykes, sir."

When I started to react, he frowned with a quick shake of the head, missed by Darnell, who was anxious to be off. He wanted to be home by sundown. He said,

"Stanfield, are you coming freely, or do you intend to resist?"

"Resist?"

"If you do, I am required to bind you."

I promised to behave. Annie had put together a bag for me. I mounted the spare horse, she lifted the bag to me, and we kissed, tears in her eyes. The children, unaware, waved goodbye to me and returned to playing in the snow.

Darnell led the way, setting a fast-walking pace, the snow now only a few inches deep. Sykes rode beside me and slowed our pace so that Darnell stayed about ten horse lengths ahead of us. The other guard brought up the rear.

Sykes wanted to talk, out of Darnell's earshot.

"Mr. Stanfield. I have to apologize for all this. Unnecessary, but Darnell convinced the authorities that you were a dangerous man."

"How do I know you?"

"I was a seaman on the *Sweet Rose*, *Rosie*. I was with her when she sank. A day I will never forget. I'd been with her for years. I remember the first time you came aboard. What a right cheeky lad, if you pardon me, sir. I don't think it wise to let Darnell know we know each other. You need friends in your predicament. Best for the opposition not to know. Your reputation and the escapades I was privileged to see make me believe you will soon find a solution but until you do you have friends who are there to protect you."

"Thank you, Sykes. That's good to know, but how is it that you were made my guard?"

"Mr. Trask was told to bring you in. He was worried that something might happen to you on the way back. He had a word with my skipper, Captain Gauden, who is currently in Salem with *Abigail*. I understand you and Trask sailed over here together with Captain Gauden in '28. I was on another boat then. Gauden was aware that I knew you and volunteered my time with another seaman, Charlie here," and he jerked his thumb over his shoulder, "to make sure nothing happened."

We talked about the past, the incredible adventures we had on *Rosie*, our sadness that she had gone, our old shipmates and what he was doing. He told me that after *Rosie*, he had stayed close to Tiny Hadfield. He was grateful for the money I had given to the crew, as well as the families of those who had been killed after *Rosie* sank, it had saved a lot of crewmen from destitution. When Tiny had been given the job to run a maintenance crew for the *Argossy*, he couldn't believe his ears. It was the absence of the *Argossy* that resulted in *Rosie* being sunk. Tiny asked Sykes if he would like to sign up, which he was delighted to do. A number of the surviving crew members were part of that crew. Then, Gauden needed some experienced sailors to fill positions on this latest voyage, which paid more than they were getting as maintenance crew, so Tiny let Sykes go provided he kept in touch.

There were rumors that somehow I was involved. Tiny had no comment on that but said it might be worth Sykes' while to let him know where he could be found and not to sign on for more than a return trip.

"So, Mr. Stanfield, are these rumors true?"

I replied that they were simply rumors and would remain so until something happened which confirmed or denied them.

"You are not denying them then?

I changed the subject.

"Sykes, I need you to correct any impression you might have given to Darnell that we are friendly. If asked you should say you have been interrogating me at Mr. Trask's request. Now I need you to create an incident that will convince Darnell you are a trustworthy guard."

Sykes was quick to understand my request. He rode into my horse, unseating himself and pulled me with him, shouting curses at me. Darnell turned in his saddle and saw me on the ground with Sykes on top of me and Charlie dismounting and standing over us with pistol raised. My head had hit the ground and I was bleeding from a cut, caused by an icy patch on the trail, over my right eyebrow, superficial but looked worse. I pretended to be stunned. Darnell trotted back to us and demanded to know what had happened.

"It's fine now sir, we have the bastard under control. He became fractious with the questions I was asking him. His horse banged into mine. Perhaps he was trying to escape. Anyway, I wasn't taking chances. I grabbed him and pulled him off his horse. I think we need to bind him."

"Is he alright? He's bleeding. Is he alive?"

"Mr. Darnell, does he need to be? He could have been shot while trying to escape."

Darnell stared at Sykes, his mind working.

"Could we get away with it?"

Sykes shook his head. He said,

"Sorry, it was a stupid idea. More trouble than it's worth. Stanfield will probably be hanged as a traitor. Why cause problems for ourselves? Interesting idea though."

Shortly thereafter we arrived on the bank of the North River and took a ferry with our horses to Salem where I was taken to William Trask's house and was ushered in, the door closing on Darnell's angry face. I told Trask what had happened. He said,

"That proves Darnell is altogether too eager, suspiciously so, to seek the severest punishment for your alleged crimes, convicted without trial if possible. Darnell expected me to congratulate him and issue instructions for you to be hauled away to gaol forthwith."

He went on, "Endecott was told by Governor Winthrop to find out the truth of the accusations against you, preferably without it all coming to trial. In turn, Endecott asked me to investigate and report back to him. Endecott being a cautious man prefers you to be easily accessible and under watch while that investigation proceeds. Mindful of the need to be seen to be neutral, I have allowed myself to be persuaded to keep you under house arrest, as an enforced guest in my household."

I thanked him for his hospitality. He laughed.

"We will try to make your stay as comfortable and as short as possible."

I asked him,

"If you don't trust Darnell, why did you send him to arrest me?"

Trask explained.

"Darnell is on the staff of the Governor and volunteered. Endecott thought it was diplomatically expedient that Darnell be allowed to do the job, but he was ordered by Endecott only to request your presence here, not to arrest you. However, I made sure that the guards ordered to accompany him could be trusted, which meant not in the employ of, and receiving their orders from, possibly interested parties. That's why I approached Captain Gauden."

Again, I thanked Trask for the care he took.

"Mr. Stanfield, I have my doubts about Darnell's involvement in this conspiracy as it seems to be being called. He came late to the party with his accusation that you are a Gorges spy. He was eager to accept that accusation at face value. He can't have had any knowledge of your presumed spying when he was in England. I remember he accused

264

you of being disloyal to Governor Endecott, on *Abigail*. He certainly made no mention then of you being a spy. He said nothing for two years until now. Why?"

I said that I was puzzled as well. I commented that Maverick also joined this conspiracy a short while ago. At least he was being a bit more circumspect, seeking corroboration before making a formal accusation. I asked Trask if he knew where Maverick was. I said I would like to talk to him. Trask said that wouldn't be possible for a while. Maverick was sailing to Bermuda out of New Amsterdam. I asked how he knew. He replied that John Woodbury told him, his son Humphrey was sailing with him. New Amsterdam, again, what was the connection?

CHAPTER 40

Journal entry – *March - April 1631*

The Trask family were hospitable in trying circumstances. I was allowed a certain degree of freedom. Sykes had become my escort. He had returned to *Abigail* and pleaded with his skipper that I was in a fairly desperate state and needed someone to look after me. Henry Gauden was loathe to lose an experienced seaman but Sykes had found a replacement sailor looking for passage home. So, Sykes was paid off and Trask employed him to keep an eye on me.

I received a short letter from David Tremaine. He had been told by Scroud that a judgement had been made and *the Argossy* was being returned to the original owners. An appeal had been filed but Scroud said that the issue was no longer a legal one, but who had the ear of the King. The owners were London based, which gave them a significant advantage. David was working with Scroud to deal with the consequences of that decision, especially with respect to Tiny Hadfield and the maintenance crew. It was expected that some if not all would continue as crew of the *Argossy*. That was a bitter blow to add to the conspiracy against me. Matters became worse.

I returned from a walk with Sykes and was met by a grave Trask. Darnell had, after several attempts, managed to get Winthrop's ear. He told him about my attempted escape and complained that I was being allowed too much freedom. He had insisted I was a spy and still free to continue being so. As a result, Winthrop had issued instructions to Endecott that I be confined and Trask had been told to comply. I asked about Sykes. He had clearly proved himself to Darnell's satisfaction and presumably to Endecott. Trask said he would keep him available, for the time being. I asked Trask to send Sykes to my family with a letter from me. I was allowed time to write the letter before I was taken to the gaol. I wrote to Annie telling her what was happening. She was not to worry. I have allies who are helping me deal with these challenges. I told her Sykes was one such ally. He could be trusted absolutely and would explain how we know each other. I gave the letter to Sykes to take to Annie, who I expected would want to send a letter back. Before leaving, he shook my hand and said he looked forward to participating in another Stanfield adventure.

Trask took me to the gaol and advised me that he would ensure I had whatever legal representation was available in Salem. He wasn't a lawyer, but in England the common law Habeas Corpus clause would curtail any confinement without judicial process. He didn't know whether that applied in New England. It seemed Winthrop had assumed extra-judicial powers. Wheels turned slowly. I was allowed no visitors. I received messages of support, especially loving letters from Annie. I replied sending my love to her and the family. I insisted that her duty was to care for the twins, not to worry about me. I was becoming well rested. It was two weeks later that I was taken to meet with Endecott. Sykes was my escort.

"Mr. Stanfield. I have to say I am most embarrassed and have been placed in a most awkward position. I have been given instructions by Governor Winthrop that are somewhat contradictory. He wants you confined without it becoming a major issue. He is a lawyer and recognizes that you have been confined without trial or even a hearing, on the basis of hearsay evidence. He is highly sensitive to threats to his position here. The circumstantial evidence points to you still working for Gorges. It is known that Gorges is seeking to gain the land grants that have been lost to him. The only way Winthrop believes he can do that is to overthrow his government. That threat surmounts any legal due process. But Winthrop is also receiving adverse comments from a number of concerned people, myself included, who are supportive of you and your past and potential future contributions here. To put it simply, Winthrop wants this problem to go away. He can expel you like he did with Thomas Morton. He knows that won't resolve the situation, given the support you most certainly have back in England. In fact, Morton back in England is actively working with Gorges to rescind the Massachusetts Bay Company's patent from the King. If you were sent back, it could only aid Gorges' efforts. On the other hand, it has been suggested to Winthrop that you have as much interest in resolving this issue as he does and that you should be given the opportunity to do so. Winthrop has too many other issues to deal with so has delegated full authority to me to work with you to reach a conclusion."

I expressed my sympathy to Endecott. I wished it had been otherwise. I recognized that accusations had been made. At the moment, Darnell, to my knowledge, had not disclosed his sources, which I said I found strange. Endecott shrugged.

"Darnell either is doubtful of how strong a case he has or wants to make a grand exposé in court. I am certain that whatever information he has he gained recently. I also believe Maverick has been questioning your loyalty. Again, it must be based on information he has gathered in New England. Governor Winthrop said there was a third accuser, Mr. Gott, who states he has received a copy of a letter from Gorges to you which clearly incriminates you."

I asked him if he had the letter or read it. "I have seen the supposed letter but not read it."

I said, "It would be difficult for me to respond to the accuser without knowing more about the letter. When was it written? What did it actually say? How do we know it was from Gorges? His signature could be a forgery. How certain is it that the letter was actually written to me? How did Mr. Gott get hold of the letter?" Endecott shrugged again.

"All good questions, Mr. Stanfield. Questions that your defense council in court would raise. But only if your case comes to court. You see my dilemma. There are many, and obvious, questions that can be raised with respect to the accusations against you. The circumstantial evidence is strong. Enough to have you tried in court. But Governor Winthrop does not want the publicity of a court case that raises the visibility of Sir Ferdinando Gorges."

"Then, Governor Endecott, allow me enough freedom to deal with this. I believe that New Amsterdam somehow holds the key. I want to go there. I also need to see a copy of the supposed letter Sir Ferdinando wrote to me. At the very least, I need to know from whom Gott received the letter."

Endecott pondered his options.

"If I could trust you to carry out this investigation without absconding, I believe your suggestion is the way to go. In addition, I do not have a pertinent resource available to escort you."

"What kind of surety do you need? My household and family are located and firmly embedded within your jurisdiction, including twins born a few days before I was dragged here by one over-zealous accuser."

"I apologize for Darnell's behavior. Trask told me and I have taken Darnell to task. I did not know that Mistress Stanfield gave birth, let alone to twins. How are she and they? Please do give the dear lady my felicitations. She was so good to my first wife."

"Thank you. I am pleased to say the confinement was brief and all are doing well, based on my last communication with them."

Endecott asked me about my relationship with Mr. Dawkins, who he remembered as being part of my household. I said that he and I had fallen out over a personal issue. The result of which was that Mr. Dawkins and I were estranged. Endecott said that he had heard that Dawkins had made it plain he was no longer a friend of mine. How would it be, he said, if he arranged for Dawkins to escort me? I kept a straight face and admitted it would be uncomfortable, probably for both of us. I also said, given the circumstances, I would find it easier if Sykes, brutal as he was, continued in that role. Endecott smiled and said it probably would be. He then had me taken back to the gaol and told me to await developments.

The next day, Trask came and invited me back to his house where he was to resume his guardianship over me. When we were back behind closed doors, he clapped me on the back and asked how I had managed to both persuade Endecott to release me into his charge and allow me to investigate my accusers? I said that I had the opinion that Endecott felt that I had been falsely accused and was more motivated to clear up this mess than anyone else. Trask agreed and added that Endecott thought I was probably more capable, as well. A short while later there was a knock on the door. Johnny was invited in and, again, behind closed doors gave me a hug. In my absence he had been to New Barrow and had been introduced to the twins. He said he had been in trepidation about going back with Jeannie still there in his mind. Seeing Annie and the children did much to chase away the sadness. He was also introduced to Patience, whom he said seemed pleasant. I raised my eyebrows when he told me that. He continued, ignoring my reaction, by asking me what my plan was to clear my name.

As I had already told Trask of my conversation with Endecott, while he left the room to organize some refreshments I gave Johnny a full account. With Trask back in the room and tankards of beer in front of us, I said,

"We need to find the source for the rumors. We can't get to Maverick as he is in Bermuda, at the moment. We can get to Darnell. We need someone he trusts or has talked with to see if we can extract that information."

Trask suggested that he would probably be the best person to deal with that. He had already asked Darnell to give him more information to support his accusation, but he had refused, saying he was keeping it for the trial. Trask needed someone close to Darnell to ask the question. Another reason was that by now Darnell would know I was back under his roof and therefore as far as Darnell was concerned, he, Trask, was suspect. Trask would have used Humphrey Woodbury, who is friendly with Darnell, but he is with Maverick. Anyway, he will work on it and get back to me.

Gott was also keeping the letter securely. Even Endecott hadn't been given access to it. It almost seemed Gott suspected it wouldn't stand too careful an examination. Perhaps the best plan would be to stay away from trying to get him to show the letter, rather to try to find out where he got it. I knew it had to be a forgery, so it mattered less what was in it but more where it had come from. Was it sent, delivered to him in Salem by someone, or did he go somewhere to get it? My sense was that someone had talked to him trying to persuade him of my guilt and used the letter to support his claim.

Johnny said he would go to New Amsterdam and force Grindle to divulge who was behind his activities. He also wanted to talk to Hoekstra. He would arrange for *Marie* to make another trip down there. Easy enough as he was still the quartermaster. While he was there, he would identify the people I needed to talk to.

"No Johnny, that seems unnecessary. I will come with you, with Sykes as my escort. Once there, I can meet with these people myself."

"Too dangerous, Isaac. Remember, Grindle wants to kill you."

"That's another reason for me to come down. I need to find out if Grindle really is Seth and if not who, and why he wants to kill me. It's too much of a coincidence that Grindle and whoever we seek are not somehow involved with Maverick's, Darnell's and Gott's sources. It is entirely possibly there is just one man behind this who has an almighty grudge against me. Grindle knows me, so I must know him. When I see him, we will be well on the way to solving the problem."

CHAPTER 41

Journal entry – *April - May 1631*

It took Johnny a couple of weeks to organize a trading voyage to New Amsterdam on *Marie*. It gave me time to go to New Barrow on a clear, bright Spring morning. The snow had long gone, and shades of green were everywhere. Sykes was my vigilant escort. Trask had provided us with horses. We arrived early in the afternoon. Annie was surprised and overjoyed to see me, as I was her. Sykes discreetly looked elsewhere while we kissed and hugged each other, I had been away for six weeks. Nestling close with both hands firmly holding my arm, she took me on a tour, with Sykes following. The children were at the stables. They ran to meet me, a lovely family hug, until James remembered himself and drew back, shook my hand and said, "Welcome home, Daddy." Quite the man of the house. Giles and Kate were out bringing the cows, with their calves, back for milking. Beth and Abigail were excited to tell me the calves' names. Kate had decided to keep them. The three heifers were called Mable, Dot, and Edith; the bullock, Adam. Abigail, serious for a moment, said that Eight had been eaten by a wolf.

"Eight," I exclaimed, "that's most of the animals!"

"No, Daddy, Eight the goat. That's why the sheep had been kept in their pen. Oh! While you were away four more does have been born, not yet named because Kate thinks they should be sold."

I was surprised. I didn't even know the goats were pregnant. I realized that I was not intimately involved with our goats and decided I should remain so. The horses Samson and Penny had followed the cattle and were at the fence waiting for me and Annie. As I felt their soft muzzles and their warm breath on my hand, I turned to Annie. "Takes you back, doesn't it?"

Annie hugged me and murmured wistfully,

"Maddy and Tess, I wonder how they are. I do miss those wonderful horses. But now we have these two. Long may they provide the same love and support. It's time to come and see Nathaniel and Hannah. They will have woken from their nap by now. Which reminds me, Isaac, we need to have them both baptized."

"Sorry, my love, baptism will have to wait. We don't have an Anglican church yet and the Puritans will only allow a church member's child to be baptized. We are not church members."

Patience was waiting for us with the babes swaddled in her arms. She gave one to Annie and one to me. I glanced at Annie hoping she would tell me which was which, but her head was down, focusing on bringing a baby to her breast to feed. Patience told me I was holding Nathaniel. Swaddled as they were, they looked identical, all pink with wispy brown hair.

That evening Annie and I went to our bed early. We had need of each other after so long away. After a long and gentle coming together, we nestled in each other's arms, and I told her all that had happened.

Annie listened without interrupting. Then she said,

"You make it all sound so simple. Just find the man who has a grudge against you and all will be well. If Winthrop decides that, come what may, he doesn't trust you, he could have you expelled like poor Mr. Morton. Doesn't he have the power to take away the land grant you had been given? If the Massachusetts Bay Company can take over Sir Ferdinando's land grant, they can certainly take yours away."

Annie was right. We were in a difficult position. We had a burgeoning farm, thanks to Kate and Giles. We were increasing the acreage in use, although still only a small percentage of the 200 acres given to us. Notwithstanding Gavan's departure, we had substantial standings of woodland, capable of providing rich harvests of wood. If those were all taken away from us, we would be forced to join a settlement in much reduced circumstances. With small likelihood of recovering anything from the *Argossy* episode, David would need to find employment for himself. I would need to find Kate a farm of her own, presumably with Giles. At least Johnny was now gainfully employed. Annie and I drifted off into troubled sleep. Sykes and I returned to Salem the following morning.

Johnny, Sykes, and I sailed down to New Amsterdam on *Marie*, at the beginning of May. Johnny was brought up to date with all the issues. He was dismayed at the implications for the Stanfield family. I said I wanted to see Grindle and then Hoekstra. He thought it would be better if I could observe Grindle without being seen, not knowing what he might do. Once I knew whether or not he was Seth, I could decide what my next step was. With respect to Hoekstra, I said a meeting should be arranged. I am a shipowner with trading interests in Europe, England, and Bermuda. I will use an assumed name, Jude Tattershall as he is aware of the name Stanfield. Johnny asked where that came from. I told him it was the name I used while searching for the kidnapped James in Bermuda.

We arrived at New Amsterdam late in the afternoon. I stayed on board while Sykes and Johnny went ashore, Sykes to become familiar with the lie of the land and Johnny to find Grindle, hopefully through Doncker. A while later, Johnny returned. Grindle was in his customary tavern, De Druif, drunk. He wouldn't recognize anyone if they sat right next to him. He suggested we go there right now. Sykes appeared and we went together. The tavern's bar room was dark, crowded, noisy and smelled of piss and beer. Johnny worked his way into a far corner, where a disheveled figure sat, head bent over his mug of ale. Johnny went up to him, sat down and said something. The figure looked up. Too far away for me to see his features. I pushed my way through the patrons with Sykes close behind. One of the patrons had a tankard of ale in his hand, it spilt over his shirt when I pushed past him. He took exception and swung a fist at me, caught by Sykes. A brawl ensued. By the time it had been cleared Grindle and Johnny had disappeared while Sykes and I were thrown out of the tavern. Perfidious English, always causing problems for poor innocent Dutchmen. Johnny joined us with a grin on his face. He had enjoyed himself, as had Sykes. When the brawl became more widespread, there were English sailors there who had joined in, Grindle had lurched to his feet and escaped out of a side door. Johnny noticed and followed him. Grindle had gone to ground in a house close by. Johnny imagined he was now in a drunken stupor. We returned to *Marie*, bruised, battered, and a little bloody. We needed to clean up and arrange my meeting with Hoekstra.

Johnny left to go to Hoekstra's office to make an appointment for me. He returned a short time later. Hoekstra's assistant said he would be available at 8:00 the following morning. I was there at the appointed hour, alone. Johnny had gone with Sykes to find Grindle. Hoekstra was a tall, thin austere looking man with a pointed beard, a full wig and deep, dark eyes.

"Mr. Tattershall, good day to you. What can I do for you?"

I introduced myself and Hoekstra said he understood I was a shipowner with business interests in Europe and Bermuda.

"Yes, I am looking to extend my international business interests to include New Amsterdam and Virginia. I have been given your name as someone from whom I should seek advice about how I might accomplish that."

An assistant came in with a tray containing a tall, thin necked, white porcelain jug with a spout, together with two small delicate cups on saucers. Hoekstra asked me if I would care for some coffee. I had never drunk coffee before. Forewarned by Johnny I said I would be pleased to but would prefer it with a little sugar. Hoekstra nodded and said he was impressed that I, an Englishman, was a coffee drinker. Coffee had only recently arrived in New Amsterdam, as far as he knew the only location in North America. I was obviously much travelled. He asked where my travels had taken me. I told him and he gently tested me by asking me questions about La Havre, Delft, Leiden, Rochelle, Bilbao, Malaga, and Bermuda, all of which he knew from direct experience.

By the end of that not subtle interrogation and our second cup of coffee, which I have to admit I began to enjoy, Hoekstra leant back in his chair and began to fill a pipe. He asked me if I smoked tobacco. I said I didn't. He asked if I minded him smoking. I said I didn't. He became much more relaxed. I had passed a test. As far as he was concerned, I was an experienced international trader.

He asked me the name and size of my ship. I said it was currently in a refit in Weymouth, recently acquired, originally called the *Argossy*, 350 tons, but was being renamed the *Sweet Rose*. I had leased or otherwise contracted to make use of other merchantmen, one of which was called the *Sweet Rose*, sadly sunk after action with a pirate a few years ago. I liked the ship and the name, so I have decided to use it. Hoekstra said he knew of the *Sweet Rose* and her sad end. I asked if he knew the owner. He said, only by reputation, a Mr. Isaac Stanfield. I wondered what had happened to him after the sinking. He understood he had moved to New England. He didn't know what he was doing there but said he had a fine reputation. I remarked that I thought Salem and Boston were a bit rough and politically unstable at the moment. I had come from New Plimouth which seemed more settled, but still quite small in terms of population. New Amsterdam was larger with many more commercial opportunities. Hoekstra laughed.

"Mr. Tattershall, I think our reputation has outstripped the reality of our situation. It is true that New Netherland is a province of the Netherlands and claims much territory to the north, east and west of us. However, we are employees of the Dutch West India Company and our effective area of interest is the Hudson River. We have established trading posts at certain points up the river but all but a few of the thirty families we brought over from Holland were located here in New Amsterdam in 1624. We now have a population comprising perhaps 250 men, women, and children. We trade with the local Indians for beaver skins. In that enterprise we are successful and can afford to import some of the finer things in life for our comfort and enjoyment as well as being valuable commodities to be traded."

I expressed surprise. He said that a major difference between this

Dutch settlement and that of the English was that there was no conflict here. They were able to focus on the business opportunities available. He observed that Governor Winthrop needed to assert his authority and King Charles had to support him. I asked what he meant. The King should not allow different claims to continue to confuse and upset the stability of the settlement. There were too many commercial opportunities to be exploited. I asked what the different claims were. He said he wasn't an expert but felt the Massachusetts Bay Company had possession and a governing structure in place. There was a claim from a man called Sir Ferdinando Gorges that he had a prior right to the territory. Hoekstra said he didn't know much more but, interestingly enough, Stanfield's name had been mentioned as being a Gorges agent. I expressed surprise. Hoekstra asked me if I knew the name Maverick. I said I was aware he was a merchant trader. Hoekstra said it was Maverick who mentioned it to him. We continued the conversation focusing more on the commercial interests I had. At the end of which Hoekstra said he would be pleased to establish a trading relationship with me. As soon as my ship was ready, he would be prepared to agree a contract between us.

—— CHAPTER 42 ——

Journal entry – *May 1631*

Back on *Marie*, Sykes was waiting for me. Johnny was ashore trans-
acting *Marie* trading business. The crew had offloaded the incoming freight and had started loading the outgoing. A problem had occurred—the manifest didn't match all the items to be loaded. Johnny was sorting it out. Sykes said that he and Johnny had gone to the
house where Grindle was believed to be. Johnny had entered and found
Grindle, in a stupor still. He told Sykes to tell me that from what he
remembered Grindle would make his way back to the tavern around
midday to spend the afternoon getting drunk again. A sad and continuing cycle of despair.

Shortly before 12:00, Sykes and I went ashore and Sykes led me to
Grindle's house, more of a hovel really. Sykes went in to see if Grindle
was still there. He was and indignantly asked what the hell Sykes was
doing there. Sykes apologized and said he was looking for someone.
Grindle didn't make much of a fuss. Sykes nearly filled the filthy room.
We waited round the corner on the way to the tavern, for Grindle to
appear. When he did, I stepped into a doorway while Sykes stood in
front of me. I heard the shuffling feet approach and round the corner.
Grindle, with a hat pulled down covering most of his face, walked
past. Sykes bumped into him knocking him off his feet. Apologizing,
he lifted the angry and protesting Grindle back onto his feet, picked

Grindle's hat off his head and used it to dust down Grindle's clothing. It was Seth. A poor shadow of his former meanness. Life had been hard. He looked deathly ill. Difficult not to pity him. Sykes let him go and he wandered off, muttering. I would choose my time when to confront him, but I would need to do it soon. I doubted he would last the summer. I wondered why he had been reduced to his current state so quickly from the man Johnny had met in New Plimouth and the man who had shot at me in Salem. Whoever had been using him must have ceased doing so, abandoning him to a miserable half existence.

Johnny returned, his problem resolved. The loading of freight continued with some urgency, as *Marie* would be leaving first thing in the morning. I told Johnny about our encounter with Seth. I thought we needed to move quickly if we hoped to obtain any useful information from him. Johnny said that if I was right and he had been abandoned, now was the time to confront him. Johnny suggested that he and Sykes go and collect him from De Druif and bring him back to *Marie*. Sykes, who had been fully briefed about the conspiracy, asked an obvious question. If Seth confesses to having shot at me, why not take him back to the authorities in Salem? I had another idea, a signed confession. We must get him to act as a witness for my defense, as well.

Without causing a scene at the tavern, Sykes and Johnny returned with Seth. I was sitting on a crate on the dock with my back to their approach. When they came up to me I turned and looked at the miserable Seth. With sudden recognition, he started back but was held by Sykes and Johnny. My initial anger and desire for instant retribution dissipated. Seth was a quivering wreck. I let my anger quell while I studied him.

"Seth, I wish I could say how nice it is to see you after all this time. We need to have a long conversation. Please sit on the crate in front of you. You look thirsty. Can we get you something?"

Seth sat, shocked and scared, was too beaten down to resist. Johnny found a beaker of beer for him which he hugged to himself, as if to preserve his life. I suggested to him that he had nowhere to go and no future in New Amsterdam. His prospects were decidedly dim, and he seemed in very poor health. He slouched down nursing the beaker, taking an occasional sip, saying nothing. I asked him if he had a wish where would he like to go. He looked up at me, bleary eyed. "What do you mean?"

"I don't believe New England is a particularly healthy place for you. Why don't you leave?"

"I don't have the means."

"If you were provided with the means, where would you go?"

"England."

"I think that could be arranged. However, there is something you can do for me in exchange."

"What's that?"

"I will write a statement for you to sign, witnessed by these two gentlemen. In return for which I will arrange for you to be shipped, as a passenger, back to England."

Seth mumbled a response. I leaned towards him and asked him to repeat what he said.

"Show me the statement and I might sign."

I rose to my feet and Seth looked up at me. "How do I know you will help me if I do?"

"Seth, I do not want you anywhere I might ever have to see you again. What you have done to my family is more than enough for me to take you back to Salem and drown you on the way. No one will know and I doubt anyone will grieve. This is your one last chance to save what's left of your life."

Leaving Seth under Sykes' watchful eye, I went on board *Marie* with Johnny who took me to the main cabin. He provided paper and a quill with ink. I sat a desk and wrote:

I, Seth Tremont also known as Septimus Grindle and sometimes known as Carson, of my free will declare that I attempted to shoot Isaac Stanfield in Salem on or about 20 August, 1629. I declare that I forcibly persuaded Arthur Beamish to admit that he had fired the shot instead of me. I also told Arthur Beamish that Isaac

*Stanfield was a spy working for Sir Ferdinando Gorges. I know
this to be a lie.*

*Further, I declare that I paid a crewman called Spiggott on Ab-
igail in 1628 to attempt to take the life of Isaac Stanfield and later
in Naumkeag to attempt to kidnap his son James Stanfield.*

I made three copies which I took back to Seth and made him read
and sign all three. He objected but was persuaded that the admissions
were for the attention of the authorities in New England. They would
have no effect back in England. Johnny and Sykes also signed the copies as witnesses. Sykes, who couldn't write, signed it with his mark.

One more thing, I said to Seth.

"I know you have a grudge, ill-placed though it is. I know you escaped being hanged because neither Tremaine nor I were there to act
as witnesses to your kidnapping James and taking him to Bermuda,
but how did you manage to come to New England? Who helped you?"

Seth seemed past caring at this stage. He said simply, "Hook." I
asked him why. He simply shook his head and would say no more. I
told him we would take him to Salem and find room for him on the
first available boat returning to England. He just nodded. We took
him onboard and sailed back to Salem the following morning. Seth
slept the whole way.

On the way back, we reviewed what we had learned. We now knew
that Maverick had informed Hoekstra of my possible role as a Gorges spy. Grindle was Seth and Seth had been sent to New England by
Hook. Having eliminated Seth from our deliberations, we now needed to find out from Maverick who had told him about me. Could it
have been Hook? Where was Hook? How do we go about tracking
him down? Then there is the secretive Darnell. Johnny expressed surprise that I had given Seth back his life. He felt Seth should have been
hauled back to face trial and likely execution. I told him, Seth was, in
all probability, dying. I did not want his past, sordid life recounted in
a court of law. Annie, as his cousin, would have been brought into it,
as would the kidnapping of James. All those horrors and the wounds

they caused being raked over. I refused to let that happen.

Back in Salem, Sykes and I left *Marie*, taking Seth with us. It was a few days before I found a passage back to England for Seth. A fishing boat was due to leave in a week. They agreed to take him for £5. It would be an uncomfortable ride, but he didn't seem to give a damn. We kept him fed and secure in a hut until it was time for him to leave. I hoped he was sailing out of our lives forever. I wondered if he would survive the journey.

Now, how to find Hook. I remembered my remark that once we knew who was behind Grindle we would be well on the way to solving the problem. I had spoken too soon. Grindle was no longer our target, Maverick was. We would have to wait till he returned from Bermuda, which wouldn't be before June we were told. He was going to Barbados before returning to New England.

I talked to Trask about the confession I had received from Grindle, as well as the report I had received from Morton about his conversation with Beamish. He said that Endecott would be pleased. He hadn't told Winthrop but he lived in fear that a letter would land on Winthrop's desk complaining about the treatment of his son. He understood that Arthur Beamish was a friend of the Governor's son, Jack. It would be more than reasonable to expect the young Beamish to write to the young Winthrop. It would make Endecott more sympathetic towards me but there were accusations outstanding. I gave copies of both documents to Trask to deliver to Endecott and asked him to tell Endecott I would be pleased to discuss both with him.

The following day, I was asked to attend Endecott in his house. He welcomed me with a smile and a handshake. He congratulated me on finding Grindle and resolving the problem he had with Beamish. While Winthrop would probably be upset, he had been left in the dark about the young man, he would be able to write and tell his father that after an exhaustive investigation, the real culprit had been found. Young Arthur should no longer be held to a confession forced on him by the culprit. If asked by Winthrop why the culprit had not been apprehended, Endecott said he would say it was to save the Governor embarrassment. He then asked me to give him the details of my investigations to date, which I did. He asked me why Grindle bore me such a grudge. I gave him brief details stemming from his younger brother being executed for several crimes, including trying to kill me, only averted by the courageous action of my wife. Endecott leaned back and clapped his hands together.

"I must hear the whole story sometime. What a splendid wife you have."

I continued by saying the older brother Seth, who called himself Grindle, swore vengeance and kidnapped my son James and took him to Bermuda. He went there as an agent for Hook, who was a smuggler. I rescued James and took Seth back to England to be tried and I presumed executed for the kidnap. Somehow, he avoided that fate.

Endecott could hardly contain himself.

"I do love to hear stirring tales. Stanfield, one evening you and the dear Mistress Stanfield must come to dinner and regale us with these stories. They only add to the reputation you had before we first met."

He regretted however that there were a number of accusations against me. Seeing that I had been successful with regard to Grindle, he was confident that given time I would resolve those other accusations as well, before the Governor turned his attention to the problem. He did tell me that the Governor's request for the documents pertaining to my land grant weren't aimed at me. He apologized to me for having given me that impression. All land grants made by the Council for New England were to be reviewed by the new land court, as Endecott had told me before the new Governor arrived in New England.

We left in as fine a fellowship as we ever had, with him calling after me to remember him to my dear wife.

—— CHAPTER 43 ——

Journal entry – *June 1631*

Endecott was happy for me to return to New Barrow, provided I had my guard with me. I wanted to be back in Salem by the beginning of June, when Maverick was expected to return from his trip to the Caribbean. Friday, 3 June was a week away. Sykes was happy to accompany me, even if it was a long walk to and from. The weather was clear, a gentle breeze and summer had arrived. Annoyingly, so had the mosquitoes. To deter them we used the paste that Kimi had given Annie, produced from a certain type of boiled bark and herbs. I also had a pot of rancid fat, only to be used in extremis. I think Sykes had an eye for Patience. On arrival, I was greeted royally and quickly settled back into my family's warm embrace.

The next morning, Annie announced that we should go for our first ride together, on Samson and Penny. They had been broken to the saddle and Giles had been working them. But they were young and fresh. It had been a long time since I had last ridden, I quickly realized my muscles and bum were much out of condition. Annie and James had been riding the more sedate Penny on a regular basis. We rode through the extent of our property, from the mouth of the Erichuck River along the cliffs above the Merrimack to our house in the coomb and up the slope a few hundred yards beyond, then southeast away from the river through woods and open fields for half a mile and then back to the

Erichuck along the bottom rectangle of the property, skirting the Indian village. Villagers, all back for the summer, acknowledged us as we rode past, the women and children waved, the latter following us chattering and laughing as far as the river. We agreed to do this every day to get my body used to it again. It also gave us time alone together to listen and talk about all that had been happening. When we returned to the stable and I helped Annie down from Penny, she put her arms round me, held me close and looked up into my eyes.

"My love, I can't bear it to have you gone with this great cloud hanging over us. I spend much of my day worrying about you and us, where we might be this time next year, or even sooner. Somehow it is so much worse being so unsettled, compared to the times you are away on a sailing trip. When I ride here, I realize I've come to love New Barrow. I would hate to lose it and the wonderful Indian friends we have here."

I hugged her. The little I had been able to do to confront my accusers had not provided much solace for her. She had been pleased that Seth had been found and sent back to England. Despite all the damage he had done, he was her cousin and she felt pity for the poor man.

I asked her about Kate. If we had to move, she would need to find another opportunity as a tenant farmer. She couldn't afford to buy land and start from scratch. Annie said Kate was ignoring what might happen. She was entirely focused on her farm and the animals. She had discussed with Annie her plans for developing the land further, expanding the acreage both for husbandry and crops. However, she felt overwhelmed at the idea of farming the full 200 acres that comprised New Barrow Farm. She thought 50 acres would be an ideal size for her, perhaps growing to 100 acres in a few years. She was worried about the wolves and other predators. She and Giles kept a constant lookout and the full grown Belle had shown her redoubtable abilities as a guard dog, but they couldn't keep the animals in shelter overnight, the numbers were growing. Markets were opening up with the spread of settlers. With the transport we now had, those markets were accessible. Her plans could all come crashing down. Annie said that Kate had a simple faith that I would protect everyone. Ye gods!!

I asked about Giles. Annie said that he and Kate behaved as if they were an old, married couple, content in their relationship, good companions to each other and they worked well together. To the outside world, Giles was a retainer. He was careful to treat Kate with respect and deference. They saw it as a game which they enjoyed playing. She had had no word from the authorities about her divorce and it didn't seem to concern her.

I mentioned my suspicions about Sykes and Patience. Annie laughed. He had no chance of success there. "Oh?" I questioned. Annie and Patience had become close and confided in each other. I asked if she had replaced Jeannie.

"No, no one could do that, but Jeannie had been dependent. Patience has an inner strength and is highly articulate, a different person. I see Patience much more as an equal. We talk about things I would never have discussed with Jeannie. Patience has decided that when Johnny comes back to earth and New Barrow Farm, however long that might take, she will marry him."

"Goodness, poor Johnny. That will be an interesting courtship."

Annie laughed and we spent the rest of the evening with the children and then to bed.

The week went by quickly. I was able to spend time with each of the children. I wanted to find out how they were developing, they seemed to be growing up quickly. I was concerned about Beth. She was maturing. She was twelve but looked older, her body was now that of a young woman. While sitting on a fence with her, watching the cows, we chatted. I was amazed at how grown up she seemed. Her mothering instincts had blossomed looking after Abigail but I was concerned. I remembered the girls in Dorchester when I was growing up. They were finding boys much more attractive than the boys were of them. I had seen some unfortunate incidents, which I had been glad to steer clear of, for the most part. A vision of Aby flashed through my mind. I would need to talk to Annie about Beth.

Abigail lived in a soft cocoon of love and happiness. Jeannie's death had been grieved over and quickly put aside. She had her big brother,

James, and big sister, Beth, to look after her. She lived for her goats who all loved her. No one could ask for a more perfect life. She had a Mummy and a Daddy who would always protect her from harm.

James and I went for a ride, he was on Penny. He had been riding her every day and, with instruction from Annie, Kate, and Giles, was becoming an accomplished rider, increasingly able to differentiate between the sometimes conflicting advice he was getting. We talked as we walked, James, happy to describe his many adventures. I asked him how he was getting on with his siblings. He admitted that he spent most of his free time with his Indian friends or exploring on his own. He said that Abigail and Beth spent a lot of time together which was good. I noticed a slight hesitation when he mentioned Beth and looked at him. He blushed and changed the subject. I reined in Samson, James stopped and I asked him if there was something the matter. He grimaced and said Beth made him a little uncomfortable. "How so?" I asked. He didn't want to talk about it, but I kept prodding. Eventually, he admitted that Beth had cornered him in the stable one day. He had gone to the loft to pull down some hay and Beth had followed him up. "What happened?" I asked. He slowly described what sounded like a clumsy attempt by Beth to seduce James. Beth evidently eager to explore and James alternately excited and embarrassed. The sound of Abigail coming into the stable looking for Beth stopped further activity. James admitted they put their clothes back on and as far as Abigail was concerned they were getting hay, which they threw down for her.

"James, you do remember the conversation we had a year or so ago. You asked where babies came from, and I told you. What you and Beth were doing is what a man and a woman do when they want to have a baby. You do realize that don't you?"

James was startled. He had not realized that. The excitement of touching and being touched was an amazing experience. He had not thought about the inevitable outcome. I told him that God provides man and woman with the incredible gift and responsibility to produce children. He makes the process exciting, to make them want to do it. But they must use that gift wisely.

"Imagine," I said, "if you and Beth had a baby. Better still, what would you do if Nathaniel or Hannah was your child?"

James looked horrified. How could such a simple, irresistible pleasure have such consequences? I pushed further.

"Have you any idea of the responsibility of a father, to care for the child, protect it, feed it, teach it, how having a child restricts your own life? Then there is the law. Having a child out of wedlock is unlawful. When such a thing happens, the father is required to marry the mother. Would you accept being made to marry under such circumstances, be it Beth or anyone else?"

Lesson over, we continued our ride, James now silent and thoughtful. After a while, I asked him what sort of future did he see for himself. Without hesitation he said he wanted to be a sailor. He wanted to do what I did and go to sea as a ship's boy and eventually become a captain and a ship owner. He had talked to David Tremaine who said that when he was captain, he would be happy to sign James on as crew.

Later, in bed with Annie I told her about my conversation with James. Annie sighed and said she was worried that Beth, having reached puberty, would have all the sexual urges that came and none of the understanding of how to deal with it. She would talk to Kate about it. Beth certainly knew the facts of life. Annie had sat down with Abigail one day to tell her, and Abigail said she already knew. When the goats first gave birth, Abigail had asked some questions and Beth had given her a full education on the subject. Annie also knew that James wanted to go to sea. It caused her great distress to think about losing James. He was growing up. It seemed way too soon for it to be the time that fledglings left the nest.

Sykes and I walked back to Salem at the end of the week. He said he had enjoyed the week, but he was not a farmer. He was happy to help Giles with the heavy labor, but different muscles were used, and he was sore. I asked him how he found Patience. He laughed and told me that she would make the right person a good wife, but not him. He found her attractive but much too independent. She had a good brain on her and needed to be challenged.

───── CHAPTER 44 ─────

Journal entry *– June 1631*

Maverick arrived back from his trip to Bermuda and Barbados the second week of June. Trask told me that Maverick planned to see Endecott that afternoon. and the meeting had been arranged for 2:00pm. He also told me that a message had been sent to Endecott that Governor Winthrop desired to meet with Maverick in Watertown, at his early convenience. I needed to try and get to Maverick before he saw Governor Winthrop. I didn't know the reason why the Governor wanted to see him, but if there was a chance I was being discussed, I should find out from Maverick how serious he thought the accusations were being made about me. Johnny was in town and had made surreptitious contact with me. We still maintained the perceived enmity between us. He agreed to intercept Maverick on his way to Endecott's office and talk to him on the street. If I was close by I could, by chance, bump into them. It was organized in haste and might not achieve much, but nothing ventured nothing gained.

Johnny stationed himself in the square close to Endecott's office, sitting on a bench engrossed in a religious tract. I watched him from the other side of the square, out of view, with Sykes close by. At about 1:45, Maverick appeared. He approached Johnny and acknowledged him. Then, to Johnny's surprise, he sat down on the bench. They started chatting and I sauntered over as if to pass them by. Maverick saw me and greeted me civilly. Johnny stood, wished Maverick a good day and stalked off. I apologized for having interrupted their conversation.

"Isaac, I must apologize to you for the rudeness of Mr. Dawkins. I am due to meet with Endecott in a few minutes. I was early, saw Dawkins sitting on this bench and thought I would eke out the time till my appointment. It seems you and Dawkins haven't reconciled yourselves to each other. I am sorry."

"Samuel, good to see you. Johnny is young and headstrong. Sad, but probably inevitable. He feels he must learn from his own experience not from the well-meaning advice of others. "

Samuel laughed and said he knew the problem. After exchanging pleasantries, I asked him if he remembered rescuing Grindle last year from Salem gaol. He looked puzzled.

"That was a long time ago. It was a man called Carson I had released. He had been sent to deliver a message to me in Charleston and had been detained, unnecessarily in my opinion. I remember telling you so at the time. But why do you ask?"

"Carson was actually Grindle. If you remember a young man called Beamish confessed to an attempt to shoot me and was quietly sent home to Suffolk. It was Grindle who had shot at me and persuaded Beamish to take the blame. He confessed and has also been returned to England. He also confessed to having made up a story about me being a Gorges agent."

Maverick looked uncomfortable. He said he had an appointment to keep. He would like to continue the conversation another time and asked how he could get hold of me. I told him I was staying with the Trasks. He stood, shook my hand, and left for his appointment. I returned to the Trask house, with Sykes following. A number of things I gathered from that brief meeting. Maverick might or might not have known Carson was Grindle but he was to be the recipient of the message that Grindle said he was to deliver. He was, therefore, close by when Grindle failed to appear, which was why he was able to have him released so quickly. Also, Maverick was puzzled and uncomfortable. Whatever had made him uncomfortable, I felt he would want to have resolved and would seek me out to do so. Finally, the last time we had met he had not been well-disposed towards me. That ill-disposition seemed to have gone.

I wondered when Maverick would get back to me and if I was being too optimistic, confused by his apparent warmth. Returning to the Trask house I was greeted by William Trask, with a long face.

"Mr. Stanfield, do you know a Sir Christopher Gardner?"

"I've never heard of him, why?"

"I hadn't until yesterday. It seems he is a Gorges spy. He came over here last year with a young woman he insists is his cousin and has been living in or near Merrymount. A letter was sent to the Governor stating that Sir Christopher is a Gorges man and wanted for bigamy, having a wife in England, another in France, and the so-called cousin is his mistress."

"Sounds sordid. What has that got to do with me?"

"The letter seems to imply that Sir Christopher has been asked by Gorges to contact you for assistance. But, to make matters worse, further letters have just been intercepted and read by Governor Winthrop intended for Sir Christopher, further implicating you."

I was confused.

"Letters from England? Who did the letters came from?"

"I think one of the letters was from Sir Ferdinando Gorges."

"Did the letter specifically say Sir Christopher was to contact me?"

"I don't know. If he is at Merrymount, he must have been invited by Morton, who is an agent of Sir Ferdinando. Perhaps he has been condemned because he knows Morton."

"This sounds highly suspect," I replied.

"Mr. Stanfield, however doubtful, it is evidence from yet another source that ties you to Gorges. The Governor doesn't want a court case. He wants enough believable evidence to enable him to deal with you without repercussions from England. Endecott tells me that the Governor has asked for the documents confirming the Council of New England's grant of 200 acres to you. I hate to say it, but you stand to lose that grant and the considerable money you have invested in it. The only thing in your favor, right now, is that the Governor is overwhelmed with other matters. When he read the letter about Sir Christopher, he immediately had him detained. I suspect that he considered Sir Christopher sufficiently unsavory that no one would vouch for him. He wasn't prepared to risk him joining Morton and Gorges in their campaign, so he didn't want to send him back to England. He just wanted him out of his hair and had him released. Unfortunately, Sir Christopher has disappeared and is probably on his way back to England to do exactly what the Governor did not want him to do. You are altogether a different matter."

I would have liked to have met with Sir Christopher before he left, but that would have been foolish. I had to stay clear of Sir Ferdinando's spies. Leaving him aside, I still wanted to deal with the New Amsterdam connection. I told Trask that I needed to visit New Amsterdam again. He agreed. I should take Sykes with me.

Later that afternoon there was a knock on the door. It was Samuel Maverick. Trask, Samuel, and I sat in Trask's parlor, each with a glass of sherry and Samuel told me that while he was with Governor Winthrop, my name had been raised. He asked Samuel what he knew about me, and Samuel had given him a short history to the extent he knew it. Winthrop then said he was aware that I had a long history of working for Gorges and he had been told that I was still doing so. He asked Samuel if he knew that, in fact, to be the case.

Samuel replied that he didn't know for certain. He used to think so, based on information he had been given from what has turned out to be an unreliable source. He added that he was now inclined to believe that Stanfield was who he says he is—a settler wishing to make New England his home with his family. Surely, he pointed out to Winthrop, the last thing Stanfield would want to do was anything that would jeopardize that desire and the considerable investment he has already made. Winthrop responded that there was logic to his contention but there were other sources that accused Stanfield of disloyalty, even of treason, and he could not discount them.

Samuel countered,

"Governor, I have heard of these sources. I received such information and rather than come to you, I wanted to prove the veracity or otherwise of those accusations. I have found the rumors to be highly circumstantial."

"Mr. Maverick, I want you to do something for me. Having Morton and now, probably Sir Christopher Gardner, working against the Massachusetts Company back in England to the extent of having the Privy Council involved, I don't want to add another voice to their complaints. Please, will you do what you did with the accusation you received and chase down the sources of the others and prove or otherwise their veracity as you call it?"

Samuel agreed to do that. The first thing he did was come to find me, tell me what the Governor had said and plan the next steps, with me engaged. He said he was working on the assumption that I was innocent and whoever was or were behind the accusations had some grudge against me. I told him that I had drawn the same conclusion.

We started with Carson or Grindle. Maverick had first come into contact with him through Hoekstra in New Amsterdam. Hoekstra and he had a business relationship. Hoekstra used various couriers to get messages to Samuel. One such was the person he knew as Carson. It was Carson or Grindle who told him that I was a Gorges agent when he had Grindle released. I asked why would Grindle suddenly start talking about me? Samuel said he thought it odd. Grindle was in a disturbed state when Samuel saw him in his cell. At the time, his sole interest was to make sure Hoekstra's courier was released and returned to New Amsterdam. Grindle seemed obsessed with me for some reason. That obsession was enough for Samuel to take note of what Grindle was saying. Some of what he said about my having worked for Gorges, he knew to be true. Although he found Grindle to be a distasteful individual, much of what he said seemed feasible. I said that I had been carrying out my own investigation. I had gone to New Amsterdam and had met Hoekstra, who had told me that he had heard about me and Gorges from Maverick. Samuel apologized for that, saying he had asked Hoekstra about the man he knew as Carson, to find out whether

Hoekstra was his source.

"Samuel, Grindle was the main reason I was in New Amsterdam. I suspected he was someone I knew in England, who had a serious grudge against me. It turned out I was right. Grindle is Seth, a cousin of my wife, who had every reason to want to seek his revenge."

I told him about my meeting with Seth in New Amsterdam. After a pause, he said,

"Grindle or Seth mentioned the name Hook, a businessman who has a trading business in Bermuda and Barbados. In fact, I have just returned from Barbados with him. Do you know him?"

I described the Hook I had known many years earlier and Samuel said it certainly sounded like him, though he was now a successful trader and looked the part, not an itinerant smuggler, as I had portrayed him. I asked Samuel where Hook was now. He said he left him in Bermuda, where he is based. His trading business is focused on the Caribbean and New Amsterdam. Did Hook know that Samuel knew me? Samuel didn't know. My name was never mentioned so there was no way of knowing if Hook had been acting against me.

I changed the subject and asked Samuel about his own trading business in Bermuda. He nodded his head. "Good," he said. I told him that I had spent some time in Bermuda in 1624. He said that I would find it has changed a great deal and the business was good. I asked him if he had come across a man called Trescothick.

"Argy, yes most certainly. Funny name though. I wonder how he got it. A good man. How do you know him?"

"I first met him eighteen years ago in France. He had been rescued from pirates. His given name is Jason, hence Argy."

Samuel looked puzzled. I said, "Jason and the Argonauts.""Aah! He told me about the rescue. He said that he and some of his fellow crewmen were rescued from what would have been a short life as a galley-slave and taken back to Plymouth from La Rochelle in 1613. If you knew him then, you must have been on the boat that took him back."

I said I was and asked Samuel how he knew him.

"Argy is a successful businessman in Bermuda, imports and exports.

If anyone wants to do business with Bermuda, Argy is the man you would want to deal with. He's honest, approachable, and trusted by his colleagues. Most importantly, he is trusted by the government, a rare attribute. Hook knows him. He told me that he had met him under somewhat adverse circumstances in 1624. Wait a minute, are you, Hook and Argy all connected?"

"We were. I haven't seen either of them since then."

"Funny, they never mentioned you."

"Why should they? I don't think either knew I was in New England. I was a distant memory to them. It seems then, that Hook did not cast aspersions in my direction."

"Actually, that's not quite true," Samuel said, "not about the aspersions, though. I've just realized that he must have found out you were in New England. He told me he had sent a man, that must have been Grindle, to New Amsterdam to act as his agent. Anyway, he found out that Grindle had attempted to kill someone, learned that it was you he was trying to kill and, forthwith, abandoned him."

I laughed. "That explains why Grindle looked destitute when I met him in New Amsterdam. He admitted Hook had sent him."

Trask, who had been keeping our glasses topped up with sherry, said it all sounded fascinating. But there was still the question of Darnell's apparent evidence and the letter the Governor had received about Sir Christopher Gardner accusing me of being a Gorges agent. I said I seemed to remember the letter implied I might be involved, not that I was an actual agent. Samuel felt those two items were probably beyond his capability to deal with and the meeting broke up.

After Samuel had left, Trask told me that he would talk to Endecott and get him to force Darnell to divulge the extent and source of the evidence he had against me. He wondered whether the source was the same for the letter the Governor had received. I said we should track down Darnell's source and find out the seriousness of the claims being made. Once we knew who was making the claims and why, we should go to the Governor.

CHAPTER 45

Journal entry – *July 1631*

By the beginning of July, Trask had been able to extract the information that Darnell had been guarding. It was part of a letter that had been sent to Walford from Thomas Weston. Darnell had gone to Walford to buy some ironware. While waiting for the items to finish being forged, they started chatting. Darnell asked Walford about when he first came to New England. Walford talked about his arrival with Robert Gorges in 1623 and the many people with whom he had come into contact. One such person was Thomas Weston. In fact, funnily enough, Walford had received a letter from Weston only a short time before, asking him to trace some people who had been at Wessagusset. In the letter, various names were mentioned including Isaac Stanfield, identified in caustic terms as Sir Ferdinando's whipping boy and the cause of Weston's fall from grace. Walford had laughed it off. Darnell asked if he could read the letter. Walford said it was on the table amongst a lot of other papers in his office in the next room. While Walford was occupied at the forge, Darnell sauntered over to the office, found the letter, and took the page containing the reference to me. No wonder he kept the theft quiet. Not only had he stolen the supposed evidence, it was worthless as evidence to support the claim that I was a current agent of Gorges. Darnell was made to realize that and ordered to return the page to its rightful owner. Darnell had let his dislike for me overrule his common sense.

Trask informed Endecott who went to see the Governor. It turned out that the letter the Governor had received from the Massachusetts Bay Company's office in London, alerting him to Sir Christopher, had suggested that Sir Christopher might seek to rally support for Gorges in New England. No actual mention of me had been made in the text of the letter, but my name had been added on the margin with a question mark. Winthrop had assumed that it had been added prior to the letter being sent from London. Endecott suggested that the Governor re-examine the letter, which he did. He found that one of his staff, responsible for opening and sorting all the Governor's mail into subject matter and level of importance, had made the insertion.

The Governor told Endecott that I should be released with his apologies. No charges would be made on this matter. I thanked Trask and Endecott for their help and with the faithful Sykes rode back to New Barrow on rented horses. On the way back, I advised Sykes that it remained my intention to acquire or lease a seagoing vessel at the earliest opportunity. I would be delighted to offer him a position in the crew. Sykes said he looked forward to it. He was to return to Salem with the horses, having been informed by Trask that he would continue to be employed in Salem, supporting the Constable in his duties.

It was so good to be back with Annie and my family. The last four months had been difficult for her, me being confined in Salem, for the most part, and Annie not knowing what our future might be. She had coped as only Annie could. The family well, the farm productive. I asked what the situation was between James and Beth. Kate had taken her daughter in hand. Annie didn't know exactly what was said but James was no longer bothered by a lustful Beth. Annie said that Kate and Beth had reached agreement that Beth would seek a position with a family looking for someone to mind their children. On Kate's next trip to town with a cartload of produce to sell, Beth would accompany her and Giles to seek such a position in Salem or one of the many new towns springing up. I was sad to think of Beth being thrown out of our protective family, but Annie said it was an opportunity for Beth. She was bright, could read and write, but was bored. She was constrained at New Barrow and needed a wider world with people, adults and young women of her own age, to help her mature into an attractive, sensible, young woman and find herself a good husband. I thought she was too young. Annie laughed. Beth is thirteen, going on twenty. In a few years, she will make a fine catch. I remembered the first time I had met Kate at her farm in Woodyates, nine years ago; attractive, alluring, even. Beth was definitely her mother's daughter.

I was able to reacquaint myself with the twins, Nat and Nan, as Hannah was now being called. They were nearly seven months old, mobile on their hands and knees. I remembered with James, and then several years later with Abigail, how constant attention had to be paid at that age and that was with only one child to watch. Patience was truly well-named. I assumed Nat would be the adventurous one with Nan following along behind or even staying close to Patience. Not a bit of it. We had a highly competitive pair. I shuddered to think what they would be like in a few years. I imagined open warfare, each determined to best the other, but united as one against any external threat, including from parents and Patience.

A few days later, I received a formal invitation from Governor Winthrop requesting my attendance, at my convenience, at a meeting wherein he wished to make his apology to me in person and to discuss my plans for the future. I wrote back that I would be pleased to accept the invitation and planned to be in Watertown in two weeks.

Johnny returned to New Barrow Farm, saying he had let it be known he was now reconciled to me. He told me that there had been dissention among the three co-owners of *Marie* which had become bitter, affecting her successful pursuit of trade. It seemed that the most disruptive of the owners, who was friendly with Johnny, wanted to sell his share and told Johnny before it became generally known. I asked Johnny to give me a detailed analysis of the operation of *Marie* since he had joined it. I also asked him to obtain a comprehensive survey of the ship, as soon as possible. He laughed. He said he thought that would be my reaction. A full survey had recently been completed and he had a copy with him which he gave me. He then took me through the survey in detail, giving me a much more solid feeling for the seaworthiness and her long-term viability as a coastal trader. He spent the next two days writing his operating report and went through every line with me. I asked him why the part-owner was so frustrated as to want to sell his share in what appeared to be a successful business venture. Johnny said he was pigheaded and wanted to go further offshore to Bermuda and beyond, for instance. He wasn't a sailor and didn't understand the limitations inherent in a pinnace. I was satisfied and commissioned Johnny to act on my behalf to buy the share available. He told me he wanted to remain as quartermaster, a job he really enjoyed. I agreed. Johnny's joining the crew of *Marie* had coincided with a significant increase in the trade and profitability of the operation.

Before he left, he played with Nat and Nan, as Godfather-in-waiting to them both. Annie and Patience told Johnny they were going for a walk with the twins and invited him to accompany them. He was happy to do so and carried Nat. Annie let Patience ask Johnny about himself and probe any reticence on his part, so soon they were deep in conversation. Annie, following along behind, carrying Nan and distracted by their animation wasn't mindful of where they were walking. Suddenly, Johnny stopped, handed Nat to Patience and slowly walked into the grove where we had buried Jeannie. He looked down at the grave marker bearing her name, then sat on the ground bent his head and wept. Annie took Nat and Patience, without bidding, went to Johnny and knelt beside him. She put her arm around him. Johnny turned and buried his head in her breast. Annie turned away and retraced her steps with the twins in her arms. Much later, Patience returned alone and thoughtful. She said that Johnny had returned to Salem. She said nothing more.

I received a letter from David Tremaine. It had been sent from Plymouth in May. I read it to Annie. Scroud's appeal to the Privy Council concerning the *Argossy* had been heard. *Argossy* would remain in the hands of her original owners, but a judgement was made that the owners were liable for the loss of the *Sweet Rose*, members of her crew who had died, and her freight. The sum of £1,500 had been awarded to the owners of the *Sweet Rose* in compensation and penalty, with an order for immediate payment, given the long time it had taken to settle the litigation. The amount had been paid into the hands of Mr. Scroud.

David had searched for a barque of the approximate displacement of the *Sweet Rose*. He was pleased to tell us he had found one, being fully refitted in a Falmouth boatyard, the *Margaret Anne*, 180 tons burden, five years old. He had accompanied an experienced marine surveyor he knew on an exhaustive inspection in Falmouth. The boat was in excellent condition with all known deficiencies being dealt with in the refit. The owners had run out of money to complete the refit and the boat had been left idle for a month. David had negotiated a significant reduction in the price, given the money owed and work still required to complete the refit, together with the pressing need for money by the owners to pay off significant debts. David, therefore, was pleased to tell me that I was now the owner of the *Margaret Anne*, it having cost me £500, including the expected cost to complete the refit, planned for the end of June. David was busy recruiting crew. J.B. and Obi, who had returned from Barbados and made contact with Mr. Scroud, had signed on as first mate and bosun, respectively, Tiny Hadfield, second mate. Tiny had been given the job of finding as many members of the old *Rosie* crew as possible. David wanted a full complement of six officers, to include a gunnery officer, "Guns" and carpenter, "Chips", with twenty seamen. Finally, he announced that he hoped to sail in July. He was taking the southern route via Bermuda, as he had a hold-full of freight booked to be taken there. He expected to find suitable produce in Bermuda to bring to New England. He said we should expect him in September. I put the letter down and Annie and I looked at each other, silent. Then Annie said one word.

"Redemption."

We hugged and Annie said it was all unbelievable. It was only a few months ago that our world threatened to come toppling down about us. We had learned some lessons. We had had grandiose plans to build a 200 acre farm, make a fortune from cutting and selling lumber, happily isolated from the teeming masses pouring into New England. Gavan had moved on, in part I felt, because he realized we weren't in an ideal location to build a lumber business. I still wasn't sure what Governor Winthrop had in mind when he invited me to meet with him, but I commented to Annie, I felt we could certainly do with less. Annie was concerned about the isolation we had built for us. We had been here a full year, and Annie had already made it clear she and the children really did miss the community life of a village centered on its church, as much as she loved New Barrow.

I went to talk to Kate. She confirmed her ideas about the ideal size of farm for her, now and in the future with 100 acres or thereabouts being as large as she would want. It was interesting how her perception of what she would need had already grown from 50 acres to 100. I thought that when she had fully utilized the 100 acres she would need access to more. However, as I had left her to run the farm with Giles, notwithstanding the children's help, she was finding it hard going. New Barrow Farm was isolated in wild animal country. Even in the Salem area, farms were being attacked by wolves and bears. Much livestock was being lost. She said they had been lucky. The imposing presence of Belle was a deterrent and the cows and goats had been kept close all winter. Giles was also a good shot with his gun, killing a number of wolves, as had Belle, so they had become wary. But with a planned and regular increase in stock, she would need more help, not only to look after the animals but also to open up more arable land. I asked her what she thought about the possibility that the Stanfields would be moving closer to civilization but retaining New Barrow for her to continue to run. She said she would need to think about that, but it would mean she'd become a tenant farmer, something she always wanted to do. She said she would talk to Giles and come back to me with her considered response. I had the feeling she was excited about the proposition but wanted to explore all the consequences, intended or otherwise. I respected her for it.

I returned to Annie and that night we celebrated the way we normally did, sleeping little and enjoying the continued explorations of each other's bodies in our lovemaking.

CHAPTER 46

Journal entry – *August 1631*

I took Samson and rode to Watertown to see Governor Winthrop at the beginning of August. He seemed harried, overworked, and not looking well. However, he was gracious in his welcome. It was the first time I had met him. Narrow, long face, emphasized by a trimmed beard and moustache, full brown hair almost touching his shoulders, with streaks of grey. High eyebrows, above large slightly hooded eyes. He looked like the lawyer he was, with a high brow that spoke of a keen intelligence. He apologized for the Damoclean threat hanging over me and said he was pleased to remove it. He had heard good reports about me concerning the years I had been actively engaged in the attempts to settle New England. For that he said he was most grateful. "Who knows," he said, "where we would all be today, without your efforts."

He then asked me pertinent questions arising from those efforts, which resulted increasingly detailed descriptions of the work that the Reverend John White and Sir Ferdinando Gorges had been doing, making my feeble efforts pale into insignificance. The Governor was quick to recognize John White's contribution but was more circumspect about Sir Ferdinando. He admitted that Sir Ferdinando had indeed made many attempts and spent a great deal of money but ultimately had failed. Now he was trying to salvage in the courts and other more nefarious means what he had previously lost. The Governor said it was a pity, really. Pioneers build the foundations that successors use to create edifices. The Governor asked me whether Sir Ferdinando had ever written to me after I had moved to New England. I admitted he had, shortly after I arrived. He had sought my help and I had written back saying I was unable to help him. The Governor also asked me about my relationship with John Endecott. I said that the relationship had not been a good one back in England. I felt that Endecott was a bit out of his depth but needed to show leadership. He also wanted me to work for him, which I refused to do. After working for Gorges, I no longer wanted to work for anyone else. Anyway, I said, Endecott had grown into his job. I liked and respected him, even if he could still be a little impetuous at times.

Winthrop said he was aware that I had been granted 200 acres of land by Endecott. He had received a copy of the deed. He asked how I came by that grant. I told him that it came from the New England Company under Matthew Craddock, which had inherited the land grants in place when they took over the Dorchester Company, under Sir Walter Erle. The original grant was awarded to Richard Bushrode, one of the main investors. He had, before his death, bequeathed the grant to me. Winthrop asked me why he would have done such a thing. I said Bushrode and I had been business partners. We were ship owners. In addition, Bushrode had been a strong supporter of John White and the efforts to settle New England. He had been appreciative of my assistance in that regard. The Governor asked me what my plans were for the land. I described the farm and admitted that we would probably use no more than 100 acres to start with. It was heavily wooded. I told him I had had plans to build a lumber business but had decided my interests were elsewhere.

"Mr. Stanfield, I was informed that you were a merchant trader in England. Am I to believe that you intend to continue in that line of business?"

"Yes, sir. I have plans to build a trading business, providing local shipping and trading services to the towns located in the Massachusetts Bay and up into Maine. I also plan to expand that business to trade with Bermuda, the Caribbean, and England."

"Do you have boats of your own?"

"Yes, sir. I expect to become a part owner in a pinnace for local trade and I have a barque currently on her way to Bermuda from England, whence it will come to Salem, expected next month."

"Mr. Stanfield, I'm delighted to hear it. We need to build our own New England fleet of trading vessels, not be dependent on others and see the profits going into foreign pockets. The flow of new settlers is increasing, the spread of settlements around the Bay and north of Cape Ann is already causing us major logistical supply problems. We have our own produce, multiplying rapidly, that needs to find overseas markets. Our treasury depends on that source of revenue, not only to repay our investors in England but also to allow us to build our own financial stability. I happen to have just had a pinnace built for me on the Mystic River. I call her the *Blessing of the Bay*. It has a thirty ton displacement. While I will use it for official business, I also want to have it used to distribute and deliver produce locally."

Winthrop asked me where I planned to base my shipping business. I said that Salem for the short term. I would wait to see how the development of Boston progressed before making long term plans. He asked, if that was my intention, was I still going to live on my farm on the Merrimack River. I replied that my wife and I had been talking about moving closer to a town, she missed the companionship of a tightknit community, centered on a church. We had recently had twins, adding to the two children we had brought with us from England. The children needed to grow up with other children their own age. However, we intended to keep our farm. I had a farm manager who was experienced and competent. It was already productive and would continue to be an important food source for the community.

Winthrop surprised me by saying he had sent his son, Jack Winthrop, with a party to Sagamore Masconomet at Agawam, to build on the relationship that he had established with the Sagamore when he had first arrived. There had been a bit of a problem with him. He had fallen foul of the Tarrantines, an aggressive tribe further north. They were threatening Masconomet and his people to such an extent that his relationship with the English settlers was putting those settlers at risk, so he and his people had been banned from approaching any settler until that danger had been ameliorated. He had told his son to discover all the settlers who had been given or otherwise bought land from Masconomet. They were to be evicted as Masconomet lived on land that belonged by Royal Charter to the Massachusetts Bay Company and he had no right to give the land to people not authorized to have it. I was shocked. Hadn't Conant been given land? Yes, I was told. There were exceptions. I was told that the land I had been granted could also be considered an exception, which was why the Governor was interested in my plans. He said he had noted that of the 200 acres I had been granted by the now superseded authority, I only now needed 100 acres, even though I had told him it was likely that I would expand to use the full 200 acres in the future. I realized then that beneath the seemingly benign appearance there was an austere and implacable leader.

At the end of our meeting, Winthrop thanked me for coming to see him. He had enjoyed getting to know more about me and to have it confirmed in his mind that I was an ally and would be making significant contributions to ensure the ultimate success of the enterprise that he governed. I wished him well in his efforts on our behalf. He also asked that when I next visited Bermuda, to pass his felicitations on to the Governor, Roger Wood, with whom he had been in contact. We shook hands and parted. I had learned much about our new Governor and promised myself that I would walk carefully and understand the rules being laid down by Winthrop's new government.

I returned to Salem and went to talk to Mr. Trask. I gave him a summary of my conversation with the Governor. He was pleased. I thanked him and said that I was, therefore, looking for a place to live in or near Salem. My business interests demanded that I establish a base there. Perhaps, Trask replied, we could join the Old Planters at the northeastern end of the Salem peninsula. He took me for a walk. There was land available, a pleasant spot close to the Gardners, currently wooded. There were also a few houses that were either empty, or soon would be as the previous occupants had moved away. I asked about the new settlement. Trask said that he had moved there but his family had regretted it as it was cramped, noisy, and dirty. However, he had decided his future was with Endecott and was certain that under Endecott's dynamic leadership, Salem would become a much sought after town in which to live, with a thriving community coalesced round an active church. I had enough information to take back to Annie, the one to make such decisions. I thanked Trask and sought out Johnny, but he was away on an extended trip on *Marie*. I left a message for him to come and see me as soon as he returned. I returned to New Barrow Farm.

Annie came to me as soon as I arrived and told me that Chogan needed to see me, urgently. Without dismounting from Samson, I immediately rode over to his village, which was agitated, people running about, women wailing in small groups. I went to his house and mounted the steps. He met me at his door, grim faced.

"Isaac, I'm pleased you came so quickly. A messenger has come from Masconomet. He has been attacked at Agawam, I need you to go and offer help. Tell him we will also come."

I said I would go immediately. Back on Samson, I galloped back to the farm, told Annie what had happened, grabbed my sword, pistols, and ammunition, told her to warn Kate and Giles. She should barricade everyone in the house, armed, and await my return. I then rode to Agawam. Near the village, I met Jack Winthrop and introduced myself. He had heard that Agawam was being attacked and was working out the best way to help. I told him I would try and work my way to the village and find out what was happening. By the sounds of the shouts and screams it sounded like a massacre was in progress.

I left Samson with Winthrop and using the heavily wooded approach to the village, I was able to reach the fringe of the trees with open ground of some 100 paces to the village stockade. The villagers or at least most of them had taken refuge. A large number of, presumably, Tarrantines were surrounding the stockade. Threats and jeers were being hurled between attackers and defenders. The huts and wetus were burning, I noticed some bodies lying on the ground. Beyond the village, the Tarrantines had gathered a group of captive women by the river where many canoes were drawn up on the bank. The Tarrantines seemed entirely preoccupied.

I withdrew and ran back to Jack Winthrop. He had perhaps a dozen men with him, all armed with flintlocks and swords. I suggested that we should spread out and creep to the edge of the wood. On Jack's word we'd fire a half volley at the Tarrantines and in the confusion attack them with as much noise as possible. Screaming men charging out of the smoke should give them pause. The other half volley should be fired halfway across the open ground. Any Indian standing his ground should be cut down. The intention, I suggested, was to have them retreat and remove themselves. If possible, we ought to try and rescue the captives. Jack thought the plan doable and organized his men accordingly. We crept through the trees and on Jack's command six guns were fired, the noise as much as the impact of the shots, followed by fourteen screaming English charging at them, was enough to send them running back to their canoes. The second volley caused little damage but increased the speed of their retreat. Several Indians had been hit in the first volley. They were picked up and carried away by their fellows. We ran after them but they were too quick for us and the distance too far for us to continue running. They left with their captives, paddling back down river and away.

Masconomet and the villagers came out of the stockade and greeted us with shouts and clapping. Masconomet hugged me – "Ah! Machk." Everyone returned to the stockade. After the excitement, the sadness. Seven villagers had been killed. Numerous wounded including Masconomet's brother. Ten women had been taken, including the brother's wife.

Later, Jack and I spent some time together. He was a friendly young man who seemed to know what he was doing. I told him I had just met with his father who had told me what Jack and his party were doing. He said the process of evicting, or announcing the intent to evict the English settlers who had already started to build homes here was an unhappy one, causing considerable grief. He was aware of my grant and was relieved to hear I had been given sanction to remain by his father. He had heard of me and knew my reputation and said he had not relished confronting me. He also admitted that his actions were causing Masconomet some confusion. He didn't understand our concept of land ownership. He was happy to let the English live on the land, when the English offered him much in return by their presence. If the English, in addition, wanted to give him gifts in exchange for his agreement that they could use the land, he was too courteous to refuse. I told Jack I looked forward to getting to know him better, as it was my intention to establish a base in Salem in the near future, leaving my farm in the hands of my farm manager. I returned to New Barrow. I had been away a few hours.

The rest of August, we spent gathering the harvest and supporting Kate and Giles as they continued to build the farm. Our goat and cow herds were multiplying, producing much dairy and meat which was sold, together with the surplus from Annie's garden to a growing market. A draught horse was acquired, and a larger cart built to take the produce to the market in Salem. The sheep were pregnant, as well. Annie and I spent long hours talking about the move to Salem. We admitted we were both torn, because the weather was clear. The farm was showing its abundance. Abigail, with Beth now working in the Sprague household in Charlestown, had become increasingly close to Patience who was happy to be Abigail's companion and confidant, including helping her work the animals. With my efforts focused on building my trading business, we agreed that I had to spend the weekdays in Salem, returning at the weekend. We were also not yet decided where we wanted to move to, permanently. Annie was insistent that it had to be the right community with a church she wanted to worship in. Until then, they would stay at New Barrow.

Now, Annie wanted to help find a place for me to stay in Salem. We left the children with Patience and rode Samson and Peg, as Annie now called her, down to Salem. The Gardners were pleased to see us and we stayed with them in the adjoining house we had helped build three years ago.

—— CHAPTER 47 ——

Journal entry – *September 1631*

We told the Gardners what we intended doing. They informed us they had a plot of land next to them that overlooked the North River. There was a small, dilapidated house on the plot with a cellar, with two small rooms on the ground floor and an attic under a steeply sloping, shingled roof. Perhaps of more importance it had a stone and brick fireplace with chimney and was now empty. I asked who owned it. It was built by the Naumkeag community in 1627, before Endecott arrived. It was, therefore, owned by the community. Endecott would have the final say on its disposal. Annie and Margaret Gardner went and examined the house. It had a small, overgrown garden and was set in a grove within a wood, near a stream looking over the North River. While the house had just two rooms, when renovated it would be more than sufficient for me. The kitchen would be my living space, the other room my office.

Annie described it all to me and I told her she needed to talk to her friend Governor Endecott. Without more ado, she asked me to accompany her to his office. I escorted her there, where she was welcomed into the house and I went and sat on a bench to await developments. About a half hour later, Annie returned looking slightly flustered. Governor Endecott had greeted her effusively, Annie thought embarrassingly so. Things calmed down after he introduced her to his new wife Elizabeth who stayed for the meeting. Annie explained what we were hoping to do. Mr. Endecott said he would be delighted to have someone take care of it. The whole of the peninsula was being surveyed, at the instruction of Governor Winthrop. Land not formally acquired already would be divided into one or two acre lots and sold. He would ensure that the plot, or as close to it as the completed survey would allow, would be earmarked for my use. He said that he had heard from Governor Winthrop that he had a most pleasant and productive meeting with Mr. Stanfield, who had informed Mr. Endecott that Stanfield that he was thinking of moving his family back to Salem, a move of which the Governor said he wholeheartedly approved. At the end of the meeting, Mr. Endecott said he would be pleased to inform us when it was appropriate for us to negotiate an agreement to acquire or otherwise have access to the house. Annie asked how long that might be. She was told that that portion of the survey had been completed but had not been approved by the land court. He would attempt to expedite the decision process for us. Annie advised him that much work would be needed before winter set in. He acknowledged the need for urgency and showed Annie to the door wishing her and her family the best of health. I complimented her and suggested she should be in charge of all subsequent negotiations.

We returned to New Barrow. Two days later, Johnny appeared. Patience was the first to see him, arriving on horseback. She went to meet him and we waited for the two of them to come to the house. Patience returned to her duties and Johnny came into the kitchen. He was smiling to himself. Annie greeted him with a kiss and a beaker of ale. We sat round the table and Johnny handed me three copies of an agreement to sign whereby I was acquiring one third ownership in *Marie* for the sum of £75. I read it and found a codicil attached that offered me first option rights to any additional shares that might become available. I asked Johnny whether that was possible. Quite likely, apparently. One of the other two owners had lost his wife and was thinking of returning to England. Johnny also gave me a list of the current contracted clients, with an itinerary of the committed deliveries. He also provided a list of expected future deliveries not yet committed to by last year's clients. It was expected that at least 80% of the previous year's business would be repeated over the next twelve months, with the expectation that there would be a large number of new clients, as new settlements were established. Johnny provided me with a list of potential clients, located from Pemaquid in Maine all the way down to New Amsterdam, to prove his point. I digested all this information and sat back and stared at Johnny, my mouth open. Johnny laughed. He said that I would need to return to Salem and have my signature witnessed by an upstanding citizen. Then, with a mischievous grin, he said I needed to return to Salem anyway. Why? because the *Margaret Anne* has arrived, heavily laden from Bermuda. Finally, Johnny said that he had been asked to let me know the house I intended renting was available and I needed to visit Governor Endecott's office to sign the rental agreement.

We left Patience to look after Abigail and the twins while Annie, James, and I rode Peg and Samson to Salem with Johnny on his rented horse. James wanted to ride with Johnny because he wanted to know all about Johnny's sailing adventures. The first thing we did was to meet with a lawyer who witnessed my signature on *Marie* agreement. Johnny said he would take the copies to the co-owner and arrange a meeting with him wherein I would receive one copy of the signed agreement in exchange for the full payment. I then went to Endecott's office to sign the rental agreement. Johnny said he would arrange to have the various deficiencies to the house repaired and I asked that he find some basic furniture as well.

We were rowed out to the *Margaret Anne* and welcomed aboard by a heavily bearded David Tremaine. He seemed to have grown upwards. He was certainly broader, a fit and a happy man. There was a grand reunion, J.B. and Obi joined us on the main deck. It had been four years since I had last been with these two dear shipmates. Tiny, duty officer, waved to us from the quarterdeck. The crew who had been busy making everything shipshape after offloading the freight under the watchful eye of Obi the bosun, stopped and watched our happy reunion, nudging each other. As I looked around, I noticed some familiar faces. I acknowledged each with a grin and a wave, I was saluted back. I asked Obi to take James on a tour of the ship. J.B. grabbed Johnny and they disappeared for a long conversation. David escorted Annie and me down to the captain's cabin, where his steward, Alfred, provided us with glasses of sherry. We sat and toasted David's safe arrival.

David had prepared a report for me covering the time he had left New England in April 1630 through July this year when he had left Weymouth for Bermuda, with his log and ship's manifests of the trip to Bermuda and from Bermuda to Salem. I would read these later, together with letters from Mr. Scroud, Will Whiteway, and the Patriarch. I asked him about Bermuda. He said he was not there for more than a week, just enough time to offload the part of his freight destined for Bermuda, then obtain and load freight for New England, all of which were listed in the manifests. However, he did meet with my old acquaintances, Jacob Hallet and Argy Trescothick, who wanted me to go down to Bermuda at my earliest opportunity. In fact, Argy was responsible for providing the freight loaded in Bermuda. He has become an important and successful merchant in Bermuda, and is looking for a reliable trading partner and ship owner in New England.

The conversation became more personal as Annie took over the questioning and the responses to what we had been doing while he was away. Annie covered all that had happened. After a second glass of sherry, Annie said she should leave me to talk boating business with David. She gathered a reluctant James and with Johnny as her escort returned to dry land. David took me on a tour of inspection.

Meg, as she was affectionately known, was larger and of improved design over *Rosie*. She was better armed with six saker guns per side, a keel 10 feet longer or 63 feet, which meant about 90 feet from stem to stern, with a tonnage of 180, as opposed to *Rosie's* 120 tons. She had a crew of 30. David was proud of her. She was sea kindly. David described a serious storm that hit them some 600 miles east of Bermuda which *Meg* handled without difficulty. He was reminded of the storm we had suffered in *Swallow* in much the same area of the Atlantic, eight years ago. After our tour, I left David to deal with docking and unloading his ship and spent time with J.B. and Obi. They were too busy to give full answers to my questions, but we agreed to meet the following day. I wanted to hear about their voyage to Barbados on *Swallow*. J.B. was as tall as I remembered him. It was eighteen years since he had taken me in charge, a ship's boy on *Rosie*. He had been clean shaven then, with long brown hair, a lean face, bushy eyebrows, brown eyes, and large ears pierced with small gold rings. He was now lined and bearded, with grizzled hair in a queue tied behind his head and what looked like the same earrings. Obi, big and strong, bald and clean shaven, was no longer the impetuous youth. I saw him with the crew, a tough but fair, well-respected bosun. Before leaving the now docked *Meg*, I had a word with Tiny. I was pleased to see him again and told him Sykes was in Salem and I had promised him a berth. Tiny was delighted. He would ensure the skipper was informed and told me to send Sykes to him as soon as possible.

I returned to the Gardners' and met up with Annie. Johnny had taken James down to *Marie*. We sat outside, Annie dozing while I read all the documents that Johnny had given me. Mr. Scroud provided a final report on the *Argossy* saga. The owners had been made to realize their grievous errors and had been advised that they had been lucky not to lose the *Argossy*. They had paid the £1,500 promptly under pain of an increasing penalty being applied for every day they delayed payment. The *Argossy* payment covered all the costs of completing the refit, purchasing and the provisioning of the *Margaret Anne*, the purchase of a full hold of freight and the operating costs of a return trip to New England via Bermuda, with £255 left over which Mr. Scroud had invested. My financial affairs had continued to improve, and he gave me the name of the New England bound corresponding business agent, Ambrose Cudlipp, who should by now have arrived. He ended with the comment that, in the expectation that Captain Tremaine had transacted his planned business in both Bermuda and New England, I would not be requiring further transfers of funds from England, for the meantime.

The letter from the Patriarch troubled me. He wrote telling me of the efforts he made to raise significant amounts money to buy provisions to be sent to Endecott in 1629 and then, after his arrival in 1630 to Winthrop to distribute to the needy during those hard winters, to such an extent that members of his parish had complained that the money raised would have been better spent on the poor and needy in his parish. He had heard nothing back from Endecott or Winthrop in the way of acknowledgement. He also wrote of his concern over hearing that the religious intolerance that had manifested itself in New Plimouth had infected Endecott and Winthrop. He reminded me he was an Anglican of Puritan persuasion but not nor ever would be a Separatist. He prayed that we would find a tolerant parish in which to live and bring up our children.

Will's letter was brief. He thanked me for my journal entries and begged for more. He hoped that my problems with my land grant would be resolved in my favor and was pleased to hear from David Tremaine that I was now back in the ship-owning business. He wished Annie and me well and with a sad little postscript mentioned that his wife Elenor was unwell and in deep depression. They had been blessed with six children, of which only William was alive and well. Young John, born in 1628, was ill and not expected to live. The others had all died as infants.

The next morning, I met J.B. and Obi back on *Meg*. They told me that they had sailed *Swallow* to Bermuda, on their way down to Barbados. Rough weather on the way forced them to spend time at Mr. Jacobson's boatyard for repairs. He had been pleased to see *Swallow* again. To their surprise Mr. Hallet, who had been Governor Woodhouse's agent during the James kidnapping saga, turned up at the yard. He now worked for the current Governor, Captain Roger Wood. The Governor's office was kept informed of all vessels arriving in Bermuda by the harbor master. Hallet said he remembered *Swallow* and came to find out how the James saga ended. He had been deeply involved, to our considerable advantage, although surreptitiously. He was pleased to hear the outcome and asked that his compliments be passed on to me when they returned to England, with the wish that Mr. Stanfield would grace Bermuda with his presence in the not too distant future. Argy Trescothick had also come by. As J.B. and Obi had no idea of my intention to move to New England, Argy assumed I was still in England. He also asked them to give his best wishes to me. He said that he and his family looked forward to seeing me again.

Swallow had then made passage directly to Barbados. It was an exhilarating ride, the prevailing winds in April were nor'easterly, averaging 20 knots, beam reaching or winds off larboard quarter, their speed averaged 10 knots for the passage and they made Barbados in five days. They said they had never had such a sail and probably never would again. *Swallow* had given them a wonderful farewell memory. They were stuck in Barbados with the paid off crew for several months. The crew had eventually found other positions on departing boats. J.B. and Obi had paid passage back to England via Jamestown and then Bermuda. They arrived back in Plymouth in late 1629 and reported to Mr. Scroud, who referred them to Tiny Hadfield. They were added as supernumerary officers to the maintenance crew of the *Argossy*. They had benefited from the trip to Barbados, both in terms of experience gained and the contacts made, which information they were pleased to bring to *Meg*, with respect to future trading voyages between Bermuda and Barbados. I told them how pleased I was to have them back as shipmates.

Later, I caught up with David and James. David said he was amazed at how much James knew about sailing and, especially, the rigging. David promised James that he would be having a serious talk with his father about James' future as a *Meg* ship's boy. James and I returned to New Barrow. David promised to come as soon as he had completed the sale and disbursement of the freight that he had brought with him. I preferred to defer discussion with him about the details of his trip until he joined us. However, it looked as if he had been successful.

── CHAPTER 48 ──

Journal entry – *September 1631*

Back at New Barrow, we were joined by Johnny and David. They had agreed to come together. Kate had taken produce to market and brought them back. Johnny said it had been an interesting ride. It was the first time Kate and David had been together since David left for England. Kate had been cool and formal. She informed David that she had submitted a request to the court seeking divorce due to his desertion shortly after he had left for England. No response had been received and Kate understood it was unlikely that any would be for the foreseeable future. However, it would be best for him to keep a low profile. David was affable in response, Johnny's presence being a barrier to more emotional interaction. Kate changed the subject and told David about Jeannie's death. David said later that he thought it a bit brutal, but Johnny handled it well, better than David who was most upset at Johnny's loss. Johnny told David that Annie and I now had twins to join James and Abigail. Annie had found a new person to look after the children. Her name was Patience. David caught a quick sideways glance Kate gave Johnny at the mention of Patience's name. She then caught David looking at her with eyebrows raised. She gave a quick shake of her head and nothing more was said. Johnny had not noticed the interaction.

We spent the rest of September reviewing the business we had now embarked upon. In summary, the conclusions we reached were as follows:

Kate, Johnny and David would each take a 25% share of the annual net profit from the business for which they were responsible, in addition to their monthly stipend.

Kate had been working with Annie to keep a tight control over expenditure and revenue of her farming enterprise. She showed us the accounting process that Annie had helped her set up and was pleased to say she was showing a slight profit. Additional investment was required, which included hiring another farm hand next Spring. Giles had someone in mind who was young, strong, and willing.

The freight David acquired in England, he bought outright from the *Argossy* proceeds, provided him by Mr. Scroud. David explained that he, as *Meg's* captain, had no trading history to which they could refer, and therefore no credibility with traders for them to risk him shipping their freight. As a result, Mr. Scroud had been comfortable using the penalty payment received as part of the *Argossy* settlement to buy the freight directly from the traders and carry the whole risk of the shipment arriving whole and undamaged and finding buyers for it all. High risk but high reward. The freight offloaded in Bermuda was exchanged in a barter arrangement for cedar logs and sugar. That freight consisted of woolen, linen, finished leather hides, and metal work from London. By way of Kinsale in Ireland, there were many barrels of salted pork and beef.

David had established trading partners in Kinsale and Cork, having exploited the relationships he had developed while working for Sir Ferdinando. In addition to the pork and beef, they also traded in dairy products, such as salted butter and cheese.

With Argy Tresothick in Bermuda, we would have an excellent importer and exporter. David said that Bermuda was becoming a hub for produce flowing from and to Europe and from the Caribbean and North America. Argy is the key to enable us to open that door. J.B. and Obi's run down to Barbados had also added to the store of knowledge we had of importers and exporters in the Caribbean.

Johnny provided an update to the documents he had given to me at the time I was considering investing in *Marie*. My predecessor co-owner had not wanted detailed information as he was close to the other two co-owners. The two were brothers, Smethurst by name, who were directly involved with Marie's operations and he trusted their competence and honesty. However, Johnny would ensure I received a detailed account every quarter. Given the strong possibility that one of them would also want to sell his share, Johnny said he also thought it likely that the remaining co-owner would not want to continue and would be likely to follow his brother's example. In other words, I should be prepared to assume full ownership of *Marie* in the near future.

It was clear we needed to find someone, separate from Mr. Cudlipp, to help us with our accounting. Cudlipp would arrange credit facilities for us and manage our investments in New England. At one meeting, when the subject was raised, Annie cleared her throat, having been mostly silent at previous meetings. We all turned to her.

"Isaac, my sweet, I don't mean to diminish the importance of proper business accounting, but I have been managing the bookkeeping of the Stanfield household since Aby died."

I thought back. A brief, fleeting memory of Aby, a longer memory of Annie managing the household accounts while looking after James for the years I had abandoned them, working to ensure those accounts were kept meticulously, then continuing after we had come back together and married, all to Mr. Scroud's total satisfaction. Annie had been managing our financial affairs since we arrived in New England, even to the extent of managing our own treasury, paying all the bills and restricting my access to funds on a strictly controlled basis. An awkward silence followed Annie's quiet and emphatic statement. While I was still ruminating, Annie sat looking at me, a slight blush high on each cheek, a dangerous sparkle in her eyes. Johnny grinned and looked at David, who was staring in rapt admiration at Annie. It was but a moment, but the silence hung as if forever. I came out of my reverie.

"Of course, Annie. Perfect! What would you like to do to get started?"

Annie looked round the table at each of us.

"First, is each of you happy to trust me as the company bookkeeper?"
We all said "yes', most emphatically.

"Second, David, I need to have you describe the business activities for which you need accounting. As skipper, do you deal directly with the traders? If so, how do you manage the transactions in and out, the costs and revenues. Do you need to know how much you think you will need to run your business on a month-to-month basis and what income you expect to receive?"

David said that he keeps a ledger to record and to keep track of all transactions. He said that the owner normally provides an amount to cover estimated costs for the voyage. Traders pay the owner's representative, such as Mr. Scroud, the fees charged for the freight to be shipped. A schedule of freight charges by commodity, based for the most part on volume rather than weight, has been established for *Meg*. A hundredweight of wool takes much more space than a hundredweight of iron nails, for example. Often that representative is the skipper, where there is no owner's representative in the port. The freight is detailed in full on the manifest. He has a secure metal box to keep all money received and to pay costs, including maintenance and crew wages. Annie responded, with a smile.

"Then, at the end of each voyage, I should be given your ledger for that voyage, together with the profit made. It seems straightforward. I will be the keeper of the books, rather than the bookkeeper. Then, you will give me a projection of your expected costs for each voyage out of Salem, so that I can fill your metal box."

We laughed. David, who might have taken umbrage, saw Annie's innocent intent, laughed, too. She turned to me.

"David said he generated 50% gross profit on his freight. Is that normal?"

I said he assumed a loading of 80%. The freight charges were calculated based on a breakeven loading of 40%. After the cost of overhead and duties were deducted, the net profit could be about 30%. It sounded like a good return to me, but that assumed enough freight arrived at its destination and was in fit state to be bought on arrival. The costs were the same for a voyage, whatever the amount of freight carried. We should factor those risks into an annual return closer to 15%.

"What about *Marie*? Is there any bookkeeping required?

Johnny explained that there was a similar schedule of freight charges for *Marie*. Slightly more complex, as the charges had to take into account a widely diverse distance as well as volume. A day to sail from Salem to New Plimouth and back. At least a week to make a return trip to New Amsterdam. The charges were significantly less than *Meg's*, because *Marie* was able to make multiple voyages per month so the annual operating cost could be spread over perhaps twenty return trips, as opposed to one or two for *Meg*. He also kept a detailed log of all transactions, which was copied and supplied to the owners on a quarterly basis with the profit share. Annie said she would keep the records received from Johnny, as well.

Annie asked me what was to be done with the expected flow of money into the Stanfield treasury. We had Scroud managing the money in England. What should be done with the returns coming to us in New England? I repeated what I had said earlier. We use Mr. Cudlipp.

"And what do we call this new company of ours?" said our forthright new keeper of the books. We looked at each other. Johnny broke the silence by asking where Annie and I had first met. Annie, puzzled at the question, said

"You know that - The Minerva Inn in Plymouth, Devon"

Johnny smiled. "That sounds like a good name."

We all agreed the company should be called The Minerva Partnership. We would need it to register with the Massachusetts Bay Company to become a fully licensed trading company. I went to get glasses and a bottle of wine. The five of us toasted ourselves and our new company.

CHAPTER 49

Journal entry – *October 1631*

David was anxious to get back to sea. An idle boat was money lost. Before he left Bermuda he had received from Argy a list of commodities needed in Bermuda. The shipment of cedar and sugar he had brought back had been enthusiastically purchased by Salem traders. They were anxious for more of the same. David had contracted with them to provide another shipment by the middle of November, before the winter set in. I wanted to talk to Argy about establishing regular trade between America and the Caribbean, using Bermuda as the hub. If I could be assured of a continuing supply and demand, I could build my trading network along the American coastline. I would also be able to tie *Marie* into redistribution and collection of the trade. Johnny told me that I needed to understand that the local trade carried out by *Marie* depended on having a number of regular traders. It was risky to depend on just one or two.

It was decided that I would accompany David on the next trip, leaving the following week. David asked about James. Would it not be opportune for him to get a feel for what it would be like to be a ship's boy, especially if his father was there to offer advice and encouragement? We discussed the likely weather conditions. David acknowledged that by the beginning of October, Atlantic weather tended to be unstable. However, *Meg* was seaworthy and had shown her mettle in serious weather. Annie was at first hesitant. She was worried about the sailing conditions, and I admitted they could be rough. I suggested that she was already an experienced deep-water sailor and this was an opportunity to visit Bermuda. After dealing with all the reasons why not, she decided that if her son James was making his first trip as a member of the crew, there was nothing that would stand in her way to prevent her from sharing that experience with him.

In addition, she admitted that she still held deep within her the unhealed, searing wound caused when James had been taken from her and the void of those lost months. Here was an opportunity to close the wound and fill that void with the people in Bermuda who had helped rescue her beloved son.

Johnny was persuaded to return to New Barrow to help Kate and Giles manage the property and continue preparations for winter. Giles and Kate had employed the young prospect he had found, by name, Benjamin Sturges. Patience, with Abigail's help, would look after Nat and Nan. I asked if Abigail was comfortable with us leaving her. Annie responded by telling me how when James left with David, Abigail had cried. Annie and Patience comforted her as she sobbed that the two best people in her life, Beth and now James, had left her all alone. Annie had taken her in her arms and told her that as she was now grown up, she had a special responsibility—looking after Nat and Nan, and making sure they grew up to be just like James and Beth. Patience had added that Abigail would never be alone. She was Patience's best friend. Abigail had reached out to Patience, hugged her and whispered, "You're my best friend, too."

I asked Annie how she had persuaded Johnny to come back. She smiled with a quick tilt of her head.

"Isaac, you can be myopic, at times."

By the time we had sorted out our family arrangements and Johnny had made arrangements for someone to stand in as quartermaster while he was at New Barrow, David, who took James with him back to Salem, had prepared *Meg* for her trip to Bermuda, fully loaded, crew ready, Sykes added, having been welcomed aboard by his old crewmates. A cabin was made available for Annie and me. James was introduced to the other ship's boy, a lad of twelve, Billy Proctor, who had joined *Meg* in Weymouth. Billy looked young for his age, with curly blonde hair, round, pink, open face, cheerful grin, and ears that stood away from his head. The poor lad was called Piggy but was cheerful with it. James took to him immediately.

On Monday, 3 October, Annie and I were welcomed on board by David, the crew assembled in the waist. Tiny Hadfield, officer of the watch, saluted us from the quarterdeck. J.B. behind him with a smile on his face. Although Annie had visited *Meg* when she arrived at Salem, she hadn't seen several of the crew since the loss of *Rosie*. They were pleased to see her and as Annie's prodigious memory recalled familiar faces, she approached each and said a few words. The bosun, Obi, had taken it upon himself to provide a close escort and helped Annie to put names to faces. It rather made me think of a royal welcome on a naval ship and said so to David, standing by my side. He whispered it only needed the bosun's pipe to "pipe the side" to make it so. I looked around for James. He and Piggy were standing to one side, James trying to hide behind a crewman. I knew James was desperately hoping we wouldn't pick him out. I caught his eye and gave him a quick nod before taking Annie's arm and guiding her away to the captain's cabin, following David into his lair.

An hour later we were at sea, heading southeast, winds from the northwest and moderate, to skirt Cape Cod. Annie was given the day cabin to use as her own and settled herself there while I returned to the quarterdeck with David. We discussed the route David would be taking. After rounding the northern tip of Cape Cod, we would head southwest for about six days, depending on the weather. There was a fast-moving, warm current of water flowing in a nor'easterly direction that we would need to cross between us and Bermuda. David said that on the way up from Bermuda, they had had an exhilarating ride, fast and rough. It would be against us on the way down, so he planned to skirt it to the west until Bermuda lay to our east on latitude 32, then head east to cross the current as quickly as possible. He didn't know how wide the current was, but it could take us many hours to cross it and we would be pushed northeast of our track. Once through, we would then turn south and head back to latitude 32 before turning east to make for Bermuda. The whole journey, David hoped, would take about twelve days. It sounded exciting. I wondered how Annie would handle it.

The next six days we sailed though clement weather, wind on starboard beam shifting to a nor'westerly, clear skies for the most part, winds 15-20 knots. *Meg* was in her element. Annie was able to regain her sea-legs, braced in a berth in David's day cabin whenever she felt the need. When on deck she stayed sheltered in the lee of the quarterdeck bulkhead on the main deck. When James was not on watch and was awake, I loved to spend time with him as he showed me how much he was learning about *Meg*, her rigging, especially the set of the sails, with courses now set on main and fore, and how they were adjusted as the wind direction backed and veered. Sykes, who was on the same watch with James and had become his mentor, had asked him whether he was ready to climb the ratlines to tend the mainsail. Eleven-year-old James had told him he had been climbing trees since he was a boy and that, of course, he was ready. Sykes tested him and James was up the ratlines of main mast to the maintop like a monkey. Once there he hung on with an enormous grin, as the mast swayed and tossed. He seemed to be in his element. Sykes had thought to follow him up closely in case James got into difficulties, but he couldn't keep up with him. He told me later that James was born to the sea, a natural. The problem was how to instill a modicum of caution. It reminded me of my time as a ship's boy on *Rosie* and then as able seaman, J.B. as my mentor. I said as much to first mate J.B. He laughed.

"Isaac, I keep seeing you every time I catch sight of James. It's frightening how much alike you are. Hopefully, being a few years younger than you were then, he will learn not to be quite so impetuous."

I replied that one of my early introductions to life on board as a ship's boy was being a powder monkey. David laughed and asked how was it?

"The gunnery practices were exciting. Live action was terrifying. Under fire, keeping the powder boxes and the shot trays full, while dodging constantly moving guns and frantic gunners, the noise deafening, the shouting of gun captains, the constant trundling of the cannon, recoiling, slamming against their retaining tackle after reloading, being hauled back to their firing position. The cursing and swearing, seemingly from everyone. Will you be having any gun drills on this trip?"

"No. We practiced extensively between England and Bermuda. There was a considerable risk of pirates masquerading as privateers. But much less of a risk between New England and Bermuda. Not enough traffic, at least for a while. No, James will have to wait to receive his powder monkey initiation."

Sun sights had been maintained at noon every day. Our log keeping was also kept meticulously, in true Navy fashion. We had been averaging 6 knots for the six days and had reached latitude 32. David ordered the course altered to head due east. The sails were reset with the wind now from the northwest and *Meg* headed for Bermuda with the wind 20 knots over the larboard quarter. A few hours later, David said we were approaching the fast moving current. The sea, until now was dark blue with regular four to six foot waves, becoming more irregular and confused as the current started interacting with the opposing wind. The color of the water was becoming a lighter shade of blue and the water temperature was rising. When the wind appeared to increase and veer from nor'westerly to westerly we knew *Meg* was being pushed by the current. Lifelines were rigged and Annie was asked to stay below, which she was more than happy to do, wedged into her berth in the day cabin as *Meg* became a wild, bucking horse. Tops'ls, main and fore, were doused which eased the motion and *Meg* battled through the turbulence, burying her head into a particularly belligerent wave and rising, flinging it aside, throwing up warm spray and with water cascading down the decks through the scuppers and back to the angry ocean. It was exhilarating. James, off watch, came and stood with me at the lee rail, sheltered by the fo'c'sle bulkhead, we were wearing our oilskins and sweating, the warmth of the water extraordinary.

Twelve hours later, the turbulence subsided, the wind backed as we moved away from the current. We changed course to head south. In ten hours we were back to latitude 32 and turned east into the rising sun, main and fore courses set to continue to Bermuda. Blue skies, wind 25 knots from the North on our larboard beam the water, now a blue-green color with a regular, rolling motion. Annie was invited to the quarterdeck. She had slept through the turmoil of the night. This final leg of our journey we completed in three days. We delayed our approach till daylight, the reefs required much respect. We sighted Bermuda at dawn on the morning of Thursday, 13 October. We approached from the west and stayed well clear of the reefs on the south shore until we were able to turn and work our way to the eastern end of the Island. Main, fore, sprits'l furled, both courses doused, we drifted until the pilot boat came to us. Four hours later we made our way into St. Georges harbor and anchored off the town wharf.

—— CHAPTER 50 ——

Journal entry – *October 1631*

After we had been cleared by the port authorities, David and I went ashore to pay our respects to the Governor. He was away from his office. I asked if Mr. Jacob Hallet perchance was available. A short while later, Mr. Hallet appeared. He looked older, greyer, more lined. He approached us, stopped, smiled, and welcomed us, with an outstretched hand.

"Mr. Stanfield, how good to see you again. I do trust you are in Bermuda for more pleasurable reasons than when you were last here. How is your son, James, is it? And Mr. Tremaine, happy to see you back, so soon."

I expressed my pleasure at meeting him again and congratulated him for his acute memory after over six years absence. I told him that both James and my wife were with us and that I would be pleased to introduce them to him. It would be his pleasure, he replied. He commented that much had changed in those six years, two Governors on from Woodhouse. Generally, the political climate had become less troubled, although the population had increased, both white and black. Governor Wood's focus was on getting the farmers to grow exportable produce to replace the dying tobacco business, which was one reason why he was pleased to see Captain Tremaine back, presumably seeking to fill his holds with more freight to be exported from Bermuda. I said that we hoped to meet with Mr. Trescothick shortly. He laughed,

"Jason Trescothick has done well for himself since Captain Tucker died. Deservedly so, if I might say so. He has become an important businessman. Bermuda benefits from his success. Wasn't he involved in the search for young James? Then there were the two blacks who helped you, Ezra and Anthony. At the time, I remember asking you to tell me the whole story whenever you returned."

I promised that I would, perhaps over a meal and several glasses of rum. I asked whether Ezra and Anthony were contactable. He told me that Ezra continued to be a much-respected leader of his people and a farmer on Somerset Island. Anthony has managed to keep himself out of trouble, despite the difficulties that exist with the black community, and remains the consummate fisherman. Hallet said that he continued to use Anthony as a confidential courier. He told me the best way to contact Ezra was through Anthony, whom he would let know that I had arrived. I asked him to forward my greetings to the Governor and that Governor Winthrop in Boston had asked me specifically to pass on his best wishes. As we left, he promised to be in touch with me to arrange that meal.

David then took me to the offices of Argy Trescothick. We were told that Mr. Trescothick was having a late lunch at the Anchor tavern on the Square. We went there. Argy was deep in conversation with two gentlemen at a corner table, his back to us, as we approached and stood behind him. One of his party looked up. I put my finger to my lips. He smiled and returned his attention to Argy.

I leant down and said,

"Would you be fancying another round, sir?"

Argy, without looking round, started to wave me away, then stopped. He saw his two companions smiling. He was silent then said,

"I know that voice. Isaac, by all that's wonderful!"

He stood, turned, and we embraced. Shaking David's hand, he bade us bring two more chairs, introducing us to his companions, local farmers. He asked if we had eaten and then ordered for us the lunch of the day, large red snappers with potatoes and tankards of ale. After we had a chance to eat our fish, and over a second tankard, Argy demanded to know what we were doing in Bermuda and how long we would be staying.

David said he had brought back the commodities Argy had requested, primarily lumber of pine, locust, and oak, plus ironware, domestic and farming. He was expecting to return to Salem with a repeat of his previous export from Bermuda; sugar and cedar. Argy said he would meet David later and come to the ship to inspect the manifest and the freight. David would be waiting for him. They shook hands and David returned to *Meg*. Argy and I returned to his office. We had much to talk about, but first, Argy wanted to get business out of the way.

"Isaac, the people you met at lunch are farmers who have been persuaded by Governor Wood to diversify their crops from tobacco to fruit and vegetables, such as potatoes, corn, oranges, limes, lemons, figs and bananas. They and their farming colleagues are also beginning to grow castor shrubs, to produce castor oil. We believe these will generate a significant export market for Bermuda. Would you allow me to talk to David about including some bushels of this produce to take back to Salem with you?"

I had no problem with the suggestion. I respected Argy's tact in wanting David to be involved with the decision about what to include in this shipment. It also made me realize we needed to establish the protocol for determining what gets shipped where. David was responsible for the movement of freight and for finding customers who wanted that freight moved. I was a customer, a trader, not exclusively bound to use my own ships. Argy could use *Meg* or any other vessel to ship his freight. Alternatively, I could buy his freight in Bermuda, have it shipped by whomsoever, wherever I wanted and sell it to importers on arrival.

We then spent the next hour or so catching up on each other's news. I told him I had heard that Hook was on the island. He laughed. He had wondered whether I had known that. He had become quite friendly with Hook, even though he was a trading competitor. He felt there was a dark side but couldn't put his finger on anything that might be deemed suspicious. He put it down to his past experience with him at the time James was kidnapped and brought to Bermuda. He asked if I would like him to arrange a meeting. I suggested that the best thing to do was casually let slip I was on the island for a short while. If he wanted to make contact with me then well and good.

I told Argy that Annie and James were here. He said that the three of us should stay with him and Mary. He would organize it with Mary, suggesting we should plan to come to them tomorrow. He said that his daughter, Sue, had never forgotten James and pined for him for many months after we had left for England. She was now fourteen and Mary was concerned that she should be put into service with another family with young children to look after. She was maturing into a fine young woman and needed to remove herself from the apron strings of her mother. I told him they would probably have difficulty recognizing James. He was tall, broad shouldered and self-assured, looking and acting years older than his soon to be twelve years. We covered our move to New England and what we had been doing to settle and to build a business. He described the final days of managing Captain Tucker's estate, Overplus, and Tucker's death not long after I had left Bermuda. The arrival of Tucker offspring and the opportunities presented to become involved with various Tucker enterprises, resulted in Argy branching out on his own. We parted, with Argy going to advise Mary of her new house guests and me wanting to walk down to see Mr. Jacobson at his boatyard.

Mr. Jacobson was pleased to see me, once I had persuaded him as to who I was. He remembered and had enjoyed the re-appearance of *Swallow*, being sailed to Barbados by J.B., Obi and crew a few years back, a sloop he had worked on back in Holland many years previously. I told him about my current circumstances and that I had just shipped a quantity of lumber to Bermuda for Mr. Trescothick. It was my intention to build a substantial business between New England and Bermuda. Would he have any interest in establishing a regular order with me for specialist marine lumber? He settled down, relit his pipe, thought for a while and said he was always interested in oak. I asked him about more exotic woods like walnut and locust. His eyes lit up. Locust he knew about. It had a fine reputation as marine wood but he hadn't used it. He would welcome the opportunity to try it. Walnut was only useful for decorative work. Teak he would love to have but I told him that I didn't have ready access to it. He always needed spruce and fir for spars. Those, I could provide. If he were to write an order for the supply of the different types of lumber he wanted to be delivered next Spring and pass the order to Mr. Trescothick, I would be happy to satisfy it. He said he would think about it. We shook hands and I returned to *Meg*.

The following morning, Argy came early to *Meg* and took us back to his house on Bridge Street, up from the Square, a fine, timber-built house with a wide, covered porch facing southwest, that looked over the harbor. Mary greeted us warmly. Sue, meeting James after so long, at first did not recognize him. She had long-held memories of the six-year-old James, to whom she had been devoted. James remembered and reached out with both hands and clasped hers. "Hello, Sue." They hugged. The boys, Charlie and Sam, alerted by the noise came running out onto the porch. They, too, were taken back by how much James had grown. In no time, the three boys were off and away, an apologetic glance from James to a subdued Sue left behind.

Mary showed Annie around the house, deep in conversation. Argy suggested he and I return to his office, we had much to discuss. We went first to the wharf where *Meg* was being off-loaded. Argy had inspected and accepted the manifest covering the freight, the previous evening. The lumber was stacked ready to be shipped elsewhere on the island. Carts were being filled with the ironware and taken to a nearby warehouse. We collected David and continued on to Argy's office. We settled down to negotiate the barter, what and how much we would return to Salem with, in exchange for what we had brought down. We wanted to return with a full load and Argy was an astute businessman. Agreement was reached, hands shaken. We shared glasses of rum in celebration of the completed transaction and David left to ensure *Meg* was ready to receive the cedar lumber, barrels of sugar, oranges, limes, lemons, and vegetables.

I told Argy about my meeting with Jacobson. I had not been fooled by his apparent non-commitment. Argy said he would contact him. We agreed that Argy would be our exclusive broker in Bermuda and would ensure that he could match the value of my imports into Bermuda with my required or opportunistic exports from Bermuda. He would have a contract prepared before I left Bermuda. He admitted he was somewhat concerned that the Somers Isles Company back in London, in effect the owners of Bermuda, might want to extend their control over Bermuda imports and exports by demanding that all shipments had to be undertaken by English ships. At the moment, that only applied to shipments to and from England. Governor Wood, employed by the Company, was torn. He recognized that the Company, representing the investors, wanted to maximize the revenue out of Bermuda. However, he needed the commerce with the Caribbean and North America which could only come by other means. Argy said he was keeping a close eye on developments and had the ear of the Governor.

—— CHAPTER 51 ——

Journal entry – *October 1631*

That evening, Argy told me that Anthony Pedro had stopped by *Meg* and had left a message for me, which had been passed on to Argy's office. The message said that if I wished to contact Anthony, I should use the procedure we had used before. Argy looked at me with eyebrows raised. I laughed and explained that when I had wanted to talk to him, I would leave a note in his fishing boat, the *Ezmeralda*, by the Coney Island bridge, which I proceeded to do, taking Annie with me. Walking to the bridge gave me an opportunity to spend some private time with her. I left a note, asking Anthony if he was free to take me, my wife and James to Somerset to meet with Ezra Garcia, who had brought James back to full health after his kidnapping. I told him we were staying with the Trescothicks on Bridge Street.

On the walk, Annie told me about her day. She had spent it with Mary and the children. They had gone to the beach for a swim and a casual lunch, packed into a hamper. Annie said she and Mary had become good friends. There was a connection. When I had met up with Argy in The Minerva Inn in Plymouth back in 1613, after we had rescued him and his fellow sailors from Spain, Annie, niece of the landlord, Alfred Potts, was working there as a barmaid. Mary was the daughter of a friend of Annie's uncle. The connection opened the way for many reminiscences. Mary also told Annie about James' kidnapping and rescue. A different perspective than Annie had heard from me. She was able to tell Annie how she had observed the extraordinary recuperative powers James had that enabled him to recover from that traumatic event. Annie could see how fascinated Sue was with James. Whenever he was present, Sue wanted to be with him, talk with him, ask him questions, some of which James found embarrassingly personal. Mary explained how part of James' healing process had come from Sue, who had adopted him as a caring elder sister. Annie told me, it reminded her a little of Beth, Kate's daughter, and her absorption with James. It seemed James was developing into an attractive young man and not yet twelve. Interesting to me, worrying to Annie.

Early the following morning, we found a note from Anthony on the porch, suggesting he was available that morning and would be pleased to take us to see Ezra. He would wait till two hours after sunrise. We had an hour. A hastily packed meal by Mary and warm clothes. We took our oilskins; it would be a blustery day. When we arrived, Anthony was there to greet us. James was excited to see him again, shaking his hand vigorously. Anthony had not changed by one degree, still the same; quietly gracious and welcoming. He bowed to Annie and helped her board his boat, slightly larger than his previous one, a typical Bermuda rigged sloop, a triangular mainsail and foresail with a boom holding the foot of the mainsail. It had a cuddy under the bows, a shelter for passengers from the spray. Once under sail, he offered the helm to James who was delighted to take over. Anthony sat by him, watching his helmsmanship. The variable winds, 15-20 knots, veering westerly, backing sou'westerly. After a while, he turned to Annie and me and said James had become an accomplished sailor. Just then, a sharp word from the helmsman, to watch the wind. He was worrying about a possible gybe. I was in charge of the mainsheet and had let my concentration wander. Anthony smiled as I quickly brough the mainsail back under control. James was relieved of his duty at regular intervals, unhappy as he was to give up the tiller. It was tiring work.

I asked Anthony about Ezra. He had had difficulties with Governor Woodhouse after we had left Bermuda, and subsequently with

Governor Bell. They felt he had too much independence and had been keen to add restrictions to the already constricted black community. However, Governor Wood had relaxed those attempts. Ezra had gained favor when he had, at the Governor's request, spent time with the black servants and their family that the Governor had working in his household. There were a large number of children and the Governor was anxious that they should be given a good education before they were sent away into service with other families. Ezra had established an appropriate curriculum for them and found a black teacher. Anthony was loathe to talk of himself, but Annie asked gentle questions and we realized that life was a challenge for the black people of Bermuda. But, he said, he was blessed to be able to continue his life as a fisherman and to work for the kindly Mr. Hallet.

James asked whether the *James* was still being sailed. Anthony replied that since James had presented the boat to Ezra's children as a thank you present, it had been in constant use both to teach the children how to sail and how to fish. It was kept clean and repainted every year, special attention being given to the name on the transom. James went slightly pink and went back to his sailing. I told Annie of how the children under Ezra's gentle guidance had coaxed James back into the real world.

Once we had rounded Spanish Point into the Great Sound, sails were eased and the wind dropped. The water rippled, with occasional darker areas where gusts disturbed the surface. Annie was fascinated with the colors in the water, the iridescent blues and greens, dark shadows as we passed close to a submerged reef, pale patches of sand under the clear water, shapes of fish, large and small, separately and in schools, disturbed by our gentle passage. The sun, now high above us, was warm. A soft breeze ruffling her hair, Annie trailed her fingers through the water relaxed perhaps for the first time since she boarded *Meg* in Salem.

Anthony guided us across the Great Sound to Sandys Narrow and dropped anchor off a rocky beach, close to the bridge. We all hopped overboard, the water up to our thighs and warm. Annie, like a schoolgirl, delighted in her wet dress. Anthony accompanied us up a path to the high ground overlooking the sound. James, ahead of us, shouted back that he remembered this was the spot where he and his friends would come to watch and play. We continued on down to the village to be met by a throng of happy, noisy children. James scanned the eager faces but didn't recognize anyone. His two special friends, a girl and a boy who had been heartbroken when James had left them, were probably long gone, no longer children. The noise disturbed adults who came to investigate. James approached one that he recognized.

"Good morning, sir. I am James."

The adult stared at this young man, now as tall as he was.

"James. How can it be? This is wonderful. Stay a moment. I must fetch Ezra."

He hurried away. James was surrounded by chattering curious children, touching him and asking him questions. James, happy to be back, delighted in engaging with them all. The years fell away and I saw the boy who had been rescued by a similar group of happy, carefree children six years ago. Annie was silent, fascinated, remembering all she had learnt about that time. I looked up and saw a familiar figure. He paused and watched us, especially James, a gentle smile on his weathered face. His hair was grizzled and receding from a high dark forehead. He came forward and shook my hand. "Isaac, it is so good to see you. And this must be your wife. Madam welcome to my village."

He bowed over her, clasping her outstretched hand in both of his. James, wading through the children, approached. Ezra turned to him and put his hands on James' shoulders and looked deep into his eyes, seemingly into his soul. James stilled, comfortable under that penetrating stare.

"James, you are well again. You are different, wise beyond your years. You have done well. I am so happy for you."

He then embraced him and beckoned us to follow him to seats that had been placed under a large palmetto. Anthony, respectfully, kept in the background. Ezra asked many questions and came to understand what had happened to us in all the years gone by. I asked him how the circumstances were between his black people and the white. He smiled sadly.

"It continues to regress, although there are ups and downs. The latest Governor, Wood, has more empathy towards us than the previous ones. He tries hard. He insists that there are no slaves, only servants, indentured like the whites. What he states and quite possibly believes, does not change the behavior and attitudes among the older settlers. Young, white, indentured workers flow into Bermuda. Since you were last here, much of the island is now settled and cultivated. There is not much room for these workers, so they move on to other islands in the Caribbean. The blacks cost less and work harder. Not only that, the indenture term is set at seven years, thereafter the white worker becomes free to earn his own living, no longer the living of his master. That should be the case with the black worker, but the seven years is a figment. While some blacks continue to be brought in because of their skills, many come having been slaves from elsewhere. Their children are caught in that never ending servitude. At least Governor Wood is trying to ensure all such children are given a good education, the means to better themselves. Slavery is increasing in the Caribbean and America. Pirates and Privateers capture slave ships and see the slaves as commodities, valuable ones, and distribute them wherever they can find buyers, so slavery spreads, inexorably.

Changing the subject, I asked him about his farm. How productive was he? What was his market? What did he grow?

"Cassava is our main crop, being a staple diet for my people. It is also the primary food for our pigs. It takes eight months to grow, being harvested in December. It is considered a major Christmas treat. We also grow wheat, potatoes, and onions, which we can harvest more frequently. Onions, for example, can be harvested in three months. We grow only to meet our needs on the Islands of Bermuda. We leave the white people to grow for international markets. We are concerned that we should not be persuaded or forced to plant our fields for export. We saw what happened with the tobacco growing phase. In the short time, when tobacco was profitable, few white people were growing food for local consumption. Their land was dedicated to tobacco. Now, with the Governor's active encouragement, farmers are diversifying and ensuring food is being grown."

While we were talking, Ezra's people had been preparing a meal for us. It was an opportunity for the whole village to gather and celebrate James' return. It was a joyous occasion. James was happily embarrassed and we parents were immensely proud. After the meal, Anthony whispered to me that we needed to start heading back, to ensure we arrived in St. George's before sundown. I had to tell Ezra we had to leave, with great regret and much gratitude for their hospitality. Annie, slightly tearful, holding Ezra's hand, said she was eternally grateful for returning James to her, not only healed but immeasurably strengthened. Ezra smiled and they embraced, then James was led by the children down to the waterside where *James*, painted a bright green, with varnished spars and the name printed in scarlet red on the transom, was beached. He was invited to board and the children made a circle round the boat and holding hands, sang a song for James, a gentle song of farewell and a wish that he would return. It was all very moving.

—— CHAPTER 52 ——

Journal entry – *November 1631*

David was anxious to leave Bermuda. It would be a rough trip back and delays would risk even worse weather. On our last day, Annie, James, and I were invited to lunch with Mr. Hallet at the Anchor. It was a welcome sight to see him relaxed—I can't remember ever having seen him so, before. He had a stressful job; the secret eyes and ears of the Governor. I introduced him to Annie. He took her hand and bent low over it. James had respectfully held back from our greeting. Hallet stepped forward and took the boy's hand in both of his.

"You are James."

"Yes, sir."

"I truly am delighted to meet you again after so long. You won't re-member but the one other time we met was when I came to wish you all *bon voyage* when you left Bermuda in the *Swallow*. You've grown into a fine young man. I'm so pleased. Now come, pray be seated, all of you, and tell me the full story of James' rescue."

I described James' adventures and James' answers to perceptive questions put to him by Hallet provided additional depth. We parted as friends, looking forward to our next meeting. The morning of our departure, now back aboard *Meg*, all the Trescothicks came to bid us farewell. We would be sure to see them again, perhaps next year.

We were about to depart the wharf when a slightly built gentleman wearing a large hat hailed *Meg*. David, on the quarterdeck, looked down at the figure and asked him his business. The man doffed his hat. It was Abraham Hook, clean shaven, hair tied back, the same hooked nose and prominent chin, well dressed, even debonair.

"Mr. Hook. It's been a long time. What can I do for you? We are about to leave."

"Why, Mr. Tremaine. Good day to you. Do you happen to have Mr. Stanfield aboard?"

At the mention of Hook's name, I approached the rail on the main deck.

"Mr. Hook. Good day to you. I understand from Mr. Trescothick that you are now a successful businessman and trader. Congratulations."

David invited him aboard. We shook hands.

"Isaac. It is good to see you again, if only briefly. I wanted to apologize for my inadvertent action in allowing Seth Tremont to inconvenience you. I had not known you had removed yourself and your family to New England. Shortly after I left you when the *Swallow* returned to England with your rescued son, I moved my base of operations to the Azores and subsequently Bermuda. I had a chance meeting with Seth a while back when I was on a trip to England. He had just been released from prison and he said he was desperate to leave England. I felt a twinge of guilt for what he had gone through and I wanted to build my connections with the Dutch in New Netherland. The result was me agreeing to support him as my agent in New Amsterdam. I had no idea he might have had an ulterior motive."

I told him the matter had been dealt with and Seth had been returned to England, barely alive. David interrupted our conversation, saying it was time to leave. Hook shook my hand and asked that I make contact with him when I next came to Bermuda. He hoped to do business with me. I suggested he and David establish the necessary connections, as he would be in Bermuda more frequently. With that he disembarked and strode away without a backward glance. Argy was right. There was something about him that reminded me of an observation made about him those many years ago. He was a likeable rogue.

I said as much to David.

Meg fully loaded, including a bushel of Bermuda onions I bought from one of Argy's farmer friends, we worked our way out of St. George's harbor on Tuesday, 1 November.

The voyage back started well. We sailed north in warm, sou'westerly winds for three days, then as the winds veered to the northeast, we tacked and headed northwest, to cut across the strong nor'easterly current we had experienced on our way to Bermuda. The current took us north as we crossed it at night, sixty miles of rough seas, made worse by the countervailing winds to the current's flow. Annie kept to her berth, head buried in a pillow, under a blanket wishing herself anywhere but where she was. James loved every minute, appointed, on his watch, to be time-keeper, marking every passing half hour with the correct number of strikes of the bell. *Meg* dealt with what was thrown at her without damage. The confused and angry seas, magnified in the green and red glare from the navigation lights, appeared to be hydra-headed, hideous monsters reaching out to grab the boat and her passengers as she passed, being constantly repulsed in sprays of foam, their frustration voiced by the howl of the wind through the rigging, the thundering cracks as the sails backed and filled, with an accompaniment of the constant rattle of halyards beating against the masts.

Once through the warm, fast moving current, the temperature dropped precipitously. We needed to head north, but could only make northwest, headed as we were by the wind. Another day and David was beginning to worry about the proximity of land. The sun hadn't been seen for two days. We had been at sea for five. Then on the sixth day, there was enough sun shining through the haze to get a sight, which placed us at approximate latitude 40, just two degrees, or so, south of Salem's latitude. But how far west were we? Our course plot had been maintained but the current's rate of flow we didn't know. However, on the chart we had plotted where we were when we entered the fast-moving current. We had kept a detailed log of our speed and heading which, when entered on the chart and without the influence of the current, placed us south and west of our actual estimated position. Using simple trigonometry, and knowing the current's direction, we were able to estimate the current's speed at 4 knots. With that we were able to replot our position which placed us about 200 miles southeast of the northern tip of Cape Cod. Two days later, we were in Massachusetts Bay and close to home.

After docking at Salem, I met with the importing merchants who were contracted to buy the cedar and sugar. They would deal directly with David after offloading and inspection, with duties paid. I quickly found ready buyers for the produce I had brought back. Fresh fruit and vegetables in November, ahead of the winter were much appreciated. Although not formally recognized by the authorities as an antidote for scurvy, seasoned mariners, David included, had seen how effective citrus fruit was. Anything that might reduce or eliminate scurvy was welcome. I made sure that we took a bushel of mixed fruit and vegetables back home to New Barrow with us.

Annie and I returned home on 11 November after staying the night at my rented house in Salem. Johnny had done more than I had asked. It was cozy, weatherproof, furnished, and ready for occupancy. I sent a message to Johnny at New Barrow to come and fetch us, then settled down alone with Annie and enjoyed the solitude, in our own inimitable way.

Annie sighed with contentment as we lay together, spent and sleepy. I asked her whether the trip had been all she wanted.

"My dear, dear man. The void is filled with wonderful people. I have regained the lost months in James' life – my wound is healed. I am whole again."

We kissed and slept.

James was now a seasoned *Meg* crewman and no longer permitted to absent himself from his duties. David stayed aboard *Meg*, reclaiming his cabin, that Annie had been confined to for much of the journey, to ensure offloading was finished without mishap and to complete the sale of the freight.

The next morning, Johnny rode down on Samson, leading Peg. Now we had returned from Bermuda, he was keen to return to his full-time role of quartermaster on *Marie*. While we were away, he had kept in touch with *Marie's* activities, coming to Salem a day or two per week. He also wanted to ensure that any onward local shipping of *Meg's* freight would be undertaken by *Marie*. Not to worry, I told him. I had informed my importers that I would take it as a kindness if they used *Marie* for any local deliveries. Annie asked how the month we were away had been spent at New Barrow. Johnny said everything and everyone were well. The harvesting had been completed, the produce stored, ready for winter. The animals were in good shape. Two wolves had been killed, a carcass of one hung to deter others. Ben Sturges was proving an excellent hire. Kate and Giles were pleased. Not only had he the makings of being a good farmer, he's also a competent hunter, with gun, bow and snare.

Annie said that was all excellent news but what about Patience and the children? Johnny turned slightly pink and rather too hurriedly said they were fine and proceeded to talk in glowing terms about how mature Abigail had become, now she was the queen bee, with both Beth and James gone, and that she adored but was firm with the twins.

Back at New Barrow, Patience met us carrying Nat, with Abigail carrying Nan. When the twins saw Annie, they squirmed in their keepers' arms, were put down and with bums raised, scampered on feet and hands to Annie, hauled themselves upright holding her legs and demanded to be lifted. I hugged Abigail and asked Patience how it all had been. "Wonderful," she said. Annie disentangled herself from the twins and they all trooped into the house while I went to check on Kate and the animals.

Two days later, David arrived with details of the returns we had made on our first Bermuda trip, which he handed over to our keeper of the books, together with the portion of the proceeds that had already been collected. It had been a great success financially. What had really amplified that success was the response to the fruit and vegetables. Endecott had been concerned about the deaths and illnesses they had suffered over the previous two winters. He was sure that with the right type and quantity of food, the situation would have been different. As a result, he asked David whether it was possible for *Meg* to make one further run down to Bermuda this year, to bring as much of the same fruit and vegetables back as possible. Endecott was prepared to pay a premium on the shipping cost to do so. He would provide David with sufficient funds to pay for whatever he was able to procure. David had told him that I had to be informed and agree. But he suggested that he should be able to barter for the produce with timber needed in Bermuda for building houses and ships, so long as Endecott was able to ensure sufficient was available in time. David said it would take about a week to get *Meg* ready, assuming I concurred.

We discussed the advisability of making a trip so late in the season, especially returning in December, with the winter upon us. David was comfortable with *Meg's* seaworthiness and the competence of his crew to make the trip and return to Salem before Christmas. Because there was a higher element of risk, he would add a 25% premium to the freight cost. We agreed he should go, leaving as soon as possible. Annie and I asked about James. We were told that James was as fine a ship's boy as he had ever encountered, competent, respected, and liked by officers and crew alike. One small matter that made a deep impression on everyone. James had become a close friend of his fellow ship's boy, Billy "Piggy" Proctor. James realized early on that while Billy accepted the name, he actually hated it. James quietly, with no fuss, persuaded the crew that Billy was the name to be used, and so it was from then on.

David returned to Salem. A week later, with a hold full of oak, locust, spruce, and fir, under the threat of a winter storm, *Meg* left for Bermuda. James would spend his twelfth birthday at sea.

Johnny asked that I meet with my two *Marie* partners in Salem. The Smethurst brothers had decided they wanted to sell their shares. They were selling their assets prior to returning to England. They were Anglicans and missed the parish life they had in Devon, the brothers were concerned about the increasing intolerance being shown to people who were staunchly Anglican or even Puritan-leaning. After a great deal of discussion and negotiation we agreed terms. What helped in the process was my offering to provide them with a credit note for a major portion of the price, payable in pounds sterling, back in England. They planned to leave for England in the spring. The contracted purchase date would be the last day of this year. Afterwards, I asked Johnny to prepare a full report, projecting how his operation would proceed under our full ownership and what maintenance, refurbishment or changes that *Marie* would need, to be completed before the end of the winter.

Preparations for winter continued. The house we had built for the Dawkinses was occupied by Kate. We turned a blind eye to where Giles might sleep. There was room in the stable loft accommodation for him and Ben, so we pried no further. Many cords of firewood, cut from dead, fallen trees, were hauled and stored under shelter close to both houses. A further extension, with hayloft, was built on to the stables to house our increasing livestock when bad weather demanded it. I hadn't been keeping in touch with the numbers of goats and cows that were expected to increase in 1632. Kate told me and I was impressed. We would need the full 100 acres for grazing and growing feed for the livestock. In fact, Kate had plans to extend the property under use to include another 50 acres. I had given the land court a map with an accurate layout plotted showing the 200 acres we had claimed of our grant. They had approved 100 acres but had reserved judgement on the rest. I would need to meet with them, as soon as possible.

One night, in bed, comfortably entwined, I asked Annie what the situation was between Johnny and Patience.

"Uncomfortable, for both. Patience and Johnny have become intimate. Patience wants to marry Johnny and, in exasperation over his refusal to ask her, has told Johnny that that's what she wants to do. Johnny has great difficulty. He tells her that he has been married twice and each has ended in disaster. He says he is totally ill-equipped to risk that happening again. He feels fated. He says he cares too much about Patience to put her into such danger."

We agreed that at some point I needed to spend some time with Johnny and get him to unburden himself to me, much as he had done before when conflicted about having children with Jeannie. Annie was certain that there was no danger of Patience abandoning Johnny, she loved him too much, but it was a major source of unhappiness. She wanted children. She adored the twins, the more time she spent with them, the more she wanted her own. Annie said that Patience, so true to her name, knew she needed to be patient, for as long as it took for Johnny to realize how much he needed her.

—— CHAPTER 53 ——

Journal entry – *December 1631 – March 1632*

David and James appeared one afternoon in late December on a borrowed horse. They had just returned from Bermuda with another full load of produce. It had been more than Endecott had needed and cost more than the timber he had given to David to take down and use to barter with. There was enough left over to fill *Marie's* hold. David had seen Johnny, who agreed to take it to Watertown to sell it to Governor Winthrop, which is what he was currently doing. David said the trip back had been fast and uneventful. However, he needed to make a quick turn round. Jacobson in Bermuda had come through with his order for lumber but needed it as soon as possible. Samuel Maverick in Bermuda asked David if he could take a shipload of freight down to Barbados from Bermuda. It needed to be there by the end of January. Endecott wanted another delivery of fruit and vegetables by March. Endecott had agreed to supply the timber that Jacobson wanted and was currently assembling it. It all seemed a little breathless, but these were commercial opportunities not to be missed.

Annie who had clasped James to her bosom, held him at arm's length and said how wonderful he would be back with us for Christmas. James looked at David, who said nothing. James turned to Annie.

"Mummy, I'm a member of the crew. Uncle David brought me here just to see you all before we sail for Bermuda and the Caribbean. I'm sorry to disappoint you but I know you will have a lovely Christmas."

The next morning, they had gone. Christmas came and went. Johnny shared it with us. We went hunting together, taking the role that James had performed on previous Christmases. It gave me a chance to sound Johnny out about his feelings for Patience. At first, he was reticent to say much. I didn't prompt him and slowly he started to unwind and spoke of his feelings for her. It was clear he loved her. He had also been able to store memories of Jeannie away in a deep recess in his mind. But he couldn't overcome the burden of responsibility he felt for the death of both his wives in childbirth and their babies who died with them. I asked him how Patience felt.

"There's my tragic dilemma. She wants my child. I long to give her that, with all my heart. My head asks me that if I love her so much, why would I risk her life?"

"Johnny, I think you need to think more clearly. Do you really believe that God has decided you don't deserve a wife or child? Because that is what you are saying by resigning yourself to your perception of what fate has in store for you. It is not fated that you will always lose a wife and child. It happened, sadly. But every step you take is a new step, not a repetition of an old one. Every day is the start of a new life. What happened yesterday has gone forever, just the memories remain. Don't let those memories corrupt your future actions."

Johnny smiled sadly and thanked me. He would think about what I had said. Meantime, he told me we had meat to find.

The report I asked for, covering the work needed on *Marie*, resulted in us arranging with a boatyard on the Mystic River to haul her in January and complete the work order by the end of February. Winter passed quickly. We were well set, well supplied, and kept the wild animals at bay. The Merrimack River remained open to fishing, *Rosie* was busy on the river, and we benefited from Chogan's experience and instruction to catch as much fish as we needed, including sturgeon. It seemed strange to be fishing without James.

Johnny had made frequent forays down to Salem and to the boatyard on the Mystic River. He remarked that it was as well he did otherwise other boat owners would have been given a higher priority. Patience worked her magic on the reluctant Johnny, and he asked her to marry him. Coming from England, we were used to the marriage ceremony being a religious event. In Puritan New England, it is deemed a civil contract between two consenting adults, witnessed by a secular authority. Johnny contacted Endecott's office and arrangements were made for their marriage to be duly witnessed at the end of March. Annie and I promised to be there, as well.

Marie was relaunched the first week in March. Her crew, with Johnny aboard took her on a proving run down to New Plimouth and returned to Salem with a shipment of corn. The second week of March, *Meg* returned with a full hold of cedar lumber, sugar, rum, citrus fruit, onions, and cassava. The new year promised to continue much as the old year had ended.

David and James came to spend a few days with us. James had grown and matured in the three months since we had last seen him. With David listening, now smoking a pipe, James described the voyage down to Bermuda and then on to Barbados. Clear sailing, storms, being chased by a possible pirate, gunnery practice, days ashore, swimming in warm blue waters off white sandy beaches, followed by a glowing account of his new life as a sailor. James' excited retelling of his adventures was final confirmation to Annie, that her James, the boy she had nurtured and protected, who had been kidnapped and returned to her, somehow strengthened in body and spirit, had cut the strings that had bound him to her. She was proud of him, sad but also happy for her James, who was now ready and prepared for this next stage in his life.

The evening before James and David left us, after we had had supper, James and Abigail went down to the stables to help Kate, Giles and Ben to bed down the animals for the night. Abigail, aware that James wanted to say goodbye, clasped his hand in both hers, not wanting to let him go. She looked up to gaze at his face tears in her eyes. James smiled sadly, stopped and hugged her.

"Be happy, dear sister. We are in a good place here. I will be back but we both have our lives to live."

Abigail nodded, her heart too full to be able to speak, and so they went to the stables, hand in hand, and James said farewell to all the animals, and in a way to Abigail, too.

I sat around the table with Annie, David, Johnny and Patience talking about the different journeys we had all travelled to this point. I reflected on how life seemed to repeat itself. The odyssey that James was soon to be embarking on is but an echo of my own start, with its promise of action and adventure. James has always delighted in hearing the old stories of my early days. Now it was his turn.

I lifted my wine glass and raised a toast.

"After the trials, setbacks, triumphs and challenges from all our early days of exploration, retribution visited upon us, to our present redemption, God bless us all."

ABOUT THE AUTHOR

DAVID TORY has sailed the coast of
Massachusetts and Maine for 30 years.
He brings other settings alive through his
familiarity with Dorset, England, and his
intimate knowledge of Bermuda and its
waters. Years of research give his books a
firm grounding in historic facts and figures
while allowing his imagination to use his
fictional characters to tell a compelling
story of the turbulent early history of New
England. Background information on that history can be found on
www.DavidToryAuthor.com.

40926404R00226